PUBLISHED BY

Pressision S.A. - Via Speranza, 5
6900 Lugano (Switzerland)

Copyright © 2017 by Marco Strazzi

ISBN-13: 978-88-941704-3-6

CONTENTS

PREFACE

This story starts from a form of curiosity several vintage watches lovers share. Who was the original owner of the timepiece they have just bought? Where did he/she live? What did he/she do for a living? The answers to these questions are mostly beyond our reach, and even more so in instances such as this one - a Longines WWW (Wrist Watch Waterproof) made for the British Army in the 1940s. I had some knowledge about these timepieces before my purchase, but was not a specialist by any means, my interest as an historian of watchmaking and author of a few books on the subject being focused on civilian rather than military production.

Now that I owned one of the rare and sought after WWWs, I felt I ought to learn more. My research led me to an in-depth study by T. Koenig and A. van der Meijden published in 2008 by the Horological Journal (see the bibliography of this book for references). It is a must-read for whoever is interested in such watches, as it provides a thorough overview of the companies that manufactured them, the requirements set by the British Army, the numbers produced, the dates of production. This last detail was a bit of a disappointment to me - it appears that no WWWs actually took part in the fighting, as they were only delivered after the end of the war in Europe. As far as my Longines is concerned, a confirmation of that came from the company itself. The movement was sold to Baume, their London agent, in autumn 1945. I could have left it to that - after all I knew enough not  *to make a fool of myself should somebody ask about my lived-in looking watch. But I did not. My interest in WWII, combined with the ownership of the Longines watch and a fascination with alternative history, resulted in a series of what-ifs. What*

REAL AND FICTIONAL

These pages feature a few pictures of the real watch that inspired the plot. As for the fictional watch you find in Chapters 5, 7 and 21, it is the result of some Photoshop work that modified its dial, movement, inner and outer case back, by suppressing the brand's name and serial numbers and by replacing the usual WWW markings with the engravings mentioned in the novel.

if a WWW prototype had been delivered for testing well befo-
re 1945? What if it had been strapped to the wrist of a British
Paratrooper on D-Day? What if it had been lost during a fight?
What if it had appeared in an auction house catalogue seventy
years later? What if ...
There followed two years of research, trips to Britain and Fran-
ce, interviews with historians and veterans, the building up of
an alternative reality, and writing. The result was the novel you
are about to read.

***

Wingwatch *deals with a tragic past and the present day attempts*
to get to grips with what it means. It is about war, memory, sa-
crifice and redemption; the dreams and nightmares of a young
paratrooper dropped into Normandy in 1944, and those of a
boy and his father who live
in our time. It is a heart-
rending chorus that
echoes between
the terraces of a
stadium and the
headstones of a
graveyard. It is a
voyage through
time in the com-
pany of that most
classic of time ma-
chines: a watch lost
on the morning of D-Day
and rediscovered seventy ye-
ars later in an auction house catalogue. *Fragile, scratched, with*
rusted hands and a faded dial, and yet capable of measuring
more than just the limited time of a human life.
As I pointed out in the introduction, 'there are times when the
truth is too big to fit in a book or a website, so big that we are
tempted to let it push beyond the limits of mere history and enter

the realm of fables.' So I wrote a fable, dedicating it to courage: both the extreme courage of those who fought, and the courage – more familiar as it is part of our daily lives – of a boy and his father struggling with bad memories. The reason? To give sense back to a word that tends to wear away and lose its meaning, as happens with all overused expressions.

Wingwatch *aims to redefine courage, but it makes no claims to having achieved that goal. At a certain point, while reading of his grandfather's escapades as a partisan, Cédric – the modern day protagonist of the novel – finds himself wondering who he would have been seventy years earlier, whether he would have found the courage to run such risks. A question that cannot be answered – for him, for the author of this fable and, in all likelihood, for many of its readers. Because courage is a mystery: we can describe and admire its results, but its roots run so deep that perhaps not even the men of the Ninth Battalion knew of its existence until they discovered it deep down within themselves.*

***

Originally published in a text-only edition, Wingwatch *is now available in a new illustrated version featuring over 130 pictures and a selection of additional contents. I hope the reader will appreciate the opportunity to visualize some of the objects, situations and places described in the text, as well as the chance to have a look at the sites where history was made and virtually meet up with three real protagonists of the events that inspired the novel.*

***

I would like to end with a word regarding the final image featured in this Preface (see opposite page). The site, well known to any football fan, is Anfield Road, home ground of Liverpool FC. The year is 1987, more or less the period when Cédric witnesses a match from the terraces of the Kop in Chapter Three. And the man in a jacket and tie is me, back when I was a sports writer. I chose this photo because, above the gates, you can see the title of the song that makes up the soundtrack to this story, and because I am wearing a poppy in the buttonhole of my jacket – symbol of remembrance for the fallen, given to me by the (English) photographer I was travelling with. This old slide gave me a start when it resurfaced from a cardboard box, as it featured the main elements of Wingwatch *long before the thought of buying a pre-owned watch even crossed my mind.*

I might not know exactly what courage is, but I now think I have a good idea of fate. Just like Cédric.

Marco Strazzi

WINGWATCH
ILLUSTRATED NOVEL

Marco Strazzi

translated from Italian by Ross Nelhams

For those who were there
And for those who always will be

INTRODUCTION

*This is a work of fiction inspired by historical events.
Names have been changed because it would be
improper to attribute to real people words and actions
that have been invented, no matter how plausible they
might be. However, the Ninth Battalion and its heroes
really did exist. They are as authentic as the gratitude
of those who visit the fallen at Ranville Cemetery
and who, every year on 6 June, celebrate
the veterans' return to Normandy.*

*And they are as authentic as the testimony
and the reconstructions that you will find listed in
the bibliography. Perhaps some readers will find the
time to make use of these resources as they look more
deeply into the subjects this novel deals with and will
reach the same conclusions as I have in writing it: there
are times when the truth is too big to fit in a book or a
website, so big that we are tempted to let it push beyond
the limits of mere history and enter the realm of fables.*

1. 6 JUNE 2014, 0:02

Beep-beep... click!

Two seconds to push the button. As fast as Sam-Sam Youny on the court: dribbles, shoots, scores. Too quick for anyone to have heard. I didn't think I would get back to sleep, not tonight. I can remember the 'Good luck!' the goodnight kiss, putting my hand under the pillow to check the bag was there, but that's all. It's such a stupid alarm clock, with Winnie the Pooh's arms showing you what the time is. It's for kids and I'm seven years old. No actually, eight, since two minutes ago. Luckily this is the last time. From tomorrow I'll use the new radio alarm clock, the one shaped like a basketball. They're going to give it to me at the party, I know because I looked in Mum and Dad's wardrobe. That way I won't have to remember to hide this toy every time Malik and Yves come over. They're my friends but I bet if they saw it they'd tell everyone at school: 'Did you know Théo sleeps with Winnie the Pooh like when he was five?'

I can't hear anything so I can get going, without making any noise because if Mum wakes up I'll be in trouble. She's been angry with me for two days and I can't answer back or try to explain, if I do she just gets angrier. She's different to us, it's best if she doesn't know anything, we can't make her run pointless risks. Dad's probably right, but in the meantime I'm stuck in the middle and he can't come with me because it's too late to convince Pierre. When he was explaining the mission it was like he didn't notice anything, like the time the bus driver went past our stop even though me and Mum were holding our hands out: 'Be careful, you have to do this and then this, don't forget anything, be sure to get here on time.' It was just like our teacher, except she asks whether we've understood what we have to do, and if someone says 'no', then she explains it again, while I didn't get a chance to say anything with Pierre. I had to wait until he'd finished to say that perhaps it would be better to wait for Dad.

'We don't even know what time he'll get back. And he wouldn't be any help.'

'Why not?'

'You know why.'

What could I say? He'd been right until yesterday, but now Dad gets it. Thanks to the watch, he says. I don't believe him.

If you ask me, he didn't want to admit he still had the dark inside. If only he'd understood two days sooner he could have come with me and said sorry, and that way we would have all been happy, especially me because I wouldn't have to face the hallway on my own. But instead...

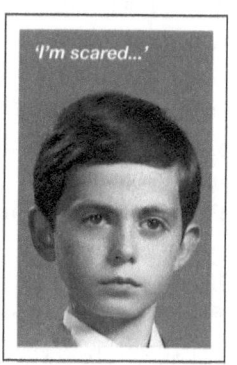

'I'm scared...'

I'm scared. I was too embarrassed to tell Pierre but he knew anyway, either from my face or because I stopped talking. I'm sure he knew because he changed the subject. He asked me about the match even though he's not interested in basketball, in fact he doesn't know anything about it. But he paid attention while I was speaking. When I said that I wasn't that bothered about it because I had other things on my mind, he got angry.

'What would your mates think if they knew? Or mine, if I told them I wasn't bothered about the mission? You need to take all

18

of it seriously: school, basketball, promises, and commitments. Otherwise how can I trust you?'

What did that mean? That he would get someone else to help him because I'm too little? I wouldn't be able to stand that. If I say I'm little then that's alright, I do it sometimes to avoid getting told off, but I don't like hearing it from other people. And what's all this about trust? Of course he trusts me, otherwise he wouldn't have given me his friends to get them ready for the mission. It took me ages and I didn't even have time to finish my French homework, but they're perfect. I'm going to take them to him now, and then we'll see if he still has anything to say about trust. I very much doubt it. In fact he's probably already forgotten about it because that's what grown-ups are like. Sometimes you can't tell what's going through their heads and perhaps they don't even know themselves, so they end up going on and on about things and making things up.

With him it's trust, with Mum and Dad it's epileptic fits. Like when we were in the shopping centre. They could have just said that they weren't going to buy me *Lost Galaxy* because it was too expensive, and that would have been it. But once they started up it was never ending, like a grammar lesson: you can't sit in front of the computer for too long, you'll damage your eyesight, a boy your age had an epileptic fit and ended up in hospital after playing for three hours solid. And they didn't even explain what an epileptic fit was, they just pulled their worried faces and that put an end to the discussion. How could I answer back if I didn't know what they were talking about? As soon as we got home I turned the computer on to check whether they'd been making it all up. There were some hard words but I understood the important bits because it was well written. Convulsions: it's when you roll about on the ground. I don't know how much it hurts but it doesn't look very nice. I wonder whether being scared can give you convulsions as well.

Back in the hallway again, at night. Like last summer.

Time certainly is a funny thing. Why is it that some things

seem so recent when they happened months or years ago? Take the bike from the raffle, for instance. I could have sworn I won it yesterday because I can remember everything. In fact it's more than just remembering because I can see and hear and smell and feel everything. The colour of the ticket, which was pink and I didn't want it but Mum and Dad talked me into it. People practically shouting so that their friends on other tables could hear them. The smell of chips. The paper napkin I kept on my knee so that they wouldn't notice the ketchup stain on my shorts. Vincent and Melissa fighting over the same ticket. The head-teacher reading the numbers out. Mum screaming, the can of fizzy orange she knocked over when she put her hand up and that luckily was nearly empty. People clapping. Grandma laughing like it was her who had won. Dad lifting me up onto the saddle. The photographer telling me to smile. To convince myself that it was two years ago I have to get on the bike and try to pedal. I can't anymore because it's gotten too small, or rather my legs have gotten too long. It doesn't matter. I've decided that was the greatest day of my life and I'll never forget it. As for the other thing, I'd have liked to forget that as soon as it happened, but even now I can't. When I told Mum about it, she just answered that it would fade with time. Is she right? And what if it sticks in my brain forever, like the raffle?

It would have been better if it was dark, that way I wouldn't have noticed anything. But at night we always leave the bathroom light on and the door a little bit open so that you can find your way if you need to go. It was hot and I was sweaty even though all the windows were open. I went to the toilet, had a wee and washed my hands, but as soon as I went back into the hallway I could feel something moving above my head. I reached into the bathroom and switched the hallway light on. I looked up and that was when I saw them: two black things going round in a circle, like the fans on the ceiling of that pizzeria where Yves' parents took us for his birthday. But we've never had any fans. Suddenly it felt as though my heart skipped a beat and my legs started shaking. Bats! Like the ones I saw on that documentary on TV, when I changed the channel because they scared me. I don't even like the pretend ones on the Carnival float – when the *Ratapignata* come past I look the other way. Dad tells me they're a symbol of the city and they can't hurt me because they're made out of paper mache, but with their wings open like that I always think they look ready to attack.

I couldn't move. I just stood there watching them, and it felt like I was puffing up, like when a strong wind blows and you keep your mouth open and it seems like there's too much air inside it. Maybe the bats knew it and they were waiting for me to explode like the baddies in games so they would have smaller pieces to eat and could lick up my blood splattered all over the walls and the floor. I shouted at the top of my lungs and then ran back into the bathroom and locked myself in. Luckily last year I didn't know about convulsions, otherwise I'm sure I would have had them then.

'What's the matter? Where are you?' It was Mum, I could hear her footsteps coming towards me.

'Bats! I hate them, make them go away!'

'Let me in.'

'No! If I open the door they'll get in as well. Call the police!'

She stayed on the other side of the door and talked and talked: she said that you can't call the police because there's a bat, that the only bats in the house were those two in the hallway, that they had got in because we'd left the windows open, that they fly around like that because they can't see, that it's not true that they drink blood or that they get into your hair, in fact if anything they're helpful because they eat the mosquitoes. But I was crying and running back and forwards in the bathroom, and when I looked in the mirror I got even more scared. I didn't recognise myself: I was bright red, my eyes were all puffy and I had a cut on my cheek. I was afraid a bat had scratched me while I was sleeping to get at my blood, but I had done it myself with my nail, wiping my face too hard to dry the tears. Mum explained all this to me, but only later on. At that moment I knew that I was caught in a trap and that not even the window being shut would save me. The bats had the house surrounded and any minute now they were going to smash the glass. I would have no way out, especially if I was there by myself. So I turned the key in the lock and Mum burst in. She hugged me and made me sit next to her on the side of the bathtub. I stopped crying but then I started again when I heard some bangs coming from the hallway. I thought more of them were coming, as big as Batman or the ones at Carnival, evil and thirsty. 'It's Dad – he's trying to push them outside with the broom.'

After a little while I heard him saying, 'You can come out, they've gone.'

'And what if they come back? I'm staying here.' It took them half an hour to get me to come out, and only after they had promised me that I could sleep in their bed.

I slept there for a week and then I went back to my own room, but we kept the windows shut at night all summer long. They moaned about the heat but I started shouting as soon as anyone talked about leaving one open, even when Dad said that he'd stay next to it to stop the bats getting in and that he'd close it before he went to bed. In the end, when spring came, and while grumbling about how much it cost, they got two air conditioners put in, one in their room and one in mine. That way, if we keep the doors open, it cools down the hallway, bathroom and a little bit downstairs, too. But in any case I never go into the hallway. I don't need to any more: ever since that night, I haven't had to go for a wee until morning.

Now, though, I have to go all the way along it and down the stairs, cross the kitchen, open the door at the end and go into the garage. It's ten times further than what I was afraid to do up until yesterday. But that's my mission, he said, and I can't chicken out now: 'Remember you're a brave soldier.' I didn't know how to answer. 'Do you know what brave means?'

'It's when you're not scared…'

'Wrong.'

'But…'

'Everyone's scared, even me and my mates. But we face up to our fear because if we can look it in the eye, it doesn't look so bad, and that makes us brave. Just the same as you, and you'll prove it on Sunday. Got it?' I said I did, but it wasn't exactly true. 'You have to be like your Dad, right?'

Dad had never spoken to me about it. In fact he seemed surprised I knew – his face even went white. He said he was tired from the journey, but once Mum explained that he does that when something bothers him. And I think he was right to be a bit shaken – it's a good story and he was brave because he didn't know that really there was no need to be afraid, apart from the dark inside. At the time I'd understood that more than what Pierre had said about things being less scary if you know your fears. I thought about that afterwards. I was thinking about it at school as well, yesterday morning, and in the end the teacher shouted at me for not paying attention. Perhaps it's like the convulsions – they scare me, but I know about them. If I get convulsions from being scared I'll know that they'll go away again after a bit, while if I hadn't found anything on the internet, I'd think that they went on forever, and perhaps they actually would. And then there's the song. If I get too scared, I'll think of that. I didn't tell Pierre, but Dad reckons it might work.

I'd better get going, otherwise I'll be late and there's no telling how angry he'll get.

I can hear something - Mum and Dad talking. And I can see through the crack under the office door that the light is on. Why are they in there this late? I'd like to listen to what they're saying. Sometimes I do – I stand behind the door and hold my breath to hear better. Maybe they have some secrets, and I like finding out secrets. One evening, before the night the bats came, they found me listening and they got angry. They weren't in the kitchen though, they were in their bedroom sighing and groaning. I didn't know what was going on so I went in. They quickly pulled the sheets over themselves and said I shouldn't just walk in like that, that…

Crack!

The floorboard that's coming unstuck! I was supposed to walk up against the wall, how did I forget that?

'What was that?'

Mum's voice. If she comes out and sees me what can I say? That I was going to the toilet? And then what? What will I do if she waits for me outside? Dad promised me that he'd take care of Mum if he needed to.

Maybe he's managed to distract her – I can still hear them talking. I feel a little bit like Pierre. I walk without making a sound, in the dark, hoping no one notices me. But he and his mates are in real danger. What could possibly happen to me? Mum could make me stay at home all morning, at worst. I don't think she'd cancel the party after all the fuss she's gone to getting everything ready.

The garage door! That's strange – I've got here without realising it. I was so worried about Mum catching me sneaking about that I forgot about the bats. Perhaps bad things only exist when you think about them, and when you stop thinking about them they disappear. Now that's an interesting thought.

'You're on time.' There he is, stepping out from behind the tool cupboard. I should be used to him by now, but the sight of him still scares me a bit. He's so tall, taller than Dad and the other grown-ups I know. 'Were you scared?'

'No.'

'You know I don't like lies, don't you?'

'Yes…'

'Well?'

'A bit…'

'How much is a bit?'

'Quite a lot…'

'So? What did you do?'

It's hard to keep up when he fires questions at you one after another. Often I can't, so I just stay quiet and wait until I know how he wants me to answer, because otherwise I'm afraid I'll say something stupid and he'll get angry. Not this time though – I want to tell him about my secret weapon straight away: 'I've found out there's another way.'

'To do what?'

'To not be scared.'

'And what would that be?'

'You don't need to look it in the eye. You just need to forget about it.'

'Great idea, maybe us lot could use it. Is that it?'

'What…?'

'Is that the only reason you've come? Because you've forgotten about being scared?'

'No, no – it's my mission.'

'Good boy.' When he smiles he looks friendly, it's a shame he doesn't do it more often, and that it doesn't last a bit longer. Now he's looking at me strangely: 'Come into the light.'

'Why?'

'I want to see something – what's that on your cheeks?'

'Nothing.' He's noticed it, even though Mum scrubbed it hard and it's practically dark in the garage because when the light bulb on the ceiling stopped working Dad just stuck the first one he happened to find in the socket, and it's too dim.

'It's us that's going, not you,' he laughs – how can he be so calm? 'Have a wash tomorrow morning, otherwise you'll look silly in front of your guests.'

I'd better change the subject, I've had enough of this one: 'You know… he remembers you now.'

'He's never forgotten me. Could you forget someone like me?'

'And the watch… he did it.'

'You both did it. You did well, too. Did you bring them?'

'They're here in the bag.'

'Empty it onto the floor.'

'Like that?'

'Perfect. Stand them up and mind you don't touch their faces

– do you remember the drawing for school?' Of course I do, I had to draw it a second time because I'd rested my hand on it and it looked like the fingerprints you see on TV. 'Close to each other, two by two. Not like that – they have to look at each other. That's it… thanks. And happy birthday.'

'I'll leave you a slice of cake, that way if you have time…'

'I'd like to, but I'll be far away. You'll have fun anyway – the house will be full of people.'

'It's your birthday too…'

'My mates will wish me the best on the plane and we'll have something to eat together. Now get going.'

'Can I stay a bit longer? Until you leave?'

'No. It's late and you need to get some rest.'

'It's Sunday…'

'Don't you want to be on good form for the party?'

'Yes, but…'

'What's the matter? You know we don't question orders.'

'No. I mean yes. But I wanted to ask you…' You can see from his face that my questions are starting to get on his nerves. It's the same face as Mum and Dad have when they say 'we'll talk about it later' or 'not now, I have to concentrate.' I have to concentrate too, when I solve an arithmetic problem, but it doesn't seem all that complicated. Maybe it's harder for grown-ups. I know I should leave him alone because he won't be staying much longer, but I won't leave until he gives me an answer: 'When are you coming back?'

2. 6 JUNE 1944, 0:02

I stared intently into the darkness, trying to make out those faint glimmers of light and convince myself that the others really were sitting just a few feet away from us. Since we had taken off I had not seen their faces, only their silhouettes. Lit cigarettes offered the only hint of their presence, strange and intermittent points of light that seemed to hang from invisible strings rather than from my mates' hands. They all sat in silence except for Captain Kadwell, who had chosen me to strike up a conversation with. This time he was not satisfied with simply teasing me to kill time like he did in the mess hall. He wanted to get a reaction out of me, to see if I was ready. When he held out the sandwich to me I did not even shake my head. I hoped he would think that I could not hear him over the roar of the engines, but he tried again, this time speaking so loudly that he was practically shouting: 'If you've gone deaf then I'm sorry, Roger. It's too late to pull a sickie.'

I could not tell him to leave me alone and nor could I tell him to go to hell. Because of his rank, apart from anything else. But I doubt whether I would have done it even if he had been a stranger I had met on civvy street. The broken nose, the light heavyweight build, that way of looking whoever he had in front of him right in the eyes ... He had picked that up in the ring, he said, to beat his opponents before he even threw the first punch. 'I can hear you, sir.'

'Then you've got no excuse: refusing sandwiches from an officer is a court-martialable offence. What's the matter, don't you like the party? But there's so many of us.'

'Yes sir.'

'Eat up and wish me a happy birthday. That's an order.'

'Happy birthday.'

'That's better,' he said as I made an effort to swallow, 'I've got no need for a moody guest. Or for a soldier who passes out cos he's hungry.'

Would he be quiet for a bit, now that I had done what he asked? I wanted to think, to find a way of forgetting about that weight between my chest and my stomach, the feeling of a foreign body that I had had since the captain had made us form up on the runway. We had lined up alongside the fuselage facing the rear of the plane, the captain near the cockpit because he would be the last to get on board and the first to jump. 'Twenty OK!', 'Nineteen OK!', we repeated just as we had done during the training jumps as we checked the parachute of the man in front of us, until the captain shouted 'All OK!'.

The first man up the step ladder started to sing and the rest joined in, even the captain. I could not be the only one not taking part so I sung as well, and as I settled onto the metal bench I tried to convince myself that we had more in common than just the months of training, the uniform and the mission. We all felt the weight of that unwelcome stowaway and we were all trying to keep it at bay with the words of an ode to beer and wenches.

But we were better off than Ted was. I had never seen him cry, not even when he had taken a bullet in the shin during the first live fire exercise. He swore like a drunkard kicked into the gutter by a pub landlord, but there were no tears and he even turned down the morphine they offered him, too furious to register the pain. That was the end of the line for him and he knew it instantly. Any other man would have let them send him home without making a fuss. But not him, he wanted to stay even if he had a limp and could not do much except for helping out in the mess hall or the armoury. When I saw him at the wheel of the truck that would take us to the runway, I was happy: my friend, the best friend I had in the platoon, was the last one I would say goodbye to when the time came to leave. I changed my mind as we shook hands in the light from the headlamps. Now he was crying alright. There were no sobs, in fact no sound at all, except for six words that he could barely bring himself to whisper: 'I should be with you lot.' I made a joke of it, I said he was in luck because I'd forgotten to close my locker and inside there was a few bob, he could buy a couple of pints on me. But it was no good. This was not the goodbye I would have wished for.

When the song ended they fell silent. A few of them lit up. Had they managed to banish the stowaway or was it that he was still there and they were trying to burn him up along with the tobacco in those glowing, red embers? For me the song had not done the trick. I needed something else. What about a memory test? The complete list of everything I had on me, dozens of objects to mentally tick off – that would help me kill time and forget all the other stuff. Better to find out that I had left something back at camp than to let myself be crushed by that nameless weight.

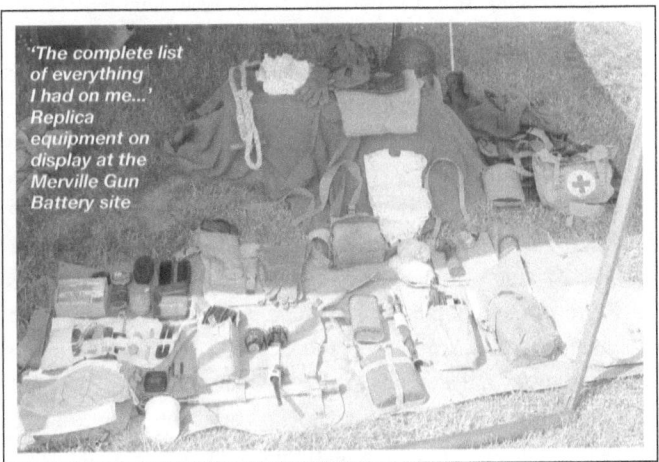

'The complete list of everything I had on me...' Replica equipment on display at the Merville Gun Battery site

Standard issue shirt with string vest and lucky jersey underneath. Battledress trousers with a 24-hour ration pack and two Mills grenades in the large pocket over my left knee. Dagger and morphine syringe in the right-hand pockets. Shell dressings in the back pockets. Denison smock with silk map sewn into the lining. Escape kit, vitamin pills and paper money in the inside pocket.

'... paper money...' The Invasion Currency
printed by the Allies prior to D-Day

Woollen hat, beret and revolver in the outer pockets. Toggle rope wrapped around my shoulders and waist. Camouflage face veil around my neck. Sleeveless jump oversmock. Lifejacket. Sten gun and magazines stuffed inside the parachute harness. Helmet with camouflage netting. Boots. Woollen gloves and socks. All the rest was in the back pack and webbing squeezed into the bag attached to my right leg. Gammon and phosphorus grenades. Spare bandolier of ammunition for the platoon's Bren. Bayonet. Pullover. Clean underwear. Cloth cape. Plimsolls. Towel. An additional 24-hour ration pack. Mess tin. Enamel mug. Water bottle. Entrenching tool in two parts. Wire-cutters. Gas-mask. Torch. Holdall containing knife, fork, spoon, razor, toothbrush, shaving mirror, comb, bootlaces, an envelope with needle, thread and buttons. And then the military paybook. The identity discs round my neck. And the battalion's maroon epaulet loops, fixed to my

'Helmet with camouflage netting...'. One of the replica helmets worn by the reenactors of the France 44 Association

shoulders at the last minute because one of the boys in the mess hall had pointed out that I did not have them: 'If the Commanding Officer notices, you'll be in trouble.

Everything where it should be, about a hundred pounds. A hundred pounds and three ounces, in fact. I forgot to mention the book, maybe because it went into the bag first, so out of place that I put it in before the real equipment. They had told us that it was important to read it carefully, although the first words seemed like a joke: 'This book has nothing to do with military operations.' I had never much cared for reading, except for comics and the sports pages in the papers, but I was not the only one who could not understand why they wanted to make us waste our time reading a manual on how to behave. Would a few instructions at camp not have been sufficient, just a quick half-hour to remind us not to call them frogs?

The man in civilian clothes – someone from the Ministry, they said – gave a serious speech, without smiling once. He wanted to watch as the books were handed out, as though he did not trust us or was afraid that someone would not get a copy. When I started reading, the bits about history, geography, customs and phrases to memorise were fairly interesting. But as for the advice, it seemed to have been written for imbeciles. Greet people. Respect everyone, in particular the women. Show understanding for the suffering endured and appreciation for the contribution of the Resistance. Try to express yourself in French, making every effort to understand and getting anything you do not understand written down. And the things we should not do, which sounded like Mum's lectures when I was a kid. Do not criticise the army that was defeated in 1940. Do not get into arguments about religion or politics. Do not accept food from civilians because they have too little to share it. Do not mess things up even in an empty billet. Do not drink yourself silly. Do not give away, much less sell, items of equipment or rations ...

'You used to eat something before matches, didn't you?' Him again.

'Matches?'

'With your little team.'

'Tottenham Hotspur aren't a little team, sir. We've won two FA Cups.'

'So you keep saying. But that was in the Dark Ages. Liverpool, on the other hand, keep on winning. 1943 champions, remember?'

'Of the League North. And Tottenham in the south, a few weeks back.'

'I didn't know that. You mean that to improve all they had to do was get rid of you?'

'I only played four times ...'

'And then they realised they'd be better off using a bloke off the street, or sticking with ten men.'

'No they didn't,' he had touched a raw nerve and, in the heat of the moment, I forgot to add 'sir.' 'It's the crowd's fault. They started whistling the minute they heard my name in the line-up because I was only sixteen and no one knew who I was. They wanted professionals, famous players ...'

'Sounds fair enough.'

'If they'd been ours then yes, but they came from elsewhere. They asked their clubs' permission, played the match for sake of the thirty shillings they made out of it and then went back where they'd come from. When one of them turned up at the last minute, they sent me to watch with the supporters even if I was ready to go onto the pitch. But it doesn't matter: those were strange championships, in fact they still are. Teams winning 9-0 one week and then losing 6-0 the next, to the same opponents ...'

'Strange? The normal ones'll start back up again soon, and then we'll see how you do. If you're as good as you say you are, I suggest you sign for Liverpool.'

I avoided answering. After all, I was in his debt. When I had asked his permission to wear the Spurs shirt under my uniform he had sighed 'yes', with the air of a bored older brother left at home to look after his younger sibling while their parents are out. He did not even listen to me as I explained that it would bring me luck because the cockerel on the team's emblem also symbolises France, and that was where they were sending us. Sitting there now, I was sure that he had no interest in football. He simply wanted to take my mind off things, and at the same time he was wondering, as he had been for months, whether I would be up to the job. As far as he was concerned I was a boy, but I was seventeen and a half, and during training I was always one of the best in the platoon. The only thing that had not gone very well was the first jump. A clumsy, rough landing, but I was back on my feet instantly. Bruised but uncomplaining, I did not say a word. 'The younger they are the more they want to be heroes,' he had muttered after witnessing the scene, without looking at me but loud enough for me to hear.

I tried to make out his features so that I could guess what he would say next to get a reaction out of me, but his blackened face was indistinguishable from his helmet, and his eyes alone seemed to penetrate the darkness. Heroes ... there was no need for heroes, he had repeated again on the truck. All we had to do was to play our part and act out what we had learnt and practised with what had become a tedious thoroughness during the last few weeks. No improvisation and above all no mistakes. The objective was identical to the mock-up they had built for us at the camp, down to the last detail. In place of the concrete there were iron, wood and fabric frames, but the machine-gun and anti-aircraft emplacements, the gun casemates, the barbed wire, the minefield and the anti-tank ditch were all exactly like those shown in the photos. Everything had been faithfully reconstructed, including the final part of the route that led to the site, and it was all to scale. The hundred yards we covered at West Woodhay would be the same hundred yards when we reached the objective, not eighty-five or a hundred and twenty. It would go just like it had during training, the captain reassured us. Why shouldn't it? He wanted to sound sure of himself but I think he must have had some doubts. Very few of us, one in twenty at most, had actually seen action. And we were all young, me most of all. The majority of the others were between nineteen and twenty-two years old. How were we going to react when we saw our comrades fall, when we heard shots fired and the cries of the wounded?

Even he was not a veteran. He had spent four years in the army but for the first three of those he had not moved from his barracks in Liverpool, much less seen the enemy. He had earned his rank in the Territorial Army and then signed up as a volunteer because, as he explained the first time I met him, he was bored of sitting twiddling his thumbs. I had no difficulty believing him because I was there for the same reason. A few weeks later though, I thought he was joking when he swore that to be brave you need to know fear and to look it straight in the eye. In fact, he went on, it is vital that you are afraid. It seemed like a strange theory coming from a boxer but he insisted, with deadly seriousness, that it was the perfect weapon. Aggression and caution: this was the recipe that had won him plenty of fights without running pointless risks and which he swore, perhaps exaggerating as he was prone to do, would have taken him to the 1944 Olympics had Hitler not decided to try to conquer the world. It did not matter, he added, as the Krauts were done for. We would deliver the knockout blow and he could go back to the ring. And to Jane.

They had married two weeks before he left for training. He was the one that insisted. They had known one another all their lives, as neighbours, schoolmates and then as boyfriend and girlfriend. There was no point in waiting, he would say to me, as though persuading her had not been enough and now he wanted to convince me as well. The war would soon be over and he would be going home all in one piece. Limping with the weight of all those medals, at worst. He – and only he – liked that joke a lot. From what I had understood, Jane did not find it very funny. He had shown me a photo: light-coloured hair down to her shoulders ('red,' he had specified, 'but fine and shiny, not like that ball of wool on the top of your head'), a forced smile on her freckled face and her gaze fixed on a point beyond the camera that gave the impression she was looking far into the future. I thought it looked like a fragile, anxious face, but I was wrong. One day I would learn that Jane was stronger than me.

How many of us would be going back home? I remembered a snatch of conversation overheard in the mess hall a few days earlier. Two medical officers were talking about preparations that would have to be made for the first casualties, as soon as possible because they were expecting a lot of wounded. When they realised I was listening to them, they got up and left. There was no need to – we had all been discussing percentages for some time. Some said nearly all of us would die, others that it would be a walk-over because the Krauts would surrender. I had plumped for fifty-fifty. That basically meant that if the captain and I had been the only ones taking part, one of us would not live to see another day. But who?

I would find out soon enough, I thought as he elbowed me in the side. He had his left hand in the large pocket of his trousers and he seemed to be trying to find something. I would have liked to say something funny, that if he had forgotten his toothbrush it was too late to go back, but I did not have the courage to, and went back to my thoughts. I was afraid, that continual weight on my stomach, but not of dying. I was afraid of going home an invalid, a burden to myself and others. And above all I was afraid the captain was right to doubt me, that I would let my mates down, that if I made a mistake then some of those boys, with whom I had passed all those exhausting months working, cracking jokes and cursing the officers that took us on marches in the middle of the night, would end up dead.

I caught a flash out of the corner of my eye and turned around. The captain was shining the electric torch onto his left wrist.

'What is it, sir?'

'I'm charging the watch up.'

3. 31 MAY 2014, 15:12

The leaden sky was a dam on the point of breaking. Sat on his scooter with one foot resting on the tarmac, Cédric Roussel listened to the gentle patter of the first raindrops on his helmet and eyed the red traffic light twenty metres ahead of him, past the queue of cars. He mulled over cutting into the left-hand lane to overtake them, putting himself in pole position before the lights changed. It was risky: there might be a cranky policeman on the other side of the crossroads. But if he got away with it Cédric could gain a few seconds and, perhaps, manage to reach shelter before the heavens opened. As he began the manoeuvre he had no need to look through the car windows in order to feel the other drivers' eyes on him. They must have been giving him the same hostile look that he used every time the tables were turned and some idiot on two wheels bumped into his wing mirror in an effort to squeeze through the space between his car door and a crash barrier.

Never mind – he was prepared to take a few horn blasts and a couple of swear-words, and even to run the risk of a fine and a point on his licence, if it meant not arriving home soaked to the skin like he had twenty days earlier. The next morning, following the same route back again in the bus and sneezing five times a minute, he had memorised every possible shelter he passed so that he would be prepared the next time rain threatened. Then in the evening, to be sure that he had found all of them, he had studied the route on Street View as well. Now, he had to admit that if he was going to find himself in the same situation once more, he was in luck: he was just two-hundred metres from safety. In the pallid light that seemed to herald an eclipse, Cédric completed the manoeuvre with a swerve to the right that placed both wheels on the zebra crossing, as though trying to ensure that he violated every possible traffic law. The sign above the chemist's in front of him, on the ground floor of the building on the corner of Pessicart, Arène and Domaine du Piol, flickered to life. The pitter patter rhythm of the raindrops was speeding up.

'... the half-curve that usually marked the limit of the city-centre traffic...'

Green! Cédric plunged into the half-curve that usually marked the limit of the city-centre traffic and the start of the way up towards his home. Not today, though – his destination was a new five-storey building, a blocky, grey affair with glass verandas and red balconies, slotted between a shorter apartment block and a small house with a pitched roof. A questionable mix of styles,

'... the entry tunnel to the car park...'

but Cédric was more interested in the entry tunnel to the car park than contradictions in town planning. As he reached the centre of the road and then crossed it, he noted the already slick tarmac and reminded himself to proceed with caution. After driving up the ramp to the garage door, he reversed the scooter so that the headlight was pointed back toward the entrance. Safe and sound, under cover and almost dry – a miracle. Just a short distance away the deafening cloudburst was hammering down on the city streets; drops as heavy and shiny as marbles which, if it were not for the splashes they produced on impact, might have been mistaken for hailstones.

His first thought was all too predictable: why had he done it? Why had he left his convenient apartment in the city-centre, which no one would have forced him out of, with school a ten-minute walk away, to chase the mirage of a house of his own, exposing himself in the process to the caprice of the weather twice a day and miring himself in debt until he retired? An idle question, little more than a way of convincing himself that his reasons were still valid two years after the move. The garden was tiny, but it was all for him, Sylvie and Théo. The garage, the fresh air, those extra thirty square metres or so. And the cost – that had been reasonable, tempting even. The owners had been in a hurry to close because they were moving to Canada, and it had seemed like a chance that could not be missed. Their savings had covered half of the price, and for the rest they had taken out a mortgage that did not seem prohibitive. They had almost two full salaries coming in, with Cédric working more than full time, thanks to the secondary school reforms which had allowed him to bulk out his hours with tutoring and training programmes, and the money Sylvie made from her part-time job. If nothing changed in the next eighteen years they would be fine. *If*.

When you fall in love you lose your head, and they had fallen in love with that house at first sight. Commuting would just be a minor detail, they had thought, mistakenly as it turned out. The family's budget, already under strain, would not stretch to buying a second car, so they had had to make do with a second-hand scooter. It was nearly always Cédric that had to use it because Sylvie's working hours meant that it was easier for her to pick up Théo after school.

A roll of thunder, closer than the others, triggered the alarm on an illegally parked sedan on the other side of the road which was acting as a breakwater in the torrent that had formed between the pavement and the road surface. Cédric turned the engine off, took off his crash helmet and hung it on the handgrip. He would have to kill time for a bit, and the only items to hand were the flyers sticking out of the letterboxes to his right, next to a panel with a series of buttons and an intercom, and his mobile with headphones. He opted for the music. At times like this, the choice was always the same: Glasgow 1976 or Birmingham 2006, thirty years apart but the same energy. It would have been a tough call had Cédric not entrusted the decision long before that to the principle of alternation. Today, it was the turn of the fortieth anniversary concert. Status Quo live, a strictly personal antidote of proven efficiency against unexpected attacks of boredom or annoyance. No one else in his circle of friends found pieces such as *Caroline* or *Down Down* relaxing; indeed, it would be more accurate to

say that no one could stand them. When in the car with his family, he felt obliged to choose something less aggressive – Ade-
le, Coldplay, Dido, the perennial charm of Abba – partly because
he could still remember something Sylvie asked him many years
earlier, almost triggering a diplomatic incident while their relationship was still young: 'Can you actually tell the songs apart?'
For when his friends or colleagues were in the car with him he
had Alizée, Celine Dion, Superbus or Mylène Farmer – mostly
home-grown pop, in an effort to discourage the jokes: Cédric the
anglophile, the one whose capital city is London, or rather Liverpool. If he actually did live in Merseyside and had to get around
on a scooter, the climate would have been enough to stop him
from being tempted to live in a house in the country.

All of a sudden, it looked as though someone outside had turned the lights back on. Cédric gave a push with his legs to move
towards the exit. The downpour had given way to a fine, dense
shower of smaller drops that shone against a sky lit up by the
sun, which had appeared somewhere to the west of the city. The
sunshine produced a pearly-grey light that was fairly encoura-
ging, albeit as rare for the French Riviera as the gloomy clouds
of a few minutes previously. It looked more like one of those English afternoons when you don't know whether to put on a short-
sleeved polo or a waterproof. As he backed up again – it was too
soon to get going – Cédric allowed himself a smile, the first since
the head teacher had given the green light for his weekend plans,
and touched the display to silence Francis Rossi's Fender Teleca-
ster. He thought he could hear something else, besides the patter
of raindrops and in between the wails of the sedan – a chorus of
voices rebounding off of thousands of raised arms and stretched
scarves. But it was a false alarm, just his memory playing up.

**

Twenty-six years earlier, another life and another world. The
Channel Tunnel did not yet exist, and neither did low-cost airlines. In those days there were charter flights, which cost less than
the major airlines but were still expensive enough to wreck the

finances of an eighteen-year-old student and put even the shabbiest of London hotels beyond his reach. But even so, he had not wanted to forgo the trip with his friends to celebrate the end of their final school exams. 'The Four Musketeers' – that was what their classmates had called them, in recognition of their rock-solid friendship. So they had slept in a Youth Hostel and eaten fish and chips every day, much to the disgust of Olivier, Damien and Wilfred. They were only half joking when they made the most of every setback to taunt him about the choice of destination. With the vile weather, dilapidated accommodation and depressing food, it seemed more like a punishment than a holiday, and an unmerited one at that – all of them had passed their exams. He still spoke to Damien now and again. He was the manager of the supermarket where Cédric and Sylvie went to do the shopping on Saturdays, leaving Théo in the supervised children's area with toys, a television, tables for drawing and occasionally an amateur clown or magician. Every time they saw one another, Damien reminded him of how he had spoilt everyone's fun with that holiday from hell.

'Bugger England!' he always said. 'I've never been back there.'

As for Cédric, he had returned once on a short study break partly paid for by the school. But the adventure worth remembering was the one with his friends who, in spite of their grumbling, had chosen to let him go on making the decisions, in recognition of the fact that his authority was based on undeniably strong foundations: his English test results and his encyclopaedic knowledge of rock music and football, the cornerstones of British culture as far as any eighteen-year-old was concerned. His position as leader had emerged unscathed even after some of the more questionable activities he had come up with during those two weeks. The concert at the Hammersmith Apollo, for instance, which had been a brutal assault on the eardrums orchestrated by an unlikely-looking, punk-era survivor and his band mates, enveloped in the acrid-smelling cloud from hundreds of smoking joints. Or the train journey to Liverpool on the first day of the football season, a mid-August afternoon that felt like November. Cold, damp and grey, a nightmare for his friends but a dream come true for Cédric. This was the place he had craved to see ever since the day he had adorned his bedroom door with a simple, hand-drawn copy of the sign that greets players as they come down the steps from the dressing rooms: a red liver bird on a white field with the words 'This is Anfield'. Anfield Road, home of Liverpool FC. A warning to visitors, a reminder to the home side, a myth for football fanatics.

This is Anfield. And he was there. He was about to watch a match from the concrete terraces of the Kop, the local supporters' area where, in those days, fans still stood to see the game. Thinking back, he could not even remember who Liverpool were playing. The team must have been small fry, otherwise they would not have been able to find tickets. He savoured the wait from within the passionate heart of Anfield, contemplating the still-empty pitch and murmuring about how there is nothing quite so green as the grass in an English football ground. Wilfred was standing at his side, listening to him with the melancholy air of someone who is forced to accept the evidence before him: that his best friend has reached a point where psychiatric hospital is no longer just an option but rather a painful necessity. Shortly thereafter it had begun to rain – the same slow, steady downpour that was forming a thin veil on the bonnet of the wailing sedan at that very moment, but ten degrees colder – and the crowd had begun to sing *You'll Never Walk Alone*, Gerry and the Pacemakers' hit that had become the Reds' anthem during the 1960s. Cédric had known the words by heart then and he still did now. Oddly enough they were in harmony with the scene outside the entrance to the car park: *When you walk through a storm / Hold your head up high / And don't be afraid of the dark / At the end of the storm / Is a golden sky / And the sweet silver song of the lark / Walk on through the wind / Walk on through the rain / Though your dreams be tossed and blown / Walk on walk on with hope in your he-*

art / And you'll never walk alone. The opportunity to sing along with fifty thousand fans at Anfield Road had been right there for the taking, but Cédric had managed nothing more than a noiseless murmur. Stock still, covered in goose pimples, with tears in his eyes and a lump in his throat, utterly overwhelmed, he wondered how on earth Wilfred and the others could laugh and make jokes about the bald, bare-chested, tattoo-covered behemoth who was singing his heart out three terraces below them. Then he had hit on the answer: they were enjoying themselves, or at least trying to, because they were at a football match. But Cédric was in church, and church was not a place for laughter. How would he be able to justify his friends' sacrilege if the faithful around him had held him responsible? It was best not to think about it. Three years after the Heysel disaster and despite the assurances Cédric had used to convince the other musketeers to accompany him, Liverpool fans still had a fearful reputation.

***

The first time, he had been seven years old. Now, at eighteen, he was amazed by how easily he could summon up the image of himself sitting in the living-room, a comic book left open on the dining table after he had been interrupted by an unusual sound,

'*Liverpool versus Saint Etienne, 1977 European Cup...*'

his gaze glued to the television, which had been left on after the news, the voice of the commentator struggling to make himself heard above the noise of the crowd, and that slow, solemn, emotional song. Liverpool versus Saint Etienne, 1977 European Cup: Cédric, as the living sports almanac that he had become, had no difficulty in slotting the different fragments into a precise context, but the memory that most stood out was the annoyance he had felt when Mum had explained to him that they had to cheer for the greens because they were French. He remembered asking himself: aren't the reds better, with their supporters' song? He had closed his comic, sat on the sofa, alone because Mum had things to do and Dad was no longer around, and watched a match from start to finish for the first time. Three one to the reds – he had been right, they were better, and it must have been the song that made them invincible.

That had been the last he had thought of it until, years later, he heard his schoolmates exchanging exciting news, or simply urban legends, of Pink Floyd's forthcoming tour in France. 'Who are Pink Floyd?' he had asked himself with the distress of a boy who, excluded by his peers, contemplates the abyss of his own ignorance for the first time. And yet, that name did ring a bell... of course! He had seen it on one of the boxes that Mum had brought with her when they had moved to Nice. A visit to the basement had confirmed it. There were three albums; apparently Dad must have liked them. This was his chance for a crash course that would then allow him to take part in his friends' discussions. What strange music, he had thought as he listened to the first tracks of *Meddle*, until a sudden thrill replaced his bewilderment: it was the reds' song, like at the match on TV! Just a few seconds at the end of the third song, followed by a rhythmic chanting: 'Li-ver-pool! Li-ver-pool!' What did it have to do with Pink Floyd? The following day, at school, he had gone up to the kids who claimed to know everything there was to know about all bands, too eager to find out the answer to be afraid of making a fool of himself, but the know-it-alls had let him down. They had had nothing useful to tell him, except what the song's English title *Fearless* meant. That was logical, he had thought: if you listen to that song you cannot be afraid of anyone, and so you win all the time, like the reds did against the greens.

His next discovery, which came at the end of the TV news, had shaken him even more than the record. Liverpool were coming to Paris, to play against Real Madrid in the European Cup Final, the following month! There was no time to lose – he had to find out everything, and make sure he was ready for when the television would play the invincibles' anthem. Why? He did not know, and nor was he interested in finding out. He had to do it, and that was that. He would look for the answer later on, when he reached the age at which he began to ask himself where his crazes had come from. And he would decide that it had been a product of the same blend of music and football, four years after the first time he had experienced it and what seemed a lifetime for a boy growing into a teenager, a coincidence which made the imminent arrival of Liverpool in France seem like some kind of prophecy.

The first thing he had done was to give up reading comics and dedicate all of his weekly pocket money to France Football, the bible of French and international football. But the match was still too far off for the magazine to run a feature on the teams. What could he do? His Mum had come up with the solution. The restaurant where she worked had English newspapers delivered to it every day as a simple and effective way of attracting British tourists. All she had to do was to ask the barman to save them instead of throwing them away at closing time, and she would bring them to Cédric. They would be almost forty-eight hours old when he read them, but what did it matter? There were four or five pages dedicated to sport every day, and at least two of them focussed on football – a veritable goldmine. That at least was the theory, but he was soon to discover that he lacked the necessary tools to reach the mother lode.

English newspapers, he had realised with horror, were written in English. How would he be able to read them? The English he had learnt in the previous months, during the two weekly hours of reluctantly endured lessons, would at most be enough to see him through the written exam. He had spent several days wondering how he could have seen it coming as the crumpled, indecipherable pages piled up on his desk, a cruel and – he had to admit – deserved punishment for his laziness. Then a headline had caught his attention, and not only because it was about a Liverpool player. He could understand it – the little he knew was enough to make out the meaning of those five words! His dejection had vanished, swept away by hope and by the discovery of a universal truth: that nothing can stop a motivated eleven year-old fighting for a good cause. Grammar book and dictionary, dictionary and grammar book: evening after evening, Cédric had figured out every last word of any articles that had 'Liverpool' in them, hours of frenzied work to overcome the barrier of hieroglyphics that stood between his thirst for knowledge and the fount of all wisdom.

In the space of four weeks, just in time for the final, his efforts had produced two memorable results. In ascending order of importance, he had got top marks on the penultimate English test of the year – the teacher seemed suspicious, how else could he have done so well if not by cheating? – and he had solved the mystery of what 'hat trick' meant. The expression had tormented him for a long time, until he had suddenly seen its connection with 'King' Kenny Dalglish's feat of scoring three goals in a single match. For some reason Mum had seemed more interested in his test marks than in Dalglish, a puzzle he mulled over as he sat in front of the TV waiting for the final in Paris to begin. Still, she was a grown-up, so she must have had a good idea of what was important in life.

It had been a dull match and the outcome was uncertain but Cédric, whose ears pricked up at every hint of singing, was not worried: the Reds were invincible. They had edged the match, just as he had expected, and three years later, by which point Cédric's obsession was beyond curing, they had become European champions once more. It had been on that occasion, during his evening inspection of the English newspapers, that Cédric had stumbled on the Holy Grail: the title and lyrics to the Kop's soundtrack. At last, the notes had become words. Despite the threatening prospect of the maths test that awaited him the following morning, Cédric had not thought twice about staying awake to translate the text and discover the secret behind the Reds' invincibility. Afterwards, more than feeling proud of his mastery of the language, which had allowed him to finish in just half an hour, he had felt confused. The words in front of him were surprising, and also slightly disappointing: sadness and hope instead of unconditional joy and certainty, a rainstorm where the blinding light of success ought to be shining.

Twelve months later, he had understood. As he trudged to school one morning in late May, after long hours filled with nightmares, his face wan and his mind replaying those horrific images – forty people dead, crushed between a stadium wall and the alcoholic rage of Liverpool's hooligans – he had felt as though he was caught in a hurricane. When he arrived, his least sensitive schoolmate had greeted him with jokes – 'Seen what your English friends have been up to?' – which he did not have the strength to answer. Then the other Musketeers had stepped in to back him up, making it clear that they would not tolerate any further jibes. A comforting thought had struck him: that what the song said was true after all, and that as long as he had friends he would never walk alone. And if that went for his schoolmates' teasing, why not believe that it could go for bad memories as well? While his passion for Liverpool plummeted, shattered by the Heysel disaster – it would take months for it to return, and when it did it was in a different, more mature form, he had assured the other Musketeers, whose doubts about this were vindicated during their trip to England – his relationship with the Kop's anthem had become deep, personal and permanent. He listened often to those few seconds at the end of Fearless, and afterwards he felt better, stronger, ready to face the storm. *Walk on walk on*

'... standing on the concrete terraces of the Kop...'

with hope in your heart / And you'll never walk alone: the message was for him, the promise of a future that would fill the void left by his most painful memory.

***

Three years later, standing on the concrete terraces of the Kop, Cédric listened to the live version of that promise, blinking back the tears that blurred his vision as he gazed at the tunnel entrance where the warriors in red appeared. Destiny had put them to the test, just as it had Cédric, but they were determined to get back their innocence, their victory, their happiness. His friends' laughter had died away, drowned out by the crowd, which rippled and roared like a stormy sea. Resistance was neither advisable nor possible; the only option was to let yourself get carried away with the crowd. But their inexperience had led them to choose a spot behind a metal bar which had rapidly been turned from an arm-rest into a kind of breakwater that the wave of fans would crash into before retreating and rushing down again. To protect their ribs they had had to move apart from one another, each one making the most of spaces left here and there by the retreating tide and managing to climb a few terraces further up. But they were no longer side by side and Cédric, on catching a glimpse through a sea of red scarves of Olivier, the shyest member of the group, who had gone as white as a sheet, had felt guilty for a moment.

But then he too had let himself be swept along with the waves, which became waterfalls every time the Reds scored, human torrents that thundered down to the advertising billboards as though they were about to stream over them and overflow onto the grass. Three or four times, that had happened. Liverpool had won easily and Cédric was radiant, despite a few bruises obtained before he had learnt how to move through the surge. Going home on the train, he had made the mistake of admitting that he had not managed to sing along with the rest of the stadium because it had been too overwhelming, and his friends did not miss their chance: 'So basically you got the best-looking girl in school into bed and then you got stage-fright.' They would say what they wanted, it did not matter. In fact, he had laughed along with them. Nothing could dampen that full, perfect satisfaction at having just experienced the most exhilarating chapter of his first eighteen years.

4. 6 JUNE 1944, 00:23

... I caught a flash out of the corner of my eye and turned around. The captain was shining the electric torch onto his left wrist.

'What is it, sir?'

'I'm charging the watch up.'

'The watch?'

'I'll need it after the jump, don't you reckon?'

'Yes, but ...'

'I can't switch the torch on every time – the Krauts would see me. So I'm doing it now.'

'I don't understand ...'

'There's phosphorescent paint on the hands and the numbers, that way they glow in the dark. If you shine a light on them, the effect lasts longer. All night, I hope. I thought you knew.'

'No ... you can't read mine in the dark.'

'What is it?', he asked, taking my wrist and shining the torch on it, 'A boy scout's watch?'

'My mother gave it to me. It keeps good time.'

'But it's not much use at night. You should have asked for one in stores. Or asked me. I'd have given you mine.'

'Yours?'

'The one I used to wear. I left it at the base.'

'You have two?'

'Yep. This one's new.' He switched the torch off and placed his wrist an inch or two from my nose with such a sudden movement that I could not help but flinch, knocking my helmet against the bar, stuck behind my sho ulders and running between two struts of the fuselage, which I would grab hold of to pull myself up. The hands, the number twelve and all the other numbers were clearly visible, looking like shards of light marble inside a bucket full of coal. 'Do you see the light worked?'

'Yes ...'

'I'll bet you'd like to know who gave it to me.'

'I don't know ... as you prefer, sir.'

'It's a present.'

'From Jane?'

'From the War Ministry. A reward, for my mission.'

'What mission?'

'In Switzerland. They chose me because I had to jump at night, in the part where they speak French. My mother taught me the language – she was born in Lyon, but then you knew that.'

'In Switzerland? When ...?'

'In March.'

'You were on the camp, in March ...'

'Apart from the time in hospital.'

'Right, but ...'

'There was no appendicitis. They made it up so no one would wonder where I was. I travelled under-cover, in civvy dress, pretending I was Swiss. No one could find out I was English.'

'Why? Is Switzerland on the Krauts' side?'

'It's neutral.'

'Neutral?'

'It's not on anyone's side. And it does business with everyone, they told me: us, the Yanks, especially the Krauts. So I had to pay attention to everything, even the little details. Had to wear only the clothes they gave me because they'd had them sent over from Switzerland, avoid expressions they only use in France, order wine instead of beer... The day of the meeting I found myself

'... in front of a factory so big I thought it must be for making cars...' The Longines manufacturing facility in the 1940s

standing in front of a factory so big I thought it must be for making cars. I gave my name – a false one, of course – to a secretary and she called someone on the phone. A bloke in jacket and tie asked to see my papers, he pretended to believe they were real and then he walked me to a room. After ten minutes he came back with a thick cardboard box and handed it to me, and sent me away without getting me to sign anything, and without offering me a drink either. It was obvious he wanted to get rid of me as soon as possible, so I left and took the first train from the local station. A shame, I would have liked to go for a walk. It's a pretty place, at the bottom of a wide valley, fresh air, still a bit of snow on the meadows. I'd like to go back there in summer, after the war, and meet that bloke again to ask him what he knew about me.'

'You went to Switzerland just to pick up a package?'

'No, but I can't talk about the rest of it. Nor about how I got back to England: now that's a good story. Just think if they'd sent Lickert, instead of me.'

'Lickert?' I was embarrassed because I was sitting right between Corporal Lickert and the captain.'

'You must have heard him boasting he can speak French. Well, if the Krauts pick him up in an hour and he tries to pass himself off as one of the locals, they'll shoot him. After having explained to him that you can recognise a cockney accent even when it's dark.'

I let out a small laugh, convinced that Lickert could not hear, but I saw him turn towards me. The captain leaned in so close that I noticed his breath smelt slightly of the marmalade sandwiches he had had before getting on the plane, the same as the one he had forced me to eat a few moments before. 'Careful. If he notices you laughing at him, he'll send you back to clean the latrines out for a month.'

I was certain I had turned red and, even if nobody could see, I preferred to change the subject: 'And the watch?'

'It was in the package I brought back from Switzerland, along with the other prototypes.'

'Prototypes?'

'Experimental watches. They made them so our army could have a look. If they're approved, they'll give them to the officers. For now there are only five, and one of them's on my wrist. As you can see, I'm an important person. But don't put on airs with your friends just because you know me.'

'No, sir.'

'When I got back I reported to an official. I was about to leave the office when he tells me to wait. He cut the string and broke the seal on the box right in front of me, pulled out five paper envelopes and put them on the desk. Then he took the watch out of one of them and held it out to me: 'Keep it, it's yours.' Before he opened the package, I didn't even know what was in it. Perhaps I could have guessed, because I'd had a peek through the workshop window when I was in Switzerland. I thought I hadn't understood him right, so didn't move. 'Well?' he asked me. I told him I didn't need it because I already had a watch. I had to take it and that was that, he answered: someone in the army had pointed out that if they wanted to test its endurance, then there was no better test than the liberation of Europe. I imagine it was an officer in the Airborne Division, the same one who put me forward for the mission.'

'One of ours?'

'Of course.'

'Who?'

'That I can't tell you, and anyway there'd be no point.' He knew I did not always believe him. I wondered how much truth there was in what he had told me this time. I would check either the following day or the week after by having a look at him while he got changed: if there was a scar near his groin then it would prove he had been in surgery and had made the whole thing up.

'... the emblem off the cap badge...'
A beret on display at IWM Duxford

In the meantime I preferred to go on listening to him because, whether they were real or not, he knew how to tell a good story. 'The bloke from the Ministry tells me as I'm leaving: 'Try it out, and come back here to tell me how it went.' He basically ordered me to make it home in one piece. I haven't had a lot of presents, not even on civvy street, so I decided to celebrate. Before I went back to base I stopped off at a jeweller's and asked if they could engrave the regimental emblem and Jane's name on the back of the watch. The shop girl explained that the letters would be no problem, I could choose whichever font I preferred, but reproducing the emblem off the cap badge would be harder because they generally do elaborate engravings on gold, not steel. Then a grey-haired gent in jacket and tie came out of the workshop. He noticed my uniform and introduced himself: he was the owner. We got talking, he told me how he had fought in France during the Great War, 'Just like you,' he added. They all knew where we were being sent, but I didn't have the authorisation to answer him. So I just smiled at him, without saying a word, so as not to be rude. He understood, and changed the subject. He promised me he'd entrust the job to the best engraver he knew and that he'd do the best he could for me. He was as good as his word. And not only that: when he sent me the package, instead of the bill he'd put a letter inside. He had paid the engraver, he said, because he didn't want to charge a Knight of Freedom. Knight of Freedom: I like it, sounds better than 'captain' or 'Sir.' If it wasn't so long, I'd order you to call me that, Roger. I wrote him a couple of lines to thank him and to promise I'd do my best too, like him.'

'Twenty minutes,' shouted the radio operator, getting out of his seat behind the cockpit and starting towards the door at the far end of the fuselage: he would act as the dispatcher during the jump.

5. 31 MAY 2014, 15:35

All clear: the sun was out and the tarmac was drying rapidly. Cédric turned the key in the ignition, thanked the apartment building in a low murmur for its hospitality and, once outside, found the road almost free of traffic and the pavements empty. Less accustomed to the rain than the fans at Anfield Road, the people of Nice preferred to wait a while before going back outside. Five minutes later he had already passed the curves that wound their way uphill, flanked by villas and apartments with their tidy gardens, and was on the lane that led past the hedges to his front gate. But before he opened it he hesitated, as though wondering about his own train of thought and not knowing what it led to. Cédric the anglophile. Or the devil's advocate, as he had been dubbed by one of his female colleagues, an implacable critic of everything that had come out of the United Kingdom, from Margaret Thatcher and the unscrupulous, post-millennium world of high finance to the wars in Afghanistan and Iraq, without of course forgetting the hooligans. But the attacks were always good-humoured; she was forced to recognise that Cédric's arguments in defence of the country went beyond Liverpool and Status Quo. His birthplace, his family's memories woven into the fabric of history with a capital H, and the nature of his work ensured that he was treated with a certain degree of forbearance even by those acquaintances who shared none of his enthusiasm for Britain's charms.

'Dad's home!' The joyful shout from an open window brought Cédric back to the present, the Mediterranean in place of the Channel. Théo was in the kitchen, as he almost always was at that hour, in theory to do his homework with his mum around and with snacks to hand, but actually because he wanted to be the first to inform Sylvie of Cédric's arrival. She played along, pretending to notice only once she had heard the official announcement, even if sometimes she saw him before Théo, who was occasionally engaged in actually writing something.

'Dad's home!' Those two words were enough to push the nuisances of the storm, the forced visit to the car park, and the mortgage to the back of his mind. Théo leapt out of the door and ran to meet him as Cédric pushed the scooter along the paving-slab path that crossed the tiny triangle of grass, bordered by the hedge on one of the long sides and by the portico overhanging the front door on the other. For Théo it was not enough merely to see him first. Cédric was well aware of this fact and avoided repeating the involuntary affront he had once committed when he had given Sylvie a peck on the cheek before the ceremonial hair-ruffling that he always gave Théo, and which had become known as the 'dry shampoo'. The little prince had taken offence and had remained in a sulk until dinner time. Since then Cédric had always respected the correct order, but now Théo could not wait and rugby-tackled his father, almost tipping him over along with the scooter: 'You're late!'

'Because of the rain. I had to stop and take shelter.' He pushed the scooter under the portico and hefted it onto the stand. As he did so his gaze rested on the football and the netless goalpost that stood over it, unstable as a rickety old table and propped up against the light-coloured stone wall that marked the end of the garden and ran alongside the short side of the lawn. It had been inherited from the previous owners. They could leave it where it was, Cédric had assured them: his son would use it. A year later though, Malik had convinced Théo to try mini-basketball and the goal had lost its appeal, turning into a mere heap of bulky scrap to be gotten rid, rather than the frame of dreams that it represented for so many of his peers. Cédric had never bothered to throw it away and it was a good job – lately, Théo had gone back to having a few shots at goal now and then.

Cédric wondered which would last longer out of the rust-stained posts and the wicker armchair that he placed his backpack on as he walked into the kitchen to greet Sylvie, reassured by Théo's smile that he was now authorised to do so. With its faded beige cushion and its improbable location next to the fridge, where no one would normally think of sitting, for the last two years it had seemed to mock the very idea of good furnishing taste. In the ultra-modern kitchen with its aluminium-clad cupboard doors, dark marble worktops, glass and steel table, and grey, imitation-leather seats, it was certainly very out of place, and a stranger might have thought it had been left there by mistake. But Cédric and Sylvie knew better, associating it with a mental image of a few years back: the apartment in the city-centre and the small balcony overlooking the internal courtyard. On occasion, they somehow managed to eat lunch on that balcony while keeping an eye on Théo, a few feet away, as he clambered onto and jumped off the armchair, its rear legs on the living room floor because it was too large to get all of it outside. Nostalgia: that was why no one had yet suggested moving it to the garden or the closet for objects awaiting elimination.

An idea suddenly came to Cédric, triggered by a chance encounter a few minutes earlier. A black and white cat had crossed the road in front of him, far enough away to allow him to slow down without using the brake. Why not? If there was a cat in the house, it could use the armchair to snooze on and the piece of furniture would be a useful object once more. Théo had said once that he would like to have a pet, although he was not insistent and nor did he specify what sort of animal. It would not be a difficult choice: there was no way they were getting a dog. Cédric hated the dumb hostility shown by certain specimens, first and foremost the doberman in the Merle family's garden, two houses down, which never failed to bare its teeth at him as he passed by. He liked cats' elegance and independence, but it was too soon to mention the thought to Sylvie, much less to Théo. He would first have to weigh up the pros and cons. With this in mind, he sat down next to Théo and his exercise book to move onto the next discussion topic: how their days had been.

No big news. Sylvie limited herself, for the umpteenth time, to cursing the virus that none of the technicians seemed to be able to remove from the computer network at the doctors' surgery where she worked, and Théo had nothing particularly memorable to pester them with, like winning a free-throw competition at break time. Cédric had something to say, but maybe he could save it for later. He would not even try for the moment, because he could see from Théo's face that he wanted to deal with the day's main item without further delay. In actual fact it had been the main item ever since last Monday: the party on Sunday. It was to be a double party because Cédric and Théo shared the same birthday. This was nothing new in itself, obviously. It would be the eighth time they had both had a birthday, but only the second in the new house.

The year before, Théo had been over the moon. When he had blown out the candles on the cake there had been twenty-two people cheering him on, instead of the maximum of five or six when they had lived in the city-centre. So, long live the house and garden, and to hell with the mortgage. Sylvie did not complain about commuting or about the financial sacrifices. She enjoyed tending to the plants – a passion that was not reciprocal, judging by the mysterious run of casualties last winter in the flowerpots lined up against the portico wall – and she had never had, perhaps never even dreamed of having, such a large kitchen. Théo missed living near his friends, but he still saw them most days because he had not wanted to change schools, and when he came home he was spoilt for choice. There was the portico for practising his basketball fundamentals, his bedroom where he could listen to CDs, the kitchen-living room for doing homework and watching TV, and finally the garage, which had become a den and games room since the car was nearly always left outside the garage door – in order to be really useful it would need to have a remote control, but they had decided that for the time being it was a luxury they could do without. Cédric and Sylvie would also have been happy to go without the air-conditioning, but they had been left with no choice when Théo had seen a couple of bats in the upstairs hallway last summer and had been left traumatised by the experience. No more open windows at night, he had made them swear, and so they had been faced with an unexpected expense. And a pointless one, given that his refusal to leave his bedroom after ten o'clock at night was still in effect and allowed for no exceptions.

But this was a time for making big plans, not for dredging up bad memories. They had to organise the party and nail down every last detail: the list of guests who had confirmed their attendance, what time they would do the treasure hunt and cut the cake, the T-shirt that the birthday boy was going to wear (official authorisation had now been granted for him to wear the yellow and blue basketball team jersey), the songs that they would listen to in the living-room (here there were no ifs and no buts, they were forbidden to disturb the neighbours by playing music in the garden), the trunk where the presents would sit waiting to be unwrapped. Sylvie would have been within her rights to feel worn out before he even started, but her patience showed no sign of strain as she handled Théo's umpteenth cross-examination. He was too anxious to notice that her answers were the same as yesterday and the day before that. Cédric, left out of the conversation even though it was also *his* party, made the most of the situation by announcing that he was going upstairs for a bit.

Once he had walked the few steps that separated the top of the stairs from his personal hideaway –small but well-lit, with a French window opening onto a mini-balcony with a view of the lawn, a world away from the broom-cupboard he had had in the apartment – Cédric sat down as his desk and looked around. He liked to take the time to appreciate the professional set-up that he had created: the desk extension for the monitor and keyboard, the two chairs on the other side of the desk and, at the end of the room, the wall covered with well-stocked bookshelves.

The only flaw was the armchair, comfortable but with no armrests. One of Théo's ideas. He had been at home when it had been delivered and, while watching it being assembled with Cédric, he had observed that it would be difficult for him to sit on his dad's lap with the armrests in the way. The objection was accepted without hesitation: every now and then, when Théo was not around, Sylvie did the same. In both cases the weight was negligible: their son was as small and slim as she was. 'Are you sure you're not Mexican?' he would ask her, partly to tease her and partly to make her notice him, when they had been merely members of the same circle of friends. Slightly protruding cheekbones, dark skin-tone, straight, black hair that obliged her to spend a long time in front of the mirror every morning and, every couple of weeks, apply a touch of hair dye to hide the first streaks of grey. And so Cédric the anglophile had found himself with a Mediterranean, if not positively Hispanic, partner. Two women in one, he would say to himself as he witnessed the nightly metamorphosis, a phenomenon that never failed to amaze him even after twelve years of marriage: her slightly elongated eyes went from quick and attentive to dreamy and defenceless the moment she took out her contact lenses. The change rendered them affectionate and exciting, an invitation to nocturnal activities that remained regular, gratifying and, since the night of the bats, relatively safe from interference by a little pest peeping round the door at the wrong moment. It was difficult to see how they would be able to protect their privacy once Théo had forgotten about his fear of flying mice.

**

Parties, cakes and candles. Children usually like them more than adults do, and as the years pass they wear thin, like an old suit. But for Cédric it was not like that. He preferred the present to the pale, gaunt face of the past, the sunken eyes looking out from behind teardrop lenses, the whispered birthday wishes rendered even more feeble by the coughing fits in the next room, the slice of cake hurriedly gobbled down at the kitchen table, in between the crumbs left over from lunch and a couple of dirty plates. His Mum had kept him company for a few minutes before putting down her fork and trying to sound happy as she announced that there would be a bit left over for the evening, and then gathering up the plates and turning to face the sink – in theory to do the washing up but actually so she could turn her back on him, and he had known she was crying. Happy birthday ... Perhaps Mum would have liked to promise him 'next year will be better', but she had held her tongue because she knew it was not true.

His sixth birthday, the last with Dad. After that, Cédric had not wanted any more cakes. He had been afraid that, as he tasted a piece of it in the kitchen or the living room, he would hear another coughing fit and see his mother hide her face to cry. It was only several years later that he had celebrated his birthday again, this time with the Musketeers in a pizzeria. But after cutting the first slice of margherita, he had hesitated for a few seconds, fork in hand. If he had heard someone clear their throat at the next table he would have run away. It did not happen, so he had carried on eating and celebrating, both on that birthday and those that followed. With time, and above all with the arrival of Théo, they had gone back to being good, happy events, worth remembering.

Cédric's second life had begun in that pizzeria, but his first remained an unanswered question that refused to be filed away, a story without an ending, incomplete. It must have been the same for anyone who lost a parent too soon. Who knew how many others could really understand him? He had found one of them, perhaps, three years previously, a few minutes he had never managed to forget. The boy at Sanremo. Where would he be now? Would he have found his Dad? Would someone have told him that, if he managed to find the strength to walk on with hope in his heart, he would never walk alone?

***

Fifty kilometres of motorway to do something different one summer Sunday, the *Riviera dei Fiori* instead of the *Côte d'Azur*, Italian instead of French as a background soundtrack and, above all, a table with a seaview and Gianni's *trofie al pesto*. Cédric was up to his waist, wading through the water to work up an appetite and towing Théo along behind him in a tiny inflatable dinghy. His son was beside himself with excitement at what seemed like a voyage on the open ocean, while Sylvie walked along the water's edge, dodging the sunbeds and waving to them.

'He's calling you': it had been Théo, from the dinghy, that had caught his attention. 'Dad! Dad!': Cédric had heard the insistent appeal, blending in to other beach sounds, but he had not thought anything of it. The voice belonged to a boy of about Théo's age, red swimming costume, short, blonde hair, running along halfway between him and Sylvie, brandishing a water-pistol. When Cédric had turned around, the boy had begun to shout even louder: 'Dad! Dad!', followed by a string of incomprehensible words, as he showed the pistol to Cédric. He was slightly taller than Théo, stocky without being fat, with wide, blue eyes. 'Dad! Dad!', the same entreaty again, the same indecipherable request: it sounded like a language from eastern Europe. Cédric had held his hands out, mirroring Sylvie's puzzled look: 'Are you lost? Can't you find your parents?' 'We'd better call the lifeguards,' she had suggested. A moment later, a woman about thirty-years old had entered the scene with a shout, approaching at almost a run through splashes of water, the hem of her skirt held in one hand to keep it dry. The boy had offered no resistance as she took hold of his arm and dragged him away from the surf, but before he had disappeared between the beach umbrellas, head hanging low, he had turned to face Cédric, showing him the water-pistol, his eyed filled with the sadness of one who watches an illusion disappear, only to be replaced by detested reality.

'Shall we go?' Théo was impatient to continue his voyage and

Cédric had appeased him. He had gone over the episode again later on in the restaurant, as Théo, hypnotised by the skill bordering on virtuosity with which a young couple sitting at the next table twirled spaghetti with seafood onto their forks, had momentarily forgotten to demand his parents' complete attention.

'How strange, for a kid to start calling a stranger 'Dad'.'

'Perhaps he really is your son,' Sylvie had laughed, 'One of the ones you don't know about.'

'I'm not joking. Did you see his face when that woman took him away? Maybe we should have ...'

'What? Théo gets annoyed too, when we tell him off. He was throwing a tantrum and his mum got angry, that's it.'

'You don't think he was being kidnapped?'

'Of course not! And the woman looked just like him.'

'I didn't notice, I was looking at him.'

'Don't worry about it, by now they've made up and she's bought him an ice-cream.'

'He might be an orphan,' Cédric had insisted.

'What do you mean?'

'He might not have a Dad. Or else he never knew him. He saw me with a boy who was calling me 'Dad', and he thought that meant I was his dad, as well.'

'No, no: he has got a dad, but someone told him you're the best one in the world, and he wanted to run away with you...'

'I give up – I can see there's no point trying to say anything serious today,' Cédric had shrugged, letting Sylvie change the subject and keeping the rest to himself. To put destiny right as though it were a screenplay to be re-drafted – was that what the boy with the water-pistol had been asking him to do? Or was it Cédric's imagination at work, attributing an impossible dream to another person in order to create the illusion that there was someone else who shared it with him, when in actual fact the look that had inspired the whole melodramatic scenario was simply the result of finding the water-pistol empty, unable to squirt water in his friends' faces and, as if that were not enough, embarrassed by his mum in front of a stranger? He had tried to convince himself that this was probably the case, but without success.

***

Master of the sky over Nice once more, it was as though the sun wanted to take revenge on the storm, giving off a light of such intensity that the shiny black monitor in Cédric's study became a mirror, reflecting an image that was clear down to the last detail. Brown hair, increasingly sparse across the temples; eyebrows, too thin to conceal the scar he had been left with as a boy when he had fallen off his bike; large, brown eyes – 'The handsomest thing about you', Sylvie would remind him, before adding with a laugh, 'In fact the only thing!' It was true: the deviated septum was not exactly film-star material, and the same could be said for his lips, so little inclined to smiling that they looked even worse than they really were. There was no call for vanity, and yet Cédric looked at that face for a long while. He was not searching for recompense, but for a memory, a reference point, a family resemblance, confirmation of what his mother sometimes told him: 'Your eyes are just like his.'

He interrupted his contemplation when he noticed the green light on the bottom corner of the monitor. Someone had used the computer and forgotten to turn it off. It was not hard to imagine who, given that Sylvie, after having finished her daily battle with the office computers, made it her business not to prolong the torture once she got home. Théo had discovered computer games and the internet a few months earlier, but he was beginning to show signs of addiction. For the time being, his parents had limited themselves to imposing certain limits – like using the internet only when both of them were at home – and refusing his pleas to buy him new computer games. The problem was that saying 'no' was never enough – afterwards there always followed a long discussion. A few weeks before, they had stumbled across inspiration in the form of a newspaper article: the story of a boy from Toulouse who had been taken to hospital after sitting for a few hours in front of a computer screen and suffering an epileptic fit. They had used it to justify the umpteenth refusal and something must have sunk in because Théo had yet to raise the subject again. Apparently though, in the meantime, he was breaking the ground rules.

'Théo!' Cédric was using his 'angry' voice, leaning his head around the study door.

'Yeah ...?' The cautious tone of the answer from downstairs pretty much amounted to an admission of guilt.

'Did you turn the computer on?'

Silence.

'Have you forgotten the rules? No internet unless me and Mum are both at home.'

Silence.

'Did you hear me?'

'Yes ... it was Pierre, he told me to.'

That was why he was so quiet: he was deciding on a defensive strategy. 'Who?'

'Pierre. He wanted to... we were playing, and he couldn't remember something.'

Should he get angry or let it go? Weighing against the defendant were his dishonesty and the fact that he was trying, it seemed, to take his parents for fools. In his favour, the apparent improvements at school – 'He seems more motivated', his teacher had announced when she had met with Sylvie at the start of the month – and the party, now so close at hand that it offered a limited and temporary immunity for minor transgressions: 'I'll let you off this time, but from now on we want to know what you're up to, when you and Pierre decide to do something. Agreed?'

'Yes Dad.'

'Try and remember.'

It was always Pierre's fault: when Théo ran to the garage halfway through dinner, normally just at the moment he had to eat some vegetables ('We agreed to meet'), when he tried to gain a few more minutes in front of the TV ('Just to the end of the film, he likes it'), when he began fitness programmes that had nothing to do with basketball ('He says I need to do push-ups to strengthen my arms'), even when he had disappeared, scaring his mother half to death. It had been a Wednesday, a free day both for Théo and Sylvie, and she had been keeping an eye on him from the kitchen as he played in the garden. But a few minutes later, the time it took to go to the toilet and empty the washing-machine, he was no longer anywhere to be seen. She had called for him dozens of times, searched the house from top to bottom, rung a few of the neighbours' doorbells to ask whether anyone had seen him, before her anxiety had turned to panic. She had sent two text messages to Cédric – the same message, sent two minutes apart: 'Ring me now!!' – and, when he had called back from the school, she had begged him in between sobs to run to the nearby police station with the photo of Théo he kept in his wallet, because in cases of kidnapping they needed to act fast. And then, before she could hang up, she had let out a scream so piercing that it could have done long-lasting damage to Cédric's hearing: 'THERE HE IS!' She had seen him walking calmly along the pavement in front of the house and raced outside. 'Where were you?!'

'Pierre had never seen our road, so we went for a walk. You know the Merles' dog, when we walked past, it started whining and ran off. The next time I go out I'll take him with me again.'

'The next time you go out without telling me, I'll lock you in your room for a week!' she had shouted at him, so beside herself with emotion that Théo, that evening, had admitted to Cédric that he was a little bit worried about Mum.

It was about time he stood up to Pierre and told him that they could not carry on like that. After having given him the chance to explain himself, of course. The problem was that Pierre could no more defend himself than he could be punished, because he did not exist. It was very clever of Théo, this imaginary friend, a play partner or a scapegoat according to what the situation called for, and Cédric had no problem remembering when he had entered their lives. It was the week when they had all watched an old film with Gérard Depardieu and Whoopi Goldberg together.

Depardieu played the imaginary friend of an eight-year-old boy, the same age as Théo, who helped him to get over the trauma of losing his mother.

The next Saturday morning Théo had walked into the kitchen and, without even a glance at the bowl of cereal on the table, announced that he too had a friend like the one in the film, but that his name was Pierre, and not Bogus. He could have thought of a more imaginative name, Cédric had thought, as he winked at Sylvie. It had not been enough merely to take note of the news. Théo had wanted his parents to follow him so that he could introduce the new arrival: he was in the garage because that was where he was staying. Taken by surprise, Cédric and Sylvie had been forced to put off their breakfast and morning perusal of the newspapers to appease him, asking themselves how they were supposed to behave in a situation such as this. Should they pretend to see the ghost, or speak to it, or ask it whether it was satisfied with the lodgings it had been assigned? Or should they start immediately, albeit delicately, to dismantle the illusion? What happened if the father chose the first solution and the mother the second, or vice-versa?

There was no time to agree on a united front – they had had to improvise. Then again, all parents have to improvise: the illustrated manual by the distinguished and refined paediatric psychologist that Cédric and Sylvie had bought when she was pregnant was still sitting in the cupboard, in the box where it had been put when they had moved, and nobody had felt the need to get it out again.

'Mum and Dad, this is Pierre. Pierre, this is Mum and Dad.' A perfect introduction; if only Théo paid that much attention to his manners when they had real visitors. Cédric had touched Sylvie arm lightly with his hand and, having received a nod of assent, addressed himself to the garage door: 'A pleasure to meet you, Pierre. Do you like staying here with us?'

'What are you doing?' Théo had rebuked him.

'What do you mean? I'm saying hello ...'

'Then look at him. He's next to the locker.'

'Sorry, I couldn't see him very well. The light isn't bright enough, I'll have to get a move on and change that bulb, otherwise Pierre won't even be able to read.'

'Don't worry, he said it's ok as it is. In the beginning I had trouble seeing him as well. With that black face and all ... But his hands are white, you can see them immediately.'

'White?'

'Well, no. Pink, like ours.'

Apparently Théo had come up with his own personal solution to the problem of integration, a guest who was both black and white at the same time. Either that or he had created Pierre by mixing together elements of his two real best friends, Malik and Yves. 'See you again soon, Pierre. And have a nice day.'

Théo had seemed satisfied: now that all the family members had met, he could get back to what he was doing. Lately though, the amount of time he had been dedicating to Pierre had increased and the habit of blaming him for initiatives his parents did not approve of was starting to become annoying. 'We should have watched a different DVD,' Sylvie had sighed a few evenings before.

Cédric had smiled: 'Not necessarily. If space mutants had arrived instead of Pierre, there wouldn't even be room for the scooter in the garage.'

'Why does he need an imaginary friend? He's got real ones.'

'And why do you need to watch Reese, the one out of *Person of Interest*? You've got me.'

'He's real.'

'The actor is, but not the character.'

'Let's try telling him that he's left.'

'Who, Reese?'

'Sometimes I worry you're *not* doing it on purpose.'

Cédric had always played for time, up to today. He was satisfied with the solution he had come up with a moment earlier. If Pierre's projects could be assessed by Théo's parents first, then that was fine. If not, he would need to think of a more drastic solution. But not before the party: Pierre was a guest of honour and the only one with a reserved seat, right in front of the TV, 'That way he won't get bored', which Théo was going to tell everyone not to sit on. The day before, Cédric and Sylvie had negotiated over the concession, getting Théo's word that he would make his own bed for a month. It was a good deal, they had agreed before they went to sleep, and one that deserved to become a permanent addition to the house rules. They might be able to reach the next agreement on spinach. The problem was finding an offer enticing enough to make him eat it once a week instead of just once a month.

***

He had better check what Théo was up to on the computer. Cédric touched the mouse and an image appeared on the screen that seemed to have nothing to do with basketball or – heaven forbid – school research, but nor did it raise any suspicion of dangerous virtual relationships. It was a round, silver-coloured disc on a black background, with six rectangular grooves spaced equally along the outer edge, like sunbeams, and an elaborate

'... a round, silver-coloured disc...'

design in the centre with the word 'Jane' written above in italics. A medal? On the address bar Cédric could see the usual 'www' followed by a long series of words that meant nothing to him, broken up by slashes and punctuation marks. He was about to click 'back' when he stopped. The design. Or rather, the emblem. For the average gameshow contestant it would have been an esoteric symbol worth a hundred thousand euros, but for him it was the dustjacket of an encyclopaedia he knew by heart, line by line and cover to cover. The parachute with a crown and a lion above it, with wings on either side. Parachute Regiment, the elite of the British army, both now and in the past: Afghanistan, the Falklands and, above all, D-Day. If he really had been on a gameshow the host would have done well to cut his losses, sign the cheque and end the programme there and then, because otherwise Cédric would have bored the audience to tears with an interminable monologue. But there was no cheque. Why did they never ask the right person the right question?

The right person; earlier that day, even the head-teacher had given him some recognition, in his own way – he was not the expansive type. That was what he would have liked to talk about when he had got in, before the avalanche that was Théo launched himself into Sylvie with his concerns about the party, forcing Cédric to beat a hasty retreat. Aurélien Rascoussier, strict Latinist (*nomen omen*, as he would say), *asking* if he could observe Cédric's history lesson, instead of simply announcing the visit as he usually did with the teachers. Indeed, it had not been one of the routine observations as part of the normal rotation, but an unscheduled one connected to Cédric's request. The head-teacher had seemed annoyed: why did he not know about this book? Cédric had explained that he did not like to boast. 'Not boast, but at least mention it,' his boss had shot back, perhaps regretting, a moment later, not having formulated the sentence in Latin to render it more effective. Cédric had excused himself with all the humility he was capable of; if need be he would have got down on his knees and begged. He would do everything short of bursting into tears, to get those three days of leave out of him. He would not, could not, turn down the invitation to accept his own personal Nobel prize: a book on the Normandy landings, the presentation at a bookshop in Caen, not as a spectator but as an interpreter during the public meeting with the author and, above all, the translator of the French edition, with the journey and stay both paid for. The head-teacher had kept him on tenter hooks until that morning, when – not without playing up the difficulties involved – he had announced that he had managed to sort out a substitute teacher. Then he had asked when he would cover the material from the book in class. 'Today,' replied Cédric. The seventieth anniversary was only days away and, since 6 June fell on a Sunday, he might as well teach the lesson beforehand.

Hence Rascoussier's request, and Cédric's obligatory assent. On the other hand, there was no call for anxiety regarding the presentation. Why should he be worried? He was on his home turf and knew he could count on his students. Whenever he made the mistake of boasting about it, Sylvie always made fun of him: 'Of course, you're a teacher from a TV programme. In fact, you're so unbelievable no producer would ever pick you as the star.' He pretended to be annoyed, but deep down he was pleased. What was the problem with being someone they could talk to, who allowed a bit of fun in his lessons?

Sometimes he gained advantages that went beyond mere good relations and discipline in class. Like last autumn, when Adrien, a second year student and computer whiz, had put a film he had downloaded off *YouTube* on his mobile phone: *You'll Never Walk Alone*, sung together by Liverpool and Barcelona fans before a Champions League match, enough to bring tears to his eyes just like that afternoon at Anfield. It had become his favourite ring tone, in fact the only one that had his permission to wake him up at a quarter to seven. Nice try, he had congratulated Adrien, at the same time as letting him know he should not delude himself: technological wizardry would not be enough to guarantee him even half a point extra in the next test. The boy, bespectacled and skinny as apparently all hackers were, had not hesitated to get his own back. In response to Cédric's question – 'How did you do it?' – he had given him the sceptical look of a NASA pilot wondering why he should waste his time explaining to some old dinosaur how a shuttle worked, and cut the conversation short: 'I've got to go, sir, Sandrine's waiting for me.' And with that he had rushed off, leaving Cédric to meditate on the strangeness of the adolescent world – could a geek like that really cheat on his computer with a girl, let alone a first-year bimbo like Sandrine? – and preventing him from pondering the second question: is it legal to download that stuff? He had had to make do with imagining Adrien's non-answer, represented in the same lost expression he would have worn if they had taken him to see a Chinese film without subtitles. The operating system installed in the brain of teenager.2000 treated copyright laws like an intruder that could be neutralised by the most primitive of antivirus software, and therefore irrelevant. Cédric should have thought about that before handing over his mobile phone. But he did not and now, when he heard the ring tone, he sometimes felt a slight pang of conscience. Not strong or often enough to actually delete it, though.

Teacher from a TV programme. What nonsense. He knew that, within certain limits, he had to allow them some breathing space. That was why every now and then he tolerated a bit of daydreaming, so long as it did not distract those who wanted to concentrate. When that happened, he raised his voice and threatened consequences. Normally it was with the first-year students: the events of the distant past did not seem to exert any great attraction over them and, when history was the final lesson of the day, maintaining discipline became a problem.

When they reached the twentieth century though, things changed. By that point the students had grown up a bit, and the fact that these things had occured in their grandparents' lifetimes piqued their interest. The change became visible when the subject was the Second World War and, in particular, D-Day. In those lessons, Cédric noticed, there was no need to maintain discipline. It was always the same, whether the head-teacher was in the classroom or not. That was why he was not worried. As he spoke, indicating the positions of the opposing forces on the blackboard, he had thrown a few glances at the class out of the corner of his eye, but only through force of habit: he was certain that nobody would take advantage of the situation to check their mobiles or exchange jokes with their classmates. Everyone almost motionless, elbows on desks, as silent as if they had been watching an action film. And it was thanks to him, today as on the other occasions: thanks to how he told it, how he took part in it, the tone of his voice and his gestures. Then came the questions, a lot of them: on the Resistance, on the paratroopers, on the massacre at Omaha Beach, on the artificial American harbour destroyed by the storm, on Hitler, who was asleep because no one dared to wake him at dawn and tell him what was happening on the beaches of Normandy.

Rascoussier had waited for the classroom to empty before walking up to the teacher's desk and saying, jokingly: 'Not bad, Roussel'. From him, that was worth a degree *honoris causa*. Cédric had smiled, pleased but not surprised, because he had seen in that comment a formal assent, the inevitable acceptance of a predestined decision he had never been in any doubt about. Being born in Caen, Normandy, on 6 June, was always going to mean something to a person with a relative who was involved in the events preceding and following the longest day. Grandad Jean-Jacques had passed away before he was born – 'too soon,' his father used to comment, little suspecting the omen that hid behind his affirmation – but had always been proud of the life he had led and the things he had done in those months, firstly as a runner for the Resistance and then as an informant working for the Allies. The tales of those deeds had been part of Cédric's childhood and had helped shape his consciousness. The 'Big Bang' of his love of all things English, even before Liverpool and Status Quo. And to all these memories was added, eight years earlier, yet another curious coincidence: Théo too was born on 6 June, a few minutes before midnight and a week before the date given by the gynaecologist, as though it had been important to him to respect both deadlines and family traditions.

***

After his father died and they had moved to Nice, where one of Mum's uncles had found her a job as a waitress, it had been her that had carried on the tradition. Cédric wanted to keep listening to the war stories, that way he had the impression that Dad was still around and that his grandfather, whom he had never met, was present at family gatherings. It made him feel as though he had as many relatives as his schoolmates. Poor Mum, he said to himself at times: what an effort she had been forced to make. To make him happy she probably had to read books, memorise names, dates, places and events in order to create an adequate setting for her father-in-law's deeds. Often while sitting at his bedside, she kept a notebook filled with dense lines of text open on her knees, perhaps the notes she made to be sure she was up to the job. She might well have made some parts up. He had asked her once, but the answer had been evasive and he had not insisted. What reason was there to tarnish the memory of those evenings, when Cédric refused to go to sleep unless she first told him a story, any story, about the maps of the fortifications drawn up by Grandad in the weeks leading up to the landings, about the danger he put himself in to deliver messages he had never read to people with aliases instead of real names, about the meetings with Landon, the officer to whom he passed information on German troop movements during the battle of Caen? Strange boy, she must have thought: rather than the superheroes from comics, cartoons and films, he preferred the stories of ordinary young men, some of them French and many others who came from far away to fight in places they had never heard of and, in many cases, die there.

For him they were not just war reports or family history. They were also a pretext to cultivate the memory of his roots. Holidays were permanently off the agenda: family finances would not stretch to cover them, and in any case – Mum would chide him – who needed the cold, grey Channel when they lived within arm's reach of the inviting water of the *Côte d'Azur*? To Cédric it had always sounded more like a case of sour grapes. The visits to the cemetery and relatives on his father's side continued, but they left him with a bitter taste in his mouth. These trips were rare, hurried and depressing. The minute they arrived in Caen Mum would give the impression that she was anxious to get back to the station, to such an extent that when they really did head back, a day or two later, even Cédric felt relieved. But not for long. As the train pulled out of the station and Mum deceived herself that she could leave the bad memories behind her just as easily, it was Cédric that was left crushed beneath the weight of nostalgia and regret.

The years had not removed the burden, but the emptiness was less empty. Even if he had not worked it out by himself, Cédric would have been able to read it in his Mum's eyes when he took Théo to see his grandmother every Sunday morning, in the two-room apartment five minutes from the *Promenade des Anglais* that she had not wanted to leave, even when he and Sylvie had suggested that she move into the new house with them. Too far from the shops, the church and her friends, she had explained, but the real reason was that she did not want to burden the family with her health problems. And so she made do with the weekly visit. But the following Sunday would be different from normal: Cédric would go to pick her up and take her back to the house. If the party finished late she could stay at theirs, and perhaps she could take on the task of entertaining Théo with stories of Grandad Jean-Jacques. If she still remembered them. For him it was no problem – fate had decided that one day they would inspire his choice to go into teaching, his debut as a translator and, that morning, the 'not bad' from the head-teacher. He would have liked to tell someone about it, but he would have to wait in line until Sylvie had finished reassuring Théo.

6. 6 JUNE 1944, 00:46

... 'Twenty minutes!' shouted the radio operator, getting out of his seat behind the cockpit and starting towards the door at the

'... getting out of the seat behind the cockpit...' The interior of the Dakota aircraft on display at the Merville Gun Battery Museum

far end of the fuselage: he would act as the dispatcher during the jump.

We stood up to clip our static lines to the cable running along the roof of the plane and repeated the sequence down to the 'All OK', before sitting back down to await the signal.

'Five minutes!' The captain moved up to the doorway. I followed him, with Lickert and the others behind me, parachutes, haversacks and bags getting in the way of those few steps down the fuselage. The captain leant out but pulled himself back in immediately – the wind must have been stronger than expected. As I strained to see past his helmet, following the clouds that passed beneath us with my gaze, I felt a violent jolt, and then a rumble. I only stayed standing because there was no room to fall, so closely packed was I between the captain and Lickert, who had turned around, cursing. The radio operator was lying motionless on the floor, his head and back against the tail bulkhead – he seemed to have fainted. The last two men in the line had lost their balance and tumbled back almost as far as the cockpit door. I heard someone shouting that his rifle was stuck and saw one of my mates attempting to help him, risking being knocked down himself, tossed about by the flak and by the pilot who was swerving this way and that to avoid being tracked by the searchlights.

We looked like rag-dolls in a box, rolling down a bumpy trail. But rag-dolls do not throw up, unlike Whaite. When I spotted him crouched down behind Lickert, hands on the floor, I wondered whether it had been a good idea to accept one of the captain's sandwiches. The red light to the right of the doorway lit up. We were supposed to wait another minute for the green light, but the Dakota banked hard, throwing the captain who disappeared outside, sucked into the darkness. I hesitated a second too long. 'Out!' Lickert shouted in my ear, so loudly I feared they would hear him on the ground as well.

A good thing I had no time to think about it. I jumped, just the way the instructor had bet I would never be able to, with my arms across my chest and my knees together, holding the position until

'... an instant later,
the parachute opening...'

I felt the jolt of the static line and, an instant later, the parachute opening. If the pilot had managed to maintain the correct altitude, I had jumped at six-hundred feet and had twenty-five seconds to get my bearings, avoid ending up in a tree or on a rooftop, and above all to detach the kitbag, dangling it from the rope fixed to the parachute harness so that it would absorb the initial impact. Unhooking it too quickly risked snapping the cord and losing the lot, but failing to separate it from my body would be even worse: with that amount of weight tied to my shinbone and my foot stuck underneath it, I would run the risk of breaking my leg on landing, which is what had happened to a corporal from B company during training. I grabbed hold of the rope and, when I felt it pull taut, tugged at it with all my strength, before letting it unwind as slowly as possible. As I descended, I glanced upward to look for my companions. I saw a couple of them twenty feet above me. I wondered whether they had all managed to jump.

They began to open up from below. Bursts of light-arms fire and tracer rounds: one passed right by me and went through the canopy. I had not considered this before. I knew I would be an easy target and that I might have ended up entangled on an obstacle, but the idea that my parachute could catch fire had never even occurred to me. They were firing at random, they could not see me because I was still in the clouds. And they were not only clouds, I realised then, but also the dust thrown up by the air raid that had preceded the jump and carried on the wind.

What I saw below when I left the clouds behind me froze the blood in my veins: the faint reflections of a body of water, unmistakable despite the darkness. A lot of water, everywhere. I recalled the photos taken by the reconnaissance aircraft, the valley between two rivers that had been partially flooded to obstruct parachute landings. The pilots would do their best to avoid it, they had assured us. Apparently ours had not quite managed it. Or else we should have waited for the green light, but if we had done then the captain would have found himself alone. I found a point of reference in what looked, from high up, to be the lit window of a house and grabbed hold of the lift web with my free hand to correct my descent. If I had landed in water it would have been big trouble, but there was no time to unsheathe the dagger and cut away the excess weight. I knew I was in luck when I saw the kitbag hit mud, sinking a couple of inches into it. The impact, a moment later, was the softest I had experien-

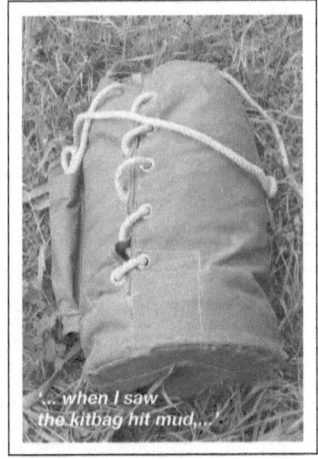

'... when I saw the kitbag hit mud,...'

ced since beginning my training.

I waited for the parachute to settle onto the water, sat up and opened the quick-release buckle. I pulled the straps off of my legs and shoulders, checked the kitbag was still closed and looked around me. The moonlight shining through the clouds reflected off of an artificial lake bordered by hedgerows on three sides and, in the distance, by a dark, irregular screen – behind those trees there must be the light I had seen coming down. I took a few steps towards the nearest hedgerow, glancing at the blades of grass sprouting up here and there, and wondering where I had ended up. What I could see had nothing to do with the pictures we had studied at the base, a clearing nestled between small plots of land, orchards and patches of vegetation. I turned around when I heard a thud, or rather a splash, from the middle of the pond, followed by a strange silence. One of my mates? Why was he not getting rid of his parachute? Where had he landed? I shuddered in horror: he was drowning, dragged down by the weight of his gear. I dropped the kitbag to run and help him, but the mud sucked at my boots and I moved more slowly with each step I took. I was wading forward with the water up to my waist when the ground disappeared from under me and I plunged downwards. I touched the bottom almost instantly, but my head was underwater. I had fallen into a trench, like him. I do not know if I would have managed to escape by myself – swimming was the only sport I had never really gotten to grips with. As I groped about I felt a tap on my helmet and, turning around, I made out the shadow of a hand moving about in the water. I grabbed hold of it and felt it give such a forceful tug that my chest was out of the water in a moment, my feet dug into what must have been the edge of the trench. I recognised a familiar, bulky silhouette: 'Thank you, sir.'

'Talk quietly,' he whispered.

'He landed there, we have to ...'

He grabbed my arm: 'It was a bag, not one of our boys.'

The surface was still, dark. The captain must have been right, otherwise we would at least have seen the parachute. But I was by no means certain and nor was he, because he said, 'We've got to go' with a voice that seemed different from normal, and without letting go of my arm. As we moved towards the edge of the field, I heard him muttering the orders we had both been given, as though someone had asked him to repeat the lesson: link up with the rest of the battalion as soon as possible, no delays. I turned around once more to look for any sign of life. Nothing, just water, darkness and silence. 'Where the hell have they dropped us?'

'Shine the light,' he said, passing me the torch and pulling the map from his trouser pocket. He unfolded it at the foot of the hedge, on a patch of grass that rose up out of the pond. 'Keep it down, next to the map.'

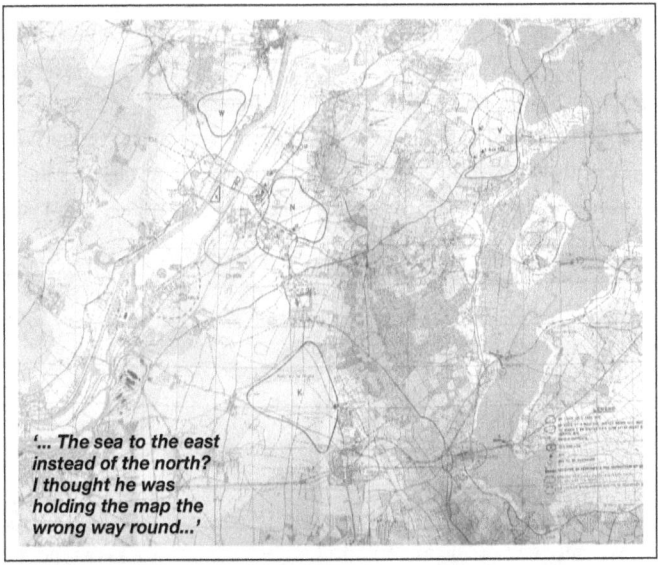

'... The sea to the east instead of the north? I thought he was holding the map the wrong way round...'

'We're here,' he whispered, indicating the squares at the centre of the light-coloured tongue of land that jutted into the blue, breaking the otherwise vertical coastline. The sea to the east instead of the north? I thought he was holding the map the wrong way round, but then I got it: what looked like the coast was actually where the flooded area and dry land met and, if he was right, the lit window I had spotted was in the village at the centre of the peninsula. He ran his index finger across the map to show me the route we would take to go around the village to the north and reach our destination, the rendezvous point, more or less three miles away. The fields we would have to cross were near to houses, but there was no other choice – just a few dozen feet further out there was nothing but water.

I felt Kadwell wrench the torch from my hand and push me down into the soaking grass. The captain threw himself to the ground and turned the light out. I saw two silhouettes moving along the hedge, about thirty yards away, crouched down low. The captain blew into the duck whistle we had been issued with to distinguish one another from strangers in the dark. No answer. He cocked his Sten and let them draw closer before whispering, 'Punch...' Although hushed, I had no trouble recognising the voice that had half deafened me on the plane twenty minutes earlier: '...and Judy!'. Strange to hear the names of those puppets there in France, in the middle of the night – the same puppets Mum and Dad had used to take me to see every now and then on Brighton seafront of a Sunday, when I was little. The Commanding Officer must have been sure the Germans would never have heard of them if he had chosen them as the watchword.

'Captain Kadwell. Who are you?'

'Corporal Lickert and Private Whaite.'

'Why the hell didn't you answer the sound, Lickert?'

'I forgot, sir. Sorry ...'

'The next time you forget something you'll get yourself shot.'

We checked our gear. Whaite had not been as lucky as me, or else his sickness on the plane had left him muddled enough to forget about the kitbag, which had come loose and plummeted down to who knew where. In the water, I hoped, wanting to find an explanation and convince myself that it really had been just a bag that had sunk, and not a friend. Lickert had lost the pouch with his rifle in it, but the rest of his gear was secure in his haversack. The captain and I had everything we were supposed to. When I wriggled free of the jump oversmock, I realised it had come in useful on the ground as well, or rather in the water: my trousers and the sleeves of my Denison smock were soaked, but my chest and back were almost dry. There was nobody nearby. The Germans must have been convinced the artificial lake would be enough. The silence was broken by the odd burst of flak, the darkness pierced by tracers chasing the aircraft as they headed for home. I remembered the advice we had been given: if you are not sure which direction to go, use the Dakotas' flight path as a reference point and go left. This corresponded both with the map and the captain's reading of it, so we started out.

7. 31 MAY 2014, 16:07

What was that enormous, silver disc filling the centre of the scre-
en? Cédric clicked back a page and another enlarged image appeared, this time accompanied by a block of text. 'British Army
WWW wristwatch' read the title. It looked battered: scratches
everywhere; hands partly rusted at the edges and a few cracks on
the light-coloured insert; black dial covered with tiny, elevated
points, like pores on skin; the numbers one to twelve arranged
around the outer border and printed in a colour some way betwe-
en orange and brown, which had run over the edges in some places. And, slightly above the point where the hands joined, there
was a symbol of the same colour, similar to a circumflex accent
but with a third line descending vertically from the top. Next to
the main image were three thumbnails, each accompanied by an
enigmatic name: 'Movement', 'Caseback' and 'Caseback interior'. When he clicked on the one in the middle, the metal disc
with the name and emblem reappeared on the screen.

He clicked back to the description again: 'Manual wind watch,
stainless steel case, screw-down back, luminous hands and in-
dexes. 1940s. Diametre 37mm, thickness 10mm. Movement: 12
lignes, 15 jewels, lever escapement, monometallic balance, flat
hairspring'. What on earth did it mean? Never before had Cédric
read two whole lines written – apparently – in his own langua-

'... hands partly rusted at the edges...'

ge without understanding a word of it. He at least had a chance with the following paragraph: 'The British Army commissioned a number of Swiss manufacturers to produce Wrist Watch Waterproof (WWW) watches during the Second World War. In this piece the broad arrow symbol, used to identify Government property, appears on the dial but not on the caseback, where a female name and the emblem of the British Parachute Regiment, which took part in the Battle of Normandy, are inscribed instead.

Comparison with watches of the same type and accompanying documents allow us to guarantee that the piece is an authentic original, despite the absence of the brand's name on the dial and on the movement's bridges, and the missing serial numbers on the caseback and underneath the lugs. Fair condition (movement overhaul recommended)'. A little underneath this, at the centre of the page and written in bold, appeared the words: 'Estimate: €2,500-3,000'

Why was Théo looking at this? Bright for his age as he was, it was difficult to imagine him grappling with an online auction, and even if he found it fun, like some sort of computer game, he would not have any credit card details to give. Clicking on the link to the homepage, Cédric found himself looking at the trademark of a Paris auction house and, going back to the watch again, at an icon that turned out to be the cover of a catalogue. On 4 June, at Deauville – the Normandy of the well-to-do and the perfect place to flog such a piece of scrap. Fair condition? And what did things in poor condition look like? And for 2,500 euro or more. A cursory glance at the rest of the catalogue was enough to see that this was one of the cheaper lots for sale.

Half past four. Cédric had no desire to empty his backpack and file the notes he had used earlier, he would do it after dinner. For now he wanted to find out where Théo had started out from in order to end up on that page. It was no use asking him, he would just drag Pierre into it again and at that point Cédric would feel obliged to get angry. What was it that made kids wind up their parents? An experiment to see how far they could push the boundaries? Craving attention? Need for affection? As far as he could remember, not even the manual buried away in that box gave any convincing explanations.

The browser history took Cédric to the *Google* homepage, where the auction house website was the ninth hit on the list for the search: 'www British Army'. So that was it: Théo was convinced that the letters 'www' were a kind of magic spell to be used all over the place, even in the search bar. The combination had taken him to the watch and the catalogue and, since it did not interest him, he had gone down to the kitchen and forgotten to turn the computer off. As for his interest in the British Army, there was an explanation for that as well, and Cédric liked to think that it was down to him, or rather the toy soldiers.

***

It had surprised him, a month or so earlier, to see them on the shelf above Théo's bed. Why had he brought out those veterans from Cédric's childhood, who had survived so many house-moves unscathed? Mum had given them to him after they had moved to Nice to provide physical back-up for the stories: a dozen British Second World War paratroopers, the ones whose emblem was on the watch, all of them a couple of inches in height. When the original box had broken, torn by heavy use, Cédric had transferred them to a tin that had originally contained Normandy butter biscuits: a fitting home, he had told himself as he placed them under his bed, safely sheltered. But as the months had passed he had been forced to think again. The first danger had been the suitcases where Mum kept their winter clothes once the flat's modest cupboard space had been filled – an armoured column which advanced under the bed, generally while Cédric was at school, forcing the paratroopers to retreat further and further back. Getting them out to play had become more difficult with each passing day, until eventually it had no longer seemed worth the effort. Cédric had grown up, the khaki heroes had given way to the champions in red, and one day Mum had gone for the sucker punch: 'Why don't we give them to Mrs Duchamp's boy? You don't play with them any more ...'

The attempt had backfired. It had reminded him of the existence of the box, making him feel guilty for having completely forgotten about it for so long, and inspiring his standpoint on the issue in the years to come: a tenacious and determined resistance against any logical argument, beginning with the idea that the little space available in the flat should be put to good use. Paratroopers never surrender, he had thought, so he too would stand firm. The skirmishes had become battles, but then Mum's offensives had palled when they had moved into a slightly larger flat equipped with a basement. After long negotiations, Cédric had managed to persuade her to let him use a corner of the lowest, ricketiest shelf in the cellar, backing up his request with the tragic tale of a schoolfriend who had left his sticker albums on the basement floor and then seen half of them ruined by a water leak. Not even his wedding or the move that followed had been enough to make him get rid of the soldiers. 'They're all I have left from when I was little,' he had explained to arouse his bride's sympathies, placing the box in the cupboard above the fridge with the defence that it was too high up for her to make use of it anyway. Actually it was Sylvie who was too short, but Cédric had gone for the diplomatic approach, fearing that the soldiers might be on the receiving end of any possible reprisal. With the acquisition of the new house the paratroopers had won the right to the most comfortable lodgings they had ever had, a well-deserved reward after thirty-five years of service: inside the tool cupboard in the garage, finally safe from the threat of elimination.

And they had stayed there until last winter, when Cédric had judged that Théo was mature enough to take his place as custodian and had given them to him. His reaction had been lukewarm. Old, plastic toy soldiers, coloured khaki from head to toe, must have seemed insignificant for someone who could count on the protection of Gyorx. The space mutant was stationed between the comics and the school books, an ideal vantage point from which to spot invaders before he could be seen and eliminate them – the exact term was 'disappear them', a synonym of the 80s' and 90s' 'terminate' – with the cyberguided weapons that sprouted from his forearms. He had arrived at the house in a bulky package underneath the Christmas tree, welcomed by Théo with the warmth and admiration befitting a hero of the war between the Lost Galaxy and the Ash Star. The saga, recounted in the latest Hollywood 3D blockbuster, had seduced almost every earthling under the age of twelve. Like every conflict, it had had a disastrous effect on the economy, in particular the wallets of parents pounded into submission by their nagging children, themselves victims of an authentic brainwashing campaign courtesy of the marketing that had been run parallel to the mega-production. As far as Cédric was concerned those responsible deserved a firm reprimand from all the organisations tasked with child protection, starting with UNICEF. During the first weeks of January the paratroopers had returned silently to the garage along with their box, almost in secret, as though Théo had been worried about having to explain himself. But Cédric had not asked him anything. In the end that was only fair: every generation had its own toys and its own heroes. Once more, it would be down to him to watch over them.

But a few months later and there they were again on the shelf, within hand's reach. As he said goodnight to his son, Cédric had not been able to hide his curiosity: 'What are my soldiers doing here?'

'They're not yours any more. You gave them to me.'

'I remember, but what happened to Gyorx?'

'He's in the garage, in the cupboard.'

'How come?'

Théo had hesitated before replying in a way which, at that moment, had been almost a novelty: 'Pierre prefers playing with them.'

'I'm glad to hear it. You know how fond I am of my paratroopers.'

'And I'm big now.'

'Really?'

'And he's a toy.'

'Who is?'

'Gyorx. I can't play with toys, I'm nearly eight.'

'It would have been good if you'd gotten big before Christmas, that way your mother and I wouldn't have bought him for you.'

Théo had pretended to yawn, his way of playing for time and considering possible diversions when a conversation headed in a direction he did not like. But instead of taking refuge behind a speech about NBA play-offs or Malik's new trainers, he had thrown his father with an odd question: 'Is it true you had the dark inside when you were little?'

'What?'

'Grandad was sick and everything looked dark to you. Even inside you.'

'I wouldn't put it quite like that, but yes, I was sad.'

'Was it so dark you couldn't tell friend from foe?'

'I don't think I'd go that far.'

'What about now? Do you still have the dark inside?'

'When I forget to turn the light on you and Mum take care of it. Who told you all this?'

'Nobody ...'

'You made it up? I don't believe you.'

'Grandma ...,' Théo had smiled before rolling over, thus signalling that the audience had ended. Cédric had had to keep his grumbles about money thrown away on already-forgotten presents to himself, as well as an observation: were the soldiers not just toys as well, like Gyorx? Not to Théo, apparently. And not to him. Otherwise, why would he have fought for so long to save them?

The following day he had phoned his mother: 'That story you told Théo, what made it come into your head?'

'Which story?'

'About me having the dark inside because Dad was sick. Was it you that told him?'

'No, why would I? All that sadness ...'

'Are you sure?'

'I would remember. I'm not as senile as you seem to think.'

So the first answer had been the right one: Théo had come up with it by himself. But how? Perhaps by embellishing something he had heard on the television or found on the internet, or listening to snippets of conversation around the home. Every now and again he hid behind doors to eavesdrop. He and Sylvie were aware of it, which was why certain topics of conversation were reserved for when he was asleep, or when they had checked that he was not in the immediate vicinity.

***

Two thousand five hundred euros: the figure had a kind of absurd fascination about it. If someone really existed who was willing to spend that amount of money on an old piece of scrap iron then there was truly no limit to the creativity of the rich. Was there anything they would not do to rid themselves of their excess wealth? The only watch of any value that Cédric had ever owned was his engagement gift, with a dedication on the back. It must have cost quite a bit – he had never asked Sylvie how much, but it was gold and, above all, new. And it still was, twelve years later, because Cédric rarely used it: his wedding, Théo's baptism and first communion, the day they had signed the contract to buy the house and the other rare occasions that demanded shirt and tie.

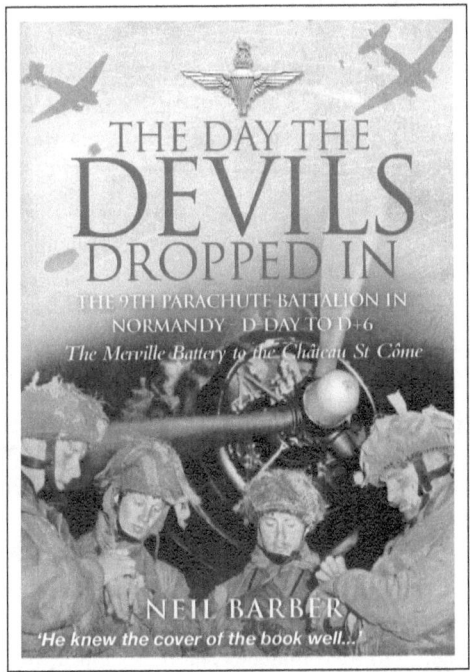

THE DAY THE
DEVILS
DROPPED IN
THE 9TH PARACHUTE BATTALION IN
NORMANDY D-DAY TO D+6
The Merville Battery to the Château St Côme

NEIL BARBER
'He knew the cover of the book well...'

Never at school, and not at home either: it was not very compatible with DIY. He had no other watches, expensive or cheap. His timekeeper was the screen of his mobile phone.

He could simply turn off the computer and not think any more of it, but that parachute with wings... Out of those participating in the auction, who knew how many would be aware of what it meant without having to consult the catalogue? One thing was certain: few individuals had access to an archive like his. Cédric stood up and pulled a book from the highest shelf on the wall. He knew the cover of the book well. The colour photo – or rather colourised after the event – was one of the most commonly used of D-Day: in the background the propeller of an aeroplane, and in the foreground four paratroopers standing in a circle, wearing camouflage jackets and helmets, looking at their left wrists, partially covered by their right hands, to synchronise watches. Which, unfortunately, were out of view.

The internet – that was where he might find something useful. Cédric went back to the keyboard and typed 'Broad Arrow', the circumflex accent with the extra leg. If the catalogue compiler had not bothered to translate the term it meant the readership knew what it referred to, and that meant *Google* knew as well. The number of results was staggering: over a million. The first on the list corresponded to a *Wikipedia* page of dense text with a couple of pictures. At the top was an elaborate emblem that only vaguely resembled an arrow. A little lower down was a milestone belonging to the Ordnance Survey, the British governmental agency tasked with drawing up maps. The symbol sculpted above the letters WD – War Department – was identical to the arrow on the watch. Apparently there were two types of broad arrow, one of them heraldic and the other used by the Government to identify military equipment, in this case a watch.

And the estimate? Cédric began with the words that corresponded to the abbreviation WWW, 'Wrist Watch Waterproof', and added the word 'price'. The avalanche of hits – eight million, this time – opened with two images. The first showed two watches similar to the one in the catalogue, but these were modern, presumably modern replicas made for enthusiasts. In the second there was an old one, almost identical. The only differences were the colour of the arrow and the numbers that showed the hours, off-white instead of orange. Cédric clicked on the other links from the first page of *Google* results, discovering a new world, the existence of which he had had no idea until that moment. Discussion groups where hundreds of collectors and enthusiasts shared friendships, advice, ideas, discoveries, the joy of a successful acquisition or the disappointment of a missed opportunity, entering a trance-like ecstasy not only when they spoke of the objects of their desire, but even while describing the cardboard boxes they were contained in, all with the aid of semi-professional photographs. And there were all kinds of prices, from the sellers present in the forums, dealers' websites, online auctions and virtual

'... he found himself staring at a pdf file...'

archives compiled with painstaking patience by bloggers. They went from one thousand five hundred euros up to four thousand, depending on their condition.

When he found himself staring at a pdf file that had the look of an essay, Cédric lingered a moment. Twenty or so pages filled with tables and diagrams, taken from a magazine and signed, according to the notes in the bibliography, by two authorities on the subject. His difficulty in reading it stemmed not from the fact that it was written in English, but from the abstruse jargon that often forced him to retrace his steps through the text in order to find the connection between words and images. He did not give up and, after an hour, he felt that he too was an expert. The article contained a little on everything there was to know on the subject: the name of the manufacturers that had produced the WWW watches for the British army; the number, estimated rather than ascertained, of watches produced; their technical features, apparently so far above average that they had only be issued to sappers and officers; the variants; the photos. The broad arrow was not only impressed in the same place on all the dials, but also engraved on the caseback, both inside and outside, and accompanied by a serial number. As the catalogue pointed out, this last feature was missing from the watch up for auction.

Although the order had been placed months earlier, the WWW watches had only begun to be delivered in May 1945, after the war in Europe had ended. None of them had therefore been used in battle. But then why did the auction house mention the Normandy campaign? Perhaps in order to render the object more desirable by associating it with an historical event, reasoned Cédric as he reopened the image to compare it with those on the pdf file and lingered on another detail mentioned in the catalogue: the watch up for sale was the only one that did not have the brand name on the dial.

The meticulous nature of a professional researcher, he told himself as he continued his investigation. When one ran into doubts it was better to clear them up rather than ignore them.

After a dozen attempts he found the clue he was looking for in a forum. The anonymous dial, explained an enthusiast in a thread regarding a watch worn in the Great War, was a precaution adopted to prevent potential investigators from tracing the origin of watches confiscated from prisoners. A wise move where Swiss producers were concerned: either side would have interpreted the supply of equipment to their enemies as a violation of the country's neutral status.

Plausible. But what need had there been for anonymity after the war had ended, when – according to the article – the WWWs had been delivered? And why were the serial numbers missing when the other examples he had seen on the internet all had them? The only certainty was that the owner had something to do with the paratroopers. If only the name had been followed by a surname ... But a 'Jane Smith' would have been useless, too common in the UK both during the 1940s and today.

Would the first owner of the watch still be alive? Unlikely – if the authors of the article were right, at least sixty-nine years had passed. The current owner could have been an heir, it was true, but how could he find out? Cédric had arrived at the foot of a wall closing off a dead end. Before giving up however, he wanted to try the only chance he had to climb up to the top and have a look at what was on the other side. The most it would cost him would be a few minutes on the phone and a euro or so. The emblem, the paratroopers, Grandad's adventures, his own work, even the toy soldiers seemed like reason enough.

It was almost six o'clock. Cédric dialled the number he had found on the contacts page quickly, as though the seconds gained would increase his chances of finding someone still in the office at closing time. 'My name is Cédric Roussel, I'm phoning from Nice. I'm interested in a watch that will go under the hammer at Deauville on 4 June. The catalogue mentions documents that show ...'

'One moment, please.' After a musical interlude, the female voice was replaced by a masculine one: 'Alain Onfray, good evening sir.' The tone resembled that of an English butler in a film, so formal as to sound fake, perhaps the style that was called for when dealing with luxury items and well-to-do buyers and sellers.

'Good evening. I would like some information on a lot that will go to auction next Friday. The catalogue says that it is a British army watch...'

'What number?'

'... Unfortunately I didn't make a note of it. I'll have a look on the internet and call you back.'

'Perhaps that is not necessary: is it the wingwatch?'

'Wingwatch?'

'The watch with the wings and the parachute on the caseback.'

'That's the one. Is that what it's called? Wingwatch?'

'No,' even his laugh had something artificial about it, 'we would have written it... that was what a gentleman from England called it yesterday when he rang for information. He referred to it as the wingwatch because the dial is anonymous, so that I would understand what he was talking about.'

'Original.'

'And effective: it worked with you as well. The number is 115, in case you were wondering. What did you wish to know? I verified its authenticity myself, and have no reason to doubt...'

'Yes, I read the website. And I saw other documents mentioned... what would they be exactly?'

'A certificate of donation dated July 1944 and a receipt from 1975.'

'Donation?'

'Stamped by Civil Affairs, Caen. A British officer gave the watch to a French citizen. The receipt refers to the transfer of the watch to a relative of its current owner.'

Caen, July 1944: that was why the catalogue mentioned the Battle of Normandy. So it was not true that the watches were only delivered after the war had ended. Not all of them, anyway. 'And the wings? The emblem, I mean. Any information on that?'

'Only what we have already written: it belongs to the Parachute Regiment.'

'Is it possible to have a look at the documentation?'

'It will be available to the public on Friday morning at Deauville along with the watch itself, at the hotel hosting the auction.'

'Would it be possible for you to send me a scan via email? It's just that I live in Nice and I don't know ...'

'I'm afraid not, sir. If everybody asked...' His attitude had changed, from obliging and formal to cold and formal. Whether by experience or because he had a nose for it, Mr. Onfray must somehow have sensed that he was not talking with an auction regular, nor even an amateur with money to burn, and would like to get rid of him as soon as possible so that he could dedicate himself to other more commercially enticing prospects, or simply to go home.

What could earn him a few more moments of the man's attention and improve his image in the eyes of the auctioneer? Quick wits and a bit of nerve: 'I have other watches like this one, but I have not been able to trace where any of them were actually used. Judging by the certificate in the catalogue it was worn during the Normandy campaign, which would make it doubly as valuable to me. My grandfather was a member of the resistance who lived in Caen, you see. I was born there as well, actually ... Do excuse me if I insist, it is very important. If I may I would like to leave you my phone number and email address, that way if you find five minutes maybe you can send me over a copy. If you need the owner's permission, pass on my details to him by all means.' He might not be able to seduce Onfray, but he only needed to plant the seed of doubt: what if the man on the phone were to become a good customer? After all, the *Côte d'Azur* conjured up images of a filthy-rich playboy, not of a teacher plagued by nightmares of mortgages, and Cédric had no reason to give details of his occupation unless they were specifically asked for.

'I'll see what I can do ... What did you say your name was?'

'I didn't. It's Roussel.'

'Roussel…?'

'Yes, R-O-U-S-S-E-L.'

'Roussel … And your first name?'

'Cédric. Shall I spell it?'

'That won't be necessary. And you're from Caen, you said?'

'I was born there, but I've lived in Nice for a long time.'

'So, Roussel without a double L and an E at the end then…'

Mr. Onfray must either have been hard of hearing or else it had been a long day – it was not exactly an unusual surname. 'That's right, without a double L and an E at the end.'

Two thousand five hundred euros: judging by the crash course he had just completed on the internet the figure was about right, at least by the standards of those lunatics that made up the world within a world. The finding irritated him. In fact, he was irritated by his own irritation. He had researched the topic and made the phone call merely to satisfy his curiosity. What did the price matter?

8. 6 JUNE 1944, 01:27

... This corresponded both with the map and the captain's reading of it, so we started out.

We stayed in single file as we moved along the narrow, grassy ground at the water's edge, brushing through leaves and branches, because using the road on the other side of the hedge would have been too risky. We had to avoid running in to anybody, above all the enemy. The mission came before everything else. In our case, four men one of whom was unarmed, it would not be difficult to resist the temptation to settle old scores, as the captain had put it.

As I moved I felt the same as when I used to walk to school before an exam, going over my final preparations. I had grown used to it: 'Englin, give me the exact positions and assault plan' was something I heard even more often than 'All OK!' It came at the end of exercises, during the daily meetings with the NCOs and the captain. Surprise tests that came as no surprise, given that I was the one they quizzed most often, the baby of the platoon. By the time we left I knew the machine-gun positions better than I did the streets back home in London.

The advance parties should have finished by now. They had left before us in two groups. The reconnaissance party had headed for the objective to prepare for the coming incursion, signalling a safe route through the minefield with white tape, crawling up to the barbed wire to identify the best spots to place the Bangalores, and positioning the mortars that would fire the signal rockets for the glider pilots who would then land inside the battery area. The rendezvous party was tasked with marking out the LZ and making it visible. This was where we were to assemble before moving against the Battery, and where the gliders were to land with the heavy equipment: jeeps, mortars, anti-tank guns, explosives, flamethrowers, mine detectors and everything needed for first aid and transmitting messages.

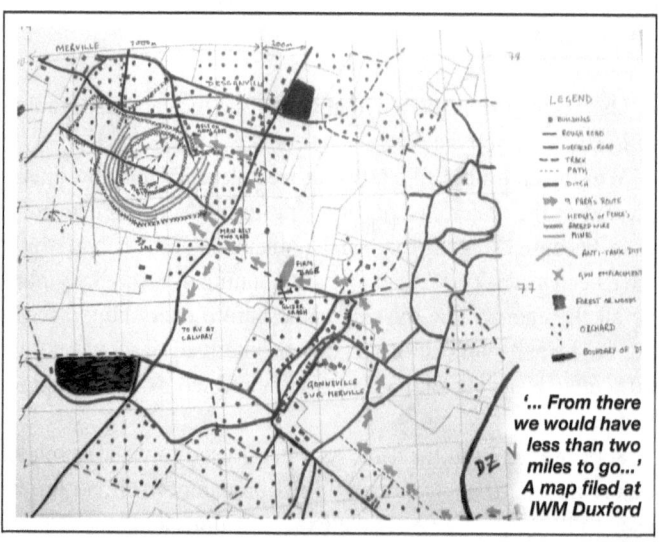

'... From there we would have less than two miles to go...'
A map filed at IWM Duxford

From there we would have less than two miles to go and, once we had gotten through the outer wire using the gaps cut by the Pathfinders, we were to divide into four groups, one for each concrete casemate. My platoon of thirty-six men was tasked with taking number one bunker, the largest. When the first glider arrived we were to blow up the inner barbed wire fence at four separate points and storm the place as our mates emerged from the gliders. A simultaneous attack that, it was hoped, would lead to confusion amongst the Germans. First objective: neutralise the machine-gun positions, following the pathways marked out by the taping party. Second: reach the casemates, use explosives to bring down the steel doors and eliminate or take prisoner those inside. Third, and most important of all: blow up the guns.

'We'll save the lives of hundreds of our boys,' the captain had told us the day before we left. It was not just something he said to motivate us. The battery was a few miles from the sea, but if those 150 mm guns were left to operate undisturbed there would be a bloodbath, and the troops who had just landed might be forced back into the Channel. After the attack, the CO would get in radio contact with the cruiser that was awaiting news about a mile from the coast. If the ship did not receive any word from us by five-thirty in the morning it would shell the Battery from the sea, but it would be impossible to obtain the same results as with a direct attack. In other words, we could not fail. We were then to arrive at and attack a village that dominated the valley through which infantry and armoured columns were later to advance, a few miles away. Our job was to clear out the enemy and hold the position until we were relieved.

Having arrived at the end of the hedge we realised the trees that had been visible from where we started were further away than they had seemed, on the other side of a crossroads and an apparently dry and passable field. One by one we ran across the canted road, between uprooted blocks of stone and other debris left by the bombardment, and threw ourselves to the ground. We waited twenty seconds before moving again, keeping our eyes on the first houses of the village, away to the left. Not a single light was on, and all we could hear was a dog barking. The captain pointed to a deep ditch running along the middle of the field before us. By following it we would reach the trees and then, once we got there, we could decide on the best way forward.

We had been walking for a few seconds when we heard a deep rumble, rapidly growing in intensity. 'Lancasters!' – Lickert and the captain whispered the same warning almost simultaneously, both diving face-down to the ground, elbows touching the bottom of the ditch and hands over their necks. Whaite and I did the same, a moment before the apocalypse began. The ground around us trembled, rose and fell, seeming almost to roar like the cows I had seen butchered in the abattoir where my uncle used to work before the war, a gigantic animal gutted by steel hooks with its insides splattering all over the place. We could only wait, immobile, covered with clods of earth from head to foot, as bombs whistled down and exploded around us.

'Idiots!' growled Lickert, the first to sit up and check he was still all in one piece after the bombers had passed. I got to my knees, reflecting that if the aim of the raid had been to put pressure on the Battery then it had failed on two counts by both missing its target and almost blowing up the attackers. However, they had succeeded in revealing the Germans' position: between one explosion and the next we had spotted tracer fire between about a hundred and fifty and two hundred yards away, on both sides of the field. All we had to do in order to avoid both emplacements was stay at the bottom of the ditch, unless of course the bombers had already hit them.

'Everyone alright?'

'Yes sir.'

As we got going we could hear orders being shouted in German and then a motorcycle roaring to life, the beam of its headlight shining in front of it. Halfway through the field the ditch ran into a crater five feet deep. As we moved around it, I realised that if we had left the boggy field thirty seconds earlier we would now all be dead. We crossed the small wood and found ourselves in a field that looked like a pincushion: dozens of pairs of stakes, ranging from eight to ten feet in height, had been placed among the waist-high wheat, with metal cables strung between them. They were obstacles for the gliders, invisible from above and too thick to cut with the equipment we had with us.

We carried on until we reached some fairly thick vegetation and, when we emerged on the other side of it, I could not believe my eyes. We had made a mistake, I told myself: that could not be the LZ. Then I recognised a lone tree they had pointed out to us on the photos, away to my right, so close to a ditch that it looked like it must fall in, and beside it an orchard. Opposite there was a clearing where a few dozen men had gathered, but no gliders, jeeps or mortars. Already headed off to the Battery, perhaps? Impossible, they would not have left so many behind. We approached after having whispered the watchword to the two nearest to us. In the middle there was a huddle of men, some officers listening to the CO. When he saw us, he stopped talking: 'Who are you?'

'Captain Kadwell with Corporal Lickert and Privates Englin and Whaite.'

'And the rest from your plane?'

'I haven't seen them, I was hoping they'd arrived before us. What about the gliders, sir?'

'There aren't any. We have a Vickers, a few Brens, a dozen Bangalores and that's it. And four fifths of the men are missing. We need a change of plan.'

9. 1 JUNE 2014, 10:37

The prefix was Caen, but the number Cédric saw on his mobile at the end of the second period did not belong to any of his relatives. As soon as he had taken in the written test and accompanied the last of the students to the classroom door, he went downstairs and walked out into the large courtyard, closed on all sides by the three-storey school building. At that hour it was virtually empty. He sat on a bench beneath the shade of one of the trees that, one day or another, would threaten to push its roots through the reddish-hued playground where a basketball and a volleyball court had been marked out. He pushed the redial button – best to make sure.

'Levasseur's office, good morning.'

'Good morning. My name is Roussel, I'm phoning from Nice. I found this number on my mobile…'

'Roussel? One moment, please. The *notaire* is busy right now, but he asked me to pass your call to him should you phone back.'

The name 'Levasseur' did not ring any bells, even with the twenty seconds or so he had to rack his brains as a piece of classical music was piped down the line.

'Hello?' the voice belonged to an older man, sixty at least.

'Yes …'

'This is Levasseur, Thierry Levasseur. And you are Mr

Roussel…'

'That's right.'

'Cédric Roussel, correct?'

'Yes …' Someone else with trouble spelling his name?

'I own the watch that will go on sale on Friday.'

'I didn't want to disturb you, all I wanted was…'

'It's no trouble. When the auction house called me, I was the one who told them I would prefer to contact you personally. They weren't keen at first – perhaps they were afraid I was going to cut out the middle man. But I convinced them in the end – I signed the sale contract a month ago and they have the watch. Of course, if I had known beforehand…'

'Known … what?'

'That you were interested. But then, how could I? So you still live in Nice …' What was he talking about? Cédric held his tongue: was it better to find a polite way to ask him, or to go on pretending he understood and wait for some clue? But the *notaire* did not give him the chance to decide: 'Are you still there?'

'Yes, I was …'

'I would like to stay on the phone with you, but I have clients waiting. What do you say to meeting in my office? Thursday afternoon, if possible. The day before the auction. I think we should have a bit of a chat. Because you will be coming to Normandy, I imagine.'

Could he not just send him the copies and leave it at that? 'To be honest I don't …'

'You tell me.' A slight note of impatience in the voice, presumably to serve as a reminder that time was money.

Why not? The man might have some interesting information, what did it matter if he had mistaken him for someone else? 'OK. Thursday afternoon.'

'Is two o'clock alright?'

'Yes …' After almost a minute spent staring at the screen of his mobile phone and the call duration displayed on it, increasing one second at a time, Cédric came to his senses and pressed the button to end the call. His next phone bill would tell him how much that little oversight had cost.

10. 6 JUNE 1944, 02:41

... 'four fifths of the men are missing. We need a change of plan.'

The captain sent us away. Lickert started making fun out of Whaite because of the unmistakable smell he was giving off: in the ditch he had evidently found not only shelter from the bombs but also a French cowpat. I did not take my eyes off the officers and did my best to listen in. Would the captain tell me something of what was going on? I felt the anxiety that had seemed to dissolve when I had jumped out of the plane and into the void. Unpleasant, but less so than I had experienced a short time earlier in the field when I could not tell the explosions from my own heartbeats, so strong they made my chest tremble, as though my heart had wanted to force a hole through my ribs and leap out of my body, so strong they echoed through my temples. Nothing like that had ever happened to me before. Perhaps, I thought, it was what they called panic, fear out of control.

Lickert and Whaite moved a short distance away to cadge a cigarette from our mates but I stayed put, preferring to be the first to know. The captain broke away from the group and walked up to me: 'We're moving out.' And then, perhaps to show me he was not worried: 'Don't forget your mug.'

'What mug?'

'The yanks say we don't go without our tea break even in the middle of a battle. It would be a shame to disappoint them, so as soon as the battery is ours we'll take a picture of all of us with mugs in our hands and send it off to Ike.'

'The battery?'

'That's what we're here for.'

'And the others?'

'We can't wait for them.' And with that he went off to call Lickert.

'... walking in two single files down the sides of a dusty road...'

We began walking in two single files down the sides of a dusty road with a balding, grassy mound in its centre. The holes gouged by the falling bombs were the most noticeable change to the countryside around us. The full moon, peeping through occasional gaps in the clouds, lit up our surroundings well enough to show any potential dangers: hedges, trees, bushes and high grass, ideal locations for laying an ambush. We advanced one stretch at a time, a hundred yards behind a patrol that went on ahead, giving us the all-clear with a duck whistle. We did not encounter another living soul until, three quarters of an hour later, someone answered the signal. I spotted a number of shadows appear from behind the trees, in front of the head of the column, and then some hand-shaking. 'The Pathfinders,' whispered the captain behind me. Their jump had gone better than ours. They had reached their objective within the scheduled time, cleared a route through the minefield up to the barbed wire and spotted a few more machine-gun positions that had been missed by aerial reconnaissance, but the signalling equipment had been lost along with the gliders.

As we followed them towards the Battery, I noticed the craters were thicker on the ground. The bombers had hit the target as well, after all. As we moved into the area between the edge of the wood and the fence that marked the beginning of the mine-field we could hear nothing except for the lowing of a few cows awoken by our arrival, and the hope came to me that the bombers might have already done our job for us. 'If they don't go back to sleep I'll kill 'em,' somebody said. 'Quiet,' ordered the captain. One of the Pathfinders who had crawled under the inner fence shattered our hopes: despite appearances the battery was not de-serted because after a few minutes under the wire he had heard voices talking in German.

The captain called ten or so names, one of them mine, and gathered us round him beneath a tree: 'There aren't enough Ban-

'... gathered us round him...'.
Both pictures in these pages feature the France 44 reenactors.

galores to blow up the fence in four places. We'll open up two breeches and two groups will go through each of them. Ours will be the first on the right hand side. We'll follow the sappers up to thirty yards from the wire. Get in there the minute the Bangalores blow and follow the Pathfinders' footprints, there's no other way to avoid the mines because there isn't any signalling tape. Our objective is casemate number one, the first one after the wire and the biggest. Don't stop for any reason: the medics will take care of the wounded. Watch for the machine-gun on top of the bunker, we need to knock it out as quickly as we can. Then we'll have to make do with what we have because the heavy explosives didn't make it in. We can throw grenades through the air vents, but don't use all of them – once we're inside we'll need them to disable the gun. Leave whatever you don't need here.'

We slipped off our haversacks and leant them against the tree trunks while the sappers, numbering around thirty and divided into two groups, passed through the hole in the wire and moved into the minefield, dragging the explosive Bangalore tubes behind them and preceded by the pathfinders, who showed them where it was safe to step.

We followed them to within about thirty yards of the inner fence, after which the captain ordered us to position ourselves next to one of the craters left by the air raid, but not inside it because of the risk of stepping on an unexploded anti-tank mine thrown to the surface by the bombs' impact and sensitive enough to be set off by a carelessly placed hand or knee. The cloud cover had thickened, but not enough to block out the moonlight completely or to prevent me from taking a closer look at the terrain separating us from the objective. What I saw amazed me, as though I had never truly believed what I had seen on the photos. Apart from the mines, we would encounter no obstacles before the barbed wire because the fifteen foot wide, ten foot deep ditch had only been finished on the far side of the Battery facing the sea before the diggers had been moved. Nobody had been able to explain

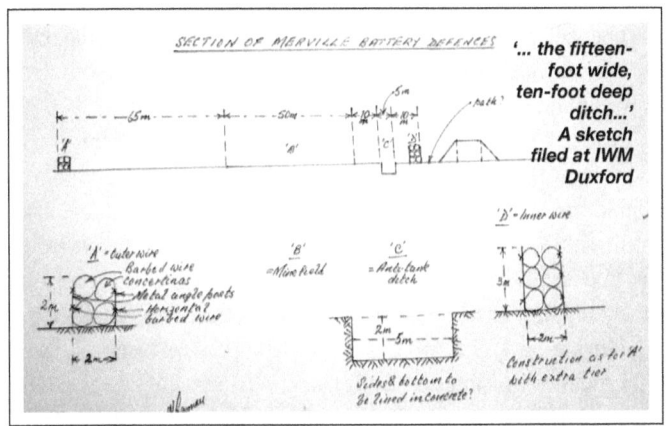

why, either at HQ or at the base.

Half a minute passed and, as I was trying to make out my mates working alongside the tangle of metal, someone tapped me on the shoulder. Skevington was pointing to a silent shadow, silhouetted against the clouds and moving toward us from the north. I guessed it must have been one of the gliders whose arrival was supposed to mark the start of the assault on the Battery, but it showed no signs of landing and disappeared to the rear of us, behind the trees. There was no way they could make out the target without the signal rockets. The garrison seemed to be awakening from its torpor: agitated orders and footsteps, metallic sounds, weapons at the ready. The glider had been no help whatsoever, serving only to put the Germans on alert. And there came another at low altitude, again from the north. This time they opened fire, a firestorm that eventually hit it in the tail. A few seconds after it had vanished from site, I heard a crash. I hoped they had made it, but they would not be able to help us anyway. Luckily I have always been a glass-half-full sort of man, able to see the bright side in any situation: at home, at school, on the pitch, at the factory, at the base, wherever. Attacking the casemate with twelve men rather than thirty-six, and without the support of the gliders, was not the end of the world: we were so few that the chances of shooting one another by mistake, even in the dark, were practically nil. That had been my biggest worry ever since they explained the plan to us.

Inside the Battery, the night was over. Flashes of tracer fire shone over the barbed wire, lighting up the branches and leaves behind us. Two machine-guns opened up almost simultaneously from within. The hiss of bullets and the impacts on the wood of the tree trunks, halfway between our groups and those on the other side, left us in no doubt: they had noticed our presence but were firing blind. I heard the CO shouting orders behind us and, a moment or two later, a rustling sound on my right. I raised my Sten but then saw a pale flash as a hand gripped the barrel, lowering it. 'It's Beltman and his lot,' said the captain, who had placed himself between me and Skevington, and was pointing at a group moving along the barbed wire, which then turned away, disappearing from our field of vision. We could hear bursts of small arms fire, explosions and shouting coming from the main entrance of the fortified area. One machine-gun fell silent while the other took the bait and turned its fire at Beltman's platoon. Then it was as though the uproar coming from inside the fence had found a wall to echo off a few hundred yards behind us, beyond the trees. Almost all of us spun around, uncomprehending. 'Brens,' whispered the captain, 'the boys on the gliders have got company.' I recalled what he had told us after a meeting with the other officers. The Brigadier himself had forewarned them: we would be going in with first-rate training and planning, but we should not be daunted if chaos reigned when the crucial moment arrived. Because it undoubtedly would.

11. 1 JUNE 2014, 13:32

'What's the matter?' Cédric raised his eyes from the plate where he was half-heartedly attempting to skewer an olive with his fork. 'Is something up?' insisted Sylvie.

'No, I was just thinking ...' Snapping out of his daydreaming proved difficult, like those mornings when he rolled over and stretched his hand out to the bedside table to switch off the ring-tone Adrien had downloaded for him, taking a while to realise he was in his own bed and not at the stadium with the other Muske-teers. Now though, he did not have the couple of minutes to come back into the real world that he did at quarter to seven in the mor-ning, because the look on Sylvie's face told him that 'I was just thinking' was not a satisfactory answer. 'Is it a problem if I leave tomorrow instead of Thursday? To go to Caen, I mean.'

'I don't know ... why?'

'Do you remember that documentary on *Planète*? The one about the American plane from World War Two they found in Bosnia, and they took it to pieces, transported it to Normandy, restored it...? We watched it together...' Why choose a complex lie rather than the nebulous truth? The answer, if there was one, lay in a corner of his mind too distant to be located in the space of just a few moments. Right then and there he was more worried about giving the game away: when something troubled him he

'... that
documentary
on Planète...'

Une coproduction

Galaxie Presse
France 3 Normandie
Avec la participation de Planète

tended to turn pale.

'I think so ...' The vagueness of her answer suggested otherwise. Why should she remember a television programme that had gone on air three years before about a subject that, in any case, was only of interest to Cédric?

'When I went to Merville museum it wasn't there yet. I'd like to see it because I'd look a fool if someone spoke about it during the presentation and I didn't know what to say. There's no problem with the school because I have my day off tomorrow. I'd leave early and visit it the next morning: it's near Caen', and Deauville as well, but there was no need to mention that. 'But I can skip visiting my relatives, that way I'll be back quicker. I haven't called them yet.'

'You ought to. If they found out you'd been to Caen without going to see them they'd be upset.'

'Agreed. Anyway, I wouldn't spend a euro more than I was going to. When they invited me, I was the one that said I only needed two nights at the hotel. I can call them back this afternoon and tell them I've changed my mind because I have to do some research at the local library.'

'If you'd thought of it sooner I would have asked for a few days of holiday and we all could have come, your mum too.'

'You know she doesn't like going back to Caen, and anyway...'

'... The party!' cut in Théo. So absorbed had he been in trying to make his story sound plausible, Cédric had forgotten about him. Théo's words came as no surprise, but the look in his eyes did. They reminded him of a middle school teacher of his – a history teacher, inevitably – who had taken a shine to him and who, after asking him a question, would watch with paternal anxiety, brightening whenever he gave the correct answer.

'You're right. You both need to get everything ready, how would you be able to come? Don't worry, Théo: I'll be back here on Saturday evening.' As he pinched his son's nose playfully between thumb and forefinger he watched Sylvie's reaction out of the corner of his eye: she stayed silent, thoughtful. He tried a joke: 'Aren't you pleased? You can ask your admirer to give you a lift in his super four-by-four ...'

'That again?!' she sighed, managing to unite three different emotions in a single expression: irritation at his teasing, embarrassment at Théo's presence and a hint of satisfaction, perceptible despite her efforts to hide it.

'I'm just a jealous guy ...,' he sang softly, not in an attempt to imitate John Lennon or Bryan Ferry but so that Théo – who was staring at him quizzically – could not understand. A moment before Sylvie could retort, he took it back: 'I'm kidding...' But that was not exactly true. Even months later, the memory still put him in a bad mood. The boss and his secretary: even more than just unpleasant, it was unbearably banal. And when the boss in question was Doctor Weber, a fifty-year-old bachelor with a reputation for extending his interest in women beyond his gynaecological practice, a dinner invitation could hardly be assumed to be merely his way of showing his appreciation for an employee's professionalism. Cédric had taken it badly, even if she had turned him down. Since then he had been trying to convince her to find a new job somewhere else. As if it was that easy, she always answered back, adding that the episode was closed and there had not been any more invitations, much less any harassment. The problem was Cédric who, at over forty years of age, had discovered that he was in fact a 'jealous guy' but did not want to admit it. And whenever he tried to make light of it he came off less convincing than a politician promising to dedicate himself to the common good. There was no point denying it: he had yet to fully digest the little smile with which Sylvie had told him the story. In fact he was still sure even now he could detect a hint – minimal, little more than a digital watermark but nonetheless visible to an attentive (or paranoid) eye – hidden behind her frown of displeasure. But this was not the time to be distracted from his main objective: 'What do you say? Will you manage if I leave early?'

'To do what?'

'You won't have the car...'

'We're both at home tomorrow. If I need anything I'll call Céline.'

'What about everything else? Théo, the party ...'

'It's only one day more. And it's not like you're a great help when you're here anyway...'

Cédric let it go, preferring a harmless dig or two to a further round of questioning. 'I promise that when I get back I'll do the shopping for a month. Actually, me and him both. Right?'

'Definitely!' Théo confirmed with enthusiasm and, instead of finishing his salad or leaving it where it was, announcing that he had to run to the garage to take a Coca-Cola to Pierre – a rather transparent ploy that would allow him to gulp down twice the daily amount permitted by the house rules, half a can – he went back to smiling like the teacher who used to tell Cédric, 'well done!' Or like a little boy anticipating the perfect Wednesday with no school and no nagging dad watching over the PC.

12. 6 JUNE 1944, 04:25

... We should not be daunted if chaos reigned when the crucial moment arrived. Because it undoubtedly would.

I was so concentrated on trying to work out what was going on at the far side of the battery and behind us that I forgot about the Bangalores until the explosion. The muffled sound of someone shouting 'Get in! Get in!' reached me through the ringing in my ears. More than hearing it, I could guess from the way the others rushed in, throwing themselves into the dust cloud masking the barbed wire. I was the last to get going but within twenty yards or so I was already near the front, catching up with the captain, when I heard him shout: 'The footprints!' I do not know how he managed to make anything out at all, what with the haze thrown up from the ground, the holes, and the darkness, pierced by the blaze of gunshots. He was running with his Sten resting on his hip: short bursts to the front and to the right, aimed to hit anyone standing, while the machine-guns seemed to be concentrating their fire elsewhere. I slowed down in an attempt to synchronise my steps with his and place my feet where his had already fallen, while two of our mates drew up alongside us. One of them was thrown into the air and plummeted back down like a rag-doll, without holding his hands out to break his fall, wounded or else killed by a mine. 'Get behind me!' I shouted at the other, but he fell too, hit by the hail of bullets now raining down around us.

I knew I could not stop to help him but I hesitated, and once I started moving again I saw the captain leaping across something. Before me lay a pit that was wider than the others: impossible to go around, as I would risk being blown to pieces by a mine as well, but I was going too slowly for my jump to clear it fully. I touched the far edge with the toe of my boot and fell into the pit up to my chest, feet scraping at the wall of soft earth, hands grasping at the grass left untouched by the bombardment in search of a handhold. Somehow, as somebody jumped over me, I managed to lever myself up on my elbows and emerge slowly from the hole, an easy target for the barrage that seemed like a solid wall, the hiss of bullets drowned out by the impacts of mortar rounds. I could see three motionless bodies lying one behind the other through the smoke, like an arrow pointing towards the wire.

I started running again, wondering whether the captain was among the mates I was moving past on the ground. As I passed the last body I was relieved to hear a groan: wounded but alive. Another lay face down in a gap through the wire, head turned towards me and feet on the other side of the obstacle. 'Over me!' he shouted. It was one of the sappers: he had lain down to form a bridge because the Bangalores had not opened a deep enough gap.

Beyond the barbed wire I could make out an enormous, dark hump, lit up on top by the flashes of machine-gun fire, and a solitary figure running up the grassy slope on its left flank; I recognised it was the captain from his short, rapid steps. The machine-gunners had not noticed him and were still pouring their fire into the breach in the wire, now behind me. Once at the base of the bunker I swerved to the left and, as I was running up the slope, I heard a few bursts from the Sten followed by some swearing. On the roof I could see the captain lying among the forest of tubes that stuck out of the grass and earth with which the cement had been covered, fumbling with the cartridge of his submachine gun, while further on, behind the sandbags, I spotted two helmets, a hand and a barrel being pointed in our direction. Still moving forwards, I grabbed a grenade and pulled the pin, throwing it when I was twelve feet or so from the nest. Two Germans leapt out to save themselves, jumping down off the bunker before I could shoot. I made to follow them, but the captain stopped me with a shout: 'Down!' I remembered and dived onto the grass. Another two steps and I would have been torn apart by my own grenade.

'... the battery looked to be caught in a storm...'
The reenactment of the assault on the Battery

After the explosion, we jumped over the sandbags. Inside there was a cartridge belt, an ammunition crate, a mess tin, the upturned machine-gun, a side cap and a Schmeisser with two cartridges, which the captain picked up after slinging the Sten round his neck: 'I'll hang on to this, I don't trust mine.' It had jammed, as it had at the base a few times. He placed a grenade underneath the machine-gun to make sure no one else could use it and we jumped out. From above the battery looked to be caught in a storm: flashes lit up figures moving between the bunkers and the anti-aircraft emplacements, rolls of thunder were followed by showers of dust, shouting, the glint of a bayonet.

Somewhere, hidden in the darkness, somebody was still firing on the wire, but it was an isolated sniper and could not prevent three of our mates from reaching us. There was no time to flush him out – we had to take care of the gun. Whaite climbed onto the roof while Loane and Jontz positioned themselves below, in front of the steel door. We threw a dozen Mills and phosphorus grenades down the air tubes and, after hearing the muffled boom, we all came down, Loane last of all because he approached one of the tubes and shouted something down it first. He did not speak German, but his meaning was clear from the tone of his voice. After a few seconds the steel door was opened slightly so that we could see a white handkerchief tied to the barrel of a rifle. 'Out!' the captain shouted. There were four of them. They came out with their hands behind their heads after having thrown the rifle and handkerchief to the ground. Only two of them wore a uniform and helmet, another had on a bloody jacket and a pair of braces dangling from his trousers as though he had only had just enough time to pull them on, and the last man a coat with the right sleeve burnt up to elbow, a woollen vest and small, metal-framed glasses with a broken lens. Stunned, terrified and unsteady on their legs, but apparently unwounded. 'Ruskis! Ruskis!' started

'... a narrow corridor broken by two apertures...'
The details about Casemate 1 as seen at Merville

shouting one of the two in uniform, the younger man. What did it mean? That they were Russians or that they thought we were?

'I don't like it,' said the captain, peeking through the open door, 'Best make them go in first.' He gestured the four men to go in ahead of us. The one in the coat shook his head without answering and lowered his gaze: he must have been certain that once we were back inside we would kill them all. The captain convinced him with a burst from his Schmeisser aimed in front of the man's feet.

Loane stopped at the entrance, next to the threshold. The rest of us followed the prisoners along a narrow corridor broken by two apertures. On the left there was a space with two doors facing one another. 'What's in there?' the captain asked, first in English and then in French. None of them understood, so he dug the barrel of the Schmeisser into the bespectacled man's back: 'Open!' A magazine, or rather two, filled almost up to the ceiling: shells on one side and crates of explosives on the other. We went on to the door on the right, torn open by the bombs. The walls were strewn with wreckage that must have been cupboards and bunks until a few minutes beforehand. I could not make out the details because the smoke had yet to settle and the beam projected by the captain's torch was moving too quickly, but those few flashes were enough to twist my stomach in knots. The dark, gaping wound in the belly of a corpse. The feathers blown to the ceiling from an exploding pillow or mattress. The dense liquid dripping onto the floor from a smashed cooking pot. Another puddle further on that had formed around a body whose legs had been reduced to a shapeless mush. And then the smells: cordite, onions, burnt flesh, urine, blood. It seemed impossible that just a few grenades had done all this.

'What is that toy?!' exclaimed the captain as we moved into the circular chamber housing the gun. Before us stood a medium-sized, old-fashioned artillery piece mounted on a wooden support, not the 150 mm monster we had been expecting. 'Whaite,' he ordered, 'take the prisoners to Loane and get them to lie down, then come back here and help Jontz. Put a gammon bomb under the elevating gear, and another on the breech block, then chuck a Mills down the barrel. We won't be able to destroy it, but they'll take a while to get it working again. Roger, with me.' Where to? I did not care, all that mattered was getting back into the fresh air, away from the stench that hung in my nostrils, on my hands, in my clothes.

13. 2 JUNE 2014, 19:29

Luckily the GPS map was up to date. After twelve hours or so at the wheel, the furthest he had ever driven in a single day, Cédric would not have enjoyed spending another hour in the traffic of Caen, turning onto one-way streets from the wrong direction in order to skirt around brand new pedestrian zones. As he arrived in Place de la République and looked around for an empty space,

'... As he arrived in Place de la République...'

he felt overcome by several urges all at once: to rest, to eat and to reach the hotel room the bookshop had reserved so he could take a shower.

But first of all he had somewhere to go. He had been thinking about it since he left, one thousand, one hundred and fifty-nine kilometres earlier, and that was the reason why he had chosen the least practical of the proposals made by the presentation organisers. A hotel with no garage in the historic centre – 'simple but modern and equipped with every comfort', the website guaranteed – was fine for someone travelling by rail, but less so for someone arriving by car. Indeed, Cédric was forced to complete three circuits of the road circling the paved area that formed the edge of the rectangular centre of the piazza with its flower beds, gravelled areas, small trees and bike ports, before he spotted the flashing indicator of a station wagon that left him an empty place in front of the tables of a café. But he did not regret his choice. The location was ideal, inside the triangle that had the race track, the Abbaye aux Hommes and the castle at its corners and, above all, a short walk from the street where he had lived when he was small.

Five minutes later he reached the crossroads where the pavement of the pedestrian zone gave way to tarmac. Like many years earlier, when his mother had given in to his insistent requests and taken him to see the front door, dragging him away again almost immediately, or the more recent occasion when Sylvie and Théo had been with him, his heart was in his throat – almost as if he did not know what he would find. And once more, thirty metres on, he felt disappointed, unconvinced, defrauded, unable to accept that his old home was really there, on the second floor of a dreary building, the facade blackened by smog, the bright, modern window frames looking like a fanciful attack of vanity. It had nothing to do with the things he would have liked to remember from those years; a nasty surprise repeating itself, an experience too unpleasant to really sink in.

The front door had been left ajar, an oversight or else someone who had nipped out for a moment. Cédric did not give it a second thought, entering without considering what story he could

'... through the window in the top part of the frame...'

use to explain his presence if one of the residents discovered him there. He did not care because the moment he pushed the door to behind him, the afternoon light of approaching summer, shining through the window in the top part of the frame and projecting intricate shadows of wrought iron onto the floor, was virtually inviting him to put his foot on the first step and grab hold of the bannister, foothold and trampoline of a little boy running up the flight of stairs, a raucous voice following him from behind with an affectionate reproach: 'Steady on, if you trip you'll hurt yourself. Why do you have to run?'

Cédric might have been five years old. Dad was already ill and could not keep up with him. But he had not felt like waiting: 'Because I'm afraid he'll get us.'

'Who?'

'Him, over there.'

'There's no one here.'

'Yes there is.'

'Then you're the only one who can see him.'

'I can't see him, it's too dark.' That afternoon the timer had not been working and everything had been plunged into darkness when they were only half way up. The only light had come from the door below, allowing them to just about make out the edges of the steps. For the rest they relied on memory.

'First you say there's someone there, then that you can't see them. You should make your mind up ...'

'I know he's there.'

'And I know he isn't. Stay closer, if you don't believe me.'

Cédric had stopped, his heart hammering and his pupils dilated, partly because of the darkness and partly from anxiety, as he tried to make out who was there. Dad had reached him and taken his hand, more breathless than his son who had just run up two flights of stairs. How weak he is, Cédric had thought as he continued looking down, behind his father's back. What would a child and a disabled adult have been able to do if the stranger decided to attack? He had felt as though it was him looking after Dad rather than the other way round, as they reached their front door. He had followed him to the living room and, after having watched him flop down into an armchair, he had gone back and turned the key in the lock, waiting with his ear to the door for almost a minute, straining to hear anything. No sounds, panic over.

After that day though, he had always found the 'grown-up' chores Mum entrusted to him unpleasant: errands to the chemist's on the ground floor, where now there was an estate agent's shop, one of several along the street. He could not refuse, Dad was nearly always ill in bed, but he was afraid. There was a presence, Cédric could feel it. And so, as he closed the door behind him to face a journey he knew was full of peril, he would try to steel himself by threatening out loud: 'Leave me alone! Dad's at home. If you come any closer I'll call him.'

The memories came flooding back, clear and also enigmatic. How had that phobia begun? Perhaps it had been the darkness that had swallowed up colours and outlines without warning, taking root in a corner of his mind where only the passing years had managed to dig it out. Or the pain: the presence had been the enemy lying in wait who, not content with snuffing out his father before his very eyes, had wanted to strike him as well, stalking him mercilessly wherever he went, tormenting him, intimidating him, shutting him in a labyrinth with no way out.

One of the first times they had gone to visit Dad after the funeral, Mum had run into an acquaintance where two avenues crossed, at the bottom end of St. Gabriel's Cemetery, where the treetops peeked out of the hedges that hid their trunks and spread overhead until they almost touched, forming the roof of a gloomy, green tunnel. She had told him to go ahead, that she would catch

'... forming the roof of a gloomy, green tunnel...'

up with him. The tomb was only a short distance away, behind the thick screen of vegetation, along a gravel path. Cédric had walked until he arrived at the dark, marble slab with the name and dates inscribed on one side and which rested, like the lid of a two-metre square box, on a base of chipped stone with moss growing between the cracks. Then he had continued on to the field where the monument to the civilian victims of the war stood, a relatively open space which he had hoped would help relieve him of the unease he had felt in the narrow alleyway between the tomb and the hedge. But he had not had the chance because he had felt something. It was not a sound or a shadow nor even a breath of air produced by someone walking past. It was the presence, like on the stairs. Enormous, ugly, evil, threatening. How had it gotten all the way there? Cédric had taken a step back, terrified and incredulous, before turning round and running back towards Dad's tomb, his eyes filling with tears and anger gradually drowning out his fears, until he had exploded in convulsive shouts: 'Go away! Go away! Go away!'

'... the narrow alleyway between the tomb and the hedge...'

The few visitors close enough to hear him had wondered who it was that the boy was shouting at and whether he needed any help, before seeing a woman emerge from behind the hedge and run towards him, enclosing him in an embrace. It was the widow of Clément Roussel, those who had known him whispered as they went back about their business. But Cédric had gone on shouting and his mother, embarrassed, had taken him away after hurriedly placing a bunch of flowers at the grave.

'What's the matter with you?' she had asked as they approached the exit, Cédric running and then slowing down to turn around, his features twisted with hate. 'If you keep it up we won't be able to visit Dad any more.'

'Yes we can, he won't be coming back.'

'Who?'

'Him. The bad man, it's his fault Dad's gone. But I chased him away.'

She had shaken her head without answering, convinced that her son had simply needed to let his anger out against somebody, even if that involved making them up.

After that, their half hour visits to the cemetery on Sunday mornings had been calmer. Cédric had taken on board the sense of composure befitting such a place so that he could help Mum place fresh flowers in the slim brass vase attached to one corner of the slab and water them gently, a few drops at a time. After they had moved to Nice the visits had grown rarer: once a year, during their trips down memory lane that Mum welcomed so little. She had never wanted to find out whether it would be possible to move the tomb to somewhere closer because, as she put it: 'It wouldn't be right. This is his city and he would want to stay here.'

Cédric was so absorbed in his thoughts that he found himself on the second floor without even realising it. It would be easy, now, to smile about his sprints up and down the stairs, about the threats, about the confrontation in the green maze of St. Gabriel. But instead he lingered, one foot on the penultimate step and his elbow on the bannister, and turned to look back down to the bottom of the flight of stairs, half expecting to see a moving figure or hear the sound of footsteps. But the only noise that reached him was a female voice from upstairs, the joking and laughter of a phone call between friends, the only interference with the gentle hum of traffic coming from below. The door, his door, was a few steps away. Cédric looked at it without going any closer, wondering whether it was still the same as then and whether, if he were to press his cheek up against the other side of it as he had used to do all those years ago in order to listen and make sure the presence had not followed him, he would still be able to make out the scent of Mum's apple cake, trapped between the wood and paintwork. He would have liked to try, but who would open the door to a stranger making a request like that? Nobody, not even if he had been a child. So he went hurriedly back down the stairs, stepped outside without closing the door and walked away, relieved. Nobody had seen him, he had not been mistaken for a burglar or a lunatic, and he had dispelled a doubt that had become disturbing: had he really seen off the presence? Because back there on the landing, he had felt as small and defenceless as when he was five years old.

14. 6 JUNE 1944, 04:51

... All that mattered was getting back into the fresh air, away from the stench that hung in my nostrils, on my hands, in my clothes.

We began following the same route back that we had taken coming in. The shooting had died down, and the little there was seemed directed elsewhere. I hoped it was all about to be over and felt a glimmer of relief, the first for hours. The sniper that had been firing on the barbed wire while we were attacking the casemate must have been taken out and the surviving members of the garrison had not noticed us moving back again. There was no one at the gap in the wire – where had the man who had acted as a bridge for me ended up? I thought he must have made it as otherwise I would have seen him still lying there, motionless. We reached the lieutenant colonel's group, which had moved up to the point where we had waited for the Bangalores to explode. About twenty men, the reserve to throw into the fray if they were needed. 'Casemate one taken, sir.'

'The gun?'

'My men are taking care of it. But I thought ...'

'Go and make sure. You two, with them.' I recognised Mortimer and Hudnell.

Back into the minefield. The captain led the group at a quick

walk and I brought up the rear, taking care not to lose sight of
him. Despite almost nothing having gone according to plan, he
seemed calm and clear-headed. I knew him well enough to be
in no doubt that, once the operation was over, he would tell the
CO in no uncertain terms what he thought of the pilot that had
dropped us into a swamp and the boys at HQ who had mistaken
a toy, as he called it, for a devastating weapon. In the meantime
however, he knew how to keep a lid on it. I envied him, and at
the same time was glad we were together: I needed some sort of
reference point.

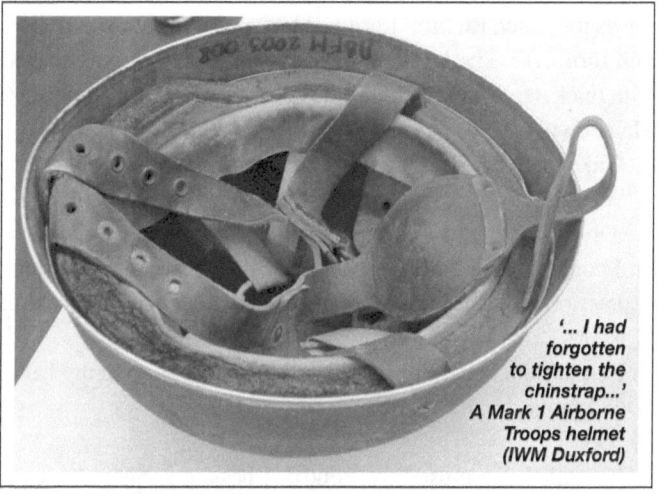

'... I had
forgotten
to tighten the
chinstrap...'
A Mark 1 Airborne
Troops helmet
(IWM Duxford)

Who, all of a sudden, I could no longer see. I had turned around
when I heard a groan and when I looked back ahead the captain
was gone. Mortimer, in front of me, was shouting 'Down!' as he
jumped into a crater, followed by Hudnell. I did the same, losing
my helmet which then hit one of them in the face: I had forgotten to tighten the chinstrap after I had unhooked it, back in the
casemate when I had felt as though I was suffocating. Mortimer
swore but the words were drowned out by a series of shots that
sounded like they were coming from a lone rifleman. The crackle

of a Bren responded from behind us. When it fell silent, Mortimer and Hudnell jumped out and ran on ahead, leaving me behind. As I picked my helmet back up, I wondered where the captain had gotten to. I spotted him the moment I was out of the hole, ten feet to my left, lying on his side. It knew it must be him because the moon was glinting off the barrel of a Schmeisser on the ground, close by. But it was not for the weapon that he was stretching his right hand out. He seemed to be reaching for his left arm as he slowly moved his legs in a circular motion. He was wounded, I thought, and trying to see if he could get back on his feet.

When he saw me kneeling over him he attempted to move, but it was too much for him. I gripped him under his armpits to help him turn over. The left side of his Denison smock was soaked with thick, tepid, sticky liquid. It was not pond water. 'Stretcher! Man down!'

'Take this!' he whispered, handing me something.

'What?'

'Give it to Jane,' he said, grabbing my arm tightly. Even though I could not see him clearly, I knew he was wearing the same expression as when I was slow to obey an order back at the base: 'Take it!'

He placed a metal object with a thin leather strap in my hand. 'Don't move, sir. I've called for help.'

'Don't ...'

'Captain?' He must have fainted. I hesitated. Should I leave him there like they had told us? Help him? How? Injecting him with the morphine syringe would have been pointless because he had lost consciousness. Go back and ask for help? I stayed there motionless for so long I would have been an easy target a few minutes earlier, but I could hear no more shooting. The battery was ours. The others did not need me but the captain did. I would wait with him until help arrived. I slung the Schmeisser and the Sten round my neck, then dragged him into the hole and sat down at the bottom. I glanced down at my right palm and it looked as though I had scooped up a dozen fireflies. The captain was right:

you could still read the watch. I would give it back to him before they transferred him to the regimental aid post.

When I heard a voice and footsteps, I hurriedly stuffed it into the pouch between the magazines I still had left. The approaching patrol was headed by the lieutenant colonel. They spotted me and someone asked if I was wounded. 'No, but the captain is. He's fainted. Where's the stretcher?'

The CO kneeled down and placed a hand on his neck. 'He hasn't fainted. He's dead.'

'You're wrong, sir. He just spoke to me.'

'He's dead, I tell you. Come with us.'

'I can't, the captain said...'

I was paralysed, unable to move. I felt someone lift me up and drag me away. There were two of them and they took me into the casemate, holding me up as if I was unable to walk unaided. I am not wounded, I thought when they left me. Why should I stay here doing nothing? I went back to the entrance, unarmed.

'Stop him.' Someone grabbed me by the arm and forced me to sit down on the floor. 'Don't move from here, got it?'

I looked up at the face before me but I could not have told you whose it was. I was too dazed even to say 'yes', and so I simply sat there, mute.

15. 3 JUNE 2014, 09:58

The flagpoles appeared as he turned onto the narrow road that ran between the villas and gardens separated by low stone walls, a short, straight stretch ending in a ring of asphalt. At its centre, an oval lawn with the French tricolour and the Union Jack. In the background, a wooden fence and a gate painted turquoise.

'... an oval lawn with the French tricolour and the Union Jack...'

Cédric parked next to the Garden of Memory, the name given by the Merville Battery website for the space recently planted with saplings to the right of the entrance, but instead of getting out of his car he dialled a number on his mobile. He had thought about it late the previous evening and concluded that deepening the misunderstanding would be pointless, or even counterproductive: 'Good morning. I have an appointment with the *notaire* this afternoon, but I would like to speak to him on the phone first, if that's possible.'

'He is not here, I'm afraid. He will be back at two. Should I pass on a message?'

'No, thank you.' Too late. The best he could hope for now was that Levasseur would simply show him the door as soon as he realised he had made an appointment with the wrong person, and Cédric would be back to square one: to see the watch and the documents that came with it, he would have to go to the hotel in Deauville, just like Onfray had explained. The worst case scenario would be that the *notaire*, instead of simply reproaching him for the time he had wasted, might charge him the full, ruinous fee permitted by the guidelines under which his profession operated.

A shame, because the day had started well. Before leaving Caen, Cédric had dropped by St. Gabriel, and what he had found there had cheered him: the bright colours of the flowers, the moist, green stems and the spotless surface of the marble showed that his relatives went there often. Dad's family was numerous, even though he was an only child – four cousins and their children, eleven in all. On the edge of the slab was another name in gold lettering: Vivienne, Dad's favourite cousin. Her funeral had coincided with Cédric's last visit to Caen, two years earlier, there and back again in a single weekend. Bruno, Vivienne's husband, was still around. If he were to call any of his relatives then Bruno would be first, but he had not yet done so and knew he would not. He told himself again that the real family reunion had already been organised for next Christmas, in Nice, and that not even the most sedentary of his relatives would be able to resist the temptation of a trip to the *Côte d'Azur* in winter. Why not drop in to visit them now, though? He had no answer for the voice inside him that kept asking this question.

His first visit to the museum had taken place a dozen years

earlier, before the plane was there – the Dakota from the TV programme, identical to those used by the paratroopers the night before D-Day, recovered in Bosnia, taken to pieces and transported to Normandy, to be finally reassembled after its eventful journey and put on show at the battery. Cédric had taped the documentary and watched it twice, struck by the commitment of dozens of amateur volunteer blacksmiths, sanders and decorators who had saved a piece of history from oblivion and destruction. Even if Jacqueline, the lady who worked in the small wooden cabin that acted as a ticket office, had not singled it out, the plane would be the first stop on his itinerary.

'... the small wooden cabin that acted as a ticket office...'

The old Skytrain, also known as the Dakota from the abbreviation of its interminable official name (Douglas Aircraft Company Transport Aircraft), looked ready to take off, as though they had just finished painting it with the colours agreed upon for D-Day: a mix of brown and bottle green background with black and white stripes in the middle of the wings and near the tail to ensure that Allied fighters would not mistake it for an enemy aircraft. Cédric circled the rounded nose that bore the irreverent acronym

'SNAFU' (Situation Normal: All Fucked Up) with which the crew had baptised their two-prop and stopped between the left wing and the tail, next to the small, metal ladder leading up to the hatch. The door had been taken off, just like on the Dakotas that went to Normandy – a measure to make sure there was no risk of it being damaged or bent by anti-aircraft fire and interfering with the jump.

'... the door had been taken off, just like on the Dakotas that went to Normandy...'

Next he went up the rungs and ducked his head to enter. Everything was as green as the outer fuselage except for the floor, grey-coloured like the asphalt of a town centre and with tracks running across it, that reminded him of tram lines. These were used for mounting seats in the civilian version of the aircraft, Cédric had read somewhere. Two metal benches ran along beneath the windows on the sides of the aircraft, facing one another. Panels with photos of the restoration work and information about the plane, from characteristics and distinctive markings to crew, had been placed where the paratroopers would once have sat. At the end of the fuselage, through a narrow doorway, he could see the navigator's instruments and the cockpit. Cédric approached to take a look and then turned back again, brushing against the strap hanging from the ceiling, hooked to the cable above his head with a clip: this was the mechanism that pulled the ripcord on the parachutes, which he had seen on DVDs about the war

'... through a narrow doorway, he could see the navigator's instruments and the cockpit...'

and on 'Band of Brothers'. He was walking in the footsteps of the paratroopers, now. Once at the doorway, he leant outside and looked up. It was a bright day, a little too cool and windy for the time of year, but the sky did not look threatening. Not like that night, when the full moon had been hidden behind cloud.

Cédric stood with his feet in the plane and his head outside, wondering how those seven hundred young men had felt as they leapt into the void, aware of the risks but oblivious to what awaited them: a chaotic nightmare rather than the mission planned down to the last detail, that they had spent the previous months training for and knew so well they could perform it with their eyes shut. Wind, anti-aircraft fire, limited visibility and pilot error had scattered most of them miles away from their objective. Many had drowned in fields deliberately flooded by the Germans and the survivors had struggled to reach the rendezvous point, only to then discover that the gliders with the heavy weapons on board had lost their way as well. Just a hundred and fifty of them, among them the commanding officer who had decided they would attempt the attack anyway, against an enemy who held the advantage in every respect: mines, two barbed wire fences, heavy weapons and armoured cement bunkers. Half of them had been wounded or killed, but the assault had achieved complete success and they had been able to sabotage the guns with hand grenades.

When the Germans had regained control a few hours later, the firepower of the battery had been so reduced it could not create much trouble for the troops landing on the beaches.

If it had been a film script it would be dismissed as merely the umpteenth example of Hollywood nonsense, seasoned with noisy special effects and bucket loads of red paint. But here the blood was real and the heroes were not muscle-bound stunt doubles covered with fake scars, replaced by the star of the moment – generally in his forties and as good looking as he was unconvincing – whenever the screenplay called for a close-up. The most senior was twenty-nine years old and the majority were no older than twenty-two. Little more than boys, volunteers accepted into the ranks of the Paras partly because a lot of them had no children of their own. That way if they fell in battle, the fate to be expected for many, they would not be leaving orphans behind.

Cédric exited the plane and covered the few dozen metres separating it from casemate number two, turned into a memorial to the battalion that carried out the attack. A space where light mingled with shade, dark and oppressive in the centre as it must have seemed to the eyes of its occupants in '44, lit by spotlights on the walls, glass cases on either side containing uniforms, weapons and helmets and the wall at the end dedicated to the battalion commander, who had passed away in 2006. Beneath the large,

'... Beneath the large, silver regimental emblem...'

silver regimental emblem rested a display case that looked like an altar. Inside it were the beret and medals donated by those who had inherited them. To the sides of the winged parachute were photographs and two monitors playing a video recording of an interview with the commander and photos of the fallen.

One of them grabbed his attention, a smiling face like the others but with something familiar about it. Where had he seen those lips with the edges turned up in an unusual smile that se-emed more like a smirk, crowned by a squat nose? The image quality was not great, the narrowed eyes reduced to little more than slits. It was the shape of the eyebrows – striking without being bushy – that set his mind whirring. Who did he look like? Someone he had studied with at university? An ex-pupil from the school? A Liverpool midfielder from the '50s? Or, more simply, himself, and Cédric had seen his face on one of the BBC do-cumentaries about paratrooper training? The image disappeared from the monitor, replaced by one of his comrades before he had a chance to read the name.

'... The words 9th Battalion - The Parachute Regiment...'

Above the exit there was a long, narrow panel. The words '9th Battalion – The Parachute Regiment' were written along the bot-tom of the photo: hundreds of soldiers posing, with those in front sitting down and those behind standing, presumably on wooden frames brought out for the occasion. Behind them, the windows and pitched roof of a building with a brick façade. The heroes all together, perhaps for the first and last time. Next to the doorway was another panel with dozens of photo portraits. Maybe Mister Smirk would be there too, but it was not worth looking for him – putting a name to the face would not be enough to dredge up the identity of his lookalike, hiding away somewhere in the recesses of Cédric's memory.

'... he walked along the path through the casemates...'

Back out of the armoured cement crypt, he walked along the path through the casemates, crossing a field interrupted by the revolving platforms where the anti-aircraft guns were positioned in 1944. Information panels described how they worked and the logistics of the battery. Inside a wooden fence loomed the menacing shape of one of the guns, a short distance away from the pedestal holding a bust of the commander. The features sculpted into the bronze looked like an attempt to conform to the news stories of the day and the testimony of the film on show inside the casemate. A tough guy, otherwise how would he have pulled it off? Attempting the assault in spite of everything. Leading the survivors through days of bitter fighting in the surrounding countryside against a numerically superior enemy. Staying in command for more than a month despite the after effects of being caught in an explosion, when the blast

'... the features sculpted into the bronze...'

wave had hurled him against a tree. As soon as circumstances had permitted he had been subjected to a medical check-up, sent back to England against his will, replaced by another lieutenant-colonel and, of course, decorated for his achievements.

A dozen years before Cédric's visit, after one of the D-Day commemorations, he had confessed that he had not found it easy to shake the hand of the German officer who had commanded the battery. Who could say what he would have thought of the sixty-fifth anniversary ceremony when, in front of dignitaries, visitors, flags and uniformed veterans with chests covered in medals, the notes of 'Deutschland über alles' had rung out before those of 'God Save the Queen', the hymn of the oppressors before that of the liberators. There was no way of knowing, as he was not around anymore. But he would have been at least as shocked as Cédric, who had seen the images on *YouTube*. And perhaps his surprise would have turned into indignation, once he learned that the military band was neither British nor French, but German. According to a newspaper article found on the internet, the ex-enemies had offered to pay their respects to the heroes because the British Defence Secretary had arranged for only one band to be made available for the ceremonies organised in Normandy. Not enough to participate in all of them, which was how Merville's had come to be saved by the most unlikely of substitutions. If that was true, Cédric had reflected, then the politicians were guilty of not practicing what they preached, urging the young to remember, but not hesitating to let spending cuts fall hardest on remembrance services.

The final stop – another new experience for him – was case-mate number one, where an audio-visual simulation of the battle took place every half hour. Not suitable for visitors of a nervous disposition, a notice read. The green light over the door signal-led that he could enter. He went down a few steps and found himself alone in another gloomy room. The visual part of the reconstruction was entrusted to manikins in German uniforms. One of them was by the wall at the side, telephone in hand. His

'... manikins in German uniforms...'

task: to transmit incoming targeting instructions from an obser-
ver a few kilometres away, situated on a piece of high ground
with a good view of the beach and the casemates. Next to him,
the gun and its crew, charged with loading and firing. The lights
dimmed, substituted by small spotlights that alternately illuminated the telephonist and the gunners, while orders were shouted
out in German, partially drowning out the explosions and crackle
of automatic weapons that seemed to come from outside. A boom
and a whiff of smoke accompanied the first shot. Between one
salvo and the next, the metallic click of reloading, further shots,
excited voices. Then came the 'Get in! Get in!' that signalled the
beginning of the attack, the shouts and small-arms fire drawing
nearer, the explosions of grenades, the clanging of shells against
the ground, the darkness split by the bluish light of a lamp on the
ceiling, English voices, first excited and then calmer. And finally
silence, followed by a tune.

Back outside again, Cédric struggled to read the screen of
his mobile beneath the sun, which had managed to warm the
air. Almost midday. He took off his pullover and placed it on
the backrest of the bench facing casemate one, a few steps away
from the eastern end of the fortified zone. Beyond the fence lay
a field and, at the end of it, a line of trees. That was where they
had come from, running in the open across a hundred metres or

so of ground laced with mines, under fire from machine-guns and mortars, in the dark. Some of them had come past where he was standing. He had the sensation that he could make out their silhouettes between the bench and the bunker that lay partially hidden in the grass, figures that stirred without advancing, held back by the weight of their weapons. But it was the six flags fluttering on their poles that were casting those shadows and the

'... the six flags fluttering on their poles...'

motionless, non-existant equipment that seemed to impede their assault, and in the silence broken only by the rippling of fabric blowing in the wind there were no shouts or gunfire to be heard, not even the subdued voices of the visitors Cédric had spotted a little earlier walking through the casemates. They had all gone, leaving him alone with a creeping disquiet he could not share with Sylvie right now. Too soon to call, her lunch break was still half an hour away. So he headed for the cabin and said goodbye to Jacqueline, without stopping to look at the books on display. Time was getting on – he had to return to Caen, have something to eat and get changed before his appointment with the notaire. As he opened the car door, he threw a quick glance at the passengers who had emerged from a coach that had just parked in front of the entrance. Old people, adults and youngsters talking in English. Cédric smiled: Merville Battery was in good hands.

16. 6 JUNE 1944, 05:17

… I was too dazed even to say 'yes', and so I simply sat there, mute.

I held my head in my hands, elbows resting on my knees. It was my first encounter with death as it truly is. The only kind I had known was that in films: solemn and slow, accompanied by tears and memorable lines. The suspicion that it was all make-believe – a guided tour, a way of preparing the audience and letting them know that something important was happening – had never occurred to me. In fact, I had never even considered it. But now I had no choice: the captain had laid the reality bare, without warning and without explanations. He was gone and that was that, in a few moments, a passenger forced onto a train without the chance to say goodbye, left to peer through the window with his nose against the glass for a last look at the faces of his loved ones, trying to see into the future. What would become of them? Of Jane, above all. Of his parents, his sisters, the friends he had made in his short life. Had he been able to give himself the answers? I thought so. He was so sure of his own strength that he must have believed there would be enough of it to go around for everyone. I tried to convince myself that it had been a good way to go, almost instant, painless and without regrets. With only one preoccupation: finding a mode of transport.

He had, or at least he hoped so. And I would not let him down. I would take the watch to Jane as soon as I could. I wondered whether she already knew about the name engraved on it, if she had had a chance to see it. I thought not: the captain had only received it a short time before, when leave had already been suspended. I poked my fingers between the magazines and fished it out from the bottom of the pouch to have a look while, every now and then, someone came to the doorway of the bunker and glanced inside, perhaps wondering why I was sitting there looking lost.

It was the first time I had looked at it properly. On the plane I had seen it for barely an instant. A bulky thing, while on the dial, apart from the hands, was a symbol that looked like a stylised letter, though I had no idea what it meant. I turned it over and saw the engravings. Whoever had done the work was as skilful as the jeweller had promised. The regimental emblem at the bottom was perfect, the feathers on the wings and the decorations on the crown identical to those of the badge on my beret. Jane's name, just above it, looked as though it had been hand-written with a pen. I was afraid of dropping it because my hand was shaking, so I put it back in the pouch.

'Everything alright?'

Lieutenant Beltman was standing in front of me. I focussed on his face only after I heard his voice. He wanted the right answer, not the truth: 'Yes ... fine.'

'Come with me.' We went outside into the cold silence as the

'... we went outside into the cold silence...' Casemate 1 now

sky was brightening. Silhouettes slid across the ground then suddenly disappeared, swallowed up by the deepest holes, only to reappear slightly further away, dark sheets that descended over bodies and then moved away, looking more like souls fleeing from their broken shells than the shadows of the living. As we walked, I turned towards the barbed wire in the hope of seeing the captain, but I knew it was hopeless: the crater where we had left him lay behind the fence, invisible from within, and by then they must have taken him away. I would no longer have the chance to sneak a look and check whether there was a scar near his groin from the operation, nor to point out that I had uncovered his lie, I thought, and then felt immediately ashamed of myself. I was like a sleepwalker who does not see an obstacle in the road and carries on walking until he tumbles to the ground, before getting up and looking around to check whether anyone noticed. Up until a moment before I had not believed it, not really. But now I did, convinced by a scar which I was not even sure existed. The jokes were over; there would be no more laughing as he offered me a cup of warm milk in the canteen, explaining that alcohol was not good for children.

Beltman led me behind casemate two, where the lieutenant colonel was kneeling beside a sergeant on a stretcher who I did not recognise because his head was bandaged and his face was like a filthy rag, with spots of congealed blood between the black of his camo paint-smeared cheeks and the whites of his eyes. He spoke with difficulty between gasps: 'I'm coming with you, sir.'

'Like hell you are, Jim. Get yourself taken care of and drink to our health. I shall see you in Paris.'

'Beltman and Englin reporting, sir.'

'I need a new batman because mine is out of the fight; they have to take him away. Do you feel up to it?'

'I ... Yes sir, certainly sir.'

'Captain Kadwell told me about you when we were at the base. He was a good officer, we will miss him. Did he teach you any French?'

'No ...'

'Never mind, I know a bit. Get your things, call Major Abbott and then come back here.'

The lieutenant colonel's batman ... You are in trouble, the captain would have said. But it was just what I needed to get my bearings back. And by staying with him, I would be the first to know what was going on.'

I knew the major: he was in charge of our company at the start of training, and had then become the CO's deputy. I spotted him as I went outside, after picking up the haversack and the Sten, and went back with him to the lieutenant colonel, who had lain down on top of the casemate and was looking towards the north-west through a pair of binoculars. I stayed back a couple of paces, but I could hear what they were saying.

'The guns?' asked the CO as he came down off of the bunker.

'They won't be using them for a while.'

'Have we sent the message?'

'Five minutes ago, after firing the only signal rocket we had. But the pigeon circled over the battery twice and then flew off in the wrong direction.'

'It would take too long to get across the Channel, anyway. Let's hope they saw the rocket. If ...' He was interrupted by the whistle of a howitzer shell, followed by a deafening roar a hundred yards or so beyond the southern fence of the battery. It was not the cruiser. 'Krauts. They know we're here. And it looks as though they are prepared to kill their own wounded along with us. We need to get going. How many of us are there?'

'Sixty-eight.'

It was five hours since the operation had begun and we were already down to one tenth of our original strength. A swear word rose to the CO's lips but he stopped it there before it could take form: 'Get the badly wounded settled inside the casemates. Those fit to be moved come to the calvary with us.'

I walked alongside him, passing small groups of three of four men, faces I could barely recognise in the half-light. Their features were twisted by a mixture of tension, open-mouthed incredulity in those who had come through our ordeal unscathed, and pain in those who had not, the latter limping along with the help of their mates. 'Put me down,' I heard Corporal Poitier tell the soldier who was carrying him on his shoulders, 'I'm safe here.' The calvary was a ten-foot high wooden statue of Christ situated where three crater-covered lanes met, strewn with branches and tree trunks. Our temporary objective, and a very fitting one we all thought, though no one said it out loud. I was sitting on the steps of the crucifix next to the CO, watched by the prisoners who we had made sit in a hole in the ground while in the distance the barrage raining down on the battery grew stronger, when we saw two of our mates appear pushing a wheelbarrow. Lieutenant Sanberg was sitting inside it with his right leg soaked in blood and a bottle in his hand: 'Great battle, what?' he shouted as soon as he saw us. Someone asked him if he had shot himself so he would not have to share the whisky and as he passed along next to us he responded that he had, adding however that we should not tell anyone. We all laughed; we needed to. We watched him disappear along with the rest of the wounded, four of our medics and two Germans, heading for the abandoned farmhouse where they would set up the regimental aid post.

'... we set out, preceeded by a patrol...'
An image from the March of Heroes set up by
the reenactors of the France 44 Association

The major came up to us: 'What's next?'

'To the village, as planned,' answered the CO.

We set out, preceded by a patrol of six men who came across mates of ours every now and then, dropped God only knew where during the night. Thirty or so in total, among them twenty Canadians who the CO ordered to bring up the rear in order to cover our backs and keep an eye on the prisoners. The vanguard was walking past the damaged walls of the first houses in the village, a few paces from a crossroads, when we heard bursts of machine-gun fire. Those at the front rapidly fell back, rounding the corner and jumping through the ground floor windows, – there was no glass left in the frames – a move imitated by half the column that had been following them on the right. The CO, myself and the others were on the left, a little way behind, next to the gaping pits gouged out of the earth by two bombs. We had no choice but to dive into the rubble of what must have been a storage shed for farm tools; I landed just inches away from the blade of a scythe with a broken handle. They were firing at us from high up, probably from the bell tower of the church that we could see in front of the crater, beyond the crossroads and churchyard. The lieutenant colonel gestured towards the end of the tree-lined road we had left behind us as we entered the village. The Canadians were coming out of it, and ran to find cover.

A mortar joined the machine-gun, its bombs landing nearer and nearer. They were using the bell tower not only to shoot at us but also to direct the mortar team down below, perhaps behind the church. 'What are our Brens waiting for?' the CO asked angrily. A moment later a prolonged burst came from inside the house. The top of the tower disappeared behind a cloud of white puffs and the machine-gun fell silent. It must have been Consalvi: for someone who could hit a bottle from quarter of a mile away, it was an easy target.

'And who the hell is that?' The lieutenant colonel stuck his head out of the crater, incredulous, and I followed his gaze. A civilian on a bike was cycling over the middle of the crossroads with a bundle on his back, a hat on his head and clothes pegs on his ankles to protect the fabric of his trousers. When he saw us, he slowed to a stop. He must have been about the same age as the captain, tall and thin with a big nose. 'Paratroopers?' he asked in faltering English, as a mortar bomb landed thirty feet or so from our crater. They had no more firing instructions, but went on lobbing rounds every five seconds anyway.

'Get down!' the CO shouted to him.

He got off his bike without betraying the slightest sign of agitation, propped it at the side of the road and hopped down into our hole. Unharmed and amazingly calm, something we had not expected from a Frenchman; he was the first we had encountered since the jump. 'Careful, the village is full of Boche.'

'How many?

'Two hundred, maybe more.'

'I don't know if we can trust him,' the CO murmured to the major, 'but it would be best to wait. The commandos should be here in a couple of hours. When they arrive we can get organised and attack. Roger, go to the others and tell Dewhurst to cover our withdrawal with two Brens. We'll fire three Sten shots when they can follow on. Abbott, take a patrol and have a look around. We need a place to hole up.'

The road could be no worse than the minefield, I thought. As I jumped up I was convinced I only had to worry about the mortar, but I heard a burst of rounds hiss over my head. Another machine-gun, this time at ground level. I reached the other side before they could adjust their aim, just as a Bren returned fire, its bullets smashing into what looked from my position like a stone table in the small gardens next to the church. I crouched down behind the corner of the building and then looked through one of the windows.

They had positioned themselves behind a heap of rubble, the remains of the wall facing the church, perhaps destroyed by one of the air raids during the last few days. The roof was gone and the internal layout could only be guessed at by the presence of a few stacks of bricks, left almost intact, that still marked where one room ended and another began. Only two walls were partially standing: the one that ran along the street and another at right angles to it, thirty feet or so from the rubble my mates had taken shelter behind. 'We're retreating,' I shouted, 'CO's orders. He wants the lieutenant and two Brens to cover us.'

'They got him,' said Sergeant Tomkins, pointing to a man lying still on the ground, 'I'll stay with Consalvi and Alden.'

The moment we emerged from behind the corner we found ourselves under fire from the Germans: now there were two machine-guns and they had started shooting from the bell tower again. Consalvi must have been short of ammo because he responded with brief, isolated bursts. As I ran I saw someone ahead of me fall face down, arms spread out before him, and MacLaury, who stopped next to him for a moment before going on, stepping to one side of the body: 'Don't stop! He's dead.' We drew near the crater – one last effort. Everyone made it across unscathed except for MacLaury, who cried out and limped to the edge, where two of our mates reached out, grabbed him and pulled him inside. It was my turn. As I jumped, I felt a sudden, forceful impact on my right flank. It is over, I thought as I plunged into the arms of the cyclist: I was about to die with only some Frenchman to bid me adieu, who for all I knew might not even be all that happy to see us. I dragged him down to the bottom with me and heard him swear – 'merde', one of the few French words I could remember – as he grabbed hold of my helmet, half strangling me. He was the first to get to his knees, looking me over as he did so: 'Lucky English!' A few of my mates moved him out the way to let the CO through: 'What are you doing down there, Roger?'

'I don't know ... I mean, I might be wounded ...'

'Doesn't look like it. I'm afraid you shall have to tag along with us for a bit longer. Get up.' I grabbed his outstretched hand as a mortar bomb landed in front of the house where we had left Tomkins and the others. 'They have to get out of there. Give the signal, Roger.'

I fired the three rounds that had been agreed on and after ten seconds or so we saw Consalvi jump out of a window and start running, drawing fire from the machine-guns, the mortars and a small cannon mounted on the half-track that had just emerged from behind the church and was advancing slowly towards out position. His only cover came from Whaite's Bren, which concentrated its fire on the bell tower and managed to silence the machine-gun nest once more. My gaze met that of the cyclist, sitting at the bottom of the crater – he must have understood he was in as much trouble as we were. When Consalvi reached us, the lieutenant colonel asked him what had happened to Tomkins and Alden. The answer was a silent shake of the head.

'Get moving.' Another single-file sprint, out in the open, but this time we had the Canadians backing us up. They had placed their mortars and a Vickers in amongst the foliage at the end of the village, and they clearly had more ammunition than we did. Their covering fire disoriented the half-track driver, who turned around and headed back behind the church.

I was running when I heard someone shouting behind me: 'English! English!' The cyclist was waving his arms. What did he want?

'He's calling us, sir.'

The CO turned around: 'He must be mad: if the Krauts see him talking with us he's a dead man. He'll be better off if we ignore him. He's too far anyway, I can't hear what he's saying.'

The Frenchman carried on gesturing. I could not understand a word, but the CO was right: all that shouting might well cost him dearly. I moved my index finger to my lips. He stopped shouting and disappeared into the crater, and I caught up with the others.

We met Abbott's patrol half a mile further on, along the tree-lined road. 'Follow us. We'll take you to the castle.'

'Castle?'

'That's right. All for us.'

17. 3 JUNE 2014, 13:43

Sylvie had reminded him to pack a jacket and tie the previous morning, when his suitcase was already closed: 'You can't turn up at the bookshop in jeans and a T-shirt.' Nor at the office of a *notaire*. Two years earlier, when he had signed the contract to buy the house, Cédric had noted that formal attire seemed to be the order of the day for all concerned: owner, buyers and agents. No doubt a habit related to the sheer amount of money involved, he thought, as he stood in front of the mirror, failing twice to do up his tie properly before settling on the third attempt – that would do at any rate. He cast his eye one last time over his hair – the only thing young about it now being its continuing resistance to any attempts to tame it with a comb – and he was ready. For a totally pointless meeting.

He did not have to wait long. Less than five minutes, before Angèle – with her outdated first name and wobbly ankles perched atop towering heels – led him along the corridor and into a room with a large, oval table at the centre: 'The *notaire* will be right with you.' Cédric took a seat on one of the leather armchairs and looked around him. Inlaid squares of parquet flooring. Wood clad walls in the spaces between the bookcases, which stretched all the way to the ceiling. The chandelier, a cascade of crystal droplets that must have been quite a sight during the evening, throwing its light out in every direction. Heavy, yellow satin curtains held in place by tie-backs next to the French doors opposite the entrance. Two console tables faced one another from the shorter walls of the room, so shiny and perfect that anyone would have said they were brand new but for the weightless elegance of the shapes, the decoration and the inlay work, all paying testimony to an ancient and forgotten art. On one of them sat a pendulum clock, its broad, white dial crowned with figures sculpted into the bronze, while on the other was a pink porcelain vase decorated with eighteenth century hunting scenes. The silence broken only by the ticking of the timepiece, the scent of aged wood and leather accentuating the sensation of a journey through time and space, towards a remote constellation with no knowledge of mortgage-related anxieties. Why did the owner of this museum want to sell a watch that would bring in at most a twentieth of his monthly turnover? Perhaps he did not like it.

The creaking door handle – only detail to clash with the general ambience – betrayed the arrival of the *notaire*. He was over sixty, just as Cédric had guessed from his voice on the phone, on the short side and thick-set, the small amount of grey hair remaining concentrated around his ears, metal glasses with rounded lenses and a slate suit with a white handkerchief protruding from the pocket. Beneath his unbuttoned jacket, a waistcoat framed the pale blue collar of his shirt and the knot of a blue tie. A good thing I got dressed up properly, Cédric thought as he held out his hand.

'Take a seat,' said the *notaire*, moving around the table and placing a leather document holder on it before sitting down opposite him. 'Cédric Roussel in my office, who ever would have thought it?'

Such a bizarre opening that Cédric could not avoid making some equally absurd associations between ideas; he could only imagine saying something like that, using the same expression, if he were to return home from school and find himself obliged by the circumstances to exclaim: 'Charlize Theron in my kitchen, who ever would have thought it?' But the chances of that happening were remote, while that stranger, smiling at him as though he were a celebrity, was an embarrassing certainty. Cédric was about to recite the short speech he had prepared – 'I'm afraid there's been some mistake', and so on – but Levasseur cut in first: 'How did you find out about the watch?'

'I came across the auction house website by chance. I'm not all that interested in the watch, but ...'

'You're not interested?'

'I mean ... I'm interested but only because of the engraving, the wings with the British Parachute Regiment's emblem. You see, I'm a history teacher and the Battle of Normandy ...' Cédric stopped because the other man's expression had changed, from cordial to vexed. A shame, Cédric thought, but hardly his fault.

'Who are you?'

'My name is Cédric Roussel. But you must have mistaken me for someone else, perhaps with the same name. I called this morning to ...'

'Same name? So you are not the Cédric Roussel born in Caen on 6 June 1970, son of Clément and Francine, who went to live in Nice in February 1977 ...'

He had given his name, place of birth and current residence to Onfray, but not the rest of it: 'Yes, but how ...?'

'I took the courtesy of checking with the registry offices before calling. To be sure it was not a mistake. But, apparently ...' The sentence was left hanging, and seemed to herald an even brisker dismissal than he had feared because the *notaire* rose to his feet. Cédric was about to do the same, but before he could the other made a request verging on an order, – 'One moment, please' – pulled a thick green volume from the bookcase behind him and opened it on the console table with the vase. When he returned to his place, he was holding a yellowed paper envelope in his hand. Inside was a small, rectangular card, which he passed to Cédric without saying a word.

'What is it?'

'I hope you can tell me, perhaps that way I can understand

who I'm talking to.' A black and white photo with two standing figures at its centre, around them bulky, white rollers and machines about two metres in height. It looked like a factory. 'Well?' prompted Levasseur.

'... the beach at Cabourg,...'

Cédric looked, perplexed and annoyed by the inquisitorial tone until, all of a sudden, the image pushed the *notaire*, the watch, the auction and everything else out of his mind. The beach at Cabourg, two shadows in movement – one long and the other short – cast onto the sand by the setting Autumn sun, a hand too big to hold all of it, eyes raised to meet a serene, reassuring smile, the same smile captured on the old photo and burning into his eyes, a blinding flash like the Provencal sun after emerging from a motorway tunnel. 'It's my Dad,' a strangled whisper more than an exclamation.

'Which one?'

'The one in the dark overalls. How did you come by this photo?' Cédric knew he had turned pale: not only could he feel it, but he could hear it in his interlocutor's voice, surprise and doubt replacing the annoyance of a few moments earlier.

'Try turning it over, it should jog your memory.'

A few words written in fountain pen, the ink – maybe black, originally – faded to a washed out reddish colour: '1973 Jean-Claude and Clément the winning team.' 'What memory?' asked

Cédric 'Who is Jean-Claude?'

'My uncle.'

'They knew each other?'

'More than that: they were friends. Not a common occurrence for a boss of a firm and his employee.'

'Firm?'

'The one in the photo. Don't you know what job your father did?'

'Typographer. But he didn't speak about it much. It upset him, having to stop working because of the illness. And when he died I was just a child.'

'I know. My uncle told me a couple of years ago, when he was in hospital. I had gone to pick up some documents from his safety deposit box and seen the watch, the one from the auction ...'

'Did it belong to him?'

'Yes. He left it to my sister and me because he didn't have any children of his own. But before that it was your father's, Mr Roussel.' Levasseur paused, as though fearing that Cédric, sitting stock still with eyes fixed on the photo, would not manage to follow him. 'It's strange that I should be the one telling you all this. Incredible, in fact ...'

'I didn't know anything about it. Any of it.'

'In that case accept my apologies. I thought I knew why you were interested in the watch, which was why I proposed to meet. Perhaps I came across as a little rude but well, you know ... I thought you were trying to pull a fast one, for whatever reason.'

'It doesn't matter ... But how did you find me?'

'It was you who allowed yourself to be found. When you called the auction house, Mr Onfray thought it might be someone with the same name, but the birth place and the grandfather being a partisan ... I wondered whether there was a link between the Roussel in Nice asking for information and the Roussel on the document.'

'Document?'

'The donation. Signed by a British officer who gave the watch to your grandfather.'

How had Onfray put it on Monday evening? *A French citizen.*
And not just any citizen, apparently: 'So my grandfather ...'

'... gave the watch to your father. And he sold it to my uncle.'
'Sold it?'

'He didn't want to. But he was ill and had to stop work just
as he was about to take over the printing workshop. They had
agreed on everything, my uncle promised he would lend a hand
as it got off the ground. But then ... with no job, a young son to
look after. Your father was afraid he wouldn't be able to make
ends meet and decided to sell the watch. My uncle bought it for
twice the amount a jeweller's in town had offered him. He wanted to show that he could count on him. And he guaranteed him
that as soon as he was better and back at work, he would sell it
back. Unfortunately ...'

'Right ...' Cédric found the strength to raise his eyes from the
photo, but not enough to articulate even one of the questions racing through his brain like branches on a surging river, no sooner passing before his eyes than they vanished again; even the
biggest one of all, seemingly easier to grasp than the others in
the moment it appeared, remained fleeting, so close and yet still
beyond his reach.

It was the *notaire* who broke the silence: 'I was wondering ...
If you didn't know, then how ...? Ah, I forgot: the internet.'

'And the regimental emblem. If I hadn't seen it, I wouldn't
be here.'

'That reminds me, I have to show you those papers. I only
have photocopies because I gave the originals to the auction house.'

Two sheets came out of the document holder. The one written
on a typewriter was faded and difficult to read. A few lines in
English with a few spelling mistakes, signed by a major named
Landon Roach, who declared that he had donated the watch on
his own initiative to thank a 'brave French patriot' for his help
during the battle for liberation, for which he had put his own

life at risk. At the top, a faded stamp accompanied by the place and date: 'Caen, July 1944.' The day and date were missing, but dotting the i's and crossing the t's was presumably not the top item on the list of priorities at the time. At the centre of the other sheet was the copy of a handwritten declaration: 'Caen, 18 February 1975. I confirm that Mr André Levasseur has paid the sum of 1,800 francs to me for the watch previously belonging to my father Jean-Jacques. Distinguishing features: emblem with winged parachute and a woman's name (Jane) engraved on the back. Clément Roussel.'

'... the copy of a handwritten declaration...'

'You can keep the photo, if you like. The one of the printing workshop.'

'Really?'

'But I would like a copy. You can send it to me when you get a chance. The photocopies ... you may as well take them too, though if you buy the watch you won't need them because they will give you the originals. I imagine you will be taking part in the auction.'

'Yes ... Or rather, I'll have to think about it. It's a lot of money.'

'If you decide to take part I will be cheering for you.'

'Thank you ...'

'I think my uncle would have liked to sell it too, but he couldn't bring himself to. He told me he kept it in the deposit box because the thought of wearing it made him sad, but he couldn't bear the idea of being parted from it. Now that he is no longer with us, my sister and I have decided to sell it. And a good thing we did: this is your chance to take it back where it belongs.'

'I hope so ...'

'I need to go now. But you can stay a while, if you want to take your time looking at the papers.'

'I believe I'll take you up on the offer ... How much do I owe you?'

'For what?'

'I've wasted half an hour of your time ...'

'Are you joking? If I charged Clément Roussel's son, my uncle's ghost would haunt me to the end of my days.' As he lowered the door handle, the *notaire* hesitated: 'Excuse me for prying, but is your mother still alive?'

There it was, the most important of the mislaid questions. 'Yes. She lives in Nice as well.'

'Ah ...' Was he going to ask? No – it was not his business. 'Send her my best wishes. And good luck.'

He must have been in a hurry, otherwise he would not have forgotten to put the volume back in its place. Cédric went up to the console table and opened it. It was an album. Family photos, a couple of familiar faces, maybe the *notaire* and his uncle many years ago. The others must have been relatives or friends; children, smiles, glasses raised in a toast around a table, dated hairstyles and clothes, a group posing with a small pedal car in the background. Big families, and probably with no one missing, either. Not like his: the photograph lying on the table, next to the photocopies, was the scar left by an amputation. But now there were Sylvie and Théo. And his son was a boy like the ones in the album. And the memories growing within him were not missing anything.

It was not right to go sticking his nose into other people's private lives, he told himself, and as he neared the cabinet to put the Levasseur family's archive in its place, among other books that betrayed a weakness for nineteenth century French fiction, he cast a last glance over the leather binding. Not a speck of dust: it was clear the *notaire* looked through the album often. It must have been important to him. And his father's photo had been there, protected in an envelope, looked after even better than the rest by a stranger who had not known that a meeting awaited him with the person for whom this message from the past was intended.

Angèle must have been too busy to offer him a coffee or a glass of water, or else she preferred to avoid moving wherever it was not strictly necessary, knowing that a topple from those heels would cost her dear. That was good. Cédric needed some time to himself to put his thoughts back in order, beginning with the one the *notaire* had brought back to him before taking his leave. Dad had worn that watch for a long time and there had never been any shortage of tales about Grandad Jean-Jacques. Why had Mum never mentioned it? She could not have forgotten – it was almost a medal of valour. His first impulse was to phone her right away, but it was the time she took her afternoon rest and, after all, there was no rush. He would see her on Sunday and they would have time to talk about it properly. His gaze wandered back to the photocopies on the table. Who had the watch belonged to originally? Roach? Maybe: logic would dictate that there was no reason why he should be in possession of anyone else's as part of his job. But why give it away? And if he was a paratrooper, as the engraving on the back would suggest, then why was he far away from the theatre of operations? Perhaps he and the other survivors of the previous battles had been conceded some leave following the liberation of Caen, when the front had moved elsewhere.

Mere conjecture, dreamt up by Cédric in a feverish but pointless attempt to sidestep the dilemma: now what? Was it harder to go back, or to press on? And if he made the wrong choice, which of the two would be the gravest error? Was it better to do something stupid or regret not having done it? Should he ask Sylvie what she thought? That was no use; he already knew her answer and it was no answer at all, only a question: 'Are you mad?' Too easy, leaving the decision up to someone else: Cédric took his leave from Angèle and, back in the street again, set off at a quick walk.

Two thousand five hundred euros. Translating the book had earned him seven thousand. Which, together with his savings, would be enough to buy a new car. The small family sedan was nine years old and had grown small; cramming in everything they needed for trips – and, above all, everything they did not need but which Théo considered indispensable – was a task that became tougher every summer. Cédric had picked out a no-frills station wagon on sale at a showroom that was just what they needed, and had agreed on a trade-in value for the old car. They had the money, the figures all added up and the time was right. But the project, conceived by weighing up every detail and following frequent consultations with Sylvie, seemed to lose its solidity with each hurried step he took towards the hotel.

Two thousand five hundred euros. When was the last time he really splashed out on anything? The flat screen LCD television, a year and a half earlier. But even then, he had not merely acted on a whim: the hefty machine with built-in VCR that they had brought with them from the apartment in the city-centre was a relic of industrial archaeology and the last they got it repaired it had cost as much as a mobile phone. They had been forced to choose a new set, and since the amount of space at the new house allowed for it, why not take the leap in the world of big-screen full HD, topping it off with a satellite dish to keep up with the English Premier League? There he had acted on a whim – indeed, Sylvie had refused to help cover the cost. But it was a one-off, an exception in a life shaped by the mortgage and dedicated to thrift, even where it came to free time. Cédric had still not taken the decision to buy himself a new pair of trainers for Friday night five-a-side, despite the fact that the soles on his existing pair were as worn out as a car's tyres after doing fifty thousand kilometres and would end up costing him an injury. His shorts and t-shirt were so threadbare that Cédric was forced to justify himself to his friends, over and over like a broken record: 'It's the Liverpool strip from the 80s, I'll go on wearing it until it rips.' Restaurants? Never, a pizza every other week at most. Cigarettes? Cédric barely knew what they were. Holidays? None longer than two weeks, since their honeymoon in the Maldives. Shows? He was not interested in theatre or opera, the giant TV eliminated the need for trips to the cinema, and the new stadium in Nice, as fine as it was, held only limited powers of attraction for a man who could watch Liverpool v Man U from the comfort of his own sofa. He had been tempted on one occasion to go and see U2 in Paris but had thought better of it – eye-watering prices. Not even the most miserly of skinflints could have called him a spendthrift.

Two thousand five hundred euros. Sunday was not only Théo' birthday, even if everyone, himself included, tended to forget it. Sylvie would get him a present as she did every year. But when was the last time Cédric had treated himself? Now that was real prehistory, long before the LCD TV. As hard as he tried, Cédric could not recall the last time he had bought something that was really for him on his birthday. The only other occasion he had really gone on a spending spree was during the long-past trip to England with his friends, when he had spent everything down to the last penny, money he had put together from his savings, earned working summer jobs, and the small reward for passing his exams that his mother had managed to scrape together and place in an envelope for him. Videotapes, books, *Spiderman* comics in their original language, records, and t-shirts, plus the tickets for the concert and the match: Cédric had left smiles on the faces of many a shopkeeper in London. But it had not been his birthday and, above all, it was another life, free of responsibilities, without a job or a family to worry about.

Cédric burst into his room after racing up the four flights of stairs, two steps at a time, too impatient to wait for the lift. Among the conveniences placed at his disposition was a free wifi network. This was the moment to make the most of it.

The web was a treasure trove of instructions and practical advice for taking part in auctions. The first tip, repeated ad nauseam: decide on a spending limit and keep your calm in the few seconds between when bidding opens and closes, to avoid being caught up in a ruinous spiral of sky-rocketing bids. But what struck him – or better, traumatised him – was a more concrete detail than the risks associated with the exhilaration of competing, brought to light as he read through the conditions set in place by the auction house. In addition to the cost of a given item, there were also taxes and commissions that could top forty per cent. In practice, as the calculator on his mobile phone revealed with implacable precision, if the watch went for two thousand seven hundred euros, halfway between the minimum and maximum estimates, the buyer would end up spending around three thousand eight hundred euros. It was a knockout blow; indeed, the ten seconds given to a boxer to get back on his feet were not enough for Cédric, nor even a whole minute. He shook himself out of his stupor only when, focussing again on the computer screen, he realised what the time was: five o'clock already, he had to make a decision. He did so with uncharacteristic speed and dashed off once more, closing the laptop without turning it off.

He knew where to go, having made a note of the address on his mobile before leaving Nice. 'You never know,' he had justified it to himself. Only a prolonged wait would have given him time to reflect, hesitate, waver and perhaps give up. But behind the re-enforced glass door there were only three employees, two sitting at the counters and another standing behind them, chatting as they awaited closing time. Three thousand eight hundred euros, not a cent more – that way it would be impossible to go any higher. As the cashier counted out the notes in front of him, Cédric felt a pang of guilt. He had earned that money with the translation, but the account was in both their names. If he won, how would he be able to summon up the courage to tell Sylvie he had blown the savings set aside for a new car on an old watch?

18. 6 JUNE 1944, 10:58

... 'Castle?'

'That's right. All for us.'

The major had been exaggerating. A large villa, more than an actual castle. We caught sight of it through the branches, a short distance beyond a broken gate with a single door hanging off its rusty hinges, as we came up the driveway, flanked by trees on both sides. In front of the wall, with its peeling plasterwork and surprisingly intact windows, the path divided in two around an oval flowerbed infested with weeds. Two floors, thirty yards by fifteen, at a glance.

The Germans had been using it as a magazine until a few hours earlier. Everywhere, from the hallway to the bedrooms, on tables and chairs, on the floor and the wardrobes with doors left ajar, were the traces of a garrison that had received orders to move off in a hurry. Clothing, weapons, ammunition, blankets, sheets, towels, a pair of binoculars and two brand new typewriters with reams of paper by their sides, even a metal cashbox filled with banknotes atop what must have been the paymaster's desk. 'I reckon I'll forget to hand that lot over to HQ,' the CO announced, 'Should cover a few rounds when they send someone in to relieve us.' An even louder cheer went up among the first men into the kitchen, who had discovered something even better than money in that it could be enjoyed immediately. The larder next door was stocked with just about everything: bread, beef, bacon, ham, butter, sacks of sugar, jars of marmalade, two metal churns full of milk and another of cream.

A stroke of luck but a warning sign as well: they might be back from one moment to the next. The lieutenant colonel sent out around thirty men divided into three groups, one to patrol the perimeter of the park and the others to find which places had the best view of the roads leading up to the villa and set up our emplacements there. As I was helping to mount the Vickers on its tripod, isolated mortar rounds fired from a farmhouse about a mile away were landing harmlessly a few yards inside the half-gate. Beltman ordered us not to return fire, partly to save ammunition that we would need until the commandos reached us and partly because the Germans were unsure of our presence, as otherwise they would be firing directly at the villa. Best to leave them with their doubts. Crossing the park to return to the CO I met twenty or so of my mates walking in the opposite direction, led by Captain Rundell, and asked myself where they were headed. I discovered the answer a short time later from a joke shared between the major and his batman as I was coming up the stairs: a sortie to dislodge the Germans from the farmhouse, at the same time as giving the impression that they were part of a numerous and well-armed enemy force. The exact opposite of what we really were.

The CO had taken possession of a room, on the first floor, that must once have been the dining room. On the pale blue and yellow striped wallpaper, torn in many places, I could make out the marks left by pictures that someone had put away for safekeeping or stolen. In front of the grey, granite fireplace lay a battered-looking sofa with matching armchairs, covered with a threadbare material of an unidentifiable colour somewhere between brown and dark red. In the middle of the room stood a rectangular table, certainly not the one around which the owners had used to sit down to dinner: more suited to a carpenter's workshop than a rich family's dining room, unvarnished and uneven. I wondered what had become of them. The lieutenant colonel was sitting on one of the chairs, each one different from the rest, that were positioned around the table, engaged in studying a map he had unfolded next to his helmet and a pair of binoculars. 'Do you need me, sir?'

'Not at the moment. Go downstairs.' The kitchen was crowded: some were eating, others smoking, and still others had found some beer. I sat down on the floor in a corner with a glass of milk and a plate I had filled with a few slices of bread and ham, and listened to the others. No one doubted that the sortie would be a success entailing no losses.

They were right. When I returned to the first floor, Rundell had come back and was talking to the CO. A few Germans had been taken out while others had fled or been captured, among them an officer. 'Shut them in the tennis court with the others and send another man to stand guard.'

He told me to sit down. I did so cautiously, wondering whether the less dog-eared armchair would bear my weight. How since we had jumped? I had lost all notion of time and it was only now, as I glanced at my wrist, that I realised my mother's gift had met an unfortunate end: beneath the broken glass, the minute hand was bent, almost crushed onto the hour hand, the time frozen at half past one. From the air raid and diving into that ditch, I thought. I remembered the captain's watch: I would use it in place of my own without actually putting it on and, once I had found out the time, would put it back where it was safe.

I lifted the pouch cover to slide my right thumb and index finger inside, mechanically and without looking as I did at the camp during rifle drill, but found only empty space. I lowered my head and saw the right-hand pocket of my uniform through a hole an inch wide. I opened the other pouch, stuffing my hand inside and pulling out the grenades. I patted my chest, my legs. Then I began to empty my haversack, throwing everything onto the floor in front of the fireplace, and got on my knees to rifle through it, trying to form a timeline of what had happened during

170

the preceding hours. When was the last time I had seen it? Before dawn, in the casemate. Then the march towards the village, the sprint to call the others, the leap into the crater... the blow to my side! It must have torn a hole in my pouch and the watch fell out of it. Perhaps it had saved my life by taking a bullet and now it was in pieces. But I could not let the captain down: if the worst came to the worst I would just have to go and find Jane with a handful of useless scrap.

'What are you doing?' I had not noticed the lieutenant colonel watching me from behind the table.

I leapt to my feet: 'I've lost Captain Kadwell's watch. He entrusted it to me, he wanted me to take it to his wife. I'm almost certain it fell out when we were pulling out of the village. I request authorisation to go back and get it. I can do it alone, sir.'

I would have done better to say nothing. The request must have sounded so bizarre that he took a few moments to realise I was not joking, and then to choose between incredulity and irritation: 'Do you think you're on a school outing? We need everyone, here. Repack your haversack and don't speak again until I ask you to.'

I felt myself blush: 'Yes sir.'

I had just finished closing the haversack when I heard a loud bang and found myself lying on the floor between the armchairs. A rush of air and an impact closer than those I had heard in the park, as I was mounting the Vickers. The lieutenant colonel had stayed on his feet by grabbing hold of the table. He neared the window. I went to stand next to him and, through a haze of smoke, saw that half the flower bed had been swallowed up by a crater. That was no mortar, nor a bomb dropped by an aircraft – we would have heard the drone of approaching engines. Artillery: the Germans who had escaped from the farmhouse had raised the alarm, and the beginning of the barrage signalled that an attack was imminent.

'Let's go downstairs.' In front of the villa, the major had gathered about forty men who were disappearing into the trees to join our comrades at the emplacements. The CO ordered me to follow them and to act as a runner between the park and the villa to keep him informed. The bombardment was intensifying, but the villa had not been hit.

I reached Beltman and his men as they were positioning themselves either side of the machine-gunners by the trees that ran along next to the main driveway, at the point where a curve in the road offered an almost uninterrupted view all the way to what was left of the gate. Then I crossed the park, where artillery rounds were shredding through the branches and sending splinters as deadly as bullets through the air, up to the pathway that led to the west-facing wall of the house. The second Vickers had been placed between the tree trunks, at the top of a small rise from

'... the second Vickers had been placed between the tree trunks...'

which it could cover the adjoining wood and, if necessary, any enemies that made it past the first emplacement. Heading back to the house, I heard the lieutenant colonel's voice. It seemed to be coming from the back of the house and I rounded the corner. 'The Kraut officer wanted to talk to him,' one of my mates guarding the fence told me. I spotted him at the centre of a circle formed by a number of prisoners, speaking with a young, confident captain who had a fairly good grasp of English.

'Englin reporting, sir.' The lieutenant colonel gestured me to be quiet as the German harangued him with the tone of a teacher reproaching his pupils: 'International conventions prohibit putting the lives of prisoners of war at risk. I demand to be moved to a safe place with my men.'

'It's your side who is shelling you, not ours. If you like, I can have you taken indoors, but I think that would be more dangerous than staying here. Your choice.'

The other did not give in: 'It is unacceptable. I wish to speak with your superior.'

'If one turns up I'll let you know. In the meantime I have a question. You seem to know about the conventions …,' a cold smile appeared on his lips.

'Of course.'

'Do you also know about Hitler's orders?'

'What do you mean?'

'I mean we received word about a note signed by the Führer. Saying British paratroopers are to be eliminated even when incapable of defending themselves. I was wondering what that had to do with international conventions.'

'You do the same.'

'What?'

'You kill prisoners.'

'If that were true, you lot would be dead already. Who told you such rubbish?'

The German lowered his gaze and fell silent beneath the stare of the CO, whose smile had vanished. The barrage was slackening: the attack would come soon. 'I have to go now, but I shall be back and I would like an answer. In the meantime, if you change your mind about where you want to be held, talk to the guards about it. Let's go, Roger.'

I would have liked to ask him a bit more about that Hitler business – it was some story. Who knew, apart from the CO? The officers, no doubt. Why had the captain not mentioned it, instead of making fun out of me? Had he been ordered not to tell anyone? Perhaps. But by then there was no way to ask, let alone have a go at him about it. And then to be fair, I had volunteered; I knew I could not expect a warm welcome. So I limited myself to muttering, 'I would have shot him.'

The CO heard me: 'Have they told you we kill prisoners, as well?'

'I ...'

'I don't think you would have killed the medical officer at the battery.'

'Medical officer?'

'Instead of going to the regimental aid post he stayed to take care of the wounded who couldn't be moved. Abbott saw him running between the casemates with a medical satchel, as the bombs were falling. He risked his skin for our boys too, not just his own. I hope he made it ... the emplacements?'

'Ready. Thirty seven men at the entrance and thirty two on the flank.'

'Go back to Beltman. Fire at will when the Krauts are twenty-thirty yards away, but only if it's a real attack. If it's a patrol, then a few bursts from the Bren so they keep their distance, nothing more.'

I stopped dead when I saw the lieutenant kneeling down a few steps from the driveway, who spun around to face me with his index finger to his lips. Among the tree trunks, a few dozen yards lower down, I could make out the first grey-green silhouettes of a column that had passed the gate and was slowly advancing. I could see thirty or so, but judging by their footsteps there might have been twice that number. Beltman ordered me down, ready to open fire: I lay down among the bushes and trees, resting the barrel of my Sten on a root protruding from the earth and keeping it in the shade of the foliage.

19. 4 JUNE 2014, 06:12

'How stupid do you think I am? That's enough now, or else no computer for a week!'

Cédric raised his head from the pillow and looked around, disorientated but then reassured by what he could see by the first rays of sunshine filtering through the blinds, washing over the shelf with the television and the desk where he had placed his laptop and charger, reaching the other side of the room and reflecting back at him by the metal coat hooks. The spartan panorama of his room; familiar surroundings after an excursion into the unknown. Too early for breakfast, the screen of his mobile told him. He reached his hand out to switch on the small spotlight embedded in the headboard, but then pulled it back.

Why was he angry with Théo? The internet, still? Cédric lay motionless, as though afraid of taking a false step and falling from the high wire strung between sleep and wakefulness, trying to regain a delicate balance, in his hands a puzzle too complete to be true and too fragile to survive the impact of reality.

Alone in the middle of a field, he had been staring down at a dark marble slab on the grass, identical to the one covering Dad's tomb, and trying, without success, to make out the words etched onto its centre: a sentence in English, not a name. He had rummaged through his pocket looking for his mobile, where he had updated the dictionary a few days earlier, but instead of the plastic shell his fingers had closed around a metal object. The sight of the watch, *that* watch, coming out of the only place he had not searched because it was too close by, too obvious, had struck him with a wave of incredulous joy, the amazement of one who finds something important long after having given it up as lost. He had put it on, buckling the strap on his wrist, and had held it to his ear, letting his eyes wander as he strained to hear its ticking. He had taken a moment or two to realize that in the meantime everything around him had changed. Or had it been that way from the start?

The field was a football pitch, he and the tomb in the middle of the centre circle. On all four sides the terraces, filled to capacity but silent. There was no shouting, no singing, not even a cou-

'... toy soldiers! English Paras from WWII...'

gh, and yet every seat was taken. Thousands of motionless spectators, all with identical light-brown boots, trousers, jackets, helmets. And faces. Toy soldiers! English Paras from the Second World War, some with a grenade in their right hand and a machine-gun in their left, others standing or kneeling to shoot, still others mid-charge with bayonets fixed to their rifles, officers in berets, binoculars round their necks and arms raised to point something out. As large as real people, they observed him from the terraces, creating in him a feeling of unease that was accentuated rather than lessened by his familiarity with the surroundings.

Anfield Road! How had he managed to get onto the pitch? What were the toy soldiers doing there? Looking down to escape their insistent scrutiny, he could not help but let out a cry: the back of his left hand was covered in a dense, red liquid, dripping down from his index finger. He was afraid he would faint, like the time when he was a boy and had seen a handkerchief soaked in blood from his nose, and looked away; then he had plucked up his courage and raised his hand to search for the wound, examining every square centimetre of skin. Nothing, not even a scratch, and yet the haemorrhage continued, unstoppable. Only when he had used his finger to lift the watch away from his wrist could he see where it was coming from. He had given a start: the metal was bleeding, not his skin. It was oozing slowly and steadily from the circular slit between the case middle and back, down through the grooves and from there onto his wrist.

Cédric had tried to get rid of the watch and throw it onto the pitch, but had found it impossible to get a firm grip on the blood-soaked strap, his sweaty fingertips slipping across it as unease gave way to anxiety and then desperation: that appendage would be stuck on him forever and no one would be able to get it off. Who could he turn to for help? Up on the terraces there were only the toy soldiers rooted to their positions, footstands resting across the seats, so impassive that now he asked himself if they really were watching him.

But who was that? At the end of the pitch, below the Kop? Théo! Unmistakable, even with his back to him and fifty metres away, talking with somebody. A woman, or rather a girl who seemed to be wearing a uniform: dark green shirt and skirt, broad-brimmed hat of the same colour with a striking red ribbon round it. Who was it? What was his son doing with her? And why was he there? He liked basketball, not football. Good for him if he had changed his mind, a thought that crossed Cédric's mind even during his waking hours: too small for a giants' sport. But he could ask him why another time. In that moment all that mattered was that he was in the right place at the right time, a promise of salvation in among the indifference of the crowd. 'Come here!' he had shouted, and Théo had turned around before setting out slowly towards him, holding the girl by her hand. 'Quick!' Théo was smiling, perhaps pleased at being seen walking around with an adult, female companion who was more attractive than his teacher, and taking his time like when he knew there was spinach for dinner. In fact he seemed not to come any nearer even though he was walking. And Cédric, instead of going to meet him halfway, had simply waited, impotent and rooted to the grass like a goalpost.

Then his attention had been captured by the illuminated scoreboard above the crowd of toy soldiers, fixed to the roof of the terraces along one side, and by two enormous numbers, yellow on a red background: 6-6, an unusual score for a football match. But what match, anyway? The only people on the pitch were him, his son and the girl.

After a minute or an hour or a day they had reached him and Cédric had held his arm out to Théo: 'Take the watch off!' But there had been no reply. 'What are you waiting for? Can't you see I ...' the question had died on his lips because there was nothing on his wrist, neither blood nor watch. Vanished – not even a trace of them on the pitch, at his feet. Where had that metallic monster with its open wound ended up? Why did its disappearance not bring him the slightest relief? And why, after taking off her hat and letting down her long, red hair, was the girl staring at him like that, silent, her freckles streaked by tears? 'Who is she? You know you're not supposed to talk to strangers.'

'She's not a stranger. She's Jane.'

Jane ... the name rang a bell, but he had never seen her before. 'Why is she crying?'

'Because you lost the watch.'

'I'm sure it's around here somewhere. If you two help me look for it ...'

'You have to do it.'

'By myself? That's impossible.'

'You're not by yourself,' Théo had answered, letting go of the girl's hand and grasping his to lead him to the marble slab, pointing at the letters etched into the middle of it.

'What does it say? I don't understand.'

'I told you, didn't I?' Théo had asked, with the air of one who knew it all.

'No ...'

'Yes I did. And so did they.'

'Who?'

'Them. Listen.' Index finger pointed at the Kop, he seemed to be counting the toy soldiers one at a time.

'I don't hear anything.'

'But they're singing.'

'How stupid do you think I am? That's enough now, or else no computer for a week!'

Odd, being able to reconstruct a dream down to the last detail, from beginning to end. Cédric had never managed to do so before. Perhaps an internet search would offer up some explanation – he would think about it tomorrow or another day, if he still felt like it. Right now he had other things on his mind. But when he decided to move, his first, instinctive gesture revealed that coming back to reality was not as simple as pressing a button on a remote control. Without looking, he felt across the top of the bedside table with the palm of his hand, in search of a watch he had never worn. He could do with a good, strong coffee, or rather two.

20. 6 JUNE 1944, 13:19

… I lay down among the bushes and trees, resting the barrel of my Sten on a root protruding from the earth and keeping it in the shade of the foliage.

Less than forty men to stop sixty or so. And having dived to the ground at the last moment, I found myself in the worst position, my view obstructed by a rise in the land, where I would only be able to see them when they were already practically on top of me. Not only that, but I had never been a great marksman: at the camp there were at least two-hundred men who were better shots than I was, which was why I had been given a Sten instead of an Enfield. From that distance even I could not miss, I told myself, but I hoped the others would force the enemy to retreat before it came to that. I was certain they must have had them in their sights because I could hear low voices speaking in German. I felt tense: what was Beltman waiting for?

All of a sudden the murmurs turned into curses and shouts, as the crackle of automatic weapons reached my ears. Who was shooting? From where? And at who? I turned to face the others. Nobody seemed to know what was happening. 'Go and have a look,' Beltman ordered the man next to him, who began crawling towards the tree line along the edge of the path. I was following him with my gaze when I heard a sudden noise and glimpsed movement in the corner of my eye, letting out a cry before I had a chance to think about it: 'Krauts, on the right!'

A dozen or so had penetrated the park after leaving the path lower down and were running towards us, dashing through the bushes and trees, When they heard me they seemed surprised, as though they had not expected to find us there. As I pulled the trigger – three round bursts like the captain had said, so that I would not find myself with an empty cartridge at the wrong moment – my only concern was the shooting coming from my mates behind me, above all the Vickers, because the Germans were strangely passive targets, slow to seek cover and return fire. It was not like at the battery, where we had been shooting at shadows. Now I could see them plainly, even spotting the small puffs of dust thrown up from their uniforms when we hit one of them. Most of them fell, some sought refuge behind tree trunks, while others joined them from behind. They seemed more like fugitives than attackers, apparently just as disorientated as those who had preceded them.

'Follow them!' The shout, in English, came from the other side of the path. The Germans abandoned their cover behind the trees and moved towards the house in an attempt to evade us. A few of them made it, disappearing into the undergrowth, but im-

... the curved silhouette of a magazine...'

mediately after more bursts of fire rang out: now it was the machine-gunners on the western side of the park who were shooting. 'More on their way!' shouted Beltman. Figures moved among the trees, fifty yards or so away, more or less where I had spotted the first wave. I took aim, but a moment before squeezing the trigger I recognised the curved silhouette of a magazine protruding from the barrel of a Bren and then, lit up for a split second by the sunlight filtering through the branches, the hem of a camouflage jacket. 'They're ours,' I shouted.

The camouflaged men threw themselves to the ground. I glanced back at Beltman, who answered with a nod of the head and gave the order to cease fire. A question reached us from behind the trees: 'Who are you lot?' 'Paras. And you?' asked Beltman. 'Commandos.'

Finally, they had arrived. Along with a rush of relief I felt a sudden ache in the back of my neck and my shoulders, tensed to take aim and open fire, pins and needles in my finger and a burning sensation on the back of my left hand, though I had no memory of where I had scratched it. 'Nice one, Roger,' said Beltman as he crawled his way up to me. No one had come out into the open: 'Move up, we'll cover you.'

One by one they emerged from the vegetation and came towards us, circling the bodies that littered the ground. There were about forty of them, led by a moustachioed officer with a strong Scottish accent: 'Who's in command here?'

'Lieutenant Beltman, sir.'

'Are you alone?'

'No. I'll take you to the lieutenant colonel. Come with us, Roger.'

Silence had fallen over the park once more. There were grey-green uniformed bodies everywhere, but one of them struck me more than the rest. He must have been about my age, blond, kneeling against a trunk, his bloody face leant against the bark, pale eyes that seemed to stare right at me, lips parted as though he were about to speak, one arm trapped between his chest and the tree, the other by his side with his hand closed in a fist. Maybe, as he was dying, he was convinced he still had the rifle with him, when actually he had dropped it somewhere. The only thing I could see near his body was his helmet, thrown onto the grass by the bullet that had struck him square in the side of the head. Though I could not know it then, that image had been branded into my memory. More than the captain, who I had barely actually looked at, still too stunned to understand what had happened to him. More than the mate I passed as I left the village, his face to the ground – it could have been anyone. More than the horrors that would pass before my eyes in the hours and days to come, dismembered corpses, features devastated by shrapnel or charred by flames. More than all of that, because what I saw before me overlapped with a hallucination. As I walked beside Beltman, dogged by the impression I was being followed by the dead man's gaze, I saw myself on the pitch in the Spurs kit, shaking the hand of a blond lad about my age, captain of a German team visiting London, saying to him, 'May the best man win' in his language as they had taught me, but convinced all the same that we were the best and that, if need be, I would demonstrate the fact by playing rough – a tackle from me and he would be taking home a nice bruise on his shin as a keepsake from his trip to England. Playing rough – how the meaning of that expression had changed. Had I killed him? No way, I had not even fired a shot in that direction. I was relieved, but a moment later felt a fool. What did it matter?

'Where on Earth were you, Roger?' we had been spotted by the CO and he was making his way towards us.

Beltman did not give me a chance to reply: 'He stayed there with us, otherwise they would have seen him. The lad did alright – noticed the enemy before the others and stopped us from firing on our guests. It's the commandos, sir.'

'We've been waiting for you a while.'

'The Krauts gave us a bit of trouble, but we gave them some back.'

'How did it go in the park, Beltman?'

'They got caught in the middle – all dead or wounded.'

'Not all,' the Commando officer corrected him. 'A few of them got away; four or five, I reckon.'

'Might work in our favour. They'll talk about what sort of a reception they had and they might leave us alone long enough to organize the attack on the village. What about us? How many casualties?'

'Four wounded in our group, sir, I don't know about the others.'

'Send Goldfield to ask and have someone relieve your boys at the emplacement. Let's go upstairs, Major. You, come with us.'

As I climbed the stairs, seemingly hundreds of them when in fact there were a dozen at most, gaze fixed on the dark terracotta steps with cracked edges, I felt tired for the first time in weeks. The officers' voices were distant background noise which I struggled to translate into words and sentences. A muffled boom from the far side of the park shook me out of my daze as I reached the landing. 'Here we go again,' I thought, attempting to predict the CO's reaction and imagining myself running outside again, but instead he gestured the major to a chair by the table, apparently unruffled. For ten seconds or so we heard nothing more. Then another boom, this time closer, followed by another pause. 'Mortars,' commented the lieutenant colonel. 'If that's the best they can do we have nothing to worry about … Roger?'

'Yes sir?'

'What are you standing there for?'

'… Nothing, sir. I mean … I'm awaiting orders.'

'At ease. And don't get any funny ideas. You will go to the village, but with us.'

I flopped onto the same armchair where I had noticed the captain's watch had gone missing, and spotted an elongated, triangular chip that recalled the shape of a rifle butt in the small left-hand column of the fireplace. I wondered whether it would be possible to seal the hole with a piece of granite like the missing chunk, fitting it in such a way as not to leave any visible mark. Were there restorers who could do that kind of a job? Did the profession have a name?

I knew neither the answers nor the reason why I should ask myself these questions. So I let my mind wander elsewhere as I sank my neck into the armchair's headrest.

21. 4 JUNE 2014, 09:47

It was the sort of place that could host a G8 summit: a luxury hotel a stone's throw from the beaches and *planches* of Deauville, five storeys of balconies and two more with windows built into the pitched roof, Haussmann style with a Norman twist. All built with the comfort of its demanding guests in mind: golf lovers, horse-racing fans and big-time gamblers from across the Channel, or from Paris. An institution, attracting the cream of the international jet-set for over a century, casting a heavy and intimidating shadow across Cédric's car. His sedan looked wrong alongside the four-wheeled offspring of the British, German and Italian automobile elites, lined up in a luxury car showroom, the 'P' sign at the entrance seeming rather an understatement. He too felt out of place as he made his way into an entrance hall the size of a tennis court, stuccoed columns lit by wall lamps flanking a concert of colour where crimson reigned supreme. It was everywhere: between the cream-coloured geometric patterns of the rugs; alternating with the ivory-white stripes of the upholstery covering the armchairs; on the round, single-coloured sofas from the centres of which towered plants with thick, polished leaves; even on the velvet stool – currently unoccupied – intended for the pianist. The lampshades sprouting from the small tables lost out in the brightness stakes to the crystal chandeliers hung from the ceiling, but the few newspaper readers seated on satin cushions seemed to find them quite sufficient. They might have been hotel guests, aspiring buyers like him, or both of these at once. Cédric hoped only his first guess was correct. He could not see himself competing with such rivals: their clothing, their accessories – leather briefcases, designer glasses, chunky gold watches peeping out from cuff linked shirtsleeves – even their facial expressions all told him he was out of his economic league.

'First floor.' The concierge in grey livery watching over the front doors from behind an imposing desk pointed to a marble staircase next to the reception. At the top of the flight of steps, panels bearing the auction house logo directed him onwards towards a corridor as wide as his garden and twenty metres longer, and from there into a room where a dozen or so people were standing in front of a cordon strung between two small, brass posts, blocking the entrance to the adjoining space. On the other side of the level crossing, a smiling man in jacket and tie was apologizing for the wait, explaining that he could not allow more than twenty people in at a time. Next to him stood a blue-uniformed security guard with the wire from an earpiece running down his neck and a frown on his face, leaving no doubts as to who was filling the role of guardian.

When his group's turn came, Cédric found himself in a room bounded by display cabinets on three sides. In front of the fourth wall, next to the entrance, was a table with two small armchairs on one side and a stool on the other, the latter occupied by a young man in white overalls with a watchmaker's loupe on his forehead and rubber pads on his thumb and index finger. At the centre of the room stood another unapproachable-looking guard dog, his attentions focused on a tanned man in his thirties with sun-bleached hair and five hundred euros' worth of moccasins on his feet, open catalogue in hand, his crime – at a guess – that he had stayed standing in a corner for too long, rather than casting his eye over the contents of the cabinets. The second sentinel too had a companion in formal dress, engaged in conversation at the far end of the room with a middle-aged couple whose every attribute – the woman's heavy make-up and flashy jewellery, the man's gesturing and the clash of bright colours that constituted his clothing – seemed to conform to a caricature of the nouveau-riche. Above, placed in the corners between the stuccoed ceiling and the walls, were two short-circuit surveillance cameras.

As the other members of the group spread out along the display cabinets, Cédric asked the uniformed guardian to enlighten him. He gave an automated response without taking his eyes off the tanned man: the objects were displayed in the same order as they appeared in the catalogue, starting with the first cabinet to the left of the door and proceeding clockwise around the room. Cédric was forced to balance on tiptoes to see over the heads of the people standing in front of him and read the metal plaques fixed beneath the displays. Number 110 closed the series running along the wall opposite the entrance where, behind the glass, heavy drapes were in place to prevent the sunshine from interfering with the contrast of the reflections glinting off of the objects and the soft lighting. All he had to do now was wait his turn in front of the first cabinet after the corner. Number 113, 114, 115 ... The plastic ring attached to the metal pedestal was empty: where had the watch gone? Withdrawn at the last minute? His crash course on the web had taught him that this sort of thing happened sometimes. That would be just his luck. But no, it was not possible – the *notaire* would have told him. The guard was mumbling something into the microphone attached to the cable, but there was no need to pester him again because the elegant chatterbox was available, having left the new-money couple and positioned himself next to the watchmaker.

'Number 115?' The timbre of the voice and its affected tone left no room for doubt: Onfray in the flesh was much like Cédric had imagined him, balding and haughty, so stiff that his perfectly pressed trousers and jacket looked made out of wood. 'Two gentlemen asked to examine it. You may join them, if you wish.'

Two men were sitting on Cédric's side of the table, one of them portly and around fifty years old, the other an older man who nodded as the expert spoke to him quietly in English, pointing at the watch, which had been placed on a velvet-covered tray with a wooden edge. Cédric sidled up behind them, hoping to see or hear something. The old man's bony hand, its web of veins so close to the surface he could practically see them pulsing, leant his walking stick against the edge of the table and touched the watch gingerly. The timepiece was not the only thing that looked familiar. The man's gaunt face and the handgrip of the walking stick, shaped like a small, ivory-coloured dog's head, both reminded him of something ...

But of course: the book presentation the evening before. After interpreting the questions from the audience and the author's answers, Cédric had taken advantage of the presence of a publishing house director, scraping an introduction from the owner of the shop. He had thanked him for the assignment and volunteered that he would be happy to work for them again, dropping in a few details from his CV as he did so. He had never had a great talent for self-promotion, but got the impression he had come across well – serious without seeming cold, polite but not obsequious – and had managed to capture his attention for longer than the few seconds big business leaders generally granted insignificant employees. Not only that, but once they had finished talking shop – a bad idea to insist and see a spontaneous offer turn rapidly into irritating begging – he had quickly grasped a joke from the bookseller and earned some extra time, contributing to an informal three-way debate about Lyon's failure in the latest Champions League. Ex-amateur footballer – his stocky build and lofty stature would have betrayed him as a centre-back even if he had failed to mention the position he played in – and long-term season ticket holder and fanatic of Olympique Lyonnais, mister Dubois had dropped the aplomb of his board of directors persona and thrown himself into an invective that spared nobody: the inept managers, the coach, dominated by the factions that had arisen in the dressing room, the mercenary players with no respect for the club or the fans, the journalists, so eager to dig up the foulest stories they could find. In between sips of orange juice, as he stoked the fire by reminding Dubois of the apocalyptic seven-nil confrontation with Real Madrid, Cédric had kept an eye on the author, engaged in an animated conversation with an old man. The exchange had shown no signs of letting up, despite the small queue of buyers that formed beside them, waiting to shake the evening's protagonist by the hand and have their copies signed by him. The historian's apparent warmth in dealing with his interlocutor had caught his attention and the dog's head atop the cane, easily visible because its owner was resting his palm on it rather than holding it in his hand, was unusual enough to be memorable. After ten minutes or so the old man had moved towards the exit with the same middle-aged man who was now sitting next to him, as Cédric threw himself heart and soul back into the agony of Lyon and the club's number one fan, too demanding a subject to allow for distractions.

But now here he was again, the old man with his walking stick, his back to Cédric as he examined the watch. He was standing so close that the younger man turned round and shot him a questioning look. 'Sorry,' Cédric excused himself in English, 'I would like to have a look too, but I can wait.' With that he backed off, but only a short distance.

The middle-aged Englishman must have been a relative of his companion, with his reddish hair, the same pale skin and average height, albeit about forty kilograms heavier; his idea of exercise was probably confined to the gesture by which he raised his finger to his nose every five seconds to push his glasses, having slipped a millimetre out of place, back where they should be. The old man was slim and, were it not for his face, covered in wrinkles and spots of dark skin, a stranger would not have guessed his age at anything over eighty, a milestone he must in fact have passed some time back. He felt the cold a lot, judging by the unseasonal waterproof he had on. He held the watch a few centimetres from his face with his right hand, but he could not see it because he had brought his left hand to his face, as though to shield his eyes from a blinding light. He shook his head when the other whispered something to him, turning the watch over once, twice, and then staring blankly into space. The expert smiled at Cédric, as though begging his pardon for a delay that was not his fault, while Onfray displayed the impassiveness of someone who saw no reason to intervene. It was the man in his fifties who resolved the impasse with a murmured question. 'Of course I'm sure!' the other snapped back touchily, before he put the watch back on the tray, picked up his stick, rose to his feet thanking the expert and made his way to the door. The speed with which he did so surprised even his companion, who – in the rush to catch up with him – seemed to forget the limits imposed by his own bulk, banging his knee against the armchair and letting out a cry.

Cédric wondered what he was sure of as his gaze followed them out, forced to admit that he too was now certain of something: he had just come across two rivals he would have to face in a few hours' time, and he was not happy about it.

'Sir?' the expert attracted his attention.

'Yes ...?'

'Would you like to examine the piece as well?'

'Thank you,' Cédric assented, sitting down and stretching his hand out towards the tray as the room began to empty. The next group would be allowed in within a few minutes.

This time it was not a dream: Dad's watch, previously belonging to Grandad Jean-Jacques and, originally, the property of a certain Major Roach. It had borne witness to one war and three generations; if that watch could talk, Cédric would have been happy to listen. Instead, he could only imagine what might have caused the deepest notch on the metal, on the right, corresponding to the two o'clock position – a blow sustained during a confrontation between British paratroopers and German grenadiers, or damage suffered from being accidentally knocked against a car door by a French father as he loaded a pushchair belonging to a toddler named Cédric into the boot? How many lives an object could hold inside it, the first of them a mystery in spite of the engravings on the back and the signature on a type-written page, the others familiar but invisible. The laboratory from one of those TV series would come in handy, to identify them from the DNA deposited over the decades by sweaty wrists.

'You can use the loupe,' the expert said, pointing to a small metallic cylinder resting on the tray. After watching Cédric try to peer through it from a distance of about ten centimetres, he added, with all the tact of one who knew how to explain something obvious to the most clueless of buyers without humiliating them: 'You need to place your eye to the wider end. And bring the object closer, so it's almost touching.'

The details studied on the computer monitor appeared before his eye: the cracked surface of the black dial, the flecks of rust on the edges of the hands, the small cracks in their inserts. And the broad arrow, raised like the numbers on the watch face and the tiny bars and points on the external ring, all of them coloured with a yellow bordering on orange, shades – as he had learnt from one of the many websites – resulting from the ageing process of the luminous paint.

'Would you like me to open it?'

'Is that okay?'

'Of course. To see the movement. It's a common request.'

Movement? Oh right, the mechanism. 'Yes, thank you.'

Watching the man use a small, rectangular instrument, inserting the hooks into two of the notches fanned out along the outer edge of the back and then cautiously rotating it anti-clockwise, Cédric could not help but shrink backwards a little. But there was no blood dripping from the fingers as they placed the steel disc and the watch face down, on the tray.

'Look at it obliquely, it's easier to see that way,' the man advised him, as Cédric tried to find the right distance between the lens and the three-dimensional X-ray he held between his left thumb and index finger. Overlapping golden wheels. Narrow silver cylinders with edges rendered jagged by dozens of minuscule teeth. Screws of three different sizes, some light-coloured and others darkened by rust. Smoothly curved plates echoing off one another, embedded with translucent, red jewels: in actual fact they were not real jewels but synthetic rubies, inserted into the metal to les-

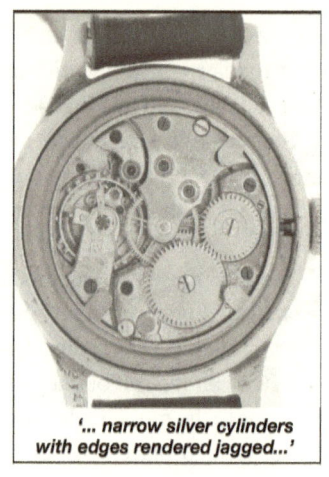

'... narrow silver cylinders with edges rendered jagged...'

sen the wear produced by the friction of the moving parts. Not bad, he congratulated himself upon realizing he had remembered that specific detail – perhaps he would be in with a chance if he were to sit a theory exam. But putting that knowledge into practice was a different story. How could he judge the condition of the mechanism, or rather, movement? To his eyes, it certainly looked its age: scratches and stains, the patina of the metal peeling away here and there, the figures on the largest plate almost illegible.

'The serial numbers should be underneath the abbreviation WWW,' said the expert, pointing at the caseback interior, which Cédric instantly associated with the photos in the pdf he had discovered on the

"... the serial numbers should be underneath the abbreviation..."

internet. 'We undertook some research, but we didn't manage to find out why they are missing, both here and on the outside, where the emblem and name appear. But the piece is authentic. We have a document proving the watch was donated during the war. If you like, I can show it to you.'

No need, thought Cédric: 'And what do you think?'

'About what?' the other man seemed surprised.

'About the condition ...' It was a naive question, but Cédric had given up pretending to be something he was not – the word 'novice' was written all over him and he needed all the information he could lay his hands on.

'Fair, considering it is a military watch. It's seen some rough use, taken a few bumps. But that lived-in look is one of the things collectors appreciate in pieces such as this. And they have certain advantages when compared to other objects from the same period. They were designed to work in difficult conditions, so they are robust, reliable and precise. Allow me to show you something.'

The latest batch of visitors was all clustered around the display cabinets and the expert made the most of it, talking at length, pleased at the opportunity to put on show not only his competence but also a genuine passion which, in a profession such as his, must have been every bit as necessary as a screwdriver. 'No one has done anything to the watch since the owner entrusted it to us. No repairs, no lubrication. It was shut away in a safety deposit box for decades. At the moment it's stopped, as you can see from the second hand – the small one, at the bottom. But look what happens if I wind the crown, just once. It starts up immediately. That tells you the workmanship is of a very high quality. The metal parts were smoothed to stop debris from building up over time and getting stuck in between the teeth of the wheels, which would obstruct them. And the case is actually waterproof, otherwise the rust stains would be much more visible. The specifications the army imposed left manufacturers with no margin for error: either they respected them or their products were rejected ... Do excuse me, but I think someone else is waiting to talk to me.'

Onfray was approaching, followed by an elegant, slender woman of around fifty, fuchsia blouse and pearls beneath features pumped so full of Botox they had been frozen into a lifeless mask, mummified caricature of a face that must have possessed a mature and aristocratic charm before its first run-in with the plastic surgeon. He placed a bracelet loaded with precious stones on the expert's tray, a tiny, rectangular timepiece at its centre.

Cédric gave up his seat, the woman attempting to shift her facial muscles into an expression vaguely resembling a smile by way of thanks, and headed for the door. Then he changed his mind and went back, waiting for Onfray to put the watch back inside its cabinet. He leaned in close, partly for one last look and partly to study the other objects surrounding it. Many were awe-inspiring: gold cases as thick as blocks of bullion, push-pieces everywhere, dials crowded with counters and hands like a dashboard, expensive-sounding brand names that even a novice like him had heard of. Next to these, the old 'broad arrow' looked like a poor relation in a threadbare suit, or at best an aristocrat fallen on hard times, a dog-eared emblem all he had left to recall his former glory. But that carried on regardless. The slightest of encouragement had been enough to get it going again, while the rest, in spite of their seductive gleam from inside the cabinet, were all stopped. Payback? The desire to be noticed? Attributing hopes, regrets and vanities to bits of old metal was childish, Cédric reflected. But it helped.

The only thing left to do was put his name down. Too early, they informed him, suggesting he wait in the adjoining room where the auction was to be held. Cédric took a seat in the front row, flicking through the catalogue they had lent him, while around him a number of workers were busy putting the finishing touches in place. The rectangular room was about thirty metres long by fifteen wide. Here too, one wall was completely covered by drapes – dark blue instead of purple, presumably even more effective at blocking the light from outside. Running alongside the curtains was a narrow table with four telephones on top, for taking offers from bidders who were participating without being physically present. The auctioneer's podium was in front of Cédric, over to the right and equipped with a side table with two computers. In the opposite corner, positioned in such a way as to be visible both from the podium and the seats, was a screen where the images of the lots would appear, accompanied by a sequence of bids in euros, pounds and dollars up to the hammer price. A quick count of the small armchairs, two blocks of twelve rows separated by the central aisle, revealed something in the region of two hundred seats.

'You may sign up now, if you wish to.' Onfray accompanied him back to the watchmaker's table, where the performers had swapped places: the expert in white overalls and his various tools had been replaced by the young man in jacket and tie who had been directing the flow of traffic at the entrance to the room, and another colleague dressed in the same way. Both had open laptops in front of them.

The interrogation went by without a hitch – Cédric had prepared himself on the internet. Name, surname, address, proof of identity, phone number, email. Payment method, if he should win? Cash, he answered unhesitatingly. He gave no credit card number – that way he would not be able to use it, a measure to prevent himself from doing anything reckless. At the end, he too had a question: 'Can I choose the number on the paddle?'

The inquisitor consulted with his neighbour, who gave a nod without interrupting his typing. 'If you like ... which number?'

'Sixty-six, if that's possible. It's my birthday, 6 June ...'

When they placed the paddle with its metal handle on the table, Cédric was not thinking about its purpose, nor about standard auction practice – holding it up meant raising the last bid by ten percent, unless the bidder shouted out a different offer – but of the number printed on the plastic and the black USB key peeping out from beneath a pile of papers between the two laptops. Cédric picked it up and held it lengthways between the two numbers: 6-6, like the score at the mysterious match. A match that had never been played, in fact.

'That's where it was!' The exclamation reminded him he had

195

the carpet of a five-star hotel beneath his feet, and not a rectangular pitch marked out by white lines.

'Sorry ... I imagine this is yours.'

'Thank you sir. And good luck for this afternoon.'

22. 6 JUNE 1944, 14:37

… So I let my mind wander elsewhere as I sank my neck into the armchair's headrest.

Why was I so exhausted? At the camp I had never been tired; Folgate had once thrown a boot at me for trying to convince him to go out for a kick around after a route march, and had not missed me by much. What was happening to me? Would I manage to get back up again? Yes, if I could just close my eyes for a minute, no more than that. Without falling asleep – just shutting them for a few seconds, then I would ready to go again. It would be for the others' benefit, not my own. One minute – my head would feel lighter and I would cut the risk of making stupid mistakes. But I had to stay awake. 'The lad', Beltman had called me. He still did not trust me, fearing I would be among the first to crack. But they were both wrong, he and the CO. School outing? Bollocks. I had warned them about the Krauts and the commandos back in the park. And I would ask again if I could go back to the village.

But I was forgetting: we would be heading back there soon, which meant no one would be able to stop me looking for the watch. Why had he given it to me? They would have sent it back home with his personal effects and it would have reached Jane, like he wanted. Why me? Maybe he trusted me, even if he had never missed an opportunity to give me a hard time back at the base. But no sooner had he given it to me than I had lost it. My haversack, not my pouch: that was where I should have put it, wrapped up safe in the cloth cape. Idiot.

What would I do if I could not find it? Pretend nothing had happened? No way: I would go all the same, to apologise to her if nothing else. If I managed to make it through alive, that was ... A note: I would write a couple of lines and keep the paper in my pocket, that way if they killed me they would send the note to Jane and she would know it had been my fault. I would do it the next day, as long as they did not shoot me in the meantime. No, better do it right away. I really should have written more notes. To my parents, to Betty ...

***

Betty! It was the first time I had thought of her in ... how long? Two days, or rather three. An eternity – certainly longer than at any other time in the previous year. Since I had gone to Mr Worthington's house to tell him I had been called up. It had been my mother who had insisted, telling me I could not keep news like that to myself. I had answered that I had never been to his house, that I would need to arrange the visit beforehand and that I would see him the following evening in any case. But she had told me to cut it out: I knew where he lived so there was no excuse, and I had to tell him because in three days' time I would be leaving. So I got on my bike. It was two o'clock in the afternoon, a beautiful Sunday in August. It was only a couple of miles away, but I had made a detour via White Hart Lane. Who could say when I would see those grounds again, my second home, place of work and stadium all in one building. And who could say when Arsenal would sling their hook. They had been playing at our home ground for four years because their own pitch had been requisitioned to set up an aid station and an anti-aircraft emplacement, and had then been bombed twice. Wartime solidarity and all that, but there could hardly have been more unwelcome guests. As I leant my bike up against the garden fence, my thoughts returned to that desecration. I tried to console myself: they were not happy either, in fact they must have been convinced the grounds brought bad luck because they had won practically nothing in years, the team who considered themselves the best.

I rang the doorbell and an angel appeared before me. Dark hair and blue eyes, lips so perfect I felt the urge to reach out and touch them to check they were real. At first glance she seemed tall as well, but that was only because she was standing two steps above me, in the doorway. I stammered that I must have got the wrong house, that I was looking for a Mr Worthington. She answered that he was her father, and asked who she should say was calling. 'Roger Englin, I play for Tottenham.' In actual fact I was still in the youth team and he was my coach. Every now and then they called me up to the first team to make up the numbers, only to send me home again when a guest turned up – that was the term they used in those days for the professionals who made ends meet by playing for whichever team happened to need them, after asking their own clubs' permission. I had gone to the grounds to play a dozen times, but had only actually made it onto the pitch on four occasions, watching the other matches from the terraces. Steering clear of the East Stand, mind – they had set up a mortuary at the top for the victims killed in air raids and I preferred to avoid even the terraces nearest the pitch.

When he appeared at the door, Mr Worthington looked me up and down as he did before matches to check everything was ship shape: hair combed, kit ironed, boots shined, not so much as a spot of dried mud on the studs. 'Remember you're wearing the Spurs kit,' he used to repeat, while pulling a face that said something like: 'Just look at what I've got to send out onto the pitch.' He asked me what I was doing there on my day off.

It was the most embarrassing moment of my life. I could not remember. It was the angel's fault – she was still there, next to her father. I stared down at the toes of my shoes, racking my brains at the same time as I tried to capture an image of her with the corner of my eye, to remember her by when she disappeared.

'I have to tell you something, sir ...' I blurted out.

'Out with it then,' he prompted, before going on, 'I'd stick with the football if I were you, doesn't look like you were cut out to be a lawyer.' I heard the sound of a giggle being smothered. It was the angel, but she seemed to be worried I would be offended and stopped immediately. Her father introduced us – she was Betty and I was Roger – and invited me in because, in his words, 'if we have to wait any longer we might as well head over to the pitch for tomorrow night's training.'

His wife was kind: she offered me a seat in a living room that marked the family as neither rich nor poor, with a large wooden radio in one corner enthroned atop a shelf that was too narrow for it, looking as though it would topple over from one moment to the next, and a black, upright piano next to the window. It was the angel, Betty, who placed a cup of tea in front of me. 'Milk, please,' I answered. That lively giggle again: no, she had asked me how many sugars I wanted. 'Poor Roger,' Mr Worthington cut in, 'today just isn't his day.' So, what did I want to tell him?

I finally remembered and launched into a monologue without stopping to draw breath, cup in hand. Army? – he jumped up – I had not even told him I was signing up. I was afraid they would not accept me, I justified myself: if my team mates had found out they would have laughed about it for weeks. I tried to soften the blow a little by saying I was sure I would make it through because, thanks to him, I was in tip-top shape and would make it through the selection process without any problems. As I spoke I stared at his right arm, like when he called us to huddle around him during training. He barely ever moved it, doing everything with his left hand; when he picked up the balls and put them away in the sack it always took him a while, but he never wanted any help. I had once asked Ritchie the caretaker about it, and he had replied, 'Dunkirk.' He had been wounded during the retreat from France and they had declared him unfit for service. Perhaps he was thinking about that, envious of the fact that I would be doing my bit for war effort. Perhaps he was afraid of what might happen to me. Or perhaps, more simply, he was wondering who he could bring in to substitute me for the next match. Walt? Possible. But I was better, he knew that as well as I did. Betty asked when I would be leaving. That pleased me. I looked her in the eye, hoping I looked a little less foolish than before: 'I start basic training next Thursday, Miss.'

No one else spoke. Betty's mother excused herself, got up and ran to the kitchen. Mr Worthington explained that she was thinking of Francis, their son, who was fighting in North Africa. Then he made a joke, telling me to try and get the war won as quick as I could so that Arsenal could put that ugly stadium of theirs back together and we could get rid us of their fans – he was sick of seeing them hanging around, he said. The quip put me in a good mood: 'Sick of them, sir? I can't stand them.'

'Well,' he agreed, 'let's say if they pass round the collection tin to get their place fixed up I'll chip in a pound, anything to get shot of them.' I burst out laughing but I noticed Betty did not seem amused. The atmosphere was strange, a little tense, so I said that I had better be getting home.

'I'll see you out, Englin,' he nodded. Englin? He had never called me that, always using my Christian name, or else simply 'boy'. He only used first names with squad members. Maybe he wanted to show me that I was a man now, at least in his eyes.

When we reached the door and he was certain nobody could hear us, he threw me a penetrating stare: 'I never expected this. Mister Fair Play turning into a cheat.'

I flushed red, uncomprehending: 'Cheat ...?'

'Remember the match last year with the Crossbrook lads?' I could – I remembered that Mr Worthington had not known whether to give me a thrashing or sing my praises. Could I remember why? Of course, how could I forget?

'I can still see that referee giving us a penalty at 1-1, five minutes from time. And you, running up to say you tripped over by yourself. No penalty, and three minutes later they scored. I felt like strangling you Roger, never mind a thrashing.'

'In the dressing room you said I'd done the right thing ...'

'After a brisk walk and a fag, though. You on the other hand, you made the right decision right away. That's why I'm so surprised to find you telling porkies now.'

I did not reply.

'What did you tell the recruiting officer?'

'That I wanted to sign up ...'

'Don't play dumb with me. I mean your age. They don't take sixteen-year-old boys.'

'I'm sixteen and a half,' I protested.

'That still isn't much. What did you tell him?'

'Eighteen ... It's not really a lie. I'm strong for my age. And by the time my turn comes I might be eighteen ...'

'Might ... Didn't you stop to think that you're too young for what they'll tell you to do? That if you balls things up it'll be your mates who pay for it?' No, I had not thought of that, but I did not want to admit it. So I stayed silent, hoping he calmed down by himself. 'What does your mother say? You've spoken to her about it, I imagine.'

'This morning, when the telegram arrived ...'

'This morning? You mean to say no one knew about any of this until today?'

'Except for Mr Davies ...' He was my other boss at White Hart Lane, in the offices that had been turned into a gasmask factory. I had been working there ever since my father had left his job there to go to sea – he was on a frigate somewhere in the Atlantic, hunting U-boats.

'What's Davies got to do with it?'

'He's the department head, I need his authorisation. I asked him not to tell anyone. It's no one's fault but mine.'

He shook his head: 'One of these days I'll have to have a little chat with Davies. And to think that in a few months' time they might have taken you on as a pro ...'

'Dodge the draft, more like.'

'You know it's not like that. A lot of them joined up in '39, before they were called up.'

'... and the rest did whatever they could to avoid going to the front.'

'If you've only joined up because they nicked your place a couple of times ...'

'No! I want to make myself useful, do my bit. Like you, sir.' I wanted nothing more than to go but I was too used to the rules of the pitch, where it was up to him to decide when I could leave.

'I hope the instructors teach you to run, at least. I've never been able to. You're fast but you waste a lot of energy because you just go hell for leather, no technique. And sometimes you trip over, like at the Crossbrook match. The referee only gave you that penalty because he didn't know you: I never would have.' He was teasing me like he did during training – perhaps the worst was over. 'Try and get back as quick as you can, got it? I need my defensive midfielder, at least until I can find one who knows how to play football.'

I thought I could make out the hint of a smile, and seized the opportunity to ask him how old Betty was. 'Sixteen, like you,' he answered. 'Sorry, I forgot, you're sixteen and a half ...'

'I bet she's got loads of boys after her, being so pretty and all.'

He had not been expecting that. His expression changed, but he looked more surprised than annoyed. Englin, daring to ask him a question like that? I was ready for a brisk 'none of your business', but instead ... 'Why don't you ask her yourself? Betty, come here.'

I gave a start and blurted out: 'It's getting on ... I'd better ...'

'If you're afraid of her, how are you going to fight the Krauts?' There she was again, the angel, with an inquisitive air. 'I'm worried about my player. Next week they'll be showing him how to use a rifle, but today I doubt whether he's up to finding his way back home. Do me a favour, will you – walk him back.'

'Me? I can go out by myself?'

'You're not by yourself – Roger's there, at least for the first bit. Don't worry, he's a good boy. Come home quick, mind.'

I was so bewildered that I asked her if she had a bike as well,

203

so we could get home faster. But Mr Worthington shot me a disapproving look, explaining that the tyres were as flat as a pancake and he did not feel like pumping them up, so we would have to go by foot. Unless, he added, I wanted to inflate them myself. I grasped that if I had volunteered to do the job he would have thrown me off the team for good, so I bid him farewell. It was the most wonderful walk of my life. And the shortest, even though I insisted we took it slowly, using the excuse that I was not used to walking with the bike. I chatted away, starting with school. I had never liked it, so much so that I was happy to find it shut when I came back to London at the end of '39, after three months on a farm where Mum and Dad had sent me to escape the bombs that would only arrive much later. The war had felt like nothing more than a long holiday, to be spent playing football and looking through the sheet-glass windows of Hamleys on Regent Street. Then my father had decided to sign up – he did not have to, I pointed out to Betty, because the factory where he worked produced war material – and I had taken his place. Ten hours a day and, every once in a while, twenty hours straight. Not much

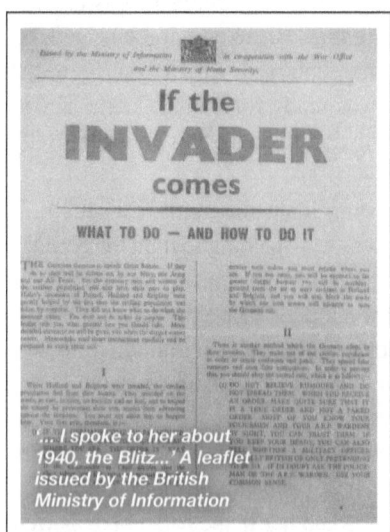

'... I spoke to her about 1940, the Blitz...' A leaflet issued by the British Ministry of Information

time left for sport, but the pay was good. We needed the money and I was the only one in the family that could work because Mum had to take care of my little sisters.

I spoke to her about 1940, the Blitz, forgetting that Betty had lived through the same experience. Nights spent down in the Anderson shelter, half-buried in the garden, trying to ignore the drone of aircraft engines, the thunder of the anti-aircraft batteries, the nearby explosions. The bomb that hit Downhills Park air raid shelter, killing hundreds of people, many of whom we both knew. Craters gaping like chasms, doors and walls riddled with splinters of shrapnel. But I made her laugh when I told her about the morning Kate, my youngest sister, had noticed our neighbours looking each other over in the garden, lost expressions on their faces: 'Look! The Black and White Family!' Mr Parks had been covered in flour from head to foot: the milling factory where he worked had been hit during his shift, the previous night. In the meantime his wife and son had taken shelter in the basement, next to the coal store, and had come out looking like a couple of chimneysweeps. When she had heard Kate shouting, my mother had given her a pinch to shut her up, but the neighbours started laughing as well. Peace was made, thanks to the war – Mrs Parks had had it in for me ever since I had hit her cat with the football, after which, she swore, Kitty had never been quite the same.

Another story Betty liked was the one about the curtain. My father had come home on leave and we wanted to celebrate, ready to tighten our belts for a week if it meant we could spend the evening up town together. Dinner for three, my little sisters at home with Nan, then the cinema – there was no danger because it was '42 and the raids had ended. For good, we deluded ourselves. They had been talking for months about the American film they were showing at the Leicester Square Empire, four hours of adventure and romance, set in the USA during eighteen hundreds. On top of that it was in colour – a real novelty, 'Technicolor' they called it. Mum was beside herself with excitement: we too were about to see *Gone with the Wind*. Like almost every woman in the cinema audience she shed a few tears, but as we were leaving she had pushed Clark Gable and Vivien Leigh out of her mind, or at least tried to, re-entering the role of housewife faced with rationing, attentive reader of government pamphlets and their tips on wartime diet and fashion. 'I could do the same thing as Scarlett,' she had thought aloud.

'What do you mean?' Dad had asked.

'Turn a curtain into a dress.'

My father and I had looked at one another: which of us was going to remind her that the only curtain left in the house was fit, at most, to be torn up into rags? My mother was still hypnotized by the magic of the cinema, I thought, but had rapidly returned to her senses and changed the subject, drawing inspiration from the documentary they had shown before the film: an ode to the nutritious virtues of the potato, omnipresent wartime foodstuff, courtesy of the Ministry of Agriculture.

When Betty managed to get a word in edgeways, she told me she missed her school, unlike me. That was part of the reason why she had tormented her parents with pleas to return home from the house they had sent her to, in order to keep her safe from the air raids. She had left shortly after me and had not been very lucky. The lady of the house had not been satisfied with pocketing the weekly billeting allowance handed out to host families, forcing Betty to miss entire days of lessons by putting her to work like a slave: washing, cooking and looking after the children. After two months of desperate letters her father had gone to collect her and bring her back to London, where he had put her name down for the Home Tuition Scheme, a school surrogate entrusted to teachers who had either retired or who had stayed in the city when their colleagues had followed the exodus of children into the countryside. The course was held when circumstances allowed for it, in private homes or in whichever space happened to be available.

It was thanks to the Home Tuition Scheme that Betty had learnt to play the piano. Mrs Walters had lost hers in the Blitz, destroyed along with everything else. Now she worked in a uniform factory and taught French in her free time, her main occupation before the war. One evening, having walked Betty home after two hours of school in a warehouse furnished with no more than a few tables and a dozen or so rickety chairs, she had seen the piano in the living room. Since then she had returned every week, partly to keep her hand in and partly to teach. On Saturdays – that was why, Betty added, I had never seen her at any of our matches. I thought the real reason was that she did not like football but did not want to admit it to me. And I was shocked that she disobeyed her father, something I had never dared to do in two years. Instead of going straight back, she stayed standing on the pavement outside my house for a good half hour. Perhaps I should have invited her in to introduce her to Mum, but then she would not have been all for me. I was about to leave and wanted to enjoy those few moments in peace. Whenever I remembered to let her say something as well, I looked at her thinking: he has never given me anything, Mr Worthington. After the best match I ever played he did no more than growl: 'See? When you train like you ought to, even you can make a go of it.' But now ... this was better than a West Stand season ticket. When I returned I would have to thank him and hope he would let her go out with me under normal circumstances, too.

When she said she really had to go, I lent her my bike. I would not be needing it for a while, and Mum could drop by to pick it up. I pretended to forget the Spurs shirt I had indoors, already washed and ironed. I should have given it to her to pass on to her father, but I did not feel like it. I would take it with me, I decided. 'Can I write to you?' I asked, to which she answered, unhesitatingly, 'Of course'. I stayed standing in the middle of the street to watch her as she rode away, until she reached the crossroads and disappeared behind the Parks' house. I did not move, hoping she had forgotten to tell me something and would come pedaling back again. Five minutes, maybe ten. Then I walked the few yards back to my house, mulling over how my life had changed in just three short hours: first the army and then Betty. And since I had only found her thanks to the telegram, I could hardly complain if I did not see her again before I left.

I wrote to her three weeks later to tell her about my new life at Fulford, where they had sent me for basic training. The vaccinations, the runs, the marches, the training on how to use the Lee-Enfield rifle and the Bren gun. My first punishment, dished out by a sergeant who must have heard my comment on his belly and who, after a ten-mile march, ordered me to run round the football pitch twice with a full haversack on my back. 'I said two!' he had shouted, after I had finished my third lap. I stood to attention a couple of steps away from him, just to show that I was not even out of breath: 'Sorry sir, I didn't hear you properly.' After that he left me alone, in fact he never spoke to me again. A few days later I was called to the CO's office. I thought another punishment was on its way – a serious one, this time. But he was cordial, asking me what I thought of the army and how I saw my future. 'I get a bit bored sir,' I answered without thinking, something I did often.

'And what can we do to liven up your time here?'

'Transfer me to the Parachute Regiment, sir.' I had done my research: the training was tough, but I was sure I would be up to it and I knew paratroopers earned one pound, one shilling and sixpence a week, three times what I was making in the King's Rifle Corps. 'One ought to be ambitious in this life,' pronounced the CO before he dismissed me. I took his smile as a promise and wrote about it to Betty, hoping to impress her: her friend Roger was about to enter into the army's elite.

She wrote back almost right away, but did not mention the Paras. Was she worried about me? She spent a long time talking about a meeting between our mothers, however. They barely knew each other, but when Mum dropped by their house to pick up the bike it was like they were old friends. They had a long chat and, to celebrate the visit, swapped recipes they had either copied down or simply conjured out of thin air, all aimed at fooling their families into thinking they were not just having the same old potatoes as always.

When I wrote to her again, I could not hide my disappointment. My month and a half of training was over, but rather than the Paras I had to put up with being transferred to the East Surrey Regiment, first at Malton and then at Uckfield. Depressing days spent in barracks with abominable latrines, where nearly everyone was either too skinny or too fat. Marches that felt like strolls, maybe because only about one in ten of them was in as good shape as me. When would the nightmare end?

Betty, on the other hand, was pleased. They had accepted her into the Women's Auxiliary Air Force and she thanked me because if it had not been for me it would have been impossible to convince her father: 'If Roger's in the infantry, why can't I do a much less dangerous job?' I was happy for her and told her so in a letter, although the fact she might not be there when I got back played on my mind. At the camp there was talk of leave and I could already see myself in uniform, ringing the Worthingtons' front door bell; impossible, I thought, that her father would deny me an hour or two with her. When I arrived in London though, my fears were confirmed: she had already left and I had to make do with chatting to her parents. Three of my former team-mates had joined up and Mr Worthington could no longer put a full squad together. His wife seemed calmer than when I had first met her a few months earlier: Francis had been hit by shrapnel and had lost three toes in the process, but they had now moved him to somewhere far behind the front lines and he was, at least, alive.

Ten days later, when I left the major's office, instead of going to pack my bags I sat down and wrote to Betty. Transfer approved! I needed to share my jubilation with someone right away, and she was the only possible candidate. My mother did not even know I had asked to become a paratrooper. I would tell her face to face, during my next leave.

Betty liked the role she had been assigned; they had picked her to work as a radar station operator, explaining that the timbre of her voice was just right for transmissions. I was not in a good position to judge: the only time I had heard it, her voice had seemed like a sound from heaven itself. She promised she would come to see my first match after the war finished because, as a way of killing time between one shift and another, she had taken up watching the boys playing in the small field next to the base, and was beginning to get into the sport.

I told her about the training, but without naming anywhere specific. Restricted information, they had warned us. The first stop was Harwick Hall for preliminary selection: marches and runs with a fully laden pack, assault courses with climbs and obstacles to get past, including rivers, trenches and barbed wire, jumping out the back of a moving truck, target practice and hand-to-hand fighting, sit-ups and weights, cross-country and boxing. Those who failed to make the grade were given an order with RTU written on it, standing for 'Return to Unit'. Back to their old units; unsuited to the Paras. I saw a dozen or so leave.

Then we moved to Ringway for simulations. A week of jumping off the beams of a wooden walkway, somersaulting off a slide to learn how to soften the impact of landing, exercises while suspended from the ceiling of a hangar by lift webs like those on the parachutes. The second week things got serious, beginning with the most hated test of all: jumping out of a cage tethered beneath a barrage balloon, seven hundred feet off the ground. We sat on the edge of the hatch and let ourselves fall the first hundred and twenty feet before the parachute opened, while the instructor, standing down below, shouted up orders to us through a megaphone. After two such jumps, the aeroplane was almost a relief: the slipstream sucking us backwards was preferable to the sensation of dropping like a stone, despite the impact and bruises of the first landing. Six jumps, after which they awarded us with the cloth emblem with the winged parachute, to be sewn onto the right sleeve of our uniform. We were real paratroopers now, and there was no turning back: from then on, anyone who refused to jump would be sentenced to eighty-four days of detention.

Before deciding on where to send me they asked whether I had any preferences. I answered that I would like to stick with Ted Withe because we had been together since the start of training and we were both assigned to the Ninth Battalion. The Bulford barracks was the best I had ever lived in, with real bathrooms and plenty of food. But the training was even tougher, including fifty-mile marches two or three times a week, often in the rain. One day they moved us to West Woodhay, where the mock-up battery had been built. It was clear that the moment of truth was drawing near. I could not write about it to Betty but her last letter, two weeks before the mission, confirmed it. She wanted to let me know we would be heading into action soon, I thought. Perhaps she had heard something, like an exchange of radio messages, or perhaps air traffic was more intense than usual.

***

As I sat on that armchair waiting for orders, I wondered where she was in that moment. She was what I had to concentrate on, that way I would have a reference point, a goal. I had no doubts as to what I would do when I got back. A quick visit to my parents, then straight to the Worthingtons. Where her father might well make me do my first training session right there and then, in the garden.

But it was best not to lay too many plans – to think about *if* I made it home. I was still in one piece then, but in a few hours' time ... We had to take the village and hold our position, and after that no one knew what would happen. She was far away, Betty – in space and above all in time. Each day was a brick, like building a house. But builders get a break every now and then. I, on the other hand, could not afford one. A minute would be enough, just one. Eyes shut without drifting off, only to enjoy the darkness for a moment. Where was the harm in it? If the CO spotted me ... but he was talking with the Commando officer and I was hidden behind the backrest of the armchair; I could simply tell him my eyes were burning and jump to attention. And then, why should I feel ashamed? I had done alright, hadn't I? At the battery, in the village, in the park. They had all seen they could trust me. What was the worst that could happen if I closed my eyes for a minute?

Unfortunately I did so, and when I opened them again the CO was standing in front of me. He was furious, telling me I was irresponsible and that had he not needed every available man he would have sent me before a court martial. Later on Beltman explained to me that he had not really meant it, and had only wanted to teach me a lesson.

They were the last twenty minutes of sleep I got for two days. A few weeks later I was promoted to sergeant in the field: I had been forgiven.

23. 4 JUNE 2014, 13:50

The mussels in themselves left nothing to be desired, but half an hour waiting for service and another ten minutes to pay was too long. By the time Cédric got back to the hotel, the room was almost full. The general hubbub of acquaintances greeting one another: auction veterans, collectors and dealers exchanged comments, pointing to pictures in the catalogue. The auctioneer was in position behind the microphone, yet to be turned on, while one of the people manning the telephones stood up and went over to the podium to hand him a slip of paper – a last minute proxy buyer?

Cédric walked slowly down the central aisle, looking for an empty seat. There they were. Not that he had got his hopes up, but seeing them there put him on edge. Halfway along the room, the section on the right. The paddle lay on the middle-aged man's knees, while the other kept his left hand on the cane, gazing straight ahead, apparently oblivious to what was going on around him. He turned round just as Cédric, still watching him, passed alongside, flashing a smile. The old man gave a nod of the head and got his companion's attention. They seemed as annoyed by his presence as he was by theirs. Cédric retraced his steps and sat down on a chair two rows behind the pair, in the section on the left next to the central aisle, where he could keep any eye on them.

Although he had been warned by his internet research, the speed of the auction still took him by surprise. A question of reflexes, not just money. The lots followed one another at breakneck speed, a process directed by the auctioneer's gestures and announcements, giving him the appearance of a traffic policeman at rush hour: paddles shooting up over people's heads as if they were on springs, excited whispers from the operators manning the phones with clients at the other end, ushers moving back and forth through the room, handing out proofs of purchase to buyers, or their representatives seated behind the table. Cédric timed a few of the contests in his head: some lasted no longer than twenty seconds and, where there were no offers, ten sufficed before moving on to the next lot. The battle for lot 111 was the longest, two minutes of offers raising the price to 120,000 euros and producing a visible reaction in the audience. Many left after the hammer had fallen; apparently this was the most anticipated lot of the day. Lots 112 and 113 remained unsold, and three offers were enough to end the bids for 114. Cédric's heart began to race as the auctioneer read out a terse description of lot 115 and named the starting price at 1,700 euros, explaining that this was a written offer received before the start of the auction.

The first offer of 1,800 euros came through the speakers, relaying a bid from one of the phone operators.

The English pair reacted: '1,900!' called the auctioneer, pointing at the middle-aged man.

Cédric raised his paddle: '2,000' came the confirmation, accompanied by a warning that from that point on each bid would signal an increase of 200 euros.

Them again: '2,200' A few seconds of silence followed. 'Any raise on 2,200?' The operator shook her head in the direction of the podium and closed the mobile phone.

Cédric returned to the fray: '2,400!'

By now it was down to him and the English pair, who conferred among themselves before making another bid: '2,600!'

This was not going well. Continuing meant breaking his own

spending limit, but letting it go for the sake of a hundred euros … One last attempt; if it failed, Cédric would go and look for the local branch of his bank to put the money back in his account. '2,800!' He was tempted to look away as he did in front of the television just before the final penalty of Liverpool-AC Milan, Champions League Final 2005, but the suspense was too great. So he turned his gaze on his rivals, trying to anticipate their reaction, split seconds that felt like hours, until the old man lowered his head.

'All closed at 2,800? No more bids? The gentlemen in the middle? Going once … going twice … sold!'

Cédric slumped against the backrest – success. He had won. If one could call it a victory. Three thousand eight hundred euros. He had an agreement with Sylvie, or at least he used to: household finances were a joint affair, and they always consulted with one another before making big purchases. A pact that had never been broken, until today.

A puffing usher appeared before him to hand over the receipt. As he slipped it into his jacket pocket, Cédric spotted the two English bidders leaving their places and moving towards the exit. The old man wore a grim expression, refusing his companion's arm and paying no attention to whatever the younger man was saying to him. Cédric got up to follow them, catching up with them in the corridor just after an usher had closed the heavy, padded door behind him: 'Good afternoon. I could see you really wanted that watch. I'm sorry, it was important to me, too.'

The middle-aged man acted as spokesperson: 'Don't worry about it. We had set ourselves a limit and we couldn't go over.'

No, they had made him go over instead: 'Collectors?'

'No … we were only interested in that watch. Or rather, my uncle was interested.' The old man gave a silent nod.

Cédric tried to involve him in the conversation: 'I saw you yesterday, as well. In Caen, the presentation of the Wilkins book. I was interpreting for him. And I translated the French edition.'

'I'm afraid I can't read it,' the voice was hoarse, that of a chain smoker or someone who had been once. 'I only speak English ...'

'I noticed you knew each other, yourself and Wilkins.'

'Actually, no,' the nephew cut in, 'We came from London for the auction, but when my uncle found out about the presentation he wanted to go. At the end he introduced himself and Wilkins was quite moved. He said he might not have been born if it hadn't been for him.'

'How so?'

'His grandfather was part of the force that went ashore at Sword Beach ...'

'I know, I translated the book. But ... your uncle?'

'He was with the paratroopers who attacked the battery near here, the night before.'

'Merville?'

'That's it. If those guns had been able to open fire, Wilkins' grandfather might not have made it through alive.'

'We did our duty,' the old man cut him short, 'And so did he.'

'I dare say, Uncle. But I reckon he would have liked to give you a hug – the only reason he didn't was that he was afraid you might not appreciate it, or else give him a thwack of your cane ...' The joke broke against the other's apparent indifference.

'Why don't we sit down for a few minutes?' Cédric insisted. 'I'd like to buy you both a drink. To make amends for the watch business ... and to explain why I wanted it so much. If you have time, of course.'

'Well ... What do you say, Uncle?'

'Alright, thank you.' The old man's eyes were bright blue; it was only now, seeing them open and attentive, that Cédric noticed them, a couple of azure spots staring out from the two dark wells beneath his brow. Eye contact, finally; for a smile he would have to wait and see.

The saloon, signalled by a glass door at the end of the mammoth entrance hall, was practically empty. Two customers stood at the bar sipping cups of coffee and chatting with the barman, perhaps buyers waiting for the auction to finish so they could retrieve their purchases. Cédric led his guests to the back of the room, next to one of the windows with a view of the internal garden. The old man leant his stick against the arm of his chair while his nephew sat down next to him and smiled at Cédric: 'We haven't introduced ourselves yet. I'm Jeremy Englin and my uncle's name is Roger. He's Englin too.'

'Cédric Roussel. My surname might ring a bell. It's on the donation certificate for the watch. But perhaps you didn't …'

'We saw it,' Jeremy confirmed, 'but I can't remember what the name was …'

'Jean-Jacques Roussel. He was my grandfather.'

'Your grandfather?' Roger repeated, sitting up straighter and hitting the cane with his elbow, knocking it onto the carpet with a soft thud. Jeremy went to get up and retrieve it, but an abrupt gesture from his uncle kept him where he was.

'That's right … I'll go and order. What would you like?'

'A beer for me and a tea for Uncle. With milk.'

'You were talking about your grandfather,' Roger began again as Cédric returned to his place.

'That was why I wanted the watch. It's a family heirloom. From my grandfather it passed to my father, who then sold it to his boss because he was ill and needed the money. And now the people who inherited it have put it up for sale.'

'On the donation it says your grandfather helped the Allies during the Battle of Normandy.' Now Cédric could read genuine curiosity in Roger's gaze.

'Exactly right. He was with the FFI, *Forces Françaises de l'Intérieur*. The Resistance, in other words. He lived in Caen and passed on information regarding enemy positions in the surrounding area. He died before I was born.'

'A pity. You would have met a hero. You know what the Krauts did to partisans, don't you?' Jeremy gave a start and, visibly embarrassed, followed the barman with his gaze as he returned to his place, after having deposited a teapot, a cup and two glasses on the table. 'Don't look so worried,' the uncle went on, 'He

217

might not even speak English.'

'Yes, but at least try to avoid using that word ...'

'Krauts? That was what we called them. What do you think will happen if they hear? At most they'll start laughing and think I'm doolally, but I doubt they'll throw me in jail. If you don't like it, put your fingers in your ears. I'm nearly ninety, you won't have to put up with me much longer.'

Jeremy shrugged as though to apologise and Cédric tried lightening the mood: 'I won't tell anyone, I promise ...'

Roger ignored them both: 'When they got hold of them they tortured and then killed them. They shot us lot right away, on the other hand: in that sense we were privileged. I would have liked to meet your grandfather and shake his hand. It would have been an honour ... so you're taking it back where it belongs. The watch, I mean.' Curious: the same turn of phrase Levasseur had used.

'By pure chance. The seller found out who I was and assumed I was interested in the watch because I knew the story. That was why he invited me to his office. Whereas actually, I knew nothing about it.'

'Really?'

'Even I can't explain it. I lost my father when I was very young, but my mother has never spoken to me about it. I'll ask her as soon as I get back to Nice ... In the meantime, perhaps you can tell me something. That Roach must have been a paratrooper, otherwise he wouldn't have had the emblem etched onto the back. I'd like to know ...'

'So would I.'

'So you don't know who he was.'

'I only know who he *wasn't*.'

'I don't understand ...'

'Never seen him and never heard of him, but then again there was no way I could know everyone in the division. But the man the watch belonged to, I remember him clearly. When I saw the photo ...'

'I showed it to him,' Jeremy jumped in, lively and cheerful despite the reproach of a few moments earlier, 'I found it in the online auction catalogue while I was looking for something regarding paratroopers – you know, my uncle doesn't talk much, so I have to do a bit of digging myself ... I saved it because of the emblem and a few days later, when he came for dinner at our house, he recognised it immediately ...'

'It wasn't hard – there's the name, along with the emblem,' Roger pointed out curtly, his tone reminding Cédric of the snatch of conversation he had caught before the auction: 'Of course I'm sure.'

'A friend?'

'Not exactly. Pete Kadwell, captain of the Ninth Battalion. I was in his platoon and Jane was his wife.'

A girl with red hair and freckles? Cédric was tempted to ask but decided against it, held back by the suspicion that he already knew the answer: 'And this Roach ...?'

'Pardon?'

'Since he has nothing to do with it ... you think ... I don't know ... that he might have stolen it ...?'

'Stolen? A thief doesn't donate his swag, does he?'

'Right ... but then how ...?'

'I had hoped you knew, seeing as the watch ended up with your grandfather. But apparently not. It looks like I'll never know what really happened ...'

Jeremy placed a hand on his arm: 'Do you want to get going, Uncle?'

'No use going back to the hotel. If I had bought it, I would have given it to the Airborne Assault museum in Duxford, so they could put it on display with the captain's name. A tribute to his memory, given it's too late for Jane to forgive me ... But never mind. Who better than the grandson of a partisan? I reckon he would agree.'

The silence lasted long enough for Cédric to realise he was being presented with an opportunity that would not be repeated:

'The captain ... What was his name ...?'

'Kadwell.'

'Now that I've bought the watch ... I'd like to know what sort of a man he was.'

'Generous, loyal, someone you could trust with your eyes shut. And a bit of a loudmouth, a boaster. Once he told me the word in French, his mother's language. I can't remember it but I'm sure you will, being French yourself.'

"... *Gascon*?"

'That's the one. He only had to open his mouth to realize what sort of a bloke he was, in fact one look at his face was enough. I would show you a photo, but I don't have it with me.'

'I'll take care of it,' another of Jeremy's contributions. 'I'll send you a scan of it by email, if you're interested.' He seemed like a nice person; and a patient one, given his uncle's temperament.

'Definitely, I would like that.' Now that the atmosphere had turned cordial, Cédric felt he could afford to run a few risks: 'You know, I ... I'm a history teacher, as well as translating that book. I've never ... I had never met anyone who was there ... I mean, French people, but never anyone from England. I'd very much like to hear any recollections you might have. In a certain sense it would make up for my never having spoken to my grandfather ...'

Despite the muddled presentation, or maybe because of it, his entreaty seemed to open a chink in his armour: 'What do you want to know?'

'I don't know, whatever you remember ...'

'Whatever I remember?' There was a hint of indulgence in his reply, like a grandfather touched by the simple candour of his grandchild: 'I'm afraid it's easier to remember than it is to forget. I'm still on that plane: every evening before I fall asleep, or when I wake up at one o'clock in the morning wondering why I'm lying in bed. I should be sitting up straight, ready to jump up behind the captain as soon as we get the signal. Instead I look up at the ceiling and take a while to remember that no one is going to shout in my face to get a move on, that I no longer have the strength to carry a hundred pounds of kit, that I'm at no risk of being burnt alive or blown to pieces by the flak, that I won't be a sitting duck as soon as my chute opens. I just have to go to the toilet or take a sip of water from the glass on my bedside table. I'm alone, the others have gone. But inside me they're still there. All of them.'

What was on the other side of the window, in the garden? No point in looking: whatever Roger was staring at did not answer to questions like 'who?' or 'where?', but must have been clear enough to relegate everything else to the background, most notably his nephew, bulky monument to the enjoyment of beer, glass half raised to his mouth and elbow resting on the arm of his chair, frozen in awe. He must never have heard his uncle speak that way before.

'We had to disable the guns pointing at the beach. Merville: they had told us the name a few hours beforehand, but I'd already forgotten it. I couldn't concentrate because the captain kept trying to strike up a conversation. He was making fun of me, about his party, about Spurs ...'

'Spurs?'

'Tottenham Hostpur. It's a football team.'

'I know,' answered Cédric: even a war veteran did not have the right to doubt his knowledge in that field. 'But ... what's the connection?'

'I played for them before joining up. On the youth team, and a few times in the first team. The captain used to tease me because he was a Liverpool man.'

Liverpool?! What were the chances? 'And the party?'

'His birthday party.'

'You mean ... He was born on 6 June?'

'Of 1920. A fine way to celebrate, wasn't it?'

Half a century: this Kadwell had been born exactly fifty years before Cédric. And eighty-six years before Théo. A Liverpool

fan, on top of that. He was starting to grow fond of him: 'And ...
what happened?'

'If you let me speak I'll tell you,' his answer clearly hinted at
a question: why keep interrupting me when you've just asked me
to tell you about it? The teacher in Cédric took note and he fell
silent. History itself was giving this lesson, not just some expert.

*'I stared intently into the darkness, trying to make out those
faint glimmers of light ...'*

24. 4 JUNE 2014, 17:39

' ... *I was promoted to sergeant in the field: I had been forgiven.*
I'm a little tired, Jeremy. Perhaps we had better get going.'

Better get going? He had spent quarter of an hour talking
about some girl, only to then wind up the Battle of Normandy in
a couple of sentences. Cédric felt he was justified in breaking the
silence: 'And the watch?'

Roger took a moment or two to realise that he, and not Cédric,
had changed the subject, and to give an answer that weighed heavily upon him: 'I followed orders, even if I had lost it. I would
have liked to go and see Jane as soon as I got back to England,
in September, but she didn't reply to my letters. Then I found out
she was in London with the Women's Voluntary Service. They
had transferred her when the V1s started raining down on the
city: there were wounded to tend to, survivors to find housing
for, high-risk zones to be evacuated. I found her reply at the barracks when I came back from Germany in 1945, and went to
Liverpool. I turned up in civilian clothing because I was afraid
she might hate uniforms, after what had happened, but actually
she was wearing the green skirt and shirt of the volunteers. And
she knew all about me, about the football, about my family. I'd
never have imagined that the captain would spend a few minutes
talking or writing to her about the youngest soldier in his platoon,

much less that she would still remember, so long afterwards. She also knew about the dedication on the watch and found it logical enough that he had entrusted it to me: what else should he have done? It was not my fault if I had lost it, and in any case the most important memories were the ones she carried inside her. Not just memories, she added: her husband was still with her, he spoke to her every day and she heard him. I felt sorry for her. The pain must have been so unbearable that ... I don't know, maybe she'd taken leave of her sense a bit. But I envied her because I hadn't managed to keep her with me. Every month that passed took something with it: her gaze, her hair, her smile, her voice, even her handwriting ...'

What was he talking about? Cédric looked for a clue in Jeremy's eyes, but the only answer he found was two eyebrows locked in a frown, totally out of place on those rounded, mild features: a clear warning he should watch his step.

'What a fool I made of myself,' Roger went on, 'I burst into tears. Like the kid I was, the captain would have said. It was the first time I'd cried since I had fallen out of a tree and dislocated my shoulder, I must have been eleven. So it was she who comforted me, the world turned on its head. The widow offering a handkerchief to the war veteran ... She thought it was because of the watch. Then I explained, in fact I let it all out. I couldn't with my parents. I had seen dozens of mates die, others lose an eye or an arm, but I didn't have a scratch, not even so much as a sprained ankle. Whereas she had done nothing more than make the most of a day off, going to visit a friend with her mother ... Where's the harm in popping into Woolworth's? Nothing, 'til a flying bomb falls on you.'

Cédric went cold, locked in a vice that was deaf to justifications. He had no reason to be ashamed for the boredom he had felt as he had listened to the story of how two teenagers had met and exchanged letters; he could not have suspected that a nightmare was hiding behind the dream of a tired-out paratrooper, and yet he felt guilty because those memories made the same, irreparable sound as the coughing fits a little boy in Caen had listened to as he watched the television. A cautionary look from Jeremy had saved him the embarrassment of an awkward question, but not the contemplation of an abyss much like the one that had swallowed him up many years earlier.

Roger's nephew also seemed ill at ease, but if it was the prospect of a tirade against the Krauts that was concerning him, he need not have worried: 'I thought of Mr Worthington again. I had gone to see him a few weeks after she ... after what happened. Half an hour spent staring at the piano, because with that ashen face and a voice you could hardly hear he was more frightening than when he used to shout at me on the pitch, telling me if I messed another pass up he would keep me there until the next day. He seemed dead as well, like Betty and his wife. But their suffering was over. Unlike his.

Roger interrupted himself to take a sip of his tea. Cédric had no need of a cue from Jeremy to know he had to wait.

'Jane asked if I would start playing again. I said I wouldn't. Why should I? Betty wouldn't be in the stands for the first match, so there was no reason for me to be there either. The army would take care of my future. I was still in service and I would be shipping back out again a short time later. For Palestine. We had to act as policemen, keep the Arabs and the Jews away from each other. Before we said goodbye, Jane made me promise I'd write to her and she got me to listen to a song.'

'A song?'

'A relative of hers had brought her a record from America. A Broadway musical, I seem to remember. It was about a woman who'd lost her man – if she could find the strength to go on, she would never be alone. Jane liked it so much she'd had the title etched onto her husband's gravestone. It would help me too, she said. I thought it would take a damned sight more than that, but I thanked her all the same. And then I really did write to her, once or twice a year. About my career as a special forces instructor after I got back from Palestine, about getting married to Maureen, that we couldn't have children ... Once I called because I wanted to ask her right away if she had heard her song on the radio. I was sure it was the same one, but it was an English group singing. What were they called? Jerry and ...? My mind's gone blank.'

'Gerry and the Pacemakers?'

'That's it, I think.'

Walk on with hope in your heart and you'll never walk alone: 'You'll Never Walk Alone!'

'The song? That's the one. Do you know it?' As to Cédric's response, signalled by a simple nod of the head, his high-school pals would have had no doubts, even twenty-six years after the shipwreck among the human waves of the Kop. 'She told me she'd bought the record because the old one was so scratched you could hardly hear it anymore. And she managed a joke: visitors to Ranville cemetery would think her husband had been a famous singer. I wanted to give a call a few years after that as well, to tell her to turn the TV on, but I was at the base. The CO had ordered us to watch the Cup Final with him in the mess hall, to celebrate Leeds' win. Actually it was Liverpool that won, and towards the end you could hear the fans singing *You'll Never Walk Alone* ... the captain was a Liverpool fan, so I thought he would have been at Wembley, or at least sitting in front of the television, if ... Well, if he hadn't stayed in France.'

A man like that would have found it in him to sing, unlike the excited schoolboy of twenty-six years ago. 'And Jane? Did she remarry?'

'No. I wrote to her saying it would do her good to begin again, but she answered that she didn't feel like she needed to. She was working as a nurse in a hospital in Liverpool and dedicating all her free time to the Voluntary Service. She had stayed in her army too, just like I'd stayed in mine. And the evenings, when she got in, she talked with him.'

'Him?'

'Her husband. An obsession, I thought, but really there was nothing wrong in it: the important thing was that she found a reason to keep going, like the song said. Her Pierre would always be with her ...'

'Pierre?'

'I almost broke my back, over that nickname ...' an amused smirk altered his features, bringing out wrinkles that had been hidden up until then: 'When we were at the camp, I took him his mail. I was happy to do it because I was the first one down at the mess hall when they handed the letters out – I wanted to know right away if there was anything from Betty. Once I saw the name Pierre Kadwell on an envelope and asked him who'd sent it. He answered that it was Jane who called him Pierre – Pete in French, because of his mother. She was so used to it that she'd written it in the space for the addressee. I didn't think it was a secret between the two of them, partly because anyone could have seen that envelope, so I told a mate of mine and the rumour got around the base in one evening. The next day, all the officers were calling him Pierre. I wouldn't dare, naturally, but it was still me he took it out on – it was my fault. I can remember the punishment even now, thirty push-ups with my haversack on. He reminded the others his name was Pete, but that if anyone fancied a bit of boxing practice with him all they had to do was say 'Pierre' and he would happily oblige, as he needed to keep himself fit for the brigade tournament. The idea of locking horns with him didn't appeal to anyone, so the nickname vanished in the space of forty-eight hours. Only Jane could call him that, he explained, because they were bound by destiny: married and born on the same day. To be fair he was born in '20 and she in '23, but the date ...'

'6 June?'

'Right. Not that it brought either of them much luck ...'

'A lot of people died, that day ...'

'In 1944, yes. But Jane died on 6 June as well. Must have been 1974 or 1975, so she was only a little over fifty. When the reverend called me, it was like watching the captain die all over again. But it comforted me to hear she'd just drifted off, without realising it. At the funeral I got the sensation I was the only one who thought her life had finished there. It must be a wonderful thing, faith. I can still remember what the padre told us, the day before the jump: 'Fear knocked at the door. Faith opened it. And there was nobody there." Glistening eyes and head held high, no sign of going to wipe away his tears with his knuckles, Sergeant Englin seemed as convinced as seventy years earlier – faith or no faith – that behind his door nobody was there.

'Mr Cédric Roussel is requested to go to the desk on the first floor for information regarding this afternoon's auction. Once again: Mr ...'

The announcement through the tannoy system and his mobile display gave him a jolt: quarter to seven, the auction must have ended some hours earlier. 'I'd better put in an appearance, otherwise they'll keep the watch ... Are you staying for the seventieth anniversary celebrations?'

'No,' Jeremy answered, finding his voice. 'We're leaving tomorrow. My uncle wants to go back to London. And you?'

'I'm going home too. But I'd like for us to stay in contact ...'

'Don't worry,' Jeremy smiled, 'I'll keep my promise.'

'Promise?'

'The photo ...'

'Oh yes, sorry, I'd forgotten. Thank you.'

25. 4 JUNE 2014, 18:55

'I thought it was about 3,800 euros ...' stammered Cédric when Onfray showed him the invoice.

'No, sir. With the commission and taxes added to the bid price of 2,800 euros, the grand total is 3,948. All of the costs are itemised here.'

He was right, of course: the withdrawal in Caen had been based on a maximum bid of 2,700 euros. A terrible idea, not registering his credit card before the auction: 'I'm afraid I've made a mistake with my sums, I don't know whether ...'

'Don't worry. If you prefer, we can send you the invoice via post or email. But we must keep the watch while we await payment, and charge you for storage and postage. It should be around a hundred euros.'

Another hundred? Not if there was any way around it. Cédric dug around in his wallet in search of the remaining 148 euros, hoping the bills from the restaurant and bar had left him enough change. The total, following feverish calculations that even included 5 cent coins, reached 143.15 euros, to which he added the 10 euro note he kept in his shirt pocket for emergencies. Throughout this process, Onfray remained unperturbed: tranquility in the face of unusual circumstances must have been one of the foundations of his professional code, acquired during long years of experience. At the end there were two piles of money on the table between them: 3,800 euros in one stack of crisp-looking banknotes and 148 in smaller notes and loose change in another. Watching all of it disappear into the cashbox troubled Cédric, who bid the auctioneer farewell and turned around to leave.

It was evident that such a scene was new even to Onfray, who allowed himself a genuine smile, maybe the first one in a day dedicated to the cool courtesy that characterised his dealings with clients: 'Aren't you going to take the watch?'

'Sorry?' Cédric answered, shaking himself out of his daze. 'Yes ... do you have a box?'

'Unfortunately no. When we have the original cases it is stated in the catalogue, and it almost never happens with pieces such as this. But you're not wearing a watch, I can see. You can put it on your wrist. I can wind it and set the correct time, if you like.'

'Thank you, that way I can see how to do it. The watch my wife gave me is battery-powered.'

'It's simple, but remember to do it before putting it on, because once on the wrist there's not enough room for your fingers and you run the risk of bending the winding shaft. You need to turn the crown in both directions until you feel a little resistance – don't try to force it because the mainspring might break. Then you pull it outwards and rotate to turn the hands until they show the right time, just the same as with your quartz watch. Finally, you press the crown down again. The important thing is to do it all gently. It is seventy years old. May I ...?' Onfray leant across the table to strap it onto his left wrist. 'As with all watches sold at auction, we recommend a movement overhaul. I prefer to remind clients of that, even if it is written in the catalogue. The strap is new, we put it on. If you wear it every day it should last about a year. When the time comes to change it because it's cracked or dirty, do try to find a similar one: it's pig leather, like the originals from the 40s.'

'Pig?'

'No lizard or crocodile: they were looking for toughness with these watches, not elegance. And bear in mind that the lugs are fixed.' The lost look on Cédris's face must have been so evident that Onfray rushed to translate: 'I mean the pins that hold the strap in place. They normally have elastic tips so that you can remove them and insert them in the eyelets. Here they are fixed in place – they are part of the case – so the strap has to be sewn on around them. It's a little complicated, but they will take care of it wherever you go to replace it. The documents are here.'

Onfray placed a file with the auction house logo on the table. The documents were inside plastic wallets that seemed to have been made to measure, one large enough to hold the donation certificate and the other smaller. Cédric gave them a quick glance to check they corresponded to the photocopies he had seen at the *notaire*'s office and took his leave – the day was not over yet.

He sat down next to a lamp on one of the satin sofas in the entrance hall in order to gather his thoughts. He slipped the watch off his wrist and held it under the light. It certainly looked as though it had seen some heavy usage, to use a technical euphemism. Had it been worth it? All that money spent, and the inevitable showdown with Sylvie still to come.

His gaze followed the only moving part that was visible: the smallest hand, at the bottom, mounted on a circle with dashes running around its edge. It fol-lowed its course, rhythm and direction immutable; proof that time was a one-way stre-et. If only the watch had come complete with a ticket back to make the hand change direc-tion, in fact all three hands, far enough to reach his father, his grandfather, the captain, the factory where someone had assembled that mechanical jigsaw, to relive all the sen-

'... the tiny, silver needle flecked with rust advanced...'

sations of everyone who had checked it, worn it or merely just touched it, then the price – any price – would have been justified. But that miracle was not for sale. The tiny, silver needle flecked with rust advanced inexorably, accompanied by its big brothers with cracks down their middle, victims of the time they measured, their wrinkles and weakness a warning to those who observed them: even if they were to stop because the mainspring was left unwound, the present would go on becoming past, the recent past slipping further and further back.

Holding the watch to his ear, Cédric had the impression he was imitating himself. And it was an image, rather than a sound, that reached him first: the dream, his dream, condensed down into a split second. The pitch, the grave, the terraces, the toy soldiers, the blood, the lit-up scoreboard, Théo, Jane, everything together and overlapping in a pile of vivid photographs, transparent, close by, within arm's reach. But they disappeared an instant later, without leaving him the *time* to put them in order. Time, as always.

26. 4 JUNE 2014, 19:47

Who said everything costs the Earth in a hotel for the super rich? When Cédric presented himself at reception to pay for the five minutes he had spent on the internet, a pleasant employee told him he did not have to pay. She would pretend that the convention for those taking part in the auction was still on, even if the only people left in the room on the first floor were the workers tasked with taking everything down and packing it away. A good job: if it had been anything over five euros he would have been forced to pay with his credit card – that was all he had left in his pocket. The search had been brief: the Commonwealth War Graves Commission website, a form to fill out with name, surname, nationality and date of death. The response had gone beyond his expectations, giving him the exact location of the grave. All he had to do was type the address into the GPS and let it lead him to the small car park, where only one other car had been left. Normal enough – too early for the seventieth anniversary preparations and too late for ordinary visitors. He saw from his mobile display it was almost eight o'clock. Cédric was not used to wearing a watch and, deep down, he did not trust it. Would it really work? He felt a tingle of apprehension as he gave it a glance, followed by relief: the extremely costly, well-used timepiece was – for the time being, at least – going just as strong as his middle-aged mobile phone.

'... the entrance was a narrow archway of light-coloured bricks...'

The entrance was a narrow archway of light-coloured bricks, a couple of metres from the roadside. The short walls on either side ran at right angles to the edge of the roadway, joining the hedge that bordered the area. 'Ranville War Cemetery' announced the lettering carved on the left-hand side; on the right there were simply two dates, 1939-1945. An ethereal veil of cloud, its edges indistinct, seemed to want to defend the gravestones from the sunshine, even now that the day was almost over. The fresh sea breeze was too weak to bother him. The place seemed deserted.

Cédric mounted a step and passed beneath the archway, pushing open a dark, wrought iron gate. Thirty or so metres ahead of him, beyond the first rows of headstones, stood a white limestone cross, as high as the arch, with a bronze sword embedded in the stone: the Cross of Sacrifice, according to the map of the cemetery. Someone had already placed something on the

'... beneath the floral tribute in the red, white and blue...'

bottom step, bright colours contrasting with the white of the stone. Cédric went nearer. Beneath the floral tribute in the red, white and blue of the Union Jack, he could see a plastic-covered note peeping out, spotted with water droplets, the light rain that had accompanied the final part of Cédric's car journey. The first lines of the text were hidden by the coloured petals, while those he could see reminded him this cemetery was not like others: '… They ask us why we do it, why we still parade now that we are getting older and just a little bit frayed. It's not for the sake of glory or the medals on our chest. It's simply that we are comrades who stood the final test. On the 6th June that fateful day, a day that we will never forget, many a lad laid down his life and paid the final debt. So when you see a veteran give the man your hand, for the medals on his chest were won in foreign lands. And when God asks the question Who are you my man, I will proudly answer: Sir, I am a veteran.'

On the other side of the cross, the pattern of headstones began again, only to be interrupted once more where two paths intersected the broad, grassy rectangle at the centre, concrete gangways marked out by columns made with bricks identical to those used in the entrance archway. At the back were an altar and small colonnade where, sheltered from the rain, someone had already set up the speaker system that would amplify the dignitaries' speeches, among them – apparently – the President of the Republic and a representative of the British Royal Family.

'… a two metre high wall that only partially blocked the view of an imposing gothic church…'

The right-hand edge of the cemetery was marked by a two-metre high wall that only partially blocked the view of an imposing gothic church with two rows of long, narrow windows along its sides. Perhaps it was worth a visit, but not now: Cédric used it as a landmark, following the wall ten paces or so towards the road. It was the front row he was interested in: an involuntary or unknowing tribute to someone who always wanted to be leader of the pack? As he covered the few metres separating him from Captain Kadwell, he read the words etched onto the neighbouring headstones: 'To my beloved husband William, who gave his life that we may live – loving wife and daughter'; 'It is better to have loved and lost than never to have loved at all – your wife Sarah'. It seemed that if they were chosen carefully, a handful of words were enough to tell the stories of five different lives.

'Captain Pete F. Kadwell – 6th Airborne Division – 6 June 1920 to 6 June 1944 – You'll Never Walk Alone.' Inspiration instead of memories; he wondered whether the idea had occurred to anyone other than Jane.

'Relative?' Cédric gave a start and, turning around, met the smile of an old man whose head was too big for his shoulders. He was wrapped in a beige waterproof, bushy grey eyebrows emphasised by his baldness, hair of the same colour reduced to a few thinning patches around his ears. 'My apologies, I didn't mean to startle you,' he excused himself in English, holding out his hand. 'My name is Lickert. I came here to visit my father. I never met him because I was born a couple of months after ... I wanted to stay with him for a while, by myself. In silence before all that hoo-ha tomorrow and the day after. You know, the police, the barriers, the dignitaries, the speeches, the helicopters ... was Captain Kadwell a relative of yours?'

'No, I'm not English.'

'French, then?'

'Yes.'

'At the end of the day so are they.'

'Who?'

'Them. They've spent longer in Normandy than they did in England. So they've become a little bit French as well.'

'I've never thought of it that way ... Well, in Kadwell's case you're right in two ways – his mother was French.'

'I know. Every now and then I read my father's letters home and his name pops up often. They spent almost a year together at the base; they were on the same plane. And they both died at Merville. I thought you were a relative, that was why I came over to you.'

Lickert? The name rang a bell. That was it: the corporal who boasted he could speak French. 'An ex paratrooper spoke to me about Kadwell a couple of hours ago: he was on that plane too. Does the name Roger Englin mean anything to you?'

'Of course! I ran into him years ago at a ceremony in London. I was glad to meet him because the letters mention him a lot. My father envied him: he wrote that he was as strong as an ox despite being so young, that he had never seen anyone quite like him. When they introduced him to me he was so slim I could have bet he was still marching thirty miles a day, just like back when he was at boot camp,' he smiled, 'I'm happy to hear he's still with us. Hopefully I shall see him at the Merville celebrations.'

'I'm afraid he won't be there. His nephew told me they're leaving tomorrow.'

'Pity. And you?'

'I need to go as well. I'm heading back to Nice because my son and I both have our birthday on Sunday.'

'Born on 6 June? You both have something in common with Kadwell ...'

'Right ...' Just something, or more than that? Cédric was not sure whether he knew every item on the list.

'I'll have to leave you to it now because my wife is waiting outside. She didn't want to come in, she says cemeteries make her sad. My best wishes to the *Côte d'Azur*.'

Cédric watched him until he disappeared behind the stone archway, and then went back to examining the grave. *You'll Never*

Walk Alone. The letters formed clear words and a complete sentence, but the longer he looked at them the more they reminded him of a picture his history of art teacher had shown once in class – one of those images that can be seen in two different ways. To him it had just looked like the portrait of an old lady, but his teacher had assured them the face of a pretty girl was concealed within those very same features. As he tried to make it out he had felt uncomfortable: why was it taking so long? Could he not see properly or, worse, was he too dim-witted? After a short time he had managed it, with a little help – look carefully and the crone's nostril and eye become the girl's chin and ear … But this time it was not working. Behind the title of the song there was something still escaping him, like the inscription on a marble slab at the centre of a football pitch. Except here there was no one who could put him on the right track, not even an eight-year-old boy accompanied by a red-haired girl.

27. 5 JUNE 2014, 08:18

Now that he was wide awake and ready for the marathon return leg, crashing out the evening before seemed all the more inexplicable. Three hours spent dead to the world, fully clothed and with the television playing to itself. When he had opened his eyes, Cédric had seen images from the night time newscast passing across the screen. He had sat up on the edge of the bed, slightly fuzzy-headed, as he usually was when he woke up from an unscheduled doze, and looked at his mobile phone. The information displayed on it had come as a shock: half-past midnight, and four missed calls from home. It had been on mute because he had forgotten to turn the sound back on after the auction. The remains of a hurried dinner littered the small table: plastic plates and cutlery, crumbs, peels. He had made the mistake of lying down 'just for a minute' before cleaning up and, upon waking, his only consolation had been the fact that he did not have to justify himself to some enraged superior. It had been too late to call Sylvie – the next morning she had to get up early and take Théo to basketball – so he had sent her a text message and, since he had woken up, had also packed his suitcase before returning to bed. Now the Anfield Road anthem, Merseysiders and Catalonians divided in loyalties but united in song, was playing from his mobile, reminding him he had to make a phone call before he left.

'Hello?' It was Théo.

'Hi, it's me. How's it going?'

'Fine. I've got to go to the gym.'

'I know. Where's Mum?'

'Outside with Céline. She's taking us. When are you coming home?'

'This evening. Hopefully before your bedtime.'

'Are you leaving right away?'

'Yes. But first I wanted to ask you something ...'

'They're beeping the horn, I've got to go.'

'Just a second. Do you remember when you left the computer on, on Monday?' Silence. Cédric could almost see the grimace of displeasure on Théo's face: why were they back on that again? Hadn't the promise not to do it again been enough? The case was supposed to be closed, dismissed, forgotten. 'Don't worry, all I want to know is why you went on that site.'

'Which site?'

'The one with the photos of watches on it.'

'It was Pierre's idea. I told you, didn't I?'

'No ...'

'Yes I did.'

Did he need to warn him again not to be cheeky, or make the threat of no computer for a week? No, once was enough: 'Oh yes, I'd forgotten.'

'I'm going, otherwise Mum'll get angry again.'

'Again?'

'She's horrible, she hurt me ...' his voice cracked, and then he hung up. He hated anyone hearing him cry.

Half an hour later the suitcase was stowed in the boot and Cédric was sitting behind the wheel, but before turning the keys in the ignition he wanted to know what was going on at home.

'Yes?'

'Hi Sylvie. Why did you take so long to answer?'

'I had to leave the changing rooms because the coach gave me a dirty look, you know how seriously he takes it all. It'd be better if we spoke later. I got your message ...'

'Just one thing. I spoke to Théo earlier, what happened?'

'What do you mean?'

'Was he playing up? Did you smack him?'

'Smack him? What are you on about?'

'He said you hurt him ...'

'Hurt him ... Well a little bit, maybe. But how else could I have got it off?'

'Got what off?'

'This morning he came down to the kitchen with black polish all over his face. Shoe polish, can you believe it? He'd taken it out of the cupboard and smeared it on his face. So we both had to skip breakfast while I cleaned it off. It probably hurt because I had to scrub quite hard to get it off. I couldn't exactly send him to the gym like that, could I? And then I had to get changed because I had polish stains on my trousers. Listen, just come home quick and have a word with your son because I'm fed up with all this Pierre business.'

Your son, a turn of phrase Sylvie generally came out with when one of Théo's less than brilliant ideas was up for discussion: 'What does Pierre have to do with it?'

'He says he wants his face to be like Pierre's, that way he'll be brave and win. We'll talk about it when you get back. But don't worry, anyway – he's fine, even if he is losing his marbles.'

She was already in a bad mood, even before hearing about the watch. All Cédric needed now was for his wife to log onto their bank's website and check the state of their account when she got home from the gym.

28. 5 JUNE 2014, 22:46

'Welcome home, hubby.'

Cédric had taken every possible precaution to avoid breaking the silence of the sleeping house, taking his shoes off the moment he stepped through the front door, gently placing his suitcase on the trunk in the hallway and climbing the stairs in the dark, barefoot. He did not feel like talking – too worn out to face the subject of the watch. The bedroom door was ajar, as always: a request from Théo, that way he felt his parents were within earshot if he needed them. Cédric made his way blindly to the bathroom, hugging the wall of the hallway to avoid the centre of the parquet flooring where a plank had come almost completely unstuck. During the wait for another job to arise before calling the carpenter out, the whole family had memorised its position and gotten used to avoiding it. No noise, but even so:

'Welcome home, hubby.'

'Sorry, I didn't mean to wake you up.'

'Sorry isn't enough. A kiss.'

Cédric hurried to obey, adding, with more passion and, he had to admit, less sincerity than usual: 'I missed you.' He needed to rack up some brownie points in view of the showdown to come.

'Well? How was it?'

'How's Théo, more like,' he responded, dodging the question.

'What's happening to the little man?'

Sylvie sat up on the bed and brushed the back of her hand against her forehead, a gesture which, in her personal body language, was an unmistakable sign of a bad mood: 'He's lost it, I told you. Today's news is that it was my fault he lost.'

'What do you mean?'

'I've never seen him like that after a match. At the gym he didn't say anything, but in the car ... crying, shouting, saying I shouldn't have cleaned his face, that I took his courage – it was crazy. I know when he's talking a lot of rot just to make me angry, but this time he really seemed to believe it. Then, the minute we got home, he calmed down. Almost too much. He must have said ten words between lunch and dinner, the rest of the time he stayed in his room. I heard him muttering something a little bit before nine o'clock, perhaps he wanted to stay awake to see you, but I think he's asleep now. You'd better have a word with him tomorrow ...'

'I'm just going to go and poke my head round the door.'

'Don't wake him up, there's the party ... which he doesn't seem to care about any more, by the way: he hasn't mentioned it in two days.'

'Now that is strange,' smiled Cédric.

**

He looked so much like her ... The same thought as always, but after a few days away it took him by surprise, as though he had found the same person in two different rooms. Sylvie in miniature: same tanned complexion, same pointed nose, same straight, black hair and – now he was asleep – even the same supine position, arms stretched out along his sides, like a soldier standing to attention. And yet the glow from Théo's night-light showed something different about him as well. He plugged the lamp into the socket by his bed every evening and removed it the following morning at seven o'clock on the dot, putting it back in its drawer in his bedside table and displaying a methodical approach evident in no other part of his daily life. Cédric had never understood why he did not simply turn it on and off at the switch.

He picked up the stool that lay upside-down at the foot of the bed and sat down next to him. His eyes were motionless beneath the lids, his breathing so light that it was only a few years earlier that Sylvie had broken the habit of her nightly check-up, where, before going to bed herself, she would gently touch the palm of her hand against his chest, the paranoia of an overprotective mother with her only child. Something different. But what? Cédric looked for a clue in his features until a sudden movement gave him the answer he sought. Théo moved his index finger to his lip, snuffing out a slight itch before it could become an irritation; nothing, not even so much as a ripple, disturbed the composure of his sleep, as he let his hand fall back against the pillow. A confident gesture; an adult gesture. Had his journey towards another self already begun? Had he needed to grow up before his time? In just four short days, while his father was far away? Far away ... Before he had even left, in a sense.

On his cheeks and forehead he could still make out the traces of polish that not even the robust scrubbing meted out by Sylvie that morning had managed to completely erase. The top of the bedside table, resembling as usual a scaled-down version of a landfill site, seemed to rule out the possibility that Théo had grown up prematurely: two paper tissues scrunched up into balls, the crumbs left over from a snack purloined from the kitchen and secretly consumed before bedtime, an empty plastic cup with a few drops of fruit juice left at the bottom, a crumpled sheet of squared paper covered with dots, numbers and arrows – game plans to learn for the next challenge on the basketball court? – and a black felt tip deprived of its lid.

And yet a careful eye could pick out a few unprecedented elements from that primordial soup. Too soon to announce a future in which the right basketball trainer might keep company with the left, hopefully on the floor rather than on the windowsill, or at least be visible somewhere in the vicinity – that, for now, was pure science fiction. Rather, an embryonic sort of harmony, behind which some kind of logic might have been at play. It was difficult to put his finger on it, though.

The Winnie the Pooh alarm clock, set to go off and with the hand pointing to the number twelve, for a start. If Théo felt so tired that he needed to be woken up at midday, then he had got his sums wrong: it would be tearing him away from the land of nod shortly, at midnight. And the toy soldiers? In two lines behind the flexible neck of the lamp, up against the wall, all of them with blackened faces. Now it was clear what the felt tip was for, although the reasoning behind the parade and cosmetic makeover was still a mystery. The corner of a yellow post-it note was poking out from beneath the base of the lamp, folded in half with the sides aligning perfectly, in stark contrast – and indicative of the transformation taking place? – to the sheet of squared paper. Opening it, Cédric found himself reading a collection of words that, just the week before, he would have found incomprehensible and forgotten about immediately: 'google www british army number 9.' It was Théo's handwriting alright, but different from usual, more hurried. Cédric could almost see him, trying to shape the letters perfectly as he was wont to do and raising his head to protest every so often, annoyed by the rapid pace of the dictation: 'Slow down! How can I keep up, otherwise?'

As he put the note back in its place, Cédric felt he was being watched. Théo's eyes – the exception to the Sylvie-lookalike rule, only part of his face that was his and his alone. Not so much the colour, halfway between Cédric's hazelnut tint and the coal black of his mother, as the rounded shape that made them seem bigger than they were. His gaze was in keeping with developments, whether imagined or presumed: the direct look of one who wanted to understand, not merely to observe. Once, on finding someone next to his bed, he would have been sitting up in no time; now, he stayed lying down, turning slightly towards him. His voice, at least, was the same as always: 'What's the time?'

'I'll only tell you if you say 'hello' first.'

'Hello. When did you get back?'

'A little while ago. Happy birthday.'

Théo threw an anxious glance at the alarm clock: 'Is it morning already?'

'Eleven o'clock at night. I wanted to be the first.'

'Thanks.'

'Well?'

'Well what?'

'It's someone else's birthday in an hour, isn't it?'

'Happy birthday, Dad.'

'And Pierre?'

Théo dug his elbows into the mattress and pushed his chest up, the air of someone who could smell a trap and had no intention of falling into it: 'Pierre?'

'When you see him, wish him a happy birthday from me.'

'...?'

'Had you forgotten? That's odd.'

'No, but ...' in Théo's wide eyes, relief was struggling to get the better of doubt – was it possible the nightmare was really over?

Cédric showed him his wrist: 'And thank him.'

'Is that it? Grandad's watch?'

'You should recognise it.'

Silence.

'You did well.'

'All I did was turn the computer on.'

'And find the right page.'

'On Monday you shouted at me, though ...'

'I shouldn't have. I'm sorry.'

'Were you pretending?'

'Pretending?'

'To be angry. And when you winked at Mum, you were laughing, and you looked the wrong way in the garage. Was it all a joke?'

'No, no joke.'

'Why, then?'

246

'I ... It's just that ... I didn't know about the watch.'

A feeble explanation, the sort a teacher came out with when he had not prepared a lesson properly. Luckily Théo was an understanding pupil, ready to rush to his aid: 'Maybe you still had the dark inside and didn't know it.'

That again: 'What's the dark got to do with it?'

'That was why you couldn't tell friend from foe.'

'I told you I've always been able to recognise my friends.'

'Then why were you mean to him when you were little?'

'Who?'

'Him. You threatened him, you shouted at him to go away. But at least you spoke to him, while now ... what's the matter with you?'

'Nothing ...'

'Your face has gone white.'

'Pale – you say pale. I must be tired. It's a long way from Caen to Nice.' But he thought he had taken twelve hours, not thirty-nine years.

'Don't worry, he's not angry. In fact, he was laughing.' Théo seemed amused as well, at his father's expense: 'He said, 'Can you imagine? A pint-sized five-year-old daring to threaten someone like me? That takes some guts. But he was brave: when your Grandma used to ask him to go down and buy something he went, even though he knew I was on the stairs and he thought I meant to hurt him. A brave soldier, like you."

'I didn't know you'd become a soldier.'

'How could I talk about it? No one listened to me.'

'Right ... At the party I'll have to say sorry to him, too.'

Théo's face clouded over: 'He won't be there.'

'How come?'

'He's leaving tonight. With them.'

'The paratroopers? Did he tell you to colour them like that?'

'It's for the mission. They're better at hiding in the dark, with black faces. As soon as the alarm clock goes off I'll take them down to the garage, then they leave. They have to get into the baddies' fortress and destroy the guns so they can't hurt their friends.'

The apprehension on Théo's face was so obvious that Cédric risked a joke to relieve the tension: 'Sounds like a job for Gyorx.'

'This isn't a film,' he answered, disappointment streaked with irritation – if Dad had really understood, then why had he started talking about toys in a moment like this? Maybe he needed a history lesson: 'And the baddies are real. To set the goodies free it's not enough to just invert the virotron flux like in *Lost Galaxy*. It's very dangerous – their lives are at risk.'

'You're right,' Cédric nodded, convinced. Before going any further he had to show he had truly grasped the concept: 'You're going into the garage by yourself? At night?'

'Those are my orders.'

'I thought you were afraid of the hallway.'

'He said if I look it in the eye it'll pass. Like you did. In fact, it was harder for you because you had the dark inside. It's a shame you wouldn't let him speak, the dark would have gone away in no time.'

'Really?'

'Yes – he wanted to help you, to say something … but you got it when you grew up, anyway.'

'I'm afraid I didn't. I must not be as clever as he thinks.'

'Yes you did … the song you listen to all the time. The one on your mobile phone, that says you'll never be alone even though you've lost someone who loved you. I don't understand the words, but he translated them for me.'

'And you can be sure he did a good job, he speaks English.'

'Does it go for everyone?'

'What?'

'The song.'

'Of course.'

'So I'll never be alone either …' The first sign of vulnerability since he had woken up: perhaps Cédric had come back in time to see him grow up after all.

'Don't worry. We're here ...'

'... and Pierre.'

'... and Pierre. And while we're on the subject: get to sleep, otherwise you'll be too tired when the alarm goes off. You don't want to be late, do you?'

'What shall I do if Mum sees me walking about? What can I tell her? She'll get angry again.'

'I'll think of something – I'll try and distract her.'

'She's horrible.' Said with such icy calm, the accusation was more unsettling than when he had shouted it through his sobs, at the climax of a (lost) battle over her permission to get two red Ys died into his hair like Sam-Sam Youny, his favourite playmaker.

'You know that's not true. She thought you'd gotten all dirty just to wind her up.'

'Wind her up? I'm not a baby. I wanted to ...'

'... be like him to become brave, I know. And you will be anyway, without having to black your face up. Look fear in the eye.'

'And if that's not enough, I'll think of the song.'

'Is that what he suggested?'

'No, that's my idea.'

'You'll see that it works.'

'But ... why do you understand and Mum doesn't?'

'She's different to us.'

'Of course – she's a woman.'

'I don't mean like that. You and I have something else in common. And Pierre too.'

'...?'

'Don't you remember what day it is tomorrow?'

It was a gust of wind that blew away the last cloud from Théo's horizon, a revelation that deserved to be celebrated by drawing on Gyorx's vocabulary, which was more creative – and on this point even Sergeant Englin would have agreed – than that in use among British paratroopers in 1944: '... That's astralflash!'

'If you want I'll come with you.'

'No!' exclaimed Théo, turning red and throwing the sheet off himself before standing bolt upright on his bed – to become taller, braver or both at once? 'I need to go alone.'

'I was forgetting: your orders.'

'And you?'

'I'll go back to the bedroom and keep an eye on Mum. She mustn't find out about the plan or what we've been talking about. That's what you do in war: never put innocent lives in danger. Got it?'

'Then she'll keep shouting at me …'

'She'll soon forget about it. The important thing is that we all do our duty. The mission depends on it.' And so did Pierre's safety, he was tempted to add, but changed his mind: Théo was already worried enough.

'I can't wait to tell him about the watch. He'll be pleased.'

'I hope so. Go to sleep, now.'

Théo snuggled back down into his bed without taking his eye off his father's wrist, letting Cédric pull the sheet up to his chest: 'Bye.'

'Good luck.' Cédric hesitated before kissing him goodnight; kids' stuff, maybe it would offend him. But no: Théo hugged him tightly and returned the kiss. That 'good luck' must have meant a lot to him.

**

Cédric was past sleeping – it happened, when he was truly tired. Instead of going back to his bedroom he went to the study and turned the computer on to check his emails. A conditioned reflex: it was unlikely anything had been sent on a Saturday. While he waited for it to boot up, he slipped the watch off his wrist and wound the crown back and forth a few dozen times before holding it to his ear. In the car he had kept doing it, at first to break the tedium of the journey and stave off drowsiness, later because he liked it. And it comforted him to discover that, when he muted the CD player and listened carefully, he could make out the ticking sound over the solid, invasive noise of the engine, the air rushing against the windscreen and the tyres on the road. Sensory compensation: forced to admit he could not understand everything he saw, Cédric had tried to convince himself that he could at least bend his hearing to his will.

Those metallic pulsations had already become part of his own personal soundtrack. And they would remain so, even if it was sure to mean Kevin would have a field day over it. The boy was a bone-idle high-school student who had reached the final year through force of inertia, dragged along by abilities that could no more be put in doubt than his laziness, and who shook himself out of his stupor and revealed his all-too-sharp skills whenever he stole centre-stage with his impressions of the teachers and their various tics. The previous November, Cédric had watched him reproduce the head-teacher's rigid walk from the doorway of the classroom, and had struggled to smother a smile as his schoolmates, who had noticed the teacher's presence, gestured to him to cut it out. A few weeks after that he had stopped himself a moment before entering the toilets because he could hear a strident female voice coming from inside – was it he or Mrs Jacquet, the art teacher, who had gotten the wrong door? He had only had to listen in for a few seconds to recognise Kevin's Provencal accent, busy describing one of Delacroix's works in the teacher's unpleasant warble, peppered with a rather more colourful choice of words than that generally employed by art critics.

It would be his turn soon. One day he would spot Kevin lift the back of his left hand to his cheek and explain to his classmates that, as a history teacher, he had to keep checking which century he was in. Never mind; he would just have to take it on the chin, and then in any case Kevin was only a few weeks from the end of school. After that the university professors would be next; if, that was, he did not find a career as a comedian more to his taste.

Instead of putting the watch back on or holding it against his ear again – dissuaded by the contemplation of his future as a laughing stock, even if he did not want to admit it? – Cédric placed it on the table, next to the keyboard, with the tongue of the buckle in one of the holes along the strap and the dial, almost perpendicular to the table top, seeming to stare back at him. As if in imitation, three smiling faces appeared on the screen when it lit up.

He often lingered over the image he had chosen as a background. It had the same euphoric effect as chocolate but without harming his teeth, and right then it swept all thoughts of the Kevin threat out of his mind. It did not seem possible that it was no more than the casual effort of a passer-by. The whole family in Aix-en-Provence, immortalised by a Japanese tourist upon their request, who had humbly protested that he was not much good, and had then – who could say whether it was down to sheer luck or to the mastery of technique apparently possessed by everyone who came from a country synonymous with cameras – given them a masterpiece: the warm light of late afternoon, the soft shadows, the balance of the composition with the group occupying the foreground and the eighteenth-century facades of the Cours Mirabeau in the background, the merest slice of sky instead of the blue vacuum that filled the upper half of the photo when a novice was behind the camera.

A wonder that could not have come off, naturally, unless its subjects had also played their part. The tanned faces of all three of them, the spontaneous smiles, the eyes open as they should be and even the colour coordination of their clothes: the pure white of Théo's freshly-ironed polo shirt above his sky-blue Bermuda shorts, Sylvie's yellow, red, blue and black dress a palette of geometric patterns printed onto bright fabric, Cédric in short-sleeved shirt, with tin green and blue stripes, and jeans. Not even a professional photo-shoot with a royal family could have produced a better result. The only person who had not been even to the task was him: when he had saved the file, after having adapted it to the dimensions of the screen, he had baptised it with the banal title 'Aix'. He had always thought the happy trio in the Provence sunshine deserved something better than that, but had been unsure how to make amends.

Now he knew. He opened the folder with the family photos

inside, clicked on the name and changed it: 'YNWA'. Why had he not thought of it sooner? Perhaps because it had seemed like something only comprehensible to the initiated, inaccessible to Sylvie and Théo, or else because he had not known that fifty thousand voices had the power to sculpt a marble slab. Inaccessible? There was always *Google* – four million hits, if he remembered correctly. And four solitary letters, enough to tell the story of a summer trip, a mood, a destiny he had been waiting for ever since the day the record-player needle had announced it to him, digging it out from between the grooves of an old vinyl.

The only new message in his inbox was from an unknown sender, one jer.eng@o2.co.uk, and was accompanied by an exclamation point: a possible threat, the antispam software warned him. A trap, brimming with state-of-the-art computer viruses? Best not to run the risk; Cédric was on the point of consigning it to the dustbin, but the image that appeared before him persuaded him to take a closer look. 'Pete and Roger,' read the subject of the email. Apparently, good old Jeremy had gone one better than merely keeping his promise – he had been quick about it too, sending the scan as soon as he had arrived home, a few hours earlier. He could make out 'May 1944' in the bottom right-hand corner, but no details regarding the location – clearly, in the weeks leading up to the mission, the secrecy surrounding the battalion's movements even extended to souvenir photos.

At the centre were a couple of smiling young men, standing next to one another in front of a picket fence, behind it what looked like a flat, grassy field, perhaps the airstrip. They were in barracks uniform, shoes shined, trousers pressed, thick shirt with pockets on the chest buttoned up to their Adam's apples, beret with the winged parachute emblem. A moment's pause, more likely – judging by their relaxed faces – at the beginning than at the end of a day's training. It was not hard to make out Roger: the light, curly hair sticking out from underneath the beret and his fresh-faced features gave him away, in stark contrast with his physique. He had been right: who could have suspected the boy had lied about his age when he was almost as tall and well-built as his superior, who was in actual fact six years his elder?

The captain: there he was, finally. Built for the part and larger than life, judging by Roger's uncertain, almost nervous, smile. The expression would have made him the ideal candidate for a film where he played himself, the paratrooper ready to invade Normandy single-handedly. A familiar, teasing grin, the lips pointed upwards only at the edges. 'Mister Smirk, I presume,' Cédric muttered. This photo was better than the portrait at Merville – more spontaneous. And more reassuring than a fearful vision hidden among the shadows of the past. His gaze was alert and focussed, but there was more. Cédric thought he could read a hint of protectiveness as well, maybe owing to his doubts on how well the overgrown puppy standing beside him would hold up when the time came – was that why he had placed an arm round his neck, like an older brother? – or maybe because he was remembering Jane. At times knowledge could impair judgement, like when you looked at a painting while the museum guide reeled off an interminable description of the artists's biography, technical details and historical facts. Interesting, but Cédric preferred to look first and ask questions later. Here it was the same thing. What effect would that gaze have had on him if he had known nothing of Pete Kadwell?

From behind Roger's neck the captain's forearm was visible, shirtsleeve pulled taught enough to reveal his wrist. There it was! Cédric zoomed in, but the image became more blurred with each click of the mouse. If it was not the same then it was very much like it, he reflected, picking up the watch and holding it next to the monitor, attempting without success to make out some particular detail that would provide definitive confirmation, proof.

Cédric put it back down next to the keyboard while one thought pushed all others out of his mind, racing at breakneck speed through the deserted, nighttime streets of his brain. Three people had worn that watch before him, and all had passed away too soon. The realisation ought to have alarmed him at least a little:

although not superstitious, he sometimes found himself repeating a series of gestures or rummaging through a drawer in search of a certain shirt he had worn on a happy occasion. Instead he contemplated it with cool detachment, like a news story from the world of high finance. The watch had been given to the captain, to his grandfather and to his father. He, on the other hand, had bought it, and he liked to think that along with the bid price, the taxes and the commission, he had also paid for a guarantee that he would live to see not only Théo but also his own children grow up. In fact, he felt sure enough to bet on it. Why? He did not know and he did not care. At this hour even the most unjustified of certainties was welcome to stick around.

'Aren't you coming to bed?' Sylvie appeared at the study door, which he had left ajar, and came closer, her light steps accompanied by the rustle of her cream-coloured pyjama bottoms. She leant a hand on his shoulder but took it back again immediately, stretching it out towards the object sitting on the table. She did not have her contact lenses in and had to hold it practically to her nose before she could be certain that it was, in effect, something new to her: 'What is it?'

The best answer that came to mind was a condensed version of the truth: 'My dad's watch.'

'I've never seen it before. Where did you have it?'

'I found it yesterday.'

'Found it?'

If he tried to play games with her he would only be making it worse for himself, Cédric thought: 'Bought it, actually. In Deauville.'

'You bought your dad's watch in Deauville? I don't follow you ...'

'There was a photo of it on an auction house website. The British Parachute Regiment emblem jumped out at me, because they took part in D-Day – this, see? So I wondered who it had originally belonged to, hoping to find out something interesting. And as it happens ...'

'May I ...?' Sylvie asked him as she sat down on his knees. She listened in silence with the watch in her hand, turning it over from time to time to examine the engravings. Onfray, the *notaire*, Merville, Roger, the auction – his report did not stint on the details. But it was incomplete, inevitably. 'Really? It doesn't sound ... I don't know ... believable.'

'I've got the documents here with me. You can see them, if you want.'

'You could have talked to me about it sooner.'

'I was afraid you'd tell me to let it drop.'

'Why would I have?'

'It cost a lot of money. It's old, to you it probably looks ugly as well. But collectors like this kind of thing.'

'A lot of money?'

'Uh-huh ... From our account.'

'Ah ...' As he awaited the inevitable request for details and, above all, explanations, Cédric wondered how Sylvie would manage to appear credible when she got angry. For starters she would have to get up, as she could hardly have a serious argument with her husband while seated on his knees, and then run to the bathroom to put her contact lenses in, her tender, short-sighted gaze being so unsuited to the circumstances. But actually she did not move, apart from to show him the palm of her hand: 'Tell me tomorrow, how much you spent.'

'Alright. I'm sorry ...'

'And don't make that hangdog face. Maybe if I'd been in your shoes ... what was that?'

'What?'

'A noise. In the hallway.'

'I didn't hear anything,' he said, feeling he could allow himself a white lie after having gotten all that off his chest.

'Then you need to have your ears tested. I'll go and see.'

Cédric took hold of her arm just before she could slip away: 'There's no need. It's Théo.'

'He never goes to the bathroom at night. Have you forgotten

about the bats?'

'He's going to the garage, not the bathroom.'

'And how do you know?'

'He told me himself, when he woke up before. A rendez-vous with Pierre.'

Sylvie's wide-eyed stare told him he had gone too far: 'Have you lost it as well, or have you agreed between yourselves to drive me crazy?'

'He's decided that Pierre's leaving and he wants to see him off.'

'See him off?'

'He promised me it's the last time. If it's not true then I'll take care of it. But if I'm right, then promise to make peace with him.'

'Who said we're at war? I'll be happy when I can cuddle him again.'

'So will he, I'm sure of it. Please ...'

'What?'

'Let him go. It's his birthday ...'

That's not fair, two against one ...' sighed Sylvie, brushing against the mouse as she put the watch back down on the table. The monitor came back to life, showing her the photo. 'Who are they?'

'The first owner of the watch and his friend, the one I met at Deauville. His nephew sent me the photo via email. Look, you can see the watch: I reckon it's this very one.'

'If you say so ... well, I'm going back to bed. As long as you haven't got any other weird stories to tell me.'

Not for now. And probably not the next day. Perhaps never: 'I don't think so. I'll be there in a bit.'

***

As he left the study, Cédric saw him coming back up the stairs and moving cautiously towards him along the hallway, illuminated by the bathroom light. He was wearing basketball socks rather than slippers on his feet. He did not seem afraid, although his eyes opened wide when he spotted his father.

'How did it go?' Cédric whispered to him.

'They left ... I think.'

'You think?'

'I wanted to wait, but he sent me to bed.'

A good job. He did not need to be there to help them check their parachutes and weapons, laugh at their jokes, salute them one by one as they got aboard the plane, watch their Dakota climb up towards the faint moon hung by a cable from the peeling concrete ceiling, or wait until he could hear the rumble of the engines no more. He could do that before he fell asleep. Or right afterwards. 'He's right. You've got to rest.'

'... the faint moon hung by a cable from the peeling concrete ceiling...'

'That's what he said.'

'Goodnight, then.'

'Dad?'

'Yes?'

'When's he coming back?'

The same question. *His* question, repeated a thousand times, until Mum had set aside her answers about heaven, which Cédric no longer listened to, and had taken refuge in a sad smile; until he had abandoned the nightly ritual of those early times, closing his eyes and pretending to be asleep the moment his head was on the pillow, convinced that a few minutes later he would hear his bedroom door open and his father stroke his cheek with his fingers to wake him up, to tell him goodnight, to say sorry for having gone off without saying goodbye and promise he would never do so again. When's he coming back? Jane must have wondered the same thing, but she knew that no one could give her the answer because she was no longer a child. But Théo was. And so had Cédric been, all those years ago. At that age there were no one-way journeys, nor convincing explanations. He could only play for time: 'I don't know. Did you ask him?'

'He said it didn't depend on him.'

'He's a soldier, he has to follow orders.'

'And then ... what did he mean, that his work here was done?'

'That he had completed his mission, I imagine.'

'What mission?'

'Why do you think he came to us?'

'To play with me.'

'... and to help you.'

'I'm the one who helped him. I got his friends ready and took them to him.'

'... by going along the hallway at night. You hadn't done that in a year. It was him that convinced you.'

'I know, but ...'

'Then he showed you how to help me. We can't ask any more of him, can we?'

'No ... but I want him to come back.'

Words were no longer enough – this needed action. Or something like it: 'Me too. I've got an idea. Do you know what we'll do? We'll wait for him together.'

'Wait for him?'

'Tomorrow night, after the party. We'll sit in the car and wait for him in the garage. If everything goes well tonight, perhaps he'll find the time to drop in and wish us a happy birthday. What do you say?' Cédric had never seen him like that: it was hard to say whether he was more incredulous or joyful, too shaken to reply. True happiness was beyond the power of words, but Cédric had no need for explanations to know what was going through Théo's head. Adults were predictable, they did not lift a finger unless it was for a good reason; his parents too, always with something to do, never a second to lose. Dad would never dream of spending an evening or a night in a car, waiting for someone who might never even show up, so there could be no doubt – he would be back. 'Well? What do you think?'

'Yes!'

'Good. But he won't like it if he finds out you didn't follow orders.'

'...?'

'He told you to get some rest, I thought.'

Théo disappeared into his bedroom without another word, le-aving the door ajar behind him, and turned on the lamp on his bedside table, the glow visible through the crack. But it went out again almost right away. What about the nightlight? He must have forgotten to plug it in. That, or he no longer needed it.

29. 6 JUNE 2014, 10:13

He had hated these moments for months. The ding-dong of the doorbell, ringing out clearly from behind the closed door, was an alarm, announcing the subtle anxiety that rose from his stomach and then swelled, jamming somewhere halfway up his neck. Cédric tried to anticipate the verdict by listening carefully to the approaching footsteps – quick and decisive or slow and dragging? – so that he would not be surprised when, at the click of the key turning in the lock, he found out what sort of a Sunday it would be. He wondered about it every week as he walked with unnecessary slowness along the second floor hallway of the reinforced-cement block of flats, as though battling against a headwind. Since when? He could remember neither the day nor the month, had purposefully removed the date from his memory, given that he could not get rid of the rest of it. A Sunday morning visit, with Théo along too – unusually glum, but Cédric had been sure his grandmother's attentions would soon sort that out. And Théo had indeed perked up the moment he saw the table had already been laid, cup ready to be filled with hot chocolate and two slices of cake on a small dish – they had not eaten breakfast at home, on Sundays they had it at Grandma's. He, on the other hand, had stopped dead. What was that grey patch in the middle of her head, a silvery puddle that seemed to be growing before his very eyes, swallowing up what little remained of the bronze-coloured dye? They had skipped their usual visit the week before because Théo's team had played a match in Menton, but what could have happened in those fifteen days?

'What's the matter with your hair?' Cédric had asked, unable to stop himself, as Mum poured the hot chocolate.

'The dye wasn't making me any younger, so I decided to stop.'

Cédric had tried, without success, to look elsewhere as he rolled up the edges of a napkin and inserted them into the collar at the back of Théo's neck. Small, worn out and as fragile as the shaking hand with which she held the teapot, the grey of her hair seemed to be reflected in everything: her eyebrows, her eyes, her lips, her wrinkles. Seventy-five years old: a few minutes before it had been just a number, but now it was a question. How many more Sunday morning visits would there be? How many years before her hand stopped shaking? She had sat down next to them, too short of breath, and watched Théo biting into a slice of cake as though she were witnessing a miracle taking place. Never before, as an adult, had Cédric been invaded by such a strong feeling of despondency. He had stood up, announcing he would leave her alone with Théo for ten minutes while he went to get a newspaper.

'But you never buy the Sunday paper ...'

'Today I want to, there's a car section.'

He had slipped outside without so much as a nod to Théo and practically run down the stairs, ignoring the lift – with no wish to run into any of the neighbours, even five seconds' wait would be too long. Once outside, on the pavement, he had managed to calm down. Somewhat. 'Everything alright?' an old man had asked him as he walked past with a dog on a lead.

'... Yes, thank you. Nothing to worry about.' It had touched him, the interest shown by that passing stranger in his Sunday best, and he had had to make an effort to ignore the cliché: the good manners of yesteryear, a teenager would simply have walked on by without a second glance, and so forth.

He had approached his car, parked in front of the building, and used the back window as a mirror. What he had seen staring back at him had convinced him to extend his walk – he could not very well go back with a face like that, reddened eyes wide like a zombie's. Mum would only have worried about him and bombarded him with questions, transmitting her own anxieties to Théo.

'And the paper?' she had asked him when he had reappeared in the doorway twenty minutes later.

'Too late. They had run out even at the *Maison de la Presse*.' He and Théo had stayed a bit longer than usual. His desperation had passed but the anguish remained. Still, he would have to learn to live with it, and the sooner he started the better.

The trouble was that there did not appear to be any remedy for the torment of those moments spent standing in front of the door, caught between fearing for the worst and hoping for nothing new, the only conceivable 'good news.' As he listened to the metallic sound of the key in the lock he felt as though he had a pistol pointed to his temple, his own personal game of Russian Roulette.

But not today. There it was, his birthday present: she was more relaxed than he had seen her for weeks, happy even. Because of the party – Théo's more than his, no doubt. Her face was expressive as it always was on her best days, emotions written across it in clear lettering, the worn out background deprived of importance. 'Here already? And Théo?'

'Asleep. He was up til late last night.'

'You did the right thing to leave him in bed, today's his day. But you ...?'

'I don't sleep much – I'm getting old. So I thought I'd come over a bit earlier. The problem is you make me feel even older. You look great.'

The usual Sunday morning joke, but this time it was not merely a way of getting her to crack a tried smile, the quickness of her riposte confirming it to him: 'Enough of your cheek. Sit down while I get ready.'

'Take your time, I told Sylvie we'd be there about lunch time.

Any coffee left?'

'In the kitchen, on the hob.'

The tepid pot was another good omen: the day had gotten off to a good start and would continue in the same vein. Now it was down to him. What to say, how to say it, when to say it. He had been thinking about it for days and had changed his strategy a hundred times. In the end he had given up: something would come to him when the time was right. But the time was right now, and nothing had come to him. Cédric dug down into the cup with a teaspoon as though hoping to find it on the bottom, where the coffee-soaked sugar had accumulated. When he had been small he used to like doing the same thing with Mum's cup, a habit before he went off to school, turning over the dark sludge to release its aroma, tasting it a few grains at a time. She had turned a blind eye – what harm could such an infinitesimal dose of caffeine do him? The taste of home. Cédric placed the handle of the teaspoon across the rim of the cup, as a reminder – that way he could begin again later on – and unfastened the strap around his wrist.

'This one or this one?' his mother's voice broke his contemplation, which had as little to do with wanting to know what time it was as it had for the last two days. In her right hand was a coat hanger with a black blouse, opaque floral designs on a shiny background; in her left, a pink one, pearl-grey neckline matching the thin stripes across it.

'It's a birthday party, not a funeral. And you're too young to dress up like a crow. If you ask me you can burn the black one.'

She feigned resentment, another ritual of her best days: 'No colour is more elegant. But what would you know? I'd do better to ask Sylvie.'

'Phone her, if you don't trust my judgement.'

'She's got too much to do. And you've left her to it, as usual.'

'I had a good reason to make myself scarce.'

'And what would that be?'

'My favourite Mum.'

'Using me as an excuse … hang your head in shame. Why not

tell me about Caen?'

'The bookshop was full. A lot of youngsters, you can see the subject of the war is still quite current. And that Wilkins is an amazing guy, he really knows his stuff. Normal enough: he's a history teacher like me ...'

'And the family? Did you see them?'

'I didn't have time, but it doesn't matter. They're coming here for Christmas. But I did find something. Why don't you sit down a minute? There's no rush ...'

As he watched her hooking the coat hangers onto the doorhandle, Cédric wondered whether a distraction and a few minutes alone would be long enough to get rid of the black blouse. 'What do you think?' he asked her, placing the watch on the table, the strap doubled up behind the case.

She threw a quick glance at it and raised her eyes, curious. Curious, but no more than that: 'What should I say?'

'I've just bought it. Have a good look at it. The back, too.'

'Looks old ...'

'Just old?' Cédric kept his gaze fixed on her, not wanting to miss a single bat of her eyelids or quiver of her lips, ready to take in the moment when no more questions would be necessary. But her reaction, after she had turned the watch over, reminded him there was no need for such an effort. Mum had never been able to hide her emotions: she tended to go pale, like him. And now she was clearly in such a state that he felt a pang of remorse. He should have prepared her for a shock, not subjected her to an interrogation.

'Where ...?' she asked, an almost imperceptible whisper escaping her lips.

'In Deauville, in an auction. It cost a bomb, but I'm happy. And I hope you are, too. It was by pure chance. I saw it on the internet.' As with Sylvie, it was not the whole story. The rest of it only mattered for him. And Théo.

'Your present ...'

'Present?'

'He always said he was going to give it to you as a school leaving present. You would have had it on your wrist for ... how long? Twenty-six years ago – today you turn forty-four.'

'But he sold it.'

'Who told you?'

'The buyer's heir, a *notaire* from Caen. But I would have preferred to hear it from you.'

'Dad didn't want to, it was humiliating. There was no reason to go back over it after ... You would never have found out about it.'

'Well you can tell me now, at any rate.'

'There's not much to tell. He always wore it, his father had left it to him, and it would have been handed down to you. Then he got sick, he had to leave his job. They were hard times, what else could he have done?'

'And Grandad? They gave me a certificate of donation with the watch ...'

'They wanted to thank him for his help. It's written in his diary; you weren't supposed to see it because it also talks about the watch, but ...'

'What diary?'

'Your grandfather's. It tells the story of what happened during those months, when he was a partisan ...'

'You've had Grandad's diary all this time and kept it hidden from me?'

'I told you that ...'

'Mum! You know what job I do, don't you? I've just translated a book about the Battle of Normandy, one day or another I'd like to write one myself. What's written in that diary ...' he was secure in his convictions but fell silent all the same, and not only because he disliked berating people, which he was not in the habit of doing, much less when the person in question was his mother; it was also his mother's smile that cut him short, more pleased than apologetic.

'... You already know it.'

'What?'

'What the diary says. Except for the watch.'

'What do you mean?'

'Maybe you don't remember, you were little. But you were already like a fussy old historian, you used to ask me if it was all true or if I was making bits up.'

'I only asked once. And you changed the subject.'

'But it was the truth, what I used to tell you.'

'The truth ...'

'If you don't believe me, check. The diary's in my room, I'll go and get it.'

She could at least pretend to be sorry, he thought as he watched her walk away. Thirty-five years of half-truths and she seemed pleased, even rejuvenated, convinced she had nothing to apologise for, the very picture of innocence. Cédric put the watch back on his wrist, traced a circle on the bottom of the cup with his teaspoon and smiled, imagining a scene that would have been taboo during her darkest days, too realistic to provide the subject material for a joke: Mum standing at the gates of heaven with Saint Peter quizzing her about why she ought to be let in, and her answering that she had always told the truth, the whole truth, *more or less*.

The blouses were still hanging on the door handle. There was now a moral justification, as well as an aesthetic one: the hateful black silk would burn to placate Cédric' indignation. But he hesitated. He himself had not told the whole truth. Before he could make a decision, Mum was back again: 'Here it is. Take a look while I get dressed.' The glance with which Cédric responded must have been unmistakable: as she gathered up the coat hangers, she added: 'Alright, I'll put the pink one on.'

30. 6 JUNE 2014, 11:04

The hour of battle draws near / The die is cast

These were the first words Cédric came upon, written where the bindings of the brown-covered notebook were becoming so frayed they were almost falling to pieces. Perhaps Grandad had copied them beneath the date 27 May because even in his day that had been the first page to meet a reader's eye when opening it; a way of memorising the words, so that he would recognise them when the time came. The signal had arrived on 1 June, while he sat with his ear virtually glued to the radio he had hidden in the attic to avoid the requisition ordered by the Germans months earlier. The transmission from the BBC, in French, had begun with the usual personal messages, dozens of coded communiqués to the various Resistance groups. But this time, as well as informing listeners that 'Clémentine may tend to her teeth' and that 'the carrots are cooked', the announcer of *Radio Londres* had recited the first part of the most eagerly anticipated phrase of all: *The hour of battle draws near* ... Jean-Jacques had not said anything to his wife – too soon. And it had in fact been another four days before the announcer had given the confirmation: ... *The die is cast*.

The scene was so vivid that Cédric had the impression he was a spectator in a theatre, watching from a seat in the front row, right beneath the stage. Jean-Jacques hurtling down the stairs and bursting into little Clément's bedroom, interrupting the story Colette had been telling in an attempt to send him off to sleep and make him forget his empty belly. Her sensing what it was without having to ask, reading in her husband's eyes a phrase that had become almost unsayable after years of waiting in vain: *they're coming*. This time it was real. *They're coming*. In a few hours' time. Not the end of the darkness, not yet, but the beginning of the end. And the chance, or rather the duty, to earn that first glimmer of light. Grandad had known for days what he would do, the morning after the announcement came: cycle a dozen kilometres to pick up a piece of paper, take off the saddle and insert the rolled-up message into the slanting tube, take it to the usual recipient. Without reading the contents, as always, even though it was not hard to imagine what they were: instructions specifying which objectives were to be sabotaged in the hours immediately following the invasion, a stretch of road or railway, a power or telephone line.

Stories Cédric had already heard, his mother had assured him. But now it was different. He was touching them on the yellowed pages, rumpled by damp; could feel their roughness as though he were travelling in a car without suspension, thrown this way and that by the lurching commentary of a railwayman turned amateur war correspondent who described life from the point of view of the French during those weeks, a frenetic roller-coaster ride of fears, hopes and disappointments, undulating lines of text behind which seemed to be hiding an outlaw, forced to write quickly and interrupt his work at the faintest of sounds from outside. The wording was laboured but the information was exhaustive and meticulous; every day a fresh page, with the date at the top.

Mum had switched on the television in her room. It kept her company while she sat in front of the mirror brushing her hair, but the list of strikes did not reach Cédric's ears, drowned out by the crackle of automatic weapons. Perhaps Grandad had been more bewildered than surprised, finding himself caught in the crossfire as he passed a crossroads pockmarked with holes, the roll of paper hidden inside the bicycle frame. Stopping would be even riskier than going on, he had told himself, and so he had kept pedalling until he spotted the group of armed men in camouflage uniforms crouching at the bottom of a hole gouged out by an exploding bomb, shouting at him animatedly in English. Already here? Was that possible? He had put his bike down at the roadside, got down into the crater with them and tried to make himself useful by warning them about the detachment guarding the village, but the officer looked as though he did not trust him. Resistance members could not wear anything to distinguish themselves, not yet.

One of the British soldiers had jumped out and sprinted to a ruined house a hundred metres further on, in front of the crossroads. It was under fire, apparently from the church bell tower. Jean-Jacques had had no choice but to stop: it was not possible to go on, the Germans would have shot him the moment he poked his head out of the hole A short time later he had seen thirty or so camouflaged soldiers leap out of the ground floor windows and run along the opposite side of the road before crossing over and throwing themselves into the crater. The last man had landed right on top of him, knocking him flying like a skittle and almost breaking his shoulder. Jean-Jacques had got to his knees, the right leg of the best pair of trousers he had left soaked in dark sludge, and had been struck by the sight and gaze of the man who had fallen on him, looking up at him from the bottom of the hole with his sky-blue coloured eyes: tall, well-built and young, no more than eighteen years old, he seemed to be wondering – and asking Jean-Jacques – whether he was wounded. Grandad had rushed to reassure him, and then the officer had arrived and ordered him to stand up. When the last man of the group, who had stayed behind to cover the others, reached the crater, they had all headed off rapidly towards the start of the road that led into the village, the same road he would have to go along.

Cédric smiled, thinking of Roger, who had wanted to shake

Grandad by the hand. In actual fact he had done one better, even if the introduction had not exactly followed the rules of etiquette. Why had Mum not ever told him about this meeting, or rather collision? The explanation came a few lines later.

As the British troops were pulling back, Jean-Jacques had spotted the glint of a metal object half buried among the rubble, at the bottom of the crater. He had reached out, and the object his hand brought back was not a bullet but a watch. One of the soldiers must have dropped it because there was a symbol engraved on the steel, like the emblem on their uniforms. He had tried to get their attention, shouting and holding the watch aloft in his left hand. The last one in the line was the boy who, after turning around and signalling him to be quiet, had continued on his way. And so Grandad had pocketed the watch and taken shelter in the crater, waiting for the Germans to cease fire.

'Halt!' The order, accompanied by a burst of machine-gun fire aimed skywards, had reached him after he had left the crater, while he was picking the bicycle back up off the ground. Five Germans came towards him on foot, preceded by a halftrack, its small cannon poking out from the steel shield behind the driver. The officer leading the patrol looked like a mastiff: stocky build, short steps and questions barked out one after another without waiting for the answers which, since he did not understand a single word, Grandad could not have given even if he had wanted to. Would they try to make themselves understood or simply shoot him out of hand? That would still be preferable to them finding the note, because then he would be handed over to the Gestapo or the French thugs of the *Hervé* gang, and a so-called interrogation expert would take care of him: fingernails ripped out, bones shattered by hammer blows and electric shocks to his testicles, the usual treatment – his recruiters had warned him when he had entered the organisation – employed to overcome suspects' reticence. Before a firing squad, whether he talked or not, wound things up. A shame he did not have a weapon – that way he could shoot first, forcing them to return fire and sparing himself the torture. Either way he was dead, he had thought. Without another chance to see his wife and son but convinced that in that crater, along with the muddy water that had soiled his trousers, he had met the first droplets of the storm that would sweep away the Boche.

Cédric tore himself away. His teeth were clenched, but it was not the pain in his jaw that was bothering him. It was the voice inside him that continued to ask, with each moment he spent reading the story of those years: Who would he have been? A hero? A villain? One of the many who tried simply to survive? It was too easy to shrug it off, answering, 'A hero, of course – what else?' How could he be sure of it, without having lived through the hunger, the fear, the worry for a father, brother, wife, son or friend? That was why it had never been merely a chapter in the history books or his family's past. As hard as he tried to put himself in others' shoes, he would never really know how he would have acted, when faced with the supreme test. Grandad, on the other hand, had passed it and then some, without knowing first what fate had in store for him: a quick end, an atrocious death or an improbable salvation.

He knew a dozen words of German and only one complete sentence: '*Ich verstehe nicht*', 'I don't understand.' He had repeated it in vain two or three times before one of the soldiers turned to the officer and offered to interpret. Probably saving his life. What was he doing there? Where had he come from? Where was he going? What had the enemy said to him? Where were they headed? It went on and on, putting him to the test, so that they could arrest him at the first contradiction. He had gone to the village to borrow some tools, he had explained, knowing the local carpenter would back up his story: it had been him who, along with the message, had handed him the bundle he was carrying round his neck, where he had placed a hammer, a rusty saw and a couple of screwdrivers. He had not seen the paratroopers, he had added – he had only noticed them once he had dived into the crater. Paratroopers?, the officer had interrupted: how did

272

he know they were paratroopers? The wings on the sleeves of their uniforms, he had answered, adding a few details he hoped might earn him the slightest hint of leniency: he had been threatened, if he dared move or even so much as draw breath he would be shot. His inquisitor had not looked

'... the wings on the sleeves of their uniforms...'

inclined to sympathy: how many of them were there? Thirty or so, he had lied, but he would not have been able to say whether there were more in the surrounding area; they had made off along the road, weapons pointed straight at him.

All of a sudden he had remembered and his heart had begun to race: the watch! What would happen if they found it on him, with the parachute clearly visible on the case? How could he explain that? The only possible justification was the truth, but even to him it sounded somewhat fanciful. One of the soldiers had bent down to pick up the bike and seated himself on the saddle. 'Nice ...' he had commented loudly after turning the pedals a couple of times. At least that was all in order: Grandad had the receipt in his pocket that they had given him after the 1943 survey. 'May I ...?' he had asked the officer, who had looked at him for a long time, a face like thunder, perhaps torn between the urge to shoot him and unease regarding a future which he knew was close at hand, and where he might well be called to answer for his actions. Finally, he had turned on his heels, walking away towards the half-track. Jean-Jacques had not dared to move until the German with the bicycle had held it out to him and the makeshift interpreter told him to move along – quickly, because if there was a second run-in he would not be so lucky again.

He had pedalled non-stop through the fields for a dozen kilometres or so, along uncared-for trails, steering well clear of the busiest roads, until he reached his contact, a small, middle-aged man with metal-rimmed glasses who he knew only as Philippe and who had looked out of place waiting for him by a barn, smoking a cigarette, with the air more of an office worker than a warrior. He had handed over the scrap of paper and left him without a word, as always. Conversation was forbidden: even a seemingly insignificant detail, divulged and noted in the course of a friendly chat, might risk giving the entire network away if either one of them were to be captured.

It was ten o'clock. A few hours earlier, as he was making his way out of the city, Grandad had heard the explosions and turned around: an air raid against the station. He could make out the bombs, little black dots falling away from the bellies of the aircraft and dropping faster and faster until they vanished into the smoke. He had wondered what would become of Michel and Valentin, the two colleagues he should have been on duty with on the platforms that morning, and hoped they had had time to run for cover. In any case he would not turn up for work and the next day he would stop in at the office to hand over one of the certificates Doctor Debailly gave him with no questions asked, leaving the space for the date blank. He had suspected the reason for those absences, but approved of them enough to run the risk.

If he had not realised it in the village, Grandad would have noticed something important was going on in the semi-deserted streets of Caen, where the queues in front of the shops were shorter than usual and the loudspeakers fixed on top of the few cars driving through the city were advising citizens to stay in their homes. The morning cloud and smoke from the air raid had thinned, letting the sun shine down and illuminate a tranquil scene that none of the passers-by seemed to trust. Instead of going back home, Jean-Jacques had extended his journey by going to visit the farm where his parents-in-law lived, in Eterville, a few kilometres south-west of the city. A surprise visit, as always, but the reason was implicit. Whenever they came by a little extra food, which sometimes happened in the countryside, they held onto it for him, hiding it on the cellar floor, behind the shelves that held the emp-

'... the farm where his parents-in-law lived...'

ty, dusty demijohns that had once been used for aging wine.

The first time they had shown him the hiding place, he had spotted a solution to his diary problem. Keeping it at home had become too risky, after the bomb had gone off at the station and some of his colleagues had been arrested. Better to keep it hidden – if he could no longer update it every day then so be it. That afternoon he had promised to put everything back as it was once he had washed the dirty laundry he had brought from home, where the water supply was unreliable, but the moment he had found himself alone he had abandoned the underwear and shirts in the stone washtub to go back down to the cellar and examine the wall more carefully. The rusty penknife he always carried with him had been enough to dig into the mortar and remove a couple of the loose-fitting pebbles at about knee-height. That would be the notebook's hiding place. And the explanation, Cédric thought, for the moisture-damaged pages.

It had seemed like a good idea. If the Germans had moved the shelves, they would have found no more than a package with a little flour inside, an egg, a handful of beans, a piece of cured meat if they were lucky, and taken it away. But they would not suspect something else might be hidden there, thirty centimetres further up the wall. Once he had put the pebbles back in place to conceal the niche, anyone would have been hard pushed to notice the difference between it and the rest of the wall – Grandad was a natural born handyman. His superiors had christened him Mister Fix-it, and every time they had a problem – which was often, now that spare parts were almost impossible to come by – they went to him. The only difficulty, during his successive visits, had been convincing the householders that he did not need any help and was perfectly able to do it by himself, picking up the provisions after he had emptied the shelves, and then pushing them back against the wall again. After a bit of hesitation they had accepted this arrangement, partly due to Colette's father's bad back, and he had always had ten minutes or so alone to write. Once his mother-in-law had walked in on him, sitting on the floor, his back leaning up against the niche. He had slipped the diary under his jacket, explaining that he had had to sit down because his head was spinning, but that he was already feeling better because he had eaten a little of the sugar they had left there. A short time later, as he put everything back in its place, he had asked himself whether he was doing the right thing. He was putting them in danger, two innocent people. Would they have been able to convince their interrogators, if it came to that? He liked to hope they would, but another doubt had joined the apprehension he was already feeling during those months, giving him sleepless nights.

On 6 June it had been easy enough to dig away a few more centimetres of space at the back of the niche. The watch had gone in behind the diary, wrapped in a handkerchief. Then Grandad had picked up the two eggs his parents-in-law had set aside for him, covering them with newspaper and placing them inside the bundle of tools, before sitting down to record the events of an extraordinary day. The pages of history would baptise it D-Day, but for him, Rommel's definition would turn out to be more fitting: The Longest Day. As he was writing, he could not have imagined that the coming hours would be even harder than those he had just lived through, nor that he would come back to the diary again so soon, on the evening of 7 June, anxious to set down on paper all he had seen, partly so he could really believe it himself and partly because he simply needed to let it out.

The drone of bombers and the explosions from Caen, at half past one, while he had still been at the farm; the fear for his family as he pedalled towards the smoke that blotted out the horizon, rent by flashes and flame; the anger he had felt at an improvised road-block, where a couple of Germans had closed the road and were turning back anyone who tried to pass; the decision to attempt it anyway, until he had found a lane that had been left unguarded; the route through collapsing walls and deafening roars; the suffocating, yellow dust; the horror of a charred corpse atop a stretcher borne by two priests; his arrival at Rue de la Fontaine, where the *Monoprix* and the school had looked like immense torches; his relief at finding the house intact and, flinging open the front door, the bump beneath the mattress, laid out at the foot of the thickest wall. Little Clément was underneath it, curled up amongst the cushions, and when his father had lifted it up to take a look he had not seemed terrified, merely worried that Mum was not there with him. Where had Colette gone? Jean-Jacques had run upstairs and found her dragging another mattress along the floor, towards the stairs. He had given her a hand and then they had both taken shelter on the ground floor, holding their son tightly against them as they waited for a let up in the bombing.

'There'll be no city left to liberate if they go on like this,' Colette had muttered, while Grandad was making a decision: they would have to escape and take shelter at his father-in-law's house, even if that meant making their way through the city-centre while the bombs were still falling, as well as missing an important rendezvous. 'Let Simone come too!' she had begged – their neighbour and Colette's best friend, in her ninth month of pregnancy, with her husband François. The moment he heard the sound of the latest wave of aircraft dying away, Grandad had left the house to look for a means of transport. A tough job: petrol was reserved for the Germans and for essential services. But an hour later he had come back again, sitting atop a van next to the baker's errand boy, the satisfied Mister Fix-it smile of a man who had just pulled off his most memorable feat. They had loaded their hurriedly-packed suitcases onto the vehicle and taken more than an hour to get out of the city, craters and rubble forcing them to change their route continually, while on Boulevard Bertrand they had been forced to travel at walking speed in order to avoid the terrified people running across the road in search of shelter; overhead, low-flying fighters were darting through the sky, looking for German positions to attack.

Once they reached the farm, all five of them had gone to the barn. There they had passed a sleepless night accompanied by the echoes of Caen's devastation and the passage of motorised columns, forced to move during the hours of darkness because they were too easy a target for Allied planes by day. The following morning, in spite of Colette's attempts to dissuade him, Grandad had wanted to return home to pick up the bicycle, which he had forgotten there in the rush to leave, hoping for a break in the bombardment that had lasted almost until dawn. Seven kilometres on foot through the fields, a bothersome journey but safer than taking the roads.

As he was passing a tumbledown house, he had heard a shout in English. There were ten or so of them in khaki uniforms and Tommy helmets, hiding in the ruins; they had spotted him and were gesturing for him to approach. What were they doing behind enemy lines? It would not have surprised him to learn they were lost, given that he had heard conflicting rumours about what was going on. The baker's errand boy had informed them that the Allies were consolidating their bridgehead. No, François had cut in: they had been thrown back into the sea, according to a policeman he had run into that morning. Both wrong, a neighbour of his parents-in-law had assured them: the landings on the nearby beaches were taking place to distract the Germans from the real invasion, which would begin shortly in the area around Calais.

The officer in charge spoke French. He had asked where he was headed and whether he had any information regarding German troop positions in the area. So the British knew where they were: they were a patrol, charged with reporting on enemy movements. Jean-Jacques had offered to go and take a look. They had agreed to meet two hours later in the same place, and then Grandad had set out again towards Caen.

A walk through hell. Among the piles of rubble of Arthur Leduc Boulevard, he had spotted what at first looked like a bundle of rags soaked in blood, but which had something inside it. Fragments of corpses, he had realised with horror, looking away and quickening his step, but slowing down again immediately to contemplate the surreal spectacle of one of the few buildings that had been left standing, deprived of its façade and sliced open from top to bottom like a dolls' house. A torn curtain flapped open repeatedly as the wind dug its way through the ruins, clinging onto its brass rail as though hoping to protect what little was left of the home's violated privacy. Through the gap one could glimpse charred roof beams, a washbasin still attached to an intact section of wall, a picture with its glass smashed to pieces, tubes and wires sticking out of what remained of floors and ceilings.

A little further on two boys from the *Equipes d'Urgence* were tending to a victim who had just been pulled from the rubble, while a colleague of theirs scattered quicklime over what had looked to Grandad like two corpses. When he had drawn nearer he had realised there was just one, cut in half: only the clothing revealed that it had been a woman. Within certain limits it had been possible to avoid looking, but there was no defence against the smell, despite the handkerchief he had tied over his nose. Jean-Jacques had been afraid he would faint in the street, where they might have mistaken him too for one of the air raid victims. But the sight of the bicycle propped up against the wall had given him heart. Both the bike and the house were still intact, an inexplicable miracle among the ruins of a street that had almost been bombed out of existence.

The detritus had impeded his movement, piles of shattered bricks that he circled around or climbed over, bike slung over his shoulder. He had looked around himself as he went, trying to memorise the positions of the few visible artillery pieces and armoured vehicles; it was hard to keep his bearings, with the city's landmarks no longer as recognisable as they had been. Once, as he turned onto the only passable boulevard he had encountered since returning to the city, there had been a frightening moment: a column of four trucks headed by a Panzer and a vanguard of three helmetless SS troops in camouflage uniform and rolled-up sleeves had been moving along it, and the men had pointed their weapons at him the moment they saw him appear from the side street. Grandad had had the impression that there would be no warning shots this time and had backed up, pedalling a few dozen metres before stopping to get his breath back, sprawling across the handlebars and amazed he was still alive: perhaps the Boche were under orders not to waste ammunition.

He had arrived almost on time at the rendezvous, but there was nobody inside the ruined building. Forced to retreat, captured, killed? Grandad had sat down, exhausted, to allow himself a short respite before continuing on his way. As a boy he had dreamt of becoming a real cyclist, a professional. In the diary there was not a trace of this fantasy, shattered by the war. Cédric only knew it because his mother had spoken to him about it once and, while he read, he tried to guess at the thoughts that would have crossed his minds during those moments of dismay, his attempts to forget about the horrors he had witnessed, to imagine himself at the finishing line of the Paris-Roubaix race, arms raised, standing atop a podium, a bunch of flowers clasped in his hands. Instead there had been no race and no training, just the wrong sport. Kilometres of cross-country cycling across ditches, craters and mountains of rubble, searching for the right route and knowing that the wrong one might lead him into the path of a bomb or a bullet, until he reached his finishing line: a ruined cottage, its split flagstone floor covered in fallen tiles, the stump of a beam left propped against the only wall that stood higher than two metres, the broken tube of a boiler his winner's trophy. And all that for nothing: the British had vanished.

Bonjour, Monsieur. There he was: Jean-Jacques had spotted him only when he had appeared at his back, from behind a wall. 'I left my men by the crossroads. That's the only place cars and motorbikes can get past.' Clearly he did not trust Grandad, and before approaching he had wanted to make sure the Frenchman had not betrayed them by bringing a platoon of German soldiers along with him. 'I am Major Landon Roach.

Roach! *The* Roach? The donation certificate was at home, in his desk drawer, but Cédric did not need to check. The rank was correct and so was the surname. On top of that, there was another coincidence that he only noticed now: the first name, Landon, like Grandad's English friend that Mum had mentioned in her stories. The same person? And what did he have to do with the watch that had been picked up the day before, fifteen kilometres away? The diary did not tell him.

Upon reaching the farm, there had been two surprises for Jean-Jacques. The Germans had positioned a machine-gun outside the front of the house, forcing his parents-in-law and everyone else to take shelter on the opposite side of the building, in the dining room. And there was a new guest: Simone's newborn baby, who had been delivered with Colette's help a few hours earlier and was fast asleep on his mother's chest. She was lying on the ground, very pale, on top of a thick blanket they had used as a makeshift mattress. 'How did you know what to do?' Grandad had asked his wife.

'Experience.'

'What experience? You're a seamstress.'

'I had a baby as well, you know.'

Passing information to the British was dangerous, he had thought, but it was easier than assisting at a birth, for him at any rate.

As evening fell the Germans had moved off with their machine-gun and the group had taken back possession of the barn. Jean-Jacques had had time to allow himself a visit to the cellar to update his diary, certain that no one would disturb him: Simone and her son were the centre of attention, her breast-feeding a public ritual in which all of them, Colette included, tried to find some sign of hope for the future.

How could he get back in contact with his comrades in the organisation? The answer lay in a farmstead at Le Mesnil, a few kilometres away, but that would include risking both his own safety and that of those who lived there. Jean-Jacques had heard about the owner of the place because he had helped Michel, his best friend, to avoid forced labour in Germany and had pointed him in the direction of certain acquaintances of his who were 'driven by a strong sense of patriotism', the very same people with whom he himself would then come into contact with. It was said that a few Allied airmen shot down over Normandy had found refuge on the farm, but Grandad had thought that impossible given that the Germans had been there since 1940. 'I'm going to Richier's,' he had mumbled to Colette, after taking her to one side. 'Maybe they'll have a bit of bread for us, too. Don't say anything to the others, no point getting their hopes up.' A nod of agreement confirmed his wife had understood the real reason for his visit.

Once within sight of the main building, already partway along the dirt track leading up to it, his first impulse had been to get away again as quickly as possible. A large, open-top car was moving towards him, occupying the entire width of the trail, headlights on even though it was not yet dark. There was no need to wait to see if its occupants were German: nobody else had the means to travel in a vehicle like that. If he had given in to the temptation to turn back he would be in trouble because they had already seen him, he thought, and so he had stood to one side at the edge of the road. There were only two of them, a driver and an officer in the back seat, and they had not even deigned to give him a second glance; in fact they had accelerated away the moment they were past him.

'My name is Roussel,' he had said to the middle-aged woman who opened the door, presumably Mrs Richier. 'I took refuge at Eterville during today's first air raid. There are eight of us ... I was wondering whether maybe you had a little bread.'

'Come in,' she had replied, keeping a certain distance despite her politeness: in those days it was hard to trust strangers.

Three men were sitting around the kitchen table, one of them in his forties and the other two somewhat younger, and they had looked up at him. Grandad had been struck by how much they looked like him, not only in their thinness but also the way they were dressed. The uniform of the French living under occupation: drab colours, shirts with threadbare cuffs and collars, crumpled trousers, shoes with worn out uppers.

'Good evening, I'm Philippe Richier,' the middle-aged one had said, standing up to shake the newcomer's hand. His hair had turned prematurely grey.

'Jean-Jacques Roussel. I'm a friend of Michel's.'

'Michel?'

'The one who asked for your help last year, to avoid a trip abroad. We really see eye to eye with each other.'

'Eye to eye?'

'On everything. Except cheese. He hates Livarot.'

'He isn't a good Norman, then,' one of the other two had cut in, his eyes dark and penetrating, stubble covering his chin.

'The important thing is he's a good Frenchman.'

'True,' his new interlocutor had smiled. 'Welcome to the club.'

He had passed the test. When they had taught him the sequence of lines he had found them pretty ridiculous, but now he was relieved he could remember them: 'From what I've just seen, this isn't a good moment to talk.'

'If you're referring to mister Richier's unwelcome guest, you can relax. He left with his driver. We are alone, and will remain so for some time, I reckon. Sounds like they need every man they can get down on the coast.' The observation had been accompanied by a venomous grin.

'My friends call me Max. And you ...?'

'Arc-en-ciel. Max? The same Max who took the note to Philippe?'

'Yes, but how ...'

'Sounds like you made it by the skin of your teeth. After all the shooting the carpenter saw you talking to the Boche. At first he suspected something, but then he saw you were in trouble. And Philippe reported that you were almost on time for the meet. Well done.'

'Today I went back for seconds,' Grandad had added, wondering whether 'rainbow' already knew this as well.

'How do you mean?'

'I almost got myself shot by the SS while I was sneaking a look at them in Caen. A British officer I met near here put me up to it. The problem is that yesterday I was supposed to meet up with Tortue. Perhaps you can reach him, tell him where I am, or ...'

'Too late,' Arc-en-ciel had answered, shaking his head.

'What happened?'

'Killed early yesterday afternoon in the air raid. Car took a direct hit.'

'Car?'

'The Gestapo's. They'd just arrested him. Our compatriots who were taking him to Rue des Jacobins died as well. Not much of a consolation.'

In the silence that had followed, Grandad had been certain everyone was thinking the same thing: that for Tortue – an appropriate *nom de guerre*, he had often laughed, given that he had once been the interschool hundred metre champion – it would have been far worse if he had reached the HQ alive. 'What shall I do now? He was the one who gave me instructions, and kept in contact with the others ...'

'I might have an idea ...' Arc-en-ciel had taken the initiative while Richier listened in silence, the third man apparently more interested in his potato and onion soup than in the conversation. 'How do you feel about doing what you did today again? Having a look around where we tell you to and reporting back to the British? Mister Richier will tell you when and where.'

'Fine,' he had answered immediately, dispelling any doubts before Colette's and Clément's faces could come into his mind. He would ponder the risk he was running of leaving a widow and orphan behind only later on, as he was climbing onto his bicycle to return to Eterville, forgetting to pick up the bread Mrs Richier had left for him on a shelf in the hallway, wrapped in a sheet of newspaper.

'Good. Now, allow me to introduce Lieutenant Pickard. He's lost his Spitfire but not the will to fight.' The man eating potatoes and onion had raised his eyes at the sound of his name, almost certainly the first word he had understood since Jean-Jacques had arrived. 'Tomorrow we're going to get him across the lines. I was here to give him instructions. And I've found myself a new informer to boot. Can't do better than that ...'

Grandad had rifled through the meagre English diary stored in his head before saying, hand outstretched: 'Friend.' The Englishman had jumped to his feet and, with a smile that had revealed a row of goofy teeth, had replied with conviction: 'Friend!' So the truth went beyond even what Jean-Jacques had considered to be no more than tall tales: an RAF pilot was staying in Richier's house, right beneath the nose of a German officer and his aide. If someone had told him that, he never would have believed it. On the other hand, who was going to believe him, if he said that he had run into the British three times in two days?

The following morning, Grandad and the others taking shelter at the farm had realised that not even Eterville was safe. The Germans had no choice: they needed to move by daylight as well now, camouflaging cars, motorbikes and armoured vehicles under branches gathered from the woods and leaping clear of them the moment they heard the drone of an approaching fighter. The scene repeated itself a dozen times a day as François and Jean-Jacques looked on; they had started digging a trench in the potato field in front of the farmhouse, and whenever the Germans scattered in search of cover, they threw themselves into it. The low-altitude flypast and bursts of machine-gun fire masked the far off rumble of cannon fire for a few seconds before the column would start out again, generally having to skirt around some smoking hulk or else push one into the ditch, and the two men would go back to shovelling earth. On 9 June they had shuddered at the sight of at least three hundred Canadian prisoners passing along the road, two abreast, escorted by SS troops, clearly proud of their booty. What was going on? And why was Richier taking so long to get in contact? Grandad wanted to know what was happening, not merely to pass on information.

The signal had arrived on 12 June, passed along by one of the hands on the Le Mesnil estate, who had told him to come to the farmstead that evening. The assignment had involved going back to Caen the following morning, taking note of what he could see on the roads and in the city centre, before reporting back to a British officer who was to turn up in civilian clothes on a bicycle. The only detail of the mission that had worried him had been the venue chosen for the meeting: one of the shelters the Germans had dug in the surrounding fields, huts sunken into the earth with their roofs at ground level. Deserted since 6 June, Richier had assured him, but the day before Jean-Jacques had listened to the tale of a tearful mother who had passed by the front of the farm with her family. She had been beside herself because she had convinced her husband that one of those huts would make an ideal shelter. They had left their suitcases and everything they had managed to salvage from the air raid inside, but the following day, when they had returned with their children, they had found the road blocked by an SS patrol, which had sent them away again, without giving them back their suitcases, naturally. Before leaving, Grandad had explained to his parents-in-law and François that he would pass by his house and the Malherbe High School, from where he would attempt to send a message to Besançon's relatives to reassure them.

The miracle had not lasted: not a whiff of smoke could be seen rising from the rubble that had once been his home, meaning the bombs must have destroyed it days earlier. What he had found

'... a twelfth century Benedictine monastery turned into a school...'

after that at Malherbe, a twelfth century Benedictine monastery turned into a school and, now, a homeless shelter, had an apocalyptic air about it. Thousands of refugees had come from every part of the city, drawn by the enormous red crosses painted on the roof and the floor of the courtyard, which, it was hoped, would be enough to save them from the air raids and artillery. People everywhere, many in pyjamas and slippers because they had fled their houses on the night of 6 June, milling around in cellars with three-metre thick walls, in passageways, offices and beneath the portico of the cloister. Classrooms transformed into mortuaries or operating rooms, with tables from the canteen standing in as hospital trolleys, the gardens given over to hurried, improvised burials. Children playing in spite of everything, next to their mothers who were busy preparing meals. Mattresses covered the ground for the sick, the only ones with a right to such luxury – everyone else made do with piles of straw.

Grandad had asked directions from a stretcher bearer drunk on exhaustion, reddened eyes and dust-covered face beneath the helmet of the Civil Defence, who had led him to the so-called post office, a storage room with a table in the middle of it. Behind it, half hidden behind a mountain of paper, sat a boy in a vest – one of the high school students? – who had taken the envelope and thrown it into a canvas sack on the floor. The letter would be sent the next day, he had said; there was no telling when it might reach its destination. Then he had pointed out the notice stuck to the wall behind him. It was an appeal, signed by the local prefect and the mayor, urging citizens to leave the city the day after and seek shelter at Trun, a few dozen kilometres further south, following a road that the Germans would leave free for the exodus. 'What do you reckon?' Grandad had asked. 'Not many will be leaving here,' the boy had answered, 'Most of them are afraid of getting caught out in the open.'

Once outside Malherbe, Grandad had been shocked to note that there were very few Germans about. He had run into the largest group, a dozen at most, in a street that had been partially spared by the bombs. They were not engaged in patrolling the town or consolidating defences, but rather in an activity that the occupiers seemed to find even more enjoyable than torture: plunder. Greedy, methodical and widespread, in spite of the notices posted here and there by the *Feldgendarmerie*, reminding the soldiery that the penalty for looting was immediate execution by firing squad. If it were any more than an empty threat, Jean-Jacques had thought bitterly, then there would have been no need for the Allies because the Boche would have taken care of killing each other. A lampshade, a colander, a threadbare rug, an alarm clock, blankets, sheets and a drawer full of cutlery; all sorts of objects were being stolen from the abandoned houses. Grandad had continued on his way, undisturbed and, in all likelihood, unnoticed by the men of the Wehrmacht as they went back and forth. A few hundred metres further on, he had witnessed a paradoxical scene. In front of the shattered doorway of a warehouse stood two rows of men, practically parallel to one another; one was made up of SS and the other of Civil Defence, and both were passing heavy sacks of flour down the line, a race between competitors who were studiously ignoring one another. The French had won, for a change: the need to feed the refugees at the homeless shelters had spurred them to redouble their efforts, with the result that three sacks were reaching their van in the time the Boche were taking to load two onto their own truck, parked nearby.

I won't have much to tell, Grandad had thought, climbing into his saddle to leave the city centre. He was wrong. As the rubble on the ground had thinned, the number of Germans had increased, until finally he was passing artillery emplacements and armoured columns beyond the city limits. The Panzers, said to be reaping a terrible harvest of British and Canadian tanks, were camouflaged beneath trees and between hedges. They had stopped him several times, sometimes firing a shot in the air, other times asking to see his identification and signalling him to turn back. Grandad had pretended to obey, altering his route until he arrived at the next roadblock, where he would explain that he did not know how to get back to Eterville. This game of hide and seek had continued until the time agreed upon for the rendezvous at the shelter, which really had turned out to be both empty and abandoned.

Roach! There he was again, with a bike even rustier than his own and minus the moustache that he must have considered to be too English, wearing ill-fitting, threadbare civilian clothes. An all-too-realistic disguise, Grandad had thought as he handed over the sheets of paper where he had drawn a rough map signalling the whereabouts of artillery pieces and tanks. When the meeting was over Roach had announced, with an air of satisfaction, that they would see each other again. But they were both running the risk of being shot as spies, a thought Jean-Jacques had done his best to push to the back of his mind as he set out once more towards his temporary home.

Indeed, they had met each other twice more. The first occasion had been 18 June, when Grandad had explained to François that he was going out to look for some means of transport: they had to flee like the inhabitants of the nearby villages, where the barrage of artillery had become more or less constant. He had not found a vehicle, but he had seen Roach. Apart from passing on the latest information, he had informed him of his decision to leave with his family. 'Good idea,' the major had responded, 'If you make it, our friends in Le Mesnil will let me know.'

As it happened, he and the other people living on the farm had been forced to spend a good deal of the next few days in the potato field, inside the trench, taking shelter as best they could from the artillery fire from both sides. It had been there, on 23 June, that Richier's messenger had found him. The reconnaissance mission had been set to take place during the early afternoon of the following day, but Jean-Jacques had brought it forward to mid-morning so that he could go to the city centre. A neighbour's son had suffered a splinter wound to the neck, an ambulance had to be sent for and Grandad was the only one who had a bicycle. After finding the van, parked in front of the Bon-Sauveur, and sending it to his neighbour's house, he had taken a lengthier look around than his other visits, and had seen the first symptom of defeat come rolling by: three Panzers headed for Vaucelles, on the right bank of the Orne, followed by a disorderly gaggle of small groups of exhausted-looking men, uniforms torn and dirty.

On 29 June the Germans had ordered the locals to evacuate Eterville, destined to turn into a battlefield a short time later. Grandad had convinced the others to take refuge at Malherbe, which had remained almost intact while the city crumbled around it. Months earlier, Jean-Jacques' parents-in-law had taken the wheels off their old, black Peugeot parked in the tool-shed, and hidden them beneath piles of straw in the barn, hoping to save the vehicle from being requisitioned. The trick had paid off; all they had to do now was reattach the wheels and pour the contents of a bottle, kept in the kitchen cupboard as though it were a fine wine rather than just petrol, into the car's tank. The masters of the house had sat in the front seat, Simone with her new born and Colette with Clément behind them; the boot was filled with everything they had managed to cram inside. After seeing them off, Jean-Jacques and François had set off on foot through the fields, avoiding the animals that were wandering around bellowing in terror at the explosions, while a German column on the road had come under fire both from artillery and fighters.

At Bretteville they had spotted the black Peugeot: his father-in-law had stopped because they had found a cartman who was prepared to take Jean-Jacques and François as far as the rubble would allow his mule to pass. They had all covered the last stretch on foot. Seeing Colette's father turn back repeatedly to look at the Peugeot abandoned alongside a church wall, shaking his head, Jean-Jacques had tried to console him: it would be difficult to steal it, with the tank almost empty. Once they reached Malherbe, they had been directed to the Party Hall – a name that sounded like a joke in very poor taste – and from there to one of the main building's cellars, with soaring vaults and reassuring stone pillars, hundreds of refugees taking shelter between them. There was only one entrance, but every room had a trapdoor in the ceiling and a step ladder, allowing its occupants to enter and exit fairly quickly. For those who wanted to take a breath of fresh air there was the cloister, inviting but also dangerous, given that nobody could guarantee that the high school's exceptional luck – it was still almost intact after three weeks of air raids – would go on indefinitely.

Seven thousand people in a building that ought to have held no more than six hundred, and yet there was food enough for everyone. The Civil Defence combed the fields looking for animals that had survived the bombs, loading them onto their trucks and taking them to the enclosures set up near the Bon-Sauveur; whenever they found one that was not long dead they took it to Malherbe, where it was butchered immediately. The emergency teams called at all of the shelters each morning, delivering fresh milk from the cows crowded into the *Prairie*; there was even cheese and wine. The only problem was water: supplied by a continuous flow of trucks carrying two hundred litre barrels of the stuff, it was still too precious and too rare to be wasted on hygiene. So the refugees ate in shifts of five hundred people, with dishes, cutlery and glasses washed just once, at the end.

Once more deprived of contacts – what had happened to Richier? Was he still alive? – Grandad had gone back to being a handyman, for which there was no shortage of work, and had signed up with the security services at the shelter, a kind of internal police force tasked, among other things, with patrolling the walls of the building by night. That would be no problem, he had thought: he would not be getting much sleep in any case, with the air raids still underway. The heaviest one, on the night of 7 July, had begun while he was playing with Clément beneath the arches of the cloister, waiting for Colette to join them when she finished her own job: she spent several hours a day sewing and mending, another essential service given that in ninety per cent of cases, when a refugee tore some item of clothing they had been wearing the day they arrived at Malherbe, they had nothing else to replace it with. The metallic cough of the anti-aircraft guns had made Jean-Jacques look up: the sky had been dark with low-flying Lancaster and Halifax bombers, no more than five-hundred metres off the ground, grouped in squadrons of twelve or twenty-four. He had not had time to ask himself which part of the city they were headed for. The first bombs had fallen closer than they ever had before, panic spreading as fast as the shockwave that had flung people against the walls of the cloister. Screams, smoke, people running desperately towards the cellars; Grandad had gathered Clément up in his arms and thrown himself towards the corridor Colette was supposed to coming out of. They had been reunited behind a pillar, almost running straight into one another, and had then rushed towards the steps that led down into the basement, where desperate people stood huddled. The Civil Defence chief had been shouting to everyone to stay calm: the planes had passed and no more bombs were going to fall anywhere near them. But the building was shaking to its very foundations and, once Jean-Jacques had managed to reach the shelter with his family, he had begun to wonder whether he had made the right choice: from below, the impacts made a dull, thudding sound that only made the sensation of being buried alive even worse. A girl, sitting on the floor beside them, had become hysterical, wailing like a banshee and starting to tear at her skirt. Convinced that it would be down to Colette to sew the shredded cloth back together the following day, Jean-Jacques had held his fist to her face and threatened to hit her if she did not calm down. Grandad must have scared the poor thing even more than the bombs because she had fallen silent and unclenched her fingers from the hem of her skirt; with those wide, staring eyes, she would have looked dead had it not been for the sobs that shook her body. Grandad had lowered his head to avoid Colette's and Clément's gaze: he was ashamed of what those catacombs had turned him into.

The longest three quarters of an hour since the Allied landings, the coup de grace for a city on its knees. The news brought by the emergency workers, coming to and departing from Malherbe, were terrifying: whole neighbourhoods spared by the earlier raids had been razed to the ground, the university library was in flames, Saint-Julien church had been literally pulverised, what was left of the town hall had collapsed. Jean-Jacques had offered to help out. They had not even asked him what he could do, putting a helmet on his head and sending him outside with a partner and a stretcher. The description of what he had seen that night was brief. Better that way: Cédric only needed a few sentences – Mum had never mentioned them, and it was hard to blame her – before he decided it was best to turn the page. One of the bodies they had

'... putting a helmet on his head...'. Two Civil Defence helmets on display at Caen Memorial (100 Objects of the Battle of Normandy)

recovered had a head but no face, melted away as if it were made of wax. And yet there had still been life in that human wreckage, air bubbling up through a blood clot roughly where the mouth or nose ought to have been – it was impossible to say which. 'We're from the Civil Defence, we're taking you to the hospital,' he had murmured to the victim before placing him on the stretcher, with all the gentleness a railwayman without the faintest idea of first aid was capable of, asking himself a moment later how a dying man without ears could have heard his reassurances.

Back at Malherbe, Grandad had flopped down beneath the arches of the cloister, his companion doing the same. And it was as though this was the first time he had seen him, as though he had not realised that he had passed hours amongst the rubble, lit up by flames, in the company of a boy who could be no more than fifteen years old. 'What is he doing here?' Jean-Jacques had thought: he should have been tucked up in bed in a pair of clean pyjamas, his biggest worry, if he had any, that he had not done enough studying for the next day's test. But he must have lost the pyjamas, the bed and the school a long time ago, and perhaps his family as well. They had bid one another farewell at dawn, after a brief rest, neither knowing any more about the other than his Christian name.

'They're here!' Grandad had been at Mass with Clément and Colette when they had heard the cry go up in the nave of Saint-Etienne on the morning of 9 July. The church next to Malherbe had been turned into a dormitory as well. The faithful followed the sermon from among the straw beds where hundreds of refugees slept, straining their ears to hear the abbot's words, interrupted every few seconds by babies crying for their milk or the groans of the sick. But they had all heard that piece of news, and those too exhausted to rouse themselves had been shaken awake by those nearby. Grandad had rushed outside along with dozens of others, without at first paying much attention to the two figures walking slowly and warily towards them, rifles in hand and dressed in khaki uniforms. He had not dreamt of liberation this way. He had expected parades, music, flowers, official speeches in front of the town hall ... Oh right, he had remembered – the town hall was not there anymore.

The two men had stopped about ten metres away and gazed at the crowd as though they could not believe their eyes. The first civilians they had encountered in Caen must have looked in even worse shape than they had been expecting, but they were not in great form themselves: staring dully and caked in dust, they had been so exhausted that even the weight of their helmets must have been unbearable. One of them had taken his off and wiped a dirty rag across his forehead, before saying in a barely audible voice: '*Bonjour. Nous sommes canadiens.*' Nobody had moved until a woman had stepped forward from the group, walked up to the helmetless Canadian, hugged herself against him and, standing on tiptoes to compensate for the difference in height, planted a kiss on his cheek. He had turned to his comrade as if appealing for help as the crowd had burst into applause. Then, in the odd kind of French they speak in Canada, he had explained the reason for his embarrassment: they had been convinced that an armoured car full of chocolate and cigarettes, to be distributed along the streets, would have passed through before their arrival. But the vehicle must have gotten stuck in one of the craters that made driving almost impossible, leaving them alone. So it had been the refugees who had offered the liberators a glass of wine before taking them through Malherbe to show them to those who could not move, as though they were trophies won at a pétanque tournament.

A few hours later a surprising piece of news had spread through the shelter: a few Resistance members had managed to bring a tricolore, with the cross of Lorraine sewn onto the white stripe, back from Vaucelles, where the retreating Germans had fixed their next defensive line. It was an undertaking he himself would have liked to take part in, Grandad had noted with a hint of envy. They had announced that the flag would be raised in the late afternoon, in the open space between the façade of Saint-Etienne and the high school's hall. Jean-Jacques could not make do with simply taking part – he wanted to be worthy of the occasion, but did not know how to get hold of one of the armbands he had seen on those who had taken part in the Vaucelles expedition. He had a piece of white cloth in acceptable condition, the one he had used to wrap the watch in when he had left Eterville – *there it was again!* – but how would he be able to draw the two-barred cross on it?

'I have an idea,' Colette had smiled, pulling a most unlikely accessory out of the battered suitcase where the Roussel family had placed what little they had left.

'You brought lipstick to the shelter?' he had asked, wide-eyed with astonishment.

'I wanted to believe I'd put it on again one day. In the mean-time you can use it.'

Jean-Jacques had started the job and ten minutes later his uniform was finished, a white handkerchief bearing the scarlet symbol of Free France ready to be tied on his arm, on his right jacket sleeve instead of the left in order to hide the most obvious signs of repair.

And the watch? Should he put it back in the suitcase, with the linen? Better to put it on his wrist, he had decided: it too had ta-ken part in the liberation, and therefore had a right to be there. He had arrived at the flagpole half an hour before the ceremony was set to begin and, next to it, had seen a group of men wearing all the official version of the armband, some in uniform and others in civilian clothes. One of them had nodded to him in greeting and separated from the group, moving towards him. Arc-en-ciel! Al-most unrecognisable: clean shaven, with a beret, military jacket, thick belt and a pistol jutting out of the holster. 'Well done on the armband. It's so nice it makes mine look fake,' he had laughed, hugging him. 'Come and see me at the makeshift town hall. We need men like you.' The courtyard had filled up quickly, people elbowing through the crowd to get closer to the young man enga-ged in attaching the flag to the wire that ran up the length of the pole; he had raised it with deliberate slowness, emphasising the solemnity of the moment.

A short man with a baritone voice had started; from where he was standing, behind dozens of heads and backs, he must have been able to see very little. He was determined to make himself heard however, and he had done: in the blink of an eye, everyone else had been singing along with him. Watching the people around him out the corner of his eye, Jean-Jacques had wondered how so many managed to sing the Marseillaise while crying at the same time, before he had realised that they could have asked the same question of him. And he had been struck by the certainty that the old grammar book he had used at elementary school had been wrong. If liberty were no more than an abstract word, as he had been led to believe, then he would not have been able to hear it, taste it, admire its colours. In that courtyard he could feel and see it all: the chorus of a thousand voices, the salty tears dripping onto his lips, the red, white and blue of the flag, left at half-mast to remember the city's fallen, the brown of the British and Canadian uniforms, worn by a small group of officers as they stood to attention, fingertips touched to the visors of their caps.

At the end Jean-Jacques had approached one of them, as he was climbing into his jeep, because he had noticed the blue-grey of his RAF uniform. 'Was it really necessary to flatten the city?' he had asked after introducing himself, careful not to sound too brusque or, worse still, ungrateful. The other had hesitated for such a long time that Grandad had started to wonder whether he had understood the question – one could hardly expect all the British to speak French – but had finally responded with a phrase that had the ring of officialdom to it. 'The final air raid was what allowed us to enter the city,' he had said, accompanying the statement with a look that contained both sadness and embarrassment. He had already been asked that question, Jean-Jacques had thought; in fact, he must have already asked it of himself, without being able to find a satisfactory answer.

For him the war was not over. In the two weeks that followed,

Malherbe had turned into a target for the German gunners dug in on the right bank, and they had hit it several times, killing dozens of refugees and forcing hundreds to board the trucks laid on by the Allies to move them to the coast, far from the front line. The people had asked themselves why the Boche were harassing a building that was still being used as a homeless shelter. Perhaps they wanted to leave a last keepsake before quitting Normandy, Grandad had commented, but he had not left. Arc-en-ciel, who he now knew by his real name, Albert Girault, had asked him to stay at Malherbe until the situation went back to normal, and he had readily agreed. He liked making himself useful, feeling he was playing an important part in the reconstruction work that was just getting underway, and Colette had backed him up, declining the invitation to follow the others, as well as her parents' offer that they could go back to live with them in Eterville.

The most unexpectedly satisfying aspect of liberation had been its funny side, being able to laugh with genuine joy, noisy, open and free. It had happened one evening, as he was telling her about the scene he had just witnessed in the canteen. Two big men armed with buckets, rags and brooms had just finished the titanic undertaking of cleaning the floor for the first time in weeks and, turning to a young man in the uniform of captain of the French Army, they had assured him with visible satisfaction that, 'It's the cleanest it's been since the Boche were in charge.' The officer had glared at them and, face scarlet with anger, unleashed a torrent of abuse in which the words 'defeatists' and 'treason' had figured prominently, before finishing with a threat to confiscate their wages and report them to the police. When the officer had finally left, it had been down to Grandad to console the two unfortunate men, reassuring them they had nothing to worry about and giving them each a dozen cigarettes after having purloined them from the storeroom he had been entrusted with having a key to. He too had become a traitor, he had commented as the story drew to a close, before being overcome by Colette's contagious laughter, just like when they had been eighteen years old. And Clément, who had never seen his parents laugh like that, had laughed along as well, without understanding why but happy nonetheless.

Jean-Jacques had not forgotten about a debt he still had to pay. 'Today I went to give the watch back,' the entry for 27 July began. He had been pedalling slowly along on the bicycle they had lent him at Malherbe – his own had been left at Eterville the day of the evacuation and his parents-in-law, upon returning home the week before, had confirmed its practically inevitable disappearance – and watching the people milling around in the rubble in search of something, anything that would remind them of the existence of the past, before all this horror. Arriving at the building on Rue d'Hastings where the Allies had set up their headquarters for Civil Affairs, he had asked around for a certain Major Roach. He had been directed to an office on the first floor where he had been greeted by a captain who had made an effort, commendable as it was ineffective, to express himself in French, informing him that Roach was not around but that he would be happy to try to help Grandad himself. At the sight of the watch with the engraving on the back, however, he had stiffened. Jean-Jacques had explained the reason for his visit twice, as slowly as possible and carefully choosing the most commonly used words in the hope of making himself understood; but it had been in vain, judging by the mistrust with which the officer had treated him. As he endured the man's questions, pronounced in an accent he would have found hilarious in any other circumstances, Jean-Jacques had begun to wonder why he had gotten himself into trouble: he was being treated like a thief or, worse, a vulture.

'Roussel! Is that really you?' had come the voice of his salvation, from behind, accompanied by the click of the captain's heels as he stood to attention. The new arrival had walked across the office almost at a run and shaken Grandad vigorously by the hand. 'What a pleasure to see you again!'

'The pleasure is mine, Major,' he had answered, never happier to have run into him. Now he could afford to indulge in civilities that the circumstances of their meetings in June had made quite impossible: 'The uniform suits you more. The moustache too.'

'Just as freedom suits you better. You made it then, thank God.'

'The thick skin of the Normans, and a good deal of luck.'

'What can we do for you? If you're after a medal, you're at the wrong place: you'll have to go and see your friends at the FFI.'

The captain, still standing to attention because Roach had not yet acknowledged his existence, had stared at them both. But, judging from the look on his face, he had no chance of understanding the reason for such familiarity between his superior and a French civilian.

'Strange: there's the symbol of the Ministry but no serial number,' the major had commented, examining the watch. 'And without that it'll be a tough job to trace its owner.'

'There's the emblem, the name ...'

'Where was it you say you saw them?'

'At Amfreville, the morning of 6 June.'

'Amfreville? I've read the reports: they had a rough time of it around there, the week after D-Day. A damned rough time of it. I'm afraid there won't be many of them left, the lads you ran into.'

And the boy with the blue eyes?, Grandad had asked himself. What had happened to him? Was he dead too? Perhaps the watch had been his. Perhaps he had a girlfriend called Jane, who had already heard the bad news. 'Can I leave it with you? If the owner has made it through alive, you're more likely to run into him than I am.'

'I have a better idea: you keep it.'

'What?'

'A gift, from the British army. You deserve it – you risked your life.' Seeing the indecision in his eyes, the officer had added: 'I'd better put something down on paper.' He had dictated a couple of lines to the captain and slipped the certificate into an envelope along, stamped and signed. 'If anyone asks where you got the watch, show them this and tell them it was me.'

If only all mysteries had such a simple explanation, Cédric thought, smiling as he read his Grandad's comment: if the British had really wanted to reward him, he would have preferred a new bicycle. Naturally, he had kept this particular thought to himself: 'I don't know how to thank you ...'

'I do. You can invite me to dinner at your house, when you have a new one,' the officer had answered, slapping him on the shoulder and walking him to the door as the captain had looked on, even more lost than he had been before. The contents of the letter had provided him with a kind of explanation, but the major's actions must have struck him as questionable, to put it mildly.

Cédric closed the diary and placed it on the table. It was his now, a birthday present that had reached its recipient decades late, bringing with it a collection of images that Mum, whether intentionally or not, had failed to mention. The best of all: Dad as a child hiding under a mattress, in amongst the cushions, worried but not terrified. Had he inherited a bit of Jean-Jacques' courage? If so, perhaps he had passed a little on to Cédric, giving him the strength to face a danger that was never really there. And to Théo.

'I'm ready,' Mum announced from her bedroom.

'So am I, nearly,' Cédric murmured, taking his mobile phone out of his bum bag to write a reminder. In the early afternoon he would have to take himself off for half an hour, or rather a whole hour, locking himself away in his study with the excuse that he had to get something done before the party, marking a test or drawing up notes for a lesson. The important thing was that he be left in peace, because photo editing required a lot of concentration and, before today, he had limited himself to removing the red-eye from portraits taken using a flash.

31. 6 JUNE 2014, 23:07

'I'm tired – I'm going to bed.' And how could he blame her, poor Sylvie? The burden of the party had fallen almost entirely on her shoulders: Cédric's mother had been right, at least about that. Or rather, only about that. All he had done was rinse the dishes and turn the dishwasher on once the last guests had left. But she had gone into action thirteen hours previously when she dropped by the patisserie to pick up the cake, and since then she had been on the go non-stop.

Everything had gone smoothly: the games; the presents; the magic tricks from Malik's dad, who had improvised an amateur conjuring routine; the candles, both Théo's, blown out in one breath, and his own, which had taken two; the sun, with a light breeze cooling the air; and the twenty-five guests, all present and accounted for, a new record for the birthday boy. Who – and this had been the only off note – had seemed somewhat absent, and not just in a figurative sense. Every so often he had vanished, only to then reappear a couple of minutes later, an inquisitive look on his face as he attempted to meet his father's eye, betraying his impatience to speak with him in private. Impossible, with all those people around, and pointless: Cédric had already known the questions, but not the answers. And so Théo's only point of reference had been an empty chair. He knew it was unnecessary, but had wanted to place it in front of the television all the same. 'You never know,' he had whispered to Cédric after lunch.

Now that Sylvie had retired to bed, so worn out that she had not even asked him when he would join her, they were alone. Seeing his father pick up the remote control, Théo got up suddenly from the sofa: 'Shall we go?'

'I want to see what's on the telly first. You go on ahead, I'll be there in a minute.'

'No, I'll wait ...'

'I thought you weren't afraid anymore.'

'Of course I'm not,' he said indignantly, 'I want to see as well.' Was he worried his dad would forget his promise? Or, even worse, that he did not think it important enough to keep?

'Don't worry; you don't need to explain anything to Mum tonight, either. I reckon she's asleep already.' Théo responded to his father's wink with a nervous, forced smile.

Weather forecast, old series re-runs, even older films, a documentary about bears, no sport. Hardly a seductive menu, but on the tenth channel he jumped to Cédric recognised a familiar place. He had almost forgotten: the seventieth anniversary, a day of celebration. The images were being transmitted from Colleville-sur-Mer, the American military cemetery, a late night round-up of

'... Colleville-sur-Mer, the American military cemetery...'

the day's event. When the channel-hopping ground to a halt, Théo – who had stayed standing, perhaps in the hope that doing so would make his father feel uncomfortable and shorten the wait – went from impatient to anxious. But he had stopped staring at Cédric as though he feared he would disappear from under his nose, and seemed intrigued by the uniformed military band, the speaker's podium, the spectator stands and the audience.

Cédric had been there twice: first as a boy, on an elementary school trip while he was living in Caen, and then again twenty years later, when he was teaching at a secondary school and, still free of family obligations, had extended his summer study break, spending a few days in Normandy instead of heading straight home from Paris. Caen and his relatives but also Colleville. He remembered it well, that day, beginning with the mishaps. He had arrived only a little over an hour before closing time because he had left his father's cousin's house too late and had taken a couple of wrong turns, but his bad mood had vanished at the first stop of his tour; instead, in the darkness and silence of the auditorium where they projected a film about the fallen, he had been overcome by emotion. His own and that of the other spectators, signalled by the handkerchiefs that, every so often, had emerged from

'... the bronze statue at its centre...'

pockets and handbags. When the lights had been turned on, he had followed the stream of visitors into the space dedicated to historical reconstructions: photographs and text on the walls and films showing on the central screens, which formed a kind of barrier between the different parts of the exhibition.

Time had been tight, so he had gone outside and, walking along a tree-lined path overlooking the beach where two thousand American officers and soldiers had lost their lives in just a few hours, he had reached the steps of the memorial, a broad viewing platform enclosed on three sides by a semi-circular colonnade. He had looked at the bronze statue at its centre before turning round to face the graves, a sight which had taken his breath away. It was the very same view the television was showing now. Beyond the rectangular pond filled with water lilies, and the small pathways running beside the long edges up to the flagpoles flying the stars and stripes, the emerald-green grass rolled away along the broad central corridor, interrupted by a small chapel; but on either side it gave way to the white of the crosses, dozens of rows that seemed more like reflections of those behind them, like images reproduced to infinity by a sequence of mirrors, while the trees, just visible in the distance, acted as the only reference point, the proof that it was not merely an optical illusion. For the first time the giant Full HD screen looked small, inadequate, and impotent. But it had been the same at the cinema, when he had seen *Saving Private Ryan*. There were no images capable of capturing the sense of vertigo that had taken hold of him, as though he had been looking down from the top floor of a skyscraper, nor sound systems advanced enough to faithfully reproduce that silence caressed by the far-off rustle of footsteps on grass, the voices of visitors condensed to a single whisper.

Cédric had walked around the pond and then up to the chapel,

'... had walked around the pool and then up to the chapel...'

where he had lingered a while over the words etched in English and French on the outer walls; then he had joined the crowd in its slow and orderly flow towards the exit. A shame he had not had the time to take his time, and murmur a 'thank you' before even just one of those crosses. Instead he had had to make do with capturing a few names as he had passed by, promising himself again that he would return, one day or another, with more time to spare.

The coverage cut to the flag-lowering ceremony, beginning with an image showing the almost perfect circle formed by the twenty or so spectators, all apparently guided by an inner voice telling them what was the right distance to maintain in order to observe without getting in the way. The cameras then followed the footsteps of an elderly man, around Roger's age, tall and thin, his hair a snowy white, as he headed slowly towards the flagpole, two children on either side of him holding his hands, each about ten years old. An accompanying soldier in a blue uniform preceded them and, once he had reached his colleague with the flag, took it as it was passed to him, holding it as though it were a tray, with both hands, and his elbows at right angles. The other soldier joined him, lifted a triangular flap and folded it down onto the part underneath, while his comrade said something to the three observers who had stayed to one side, and with a nod of his head invited the old man to come closer with the children. The bigger one, guided by his grandfather (or his great grandfather?), reached out with his hand, brushing it against the flag and following the actions of the man leading the ceremony as, one fold after another, he reduced the size of the flag until it was shaped into a broad, flat block, its sides perfectly smooth. All of it without appropriate commentary: the presenter was speaking about something else, maybe because no one had brought him up to speed regarding this particular aside. As such the identity of the elderly guest – a veteran, the brother of one of the fallen? – could only be guessed at.

The programme drew to a close straight afterwards. Viewers were given the illusion of entering the chapel and approaching the black marble altar, where a phrase written in English caught the eye and remained easily visible in the foreground, even when the theme music began to play, with the credits sliding horizontally along the bottom of the screen instead of vertically.

'... the black marble altar, where a phrase written in English...'

'What does it say?' One of the great things about Théo was that curiosity always got the better of him, even when – as was the case this evening – he had a very clear idea about the order of his priorities.

'I give unto them eternal life and they shall never perish.'

'Perish? What does that mean?'

'Die.'

'But they did die. All those crosses ...'

'Didn't you hear what they said on the TV? They fought for our freedom. We're still free, so they're still alive.' There was no need for a degree in philosophy to see through the holes in that reasoning, but Théo took note of it without objection and fell silent, eyes lowered. He had good call for allowing himself to be convinced that the Knights of Freedom really were immortal.

32. 7 JUNE 2014, 03:11

'Dad ...?' The stiffness in his neck, the pins and needles and the open magazine slipping off his lap all brought that interminable flight to the Maldives to mind, when – emerging from an uncomfortable and restless doze – he had asked himself where his right hand had gone. He had found it buried between the two seats, his own and the one where Sylvie slept with an irritatingly peaceful expression on her face, oblivious to the impending risk of gangrene hanging over her new husband, and had tugged it out with a jerk of his numb shoulder, doubtful of the prospect that it might one day go back to functioning as it had. It was the same hand that now lay unconscious beneath his leg, but Cédric could not dedicate himself to reviving it as promptly as he would have liked. 'You fell asleep ...,' Théo's voice was reproaching him.

'Looks like it. And you too, before I did.'

'What will we do now, if ...? I mean ... if he came by and we didn't notice.'

'*You* didn't notice. I did. I fell asleep afterwards.'

'After what?'

'After he left.'

'Left?! When?' Théo seemed to have forgotten that the car had four doors and threw himself into the space between the front seats to take his place next to his father, without giving him time to move to one side. The bang to his shoulder hurt. A good sign: the limb had some feeling in it, meaning it was still salvageable.

'It must have been about two.'

'And when did he get here?'

'An hour before that, I'd say. You were already asleep.'

'Why didn't you wake me up?'

'He didn't want me to.'

'Who?'

'Him. He said if he had any children he wouldn't have anyone go waking them up in the middle of the night.'

'But ...'

'It all went fine, you should be pleased.'

'And the baddies?'

'They were afraid and surrendered.'

'So he'll be back soon ...'

'You know it's not up to him.'

'Didn't he say anything else?'

'That he was pleased with you, that you're an excellent soldier. Then he wished me a happy birthday, asked how the party went. And I apologised. You were right: he's not angry.'

Frowning, his drowsiness swept away by bitterness and irritation as they hunted for a pretext to come out into the open, Théo stared at the dashboard as though the speedometer and rev counter were spools of finely lined paper, their hands the stylus of a lie-detector machine. He was clearly not convinced by what he was seeing: 'Strange ...'

'What is?'

'That he comes to see me but doesn't talk to me, and then leaves without saying goodbye ...'

'He was being kind. You were so fast asleep ... And he told me to pass on his goodbye.'

'Yeah, but ...'

'What's the matter, don't you believe me? Why would I make it up?'

'I don't know ... To convince me nothing happened to him, to make me happy, because it's my birthday …'

Cédric did his best to sound annoyed: 'Your birthday was yesterday. And fairy tales are for little kids.'

Once he would have let it go, but the D-Day version of Théo was not afraid, not of the dark, not of bats and not of his dad: 'Exactly,' he answered back, leaving the rest – *then why are you trying?* – merely implied.

'So you don't trust me. I ought to send you straight to bed and not give you your dinner tomorrow.' The threat echoed through the silence because Cédric followed it with a pause, respecting the dramatic timing he had gone over in his head before drifting off. A convincing act, judging by Théo's nervous chewing motion, perceptible beneath his cheek. All that was needed now was to close the trap: 'But I'll give you a chance instead. How much are you willing to pay for proof?'

'Proof?'

'Proof that he was here, that I spoke to him. It'll cost you, but at least you'll be sure.'

'I haven't got any money …'

'No need: you can give me back my toy soldiers.'

'The soldiers?' The previous morning he had been so happy to find them exactly where he had left them the night before, lined up two by two, face to face, that in the few minutes he had been able to spend alone with his dad, before the party, he had spoken of nothing else, certain that, after having come back safe and sound, they could expect an inspection from Pierre. That was why he had moved them only a moment before Cédric had parked his car and then lined them up again on the back seat: standing, propped up against the backrest, so that they would not be taken by surprise when their captain arrived. What should he do? Him or his mates? Certainty, bought at a high cost, or doubt?

'I almost forgot: you can rest easy because I'll make you a money-back guarantee.'

'What do you mean?'

'Do you remember the vacuum cleaner Mum bought on the

internet, the one that was supposed to do everything by itself? It didn't work, so we sent it back and got our money back. Same thing here: if you're not convinced by the proof, you can keep the soldiers. Can't ask for more than that ...' Perhaps that would have been enough, but Cédric did not want to run any risks. The final bait was irresistible; ignoring it would be too much of a blow to his self-esteem: 'But no one's forcing you to, if you don't feel up to it.'

The response was immediate, as he had foreseen: 'Alright, I'll do it.'

'Then shake my hand. That's how you make an agreement, man to man. No need for signatures. Let's go.'

'Where?'

'My study. I want to show you the proof before you go to bed, that way you can go to school happy and I can take my soldiers back. I think I'll keep them in my bedside table drawer.'

He could read a feverish agitation in Théo's eyes. Had he made a mistake? Was it too late to change his mind, tell Dad he believed him, act like a kid? Or should he accept his responsibilities? Pierre would have been in no doubt. And nor was Théo, who turned around to throw a glance at the paratroopers – his last? – before closing the car door: 'Let's go.'

33. 7 JUNE 2014, 03:28

'But how ...?' The monitor was the only source of illumination in the study, the lighthouse guiding a small sailor with eyes wide open and lips parted, torn between joy and remorse. Perhaps Théo was beginning to wonder whether it was really worth crossing the frontiers of the night and venturing onto islands known only to the adult world, if it was worth fighting with such determination for the permit he had longed for ever since his life had become too complex to be shut away inside the right angle signalled by the hands of the big clock on the kitchen wall: nine o'clock, bed time, school tomorrow. He was not ready to admit it, of course, but the idea that Mum and Dad were right to send him to bed early must have seemed less absurd than usual, because in that dark dimension he was so keen to enter, things happened that were even more inexplicable than the betrayal plotted by Ney-Zet, Gyorx's best friend, while the Emperor of the Lost Galaxy prepared his assault on the outpost of Kradabash. His relief was tangible, but so too were his annoyance and shame: how would he explain himself when Pierre came back and found out he had sacrificed his soldiers because he had not trusted his dad? Would he tell him he was a moody, spoilt kid? 'It's him ... It's really him.'

For Cédric this was payback time. He had a right to. A duty, in fact. As he spoke, he experienced a feeling of déjà-vu unlike any he had ever known before and which, instead of melting away, only grew clearer: 'I told you, didn't I?'

'No!' Théo protested.

'Yes I did.'

'No you didn't! How could I know you'd taken a picture? Why didn't you show it to me right away?'

'Because you didn't believe me, which meant you needed to be taught a lesson. What do you say now?'

'About what?'

'Are you convinced or not?'

'Who's the other one?' The same tactic as always, a question instead of an answer. How had Kipling put it? *If you can meet with Triumph and Disaster /And treat those two impostors just the same* ... Still a long way off, for Théo.

'His name's Roger, he's a friend. He had the idea of the photo.'

'He spoke to me about Roger once. So it's true he looks like a boy, the same as me.'

'Much taller than you. But he's young, that much is true.'

'Is he friendly?'

'More or less. And bright, though he doesn't talk much. I think he's shy. Or he's afraid. You know how Pierre is: he shouts at him, calls him a kid to get him angry ...'

'Why is the photo so dirty? All grey, with those stains ...'

Let's see if you can do any better, part of him wanted to reply, but he would not have said it even if he could, fearing that an hour's apprenticeship in front of the screen would see Théo reach a higher level of mastery than his father. And then the background was not bad for a forty-four-year-old, unaware until two days earlier of the very existence of a computer tool called 'clone brush', let alone how to use it. 'I must have done something wrong when I downloaded the photo from my mobile. I was in a hurry because I'd left you alone in the garage. But what do you care if you can't see the car and the cupboard? Pierre's what matters, right?'

'His face isn't black like the other times.'

'He doesn't need it any more. Mission accomplished.'

'They're smiling.'

'They're happy. They've done their duty and gone to see two friends on their birthday. I'll print it out for you, if you like. In the meantime go and fetch me my soldiers.'

'Do I have to get them right now?' he asked, his voice filled with heart-wrenching distress, but this was not the moment to go soft.

'Quick as you can, we've got to go to bed. And when you come back, knock twice: I'll shut the door because the printer's noisy.'

There was a lot to do. The clatter of cylinders inside the printer as they spat out the sheet of paper and deposited it on the plastic tray reminded him of his first task: send an email to Jeremy to thank him for the photo – no need to mention exactly what he had done with it, of course – and tell him about how a few coincidences had become seventy years of questions without answers. Roger had the right to know who Major Roach was. To smile at the thought of how a rough embrace with a French cyclist had left such a deep mark that it had endured through two generations before finally depositing itself on Cédric's wrist, like a footprint in the sand – Normandy sand, naturally – still intact after thousands of tides had passed over it.

Then there were things to do in his free time, the weekends in which Cédric already knew what he would be up to. Sylvie and Théo could go up to town by themselves, if they wanted to. He would stay home and turn on his computer to transcribe what had happened to a brave railwayman, to his family, to his friends – if he never found a publisher who was interested in those memoirs because there were already more than enough tales from the war, then so be it. But he needed to make a copy, to read from time to time in place of the original, which he would keep in the drawer of his desk, inside a plastic wallet to protect it from dust, light and fingers, and to print out for Théo to look at when he was older.

Third on his to-do list: the *notaire*. He still did not know how it had gone; Cédric had to tell him and send the scan of the photo of his uncle with Dad.

Lastly there was Sylvie, and here things got more complex. How was he going to broach the subject of the summer holidays and convince her there was a more attractive destination than Corsica? 'The man the watch belonged to wanted it to reach his wife … She's not around anymore, but … I feel a sort of duty … Just a visit to the cemetery, a few minutes to pay my respects, then we can do the tourist thing. Liverpool's not bad, you and Théo have never been; in fact neither of you have ever been to England. We could make the most of being there and take a trip to London … What with budget airlines and last minute deals we wouldn't even have to spend much …' 'Are you sure it's not an excuse to see some football match?' she would ask. And he would reply: 'Please, the television's more than enough …', hopefully without turning pale and keeping to himself the thought that there was a big difference between listening to *You'll Never Walk Alone* in his living room and singing it at the stadium. Would he have managed it if he had had the 'wingwatch' on his wrist, twenty-six years earlier? He liked to think so. He really should have had it then, a proud father's school leaving gift to his son. And if Théo were to notice that the name on the gravestone, Jane, was the same as the one on the watch? 'It's a common name in England,' he would answer, to avoid a lot of difficult explanations.

Knock knock: Théo was back, face like a funeral, fingers dug deep into his tracksuit pockets.

'Keep the photo. And you can put them in your room.'

'Them?'

'The paratroopers. They need their rest, too.'

'But you said …'

'I changed my mind. You can keep them.'

'Really …?'

'… If you promise that from now on, you'll believe what I tell you.'

Is that all? the drowsy eyes beneath the increasingly heavy

315

eyelids seemed to ask him. 'Alright.'

'Say: 'I swear.''

'I swear.'

'Off to bed.'

He could go too, now he had found the right present for Théo. He had not been thrilled by the mini basketball with the radio alarm clock, judging by the expression on his face as he opened the package from his parents. And nor by the basketball videogame, the small magnetic blackboard, the fluorescent green T-shirt with his name printed on it or the little remote-controlled car. All of it lay forgotten on the chest among the boxes, colourful wrapping paper, ribbons, shop labels and present tags. Théo had been convinced he deserved better and he was right: he was not a baby, after all.

34. 7 JUNE 2014, 07:09

'What are you doing? It's gone seven o'clock!'

Tummy ache always works. But not headache. Mum gets worried, once she wanted to take me to the hospital. Tummy ache isn't as scary, and then I know just what to say: too much ice cream at the party. She's sure to believe me, how could she have been watching me the whole time with everything she had to do? The last time I threw a sickie was back in December and I don't think she remembers that any more. A couple of times each school year – up until now there haven't been any problems because I never get really ill. What does it matter if I miss two days every nine months? Better to sleep at home than on the school desk or walk around like a zombie the way Jennifer does – she makes fun of me because I have to go to bed early while she never does before midnight, even though she's not up to doing even a simple addition before ten o'clock.

Of course I'm tired, but I'm not as out of it as Dad seems to think. There was no need for him to come in at half past six to remind me not to say anything to Mum. What does he think? That I'm so stupid I'd tell her I was up until four in the morning, after how much she's told me off over the last few days? I'm not going to school, that's all. Alone the whole morning; Mrs Yvonne will come and look in on me every now and then, and when she can't she'll phone me. Then there'll be three or four calls from Mum and Dad, too. Apart from that, total freedom, or nearly. No computer because if they realise I've used it again without saying anything there's no telling what'll happen, and no snacks or fizzy drinks because otherwise the tummy ache story won't hold up. Never mind: you can't have everything.

I'll call Mum now and tell her. Quietly, as if I had difficulty speaking, but without overdoing it. And sitting up, because if she finds me lying down she'll only start worrying. While if I'm sitting up she'll think I've tried to get up, so I'm not too ill, just a little bit, but that it's best to let me stay home as a precaution. Precaution: I like that words, it's magic. Ever since I learnt it I've used it often to save myself a lot of hassle, even though Dad started laughing once and said that spinach wasn't dangerous, so I could eat it without taking precautions.

The problem is Pierre. What'll happen if he comes back and finds me here? He'd start asking questions: 'Why didn't you go to school? Why don't you do what I tell you? Why do you tell lies?' How would I answer him? That I'm afraid of falling asleep in class and getting shouted at by the teacher? That if Mum finds out I stayed up almost all night she'll get angry and tell me I can't have any snacks for a week, after arguing with Dad because he lets me do whatever I want? I can almost hear him: 'Did you think it was enough to be brave just once? Too easy.' It wouldn't even be worth reminding him that I'd woken up at night to help him out. 'You followed orders, full stop.' Could I tell him the truth? No chance. He wouldn't understand and he might order me to go to school by myself, a five kilometre walk down the hill.

I'll take the risk. On the other hand, what can I do if people only listen to me when it suits them? In a minute's time, when Mum comes into my bedroom and I tell her about my tummy ache, the worst she'll do is grumble a bit about how she should have kept a closer eye on me because she knows how I can't help myself when I've got ice cream in front of me and just go on eating, but how could she have done with all those people here, how come she had to think of everything – the usual moans, but at least she won't be wondering about whether it's true or not. Because she trusts you, Pierre would say, to make me feel guilty. Rubbish. I think it's just because it's easier to believe the tummy ache story than the other thing.

It was like when Patrick elbowed me, during training. That time I couldn't catch my breath, but it came back again quickly. Yesterday, though, it was more annoying rather than a real pain, but it didn't go away. It had been like that since morning. Since the night before actually, when we'd said goodbye. It wasn't convulsions, I would have known if it had been. It was a weight, and I couldn't understand if it was pushing down from outside or inside my tummy, while my head felt light: I couldn't concentrate on anything, thoughts kept slipping away from me. I wasn't watching when they did the magic tricks, I didn't feel like eating – I didn't even touch the ice-cream, let alone get indigestion from it – I went off every ten minutes with the excuse that I had to go for a wee, and I couldn't wait for the party to finish, so that people would stop asking where I was and I could stay in the garage alone, in peace.

Who could I talk to about it? Only Dad, but when I woke up he'd already gone to Grandma's and after lunch we didn't have enough time by ourselves because he shut himself away in his office, and during the party he was always with someone. He'd

'... how come his friends had come back when he hadn't...'

promised me that we would wait up together, that was true. But I wanted to ask him how come his friends had come back when he hadn't, whether he was sure, and if he was sure, why didn't he know what time he was coming? The later it got the heavier the weight felt – I was starting to think that actually even Dad didn't know anything. Tummy ache, real tummy ache, would have been better than that.

Why did they send him away the very day of the party? I always knew they'd give him a mission sooner or later, but I only heard about the guns on Thursday. When I told him I was afraid he just started laughing: 'Nothing can happen to me.' So I got angry because I know when people are telling me tales, like when Sébastien swore he hadn't taken my pen, I didn't believe him and I was right because I found it in the pocket of his raincoat. I'm old enough now to know there's a difference between real wars and the ones Gyorx fights in, between Dad's soldiers and toys. He invented some kids' story to make me feel better: 'The baddies don't know how to be brave. They'll wet themselves with fright and have to put their rifles down to change their underwear, so it'll be a walkover for us.' He wanted to make me laugh but it didn't work.

What had happened to him? It was my worst birthday ever, counting the minutes and wondering when everyone was going to leave instead of having fun. So today I'm right to …

Just a minute. Now that's an idea! I could go, to school. That way the next time he'll have nothing to moan at me about and he'll have to listen. If the teacher shouts at me for not paying attention, I'll try using the tummy ache story with her. It suits Dad to pretend nothing happened because if they find out what really went on he'll be the first one to get into trouble. And Mum'll think that I really did the right thing because I went to school even though I wasn't feeling completely up to it. Brilliant. The perfect plan, just like his. Shame I won't see him if he drops by this morning. I'll leave him a note in the garage. If he wanted to speak to me, he could have done last night, he knows I have school.

Sure, it would have been fun. Waiting for everyone to leave, turning on the television to make sure no one could hear me, shutting myself in my room, jumping up and down on my bed, holding my arms up and shouting like when I win at basketball, in fact even more, like Dad when Gerard – or was it Gerrard? – scored that last minute goal and Mum got a shock because she thought he'd hurt himself. Then taking the Sam-Sam Youny poster off the door, getting the photo out of the drawer, putting a bit of tape on the corners and sticking it up high, so I can see it even when I'm lying in bed. It's not very good, of course. Poor Dad: his mobile phone's easy to use, but he still can't do it properly. He should have called me, like the time he stopped that Japanese tourist because he couldn't work out how to use the timer. Best not to remind him about that though, otherwise he'll get angry. And then anyway that was nice of him, letting me keep the toy soldiers. I wonder why. Maybe he only wanted to show me he was right, he absolutely loves being right.

Pierre too. But this time I'm right. And when we see each other I'll tell him, I'm certain of that. I'll tell him everything. That I was upset, that last night he should have woken me up, that my party was rubbish because I was afraid and so today I would've been right to take a day off to shout and laugh by myself, that I went to school just to make him happy even if I couldn't care less about the teacher or the French homework, and if he tries to interrupt me because he doesn't like listening to what I have to say then I'll just talk louder, and it doesn't matter if he punishes me then because he's an officer and I'm just a private. You're back, nothing else matters.

'Well? Do I have to pull you out of bed myself?'

'Alright Mum, I heard you! I'll get dressed now.'

APPENDIXES

THE VETERANS

Wingwatch is a work of fiction firmly rooted in historical reality and aiming to pay tribute to it. It is dedicated to the fallen, the comrades-in-arms who go back to Normandy every year to remember their sacrifice, and those who can no longer be there because, with the passing of the years, they have joined them in the resting place of heroes. These pages are about three Veterans of the 9th Battalion I met up with during my visits to Normandy.

The Veterans of 9th Para with a young fan of theirs and his proud Mum.

FRED GLOVER

The following is a summary of Fred Glover's own testimony, published by Neil Barber in The Day The Devils Dropped In (Pen & Sword Aviation, UK, 2002).

In the early hours of 6 June 1944, Fred Glover was part of a group tasked with reaching the Merville battery aboard one of the three gliders that were to begin the assault from within the fortified zone. The pilot was unable to make out the objective due to the fact that the necessary signalling materials had been lost, along with much of the material that had been parachuted in beforehand. When the glider flew over the battery, the garrison

– alerted by the first glider – was ready to open fire. Tracer fire pierced the wings and fuselage; later on, Glover would remember having seen his own legs jerk upwards, without realising in that moment that he had been hit. The pilot undertook evasive manoeuvres to escape the anti-aircraft fire, bringing the glider down in an orchard half a kilometre to the east of the objective. In the crash-landing the glider lost its wings and tail section, and the paratroopers who emerged unscathed helped the others – among them Glover – to escape through a large gash on the right-hand side; they then found cover in the craters produced by the air-raids that had taken place in the preceding days and hours.

Fred Glover signing the Denison smock of an admirer.

From there, they could make out a group of men moving towards the battery through the darkness. They could only be enemy troops, and so the paratroopers opened fire. This firefight prevented German reenforcements from reaching the objective while the attack was underway. When they realised that their comrades had taken the battery, the paratroopers who were able to move made their way towards the pre-arranged meeting point. Glover also attempted to join them, but the pain from his wounds was too great. A medic administered morphine to him and to three other wounded men (among them two Germans) before leaving them inside the crater.

They were found there by an SS patrol; luckily for Glover, one of the Germans in the crater was conscious and able to explain that a British medic had treated him. Had this not been the case, it is probable Glover would have been executed (this was the order that had come down from high command, and the fate that befell other captured paratroopers).

Glover was transferred from Merville to a German field hospital, and then moved several times before ending up at the Hôpital de la Pitié in Paris. In the capital there reigned an atmosphere of impending defeat, and Glover and the other servicemen feared that they would next be moved to a prison camp inside Germany itself. For this reason, taking advantage of an increasingly distracted guard unit and the acquaintances he had made among the French medical staff, Glover decided to attempt an escape;

Fred Glover enjoying the dance at the Veterans evening in Merville.

unfortunately, as he jumped from the infirmary roof, his wounds re-opened. The men of the French Resistance who had been waiting for him took him away and treated him, but the next day they advised him to go back to the hospital – he would receive better care there, and the fleeing Germans were abandoning the wounded prisoners anyway.

Back at the Pitié and practically ignored by the Germans who at this point cared only about getting out of Paris as soon as possible, Glover slipped into the officers' quarters and stole a Luger pistol with holster and magazines. Thus armed, he awaited the arrival of the first Allied tanks of General Leclerc's division, along the Paris Boulevards, among hundreds of thousands of deliriously happy citizens. The celebrations stopped when somebody opened fire on the crowd from the top floor of a building situated behind Glover and a comrade he had met at the hospital. They were paratroopers, and acted as such; they entered the building, mounted the stairs – with difficulty, given that both were convalescing – and came across an old lady who ran past them, screaming and pointing to a door left ajar at the end of the corridor. They threw it open and Glover, noting movement behind a curtain, fired two shots. He did not have time to check whether he had hit anyone because the room began to disintegrate in that very moment, under fire from the street by a tank that had spotted the source of the shots. Both men sped back outside to save themselves.

In the following weeks Glover, armed with a rifle, lent a hand to the partisans patrolling the streets, before his new comrades advised him to return to England to seek proper treatment for his wounds, which had deteriorated. The Resistance entrusted him to the care of an American officer and, before he left, Glover gifted his Denison smock to the head of the first Resistance group with which he had entered into contact in Paris. After a few hours spent at a field hospital, he was loaded onto a C-47 and transported to England.

GORDON NEWTON

When war broke out (1939), Gordon Newton was fifteen years old and working in a factory that produced a metal alloy using silver paper. In 1942 he signed up with the army, who assigned him to the Royal Sussex Regiment. In 1943 he presented a request for transfer to the Airborne Division.

On 5 June 1944, a paratrooper with the 9th Battalion, he was on board one of the gliders tasked with opening the assault

Gordon Newton leading the Veterans march in Merville.

from within the Merville Battery. Tall and well built, he was entrusted with the heaviest infantry weapon: a flamethrower, stowed beneath the bench where he was sitting. During the flight across the Channel, the braking parachute positioned behind the tail opened, cutting the glider's speed and altitude; it would have landed in the sea had the co-pilot not intervened by cutting the straps that held it in place. Having arrived in the target zone, the glider was greeted by anti-aircraft fire; one projectile hit the flamethrower, rendering it useless, but luckily not causing a fire that would have killed all those aboard the glider. When he believed he had spotted the battery, the pilot disconnected his craft from the Albemarle that had been towing it, but he immediately

A panel about Gordon Newton on display at Pegasus Memorial, Ranville, in 2012.

realised that he was about to land in a village (Gonneville) and swerved towards one of the flooded fields. Newton and the others emerged from the glider in waist-high water and began to wander through the countryside, only running into a group of Canadians several hours later, who then led them to the makeshift brigade HQ. From there they were sent to occupy the château Saint-Côme and the surrounding woods, south of Bréville, of crucial strategic importance because of its elevation, which offered a good view of the south and west, towards the bridges across the Orne and the Caen Canal, which had been taken during the night. Heavy and continuous German counterattacks ended only on 12 June with the taking of Bréville by a mixed contingent of paratroopers and infantry supported by armoured vehicles.

Newton and the remnants of the 9th Battalion were transferred away from the front line on 17 June, but in the following weeks they returned to carry out patrol duties. In September they went back to England, and in December they were back in action. This time they were fighting in the Ardennes, in order to blunt the last

German offensive of the war. In March 1945 Newton took part in Operation Varsity, an airborne assault against German territory east of the Rhine in order to make way for the advance of three armies under General Montgomery.

Next came a rapid push towards the Baltic, which ended at Weimar, where the battalion arrived on 2 May with orders to stop the Soviet advance at all costs. After days of tension in which armed confrontation between the two ex-allies became a real possibility, the situation stabilised following the armistice (8 May). Their next destination was the Pacific, but Japan surrendered before the battalion reached their final destination. Newton and the others were re-routed to Palestine for peacekeeping operations.

In 1947 Newton left the army with the rank of corporal. He was twenty-two, and spent the next thirty-three years in the police. Here he filled various roles, among them directing the Hendon driving school (near London). Retirement was not for him, and so – after having left the police – he employed the skills he had acquired at Hendon to train anti-kidnapping squads in various hotspots including the Philippines, Honduras, Guatemala and Colombia. In 1997 he became an honorary citizen of London and in 2005 France conferred upon him the title of Knight of the Legion of Honour. Secretary of the 9th Battalion Veterans' Association, he returns to Normandy every year to celebrate the anniversary of D-Day with the other ex-servicemen.

GEOFF PATTINSON

The following is the account of Geoff Pattinson's war experience in his own words. The text is taken from the reply he wrote to me when I informed him that I had written a novel inspired partly by the deeds of the 9th Battalion in Normandy.

'It was intended that the three gliders carrying sixty 'A' Company men, plus a few engineers and explosives, crashed inside the compound of the battery and engage the garrison from within, causing a diversion during the main attack from outside.

'Unfortunately, two of the gliders landed outside the target and the third glider force landed in England. I was in this glider. During the flight my feelings were one of apprehension, I was wondering what I had let myself into. There was no talking, each

Geoff Pattinson meeting up with Eugene Noble, the American pilot who flew the C-47 Dakota aircraft on display at the Merville Gun Battery.

with his own thoughts in the darkness not knowing how far we had travelled.

'Suddenly there was quite a jerk and a bit of a noise, we were now gliding, the tug having let go the tow rope.' The landing was very heavy and bumpy, then silence. We braced ourselves in readiness to pile out, but before we could so the officer came along the aisle instructing us to stay where we were. He climbed out, then came back shortly and told us to get out in an orderly fashion. The tug rope had snapped and as luck would have it came down on a landing strip at Odiham aerodrome in the South of England. I do not know how the others felt, but all my pent-up feelings disappeared and were replaced by a certain amount of relief.

'We were transported back to Brize Norton by road, having taken off from there. Another glider was made available and around 17.00 hrs we emplaned for a second go at getting to Normandy. Came in to land at Ranville Plain, all quiet except for sporadic gunfire in the distance. The officer marched us up hill on to a road leading to Le Mesnil crossroads, before there we got into a ditch that afforded good defence. For the next three days we defended the position against several attacks.

'Withdrawn from there, on D+3 (Friday) evening the group was moved to some woods adjacent to Château St-Côme. What remained of Battalion were there and had dug in. That night the Germans mortared the site very heavily, quieting down round about dawn.

'D+4 (Saturday) in the morning a six men patrol which included me entered the badly damaged Château to clear it out, but it had been vacated. The patrol sergeant sent a corporal and myself to get to the far side of some stables that lay behind the Château to spot any movement. Getting through the stables to the open country, we had not gone very far when a group of Germans appeared. Trying to get back to the stables the corporal made it, the Germans by now were using a light machine gun and as I just got to the opening I was wounded on both legs. Now face down on the stable floor I tried to get up and found I could. With a shambling sort of run I got to the woods and found the Regimental Aid Post. The fact that I had been shot set up some fear in me, but once I was being attended to I calmed down.

'Deemed unfit to continue, I was taken to the beachhead for evacuation back to England. I had had my baptism of fire, something I did not want to experience again. It wasn't to be.

'Rejoining the Battalion on its return to the United Kingdom, the strength was made up by volunteers pressing forward to join the Parachute Regiment.

'Late December the 6th Airborne Division was sent to the Ardennes, after which they dropped over the Rhine. Moving through Germany to the Baltic and meeting up with the Russians. The war was over, the Germans capitulating on 8th May 1945.

A hero and a dancer -
Geoff Pattinson at the
Veterans evening in Merville

'This was followed by being sent to Palestine, where I stayed with 9th Battalion until May 1947 when I was sent back to UK for demobilisation.

'Now it was really over for me. I was back to being a civilian, a survivor, not a hero.

THE SITES

MERVILLE GUN BATTERY

The starting point of the novel's plot is the daring assault on the Merville Gun Battery by the 9th Battalion of the British Parachute Regiment that took place before dawn on D-Day. Many of the pictures featured in the novel's chapters were taken on site. Here are a few more.
www.batterie-merville.com

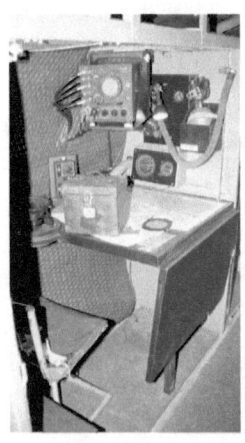

The radio operator's desk of the C-47 Dakota aircraft on display at the battery area.

The interior of the aircraft as it appeared to the Paratroopers who approached the doorway.

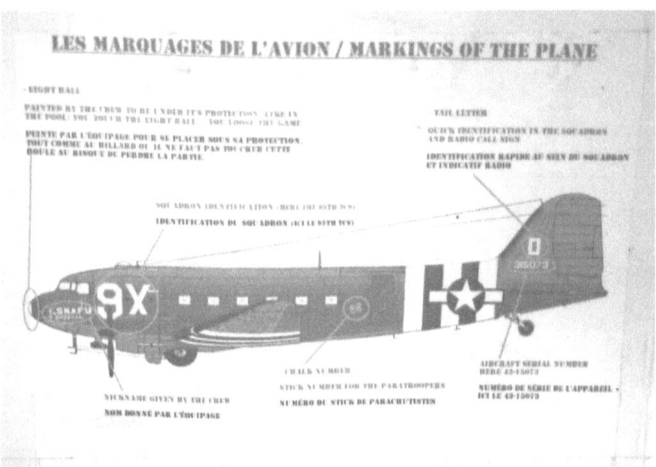

LES MARQUAGES DE L'AVION / MARKINGS OF THE PLANE

The aircraft's markings and their meaning. From left to right:
1. The white spot on a black background painted onto the nose is a propitiatory allusion to the 8 ball in pool: you touch the eight ball, you lose the match. 2. The irreverent nickname for the Dakota used by its crew: SNAFU stood for 'Situation Normal: All Fucked Up'. 3. 9X is the squadron's identification number. 4. The number 88 written in chalk refers to the Para group (or 'stick') that was to use the aircraft. 5. The '0' on the tail identifies the aircraft within the squadron and in radio communications.
6. Beneath the '0' is the aircraft's serial number.

Jean-Pierre Legrand, leader of the team that restored the aircraft after it had been located in Bosnia, disassembled and transported to Normandy. Chapter 11 of the novel mentions the documentary made to tell the adventurous story of the 'Snafu Special'. Check out www.the-snafu-special. com for further details.

The town centre as it appeared in June 2014,
when the D-Day 70th anniversary was celebrated.

Merville's tribute to Emile Corteil and Glen, his 'Paradog'.
The nineteen-year old private was charged with the handling of the
German shepherd that was trained to jump from the aircraft with
a parachute similar to that used for bicycles. Once on the ground,
the dog would run messages between the combat units, locate
anti-personnel mines and, using its acute sense of smell, signal the
presence of enemies in the area. Such a small and fast 'soldier', it was
thought, was a hard target to hit. Unfortunately, both Emil and Glen fell
victims of friendly fire as Allied fighters targeted their group, having
mistaken them for enemies. They now lie at rest in Ranville cemetery.

The information panels along the visitors' itinerary.

On the foreground, the Cross of Sacrifice. On the right, the Dakota aircraft.

This Memorial marks the point where the men of the 9th Battalion gathered before assaulting the Merville Gun battery - 'From this crossroads on the night of 5/6th June the 9th Battalion of the British Parachute Regiment, reduced to 150 men and deprived of most of its weapons and equipment but united behind its Commanding Officer Lt. Col. T. Otway departed to assault and capture the Merville Battery'.

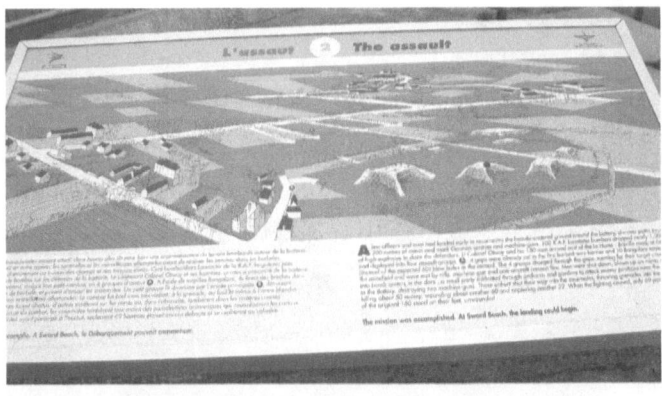

Located on top of casemate 2, this panel details how the assault was carried out - 'When the fighting ceased, only 69 paratroopers of the original 150 stood on their feet, unwounded'.

The information panel about an open gun emplacement that permitted full 360° rotation.

The weapon emplacement on top of Casemate 1 is a Tobruk pit, that is a concrete chamber with a neck-like opening.

In 2012, a few months after his passing, relatives and comrades paid this tribute to George (Jock) Moody, formerly of C Company, 9th Para Battalion.

The annual ceremony takes place in front of the entrance to the Battery area.

Ranville was the first village to be liberated in France when British paratroopers captured the bridge over the Caen canal in the early hours of D-Day. Many of the Division's casualties are buried in the local War Cemetery and the adjoining churchyard. A few pictures of the site appear in Chapter 26. Here are some more.
http://tinyurl.com/89eqaoj

This headstone is etched with the moving words addressed by a wife to her fallen husband: 'May God keep you in eternity to await our meeting, darling, just you and me - May'.

The Cross of Sacrifice stands at the centre of the graves area. The Cemetery contains 2,236 Commonwealth burials of the Second World War. There are also 323 German graves and a few burials of other nationalities.

The Stone of Remembrance.

The Churchyard contains 47 Commonwealth burials and one German grave.

The bust of Major General Richard N. Gale, commander of the 6th Airborne Division on D-Day, welcomes visitors to the Ranville public library.

SAINT-CÔME
BOIS-DES-MONTS
LE MESNIL

The areas of Château Saint-Côme and Bois-des-Monts were of strategic importance as they held a commanding position on the Eastern flank of the Allied invasion. After their withdrawal from the Merville battery, the remnants of the 9th Parachute Battalion, joined by comrades who had dropped wide on D-Day, were tasked with holding the position. They did so for six days against fierce attacks and constant shelling that involved heavy casualties.

The Ranville plain as seen from the Villa Bois-des-Monts, where the 9th Battalion Commanding Officer established his HQ and Aid Post.

The Château Saint-Côme in 1944 and now. The building and its park are located opposite the Villa Bois-des-Monts.

The entrance to Château Saint-Côme hosts a commemorative plaque, whose text reads as follows: 'During the night of 7th June 1944 9th Parachute Battalion, reduced to 85 men after Merville and Amfreville / Le Plein, occupied the Bois des Monts Château St. Côme position with orders to hold it at all costs as it overlooked the Ranville plain and the Orne bridges. In the next few days men rejoining from scattered drops increased the battalion strength to 270. It was reinforced by 5th Battalion The Black Watch and elements of the Royal Armoured Corps, 1st Canadian Parachute Battalion and other Airborne troops. Between 7 -13 June the enemy attacked with increasing strength, finally using three infantry battalions, artillery and a squadron, outnumbering the defenders by about four to one. Despite severe hand-to-hand fighting the enemy did not penetrate the perimeter and suffered very heavy casualties. On 13 June 9th Parachute Battalion was relieved by 52nd Oxfordshire and Buckinghamshire Light Infantry and moved to another front line position with only 150 men.'

Every year a group of veterans, their relatives and friends gather around the commemorative plaque at Château Saint-Côme for a memorial ceremony.

The stables of Château Saint-Côme, where a 9th Battalion reconnaissance party met up with the enemy.

Located in the park beside the Villa Bois-de-Monts, this tool shed acted as an Aid Post for the 9th Battalion's wounded. Their names are still visible on the wall.

An annual ceremony takes place at Le Mesnil crossroads, one kilometre south of Château Saint-Côme. Both Canadian and British paratroopers were involved in the defence of this key position.

The Memorial to Brigadier James Hill, Commanding Officer of the 3rd Parachute Brigade on D-Day.

THE MUSEUMS

AIRBORNE ASSAULT

Located within the Airspace Hanger of the Imperial War Museum Duxford, Airborne Assault is the Museum of the Parachute Regiment and Airborne Forces, tracing their history from inception to present day. I spent a few hours there with Francesco Di Cintio, historian and expert contributor to the institution, who proved a passionate and knowledgeable guidance through the world of Paras. These pages feature a few documents on display and filed in the archives.
https://paradata.org.uk

'Now you can enlist ...'. In 1942, a recruiting campaign was launched to attract more volunteers to the newly formed Parachute Regiment.

'Prepare for action - Fitting equipment in aircraft'. This training poster is a reminder of things to do: 1. Hook up static line to strop. 2. Secure kit-bag leg straps. 3. Attach kit-bag jettison device. 4. Attach valise leg strap. 4. Attach valise neck band.

'Control in the air'. Flight instructions as seen on a training poster: 1. Look up. 2. Ease seat strap. 3. Parachuting position. 4. Turning. 5. Checking oscillation (forward drift) 6. Checking oscillation (backward drift).

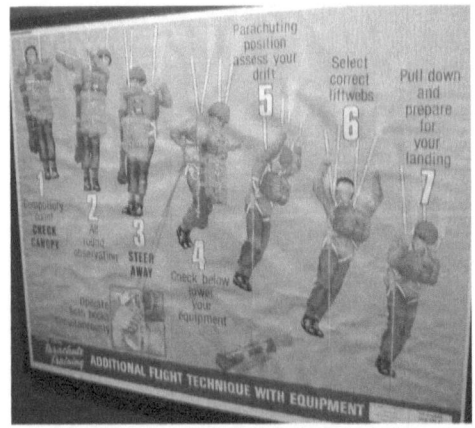

'Additional flight technique with equipment' - seven pieces of advice for a correct descent.

The account of the Merville operation as seen in the subsequent 'Immediate report', which details the problems involved, preliminary organisation, organisation on arrival, assault plan, execution and preliminary training.

CASUALTIES SUFFERED BY 6 AB DIV IN NORMANDY

Units	KILLED		WOUNDED		MISSING	
	Offrs	Soldiers	Offrs	Soldiers	Offrs	Soldiers
HQ 6 AB Div	4	2	9	13	1	6
Div HQ Def Pl	-	3	1	4	-	5
HQ 3 Para Bde incl Def Pl	4	3	5	26	2	15
1 (CA) PARA	5	60	10	152	4	97
8 PARA	5	73	14	222	3	107
9 PARA	8	54	13	154	2	192
224 Para Fd Amb	-	9	1	14	3	40
HQ 5 Para Bde incl Def Pl	-	1	4	18	-	3
7 PARA	6	84	12	236	2	112
12 PARA	4	101	26	387	3	43
13 PARA	3	76	11	215	3	51
225 Para Fd Amb	-	9	2	17	-	12
22 Indep Coy PARA	2	6	1	13	1	2
HQ 6 Airlanding Bde incl Def Pl	1	1	6	18	-	-
12 DEVON	4	33	14	212	1	12
2 OXF BUCKS	9	61	19	238	-	13
1 RUR	6	42	18	217	1	34
195 Airlanding Fd Amb	-	4	1	14	-	1
HQ RA	-	1	2	2	-	-
53 Airlanding Lt Regt	4	11	2	27	1	1
2 Airlanding LAA Bty	-	-	-	-	-	-
3 Airlanding ATk Bty	-	10	2	27	-	4
4 Airlanding ATk Bty	1	12	-	24	3	9
HQ RE	1	-	2	-	2	1
3 Para Sqn RE	1	14	2	27	1	1
591 Para Sqn RE	2	5	3	18	4	16
249 Fd Coy RE	-	4	1	36	-	-
286 Fd Pk Coy RE	1	4	-	3	-	1
CRASC	-	-	-	-	-	-
716 Coy (AB Lt Comp)	2	13	1	33	-	9
398 Coy (AB Div Comp)	-	7	1	28	-	5
63 Coy (AB Div Comp)	-	-	-	6	-	44
HQ REME	-	8	3	8	-	6
Div Wksp	-	-	-	-	-	-
Armd Recce Regt	-	10	6	26	2	8
Div Sigs	3	20	7	71	1	21
Div OFP	-	-	-	-	-	-
Div Pro Coy	-	4	-	-	1	13
Div POCU	-	-	-	2	-	-
317 Fd St Sect	-	-	-	2	-	2
TOTAL	76	745	199	2510	41	886

Summary: Wounded   2709
          Killed and Missing   1748
          Total Cas   4457

Note: These figures rep the sit when 6 AB Div returned to UK in Aug 44. Many of those posted 'missing' were captured and emerged from PW camps at the end of the war. Only 49 offrs and sldrs remained classified as 'missing' at the conclusion of hostilities.

The official list of casualties suffered by the 6th Airborne Division in Normandy.

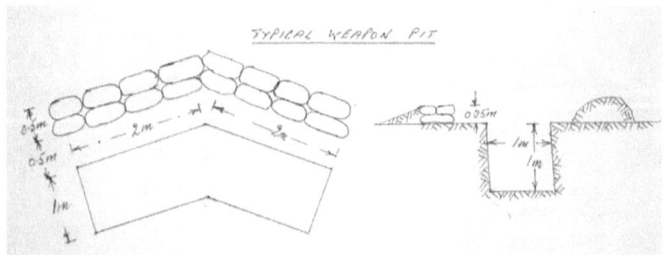

TYPICAL WEAPON PIT

A sketch showing a German machine gun emplacement like those of the Merville Battery at the time of the British Paras' assault.

PEGASUS MEMORIAL

Located in Ranville, the Pegagus Memorial was inaugurated in 2000 by HRH the Prince of Wales. It is dedicated to the men of the 6th Airborne Division and their role during the Battle of Normandy from June to September 1944. Here are just a few of the hundreds of objects on display on the site. http://www.memorial-pegasus.org/mmp/musee_debarquement/index.php

A diorama of the Merville Gun Battery as it looked like in 1944.

A showcase displaying the Paras' medical equipment. In the foreground, the morphine syringes used for injection into those who were severely wounded in order to alleviate their pain. The letter 'M' was marked on the forehead to show they had been so injected.

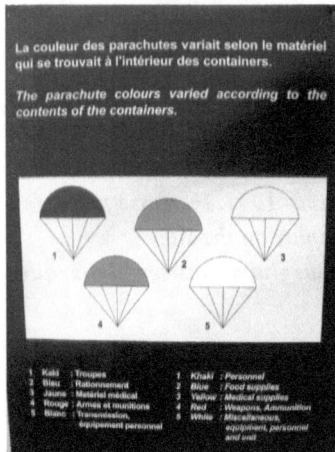

La couleur des parachutes variait selon le matériel qui se trouvait à l'intérieur des containers.

The parachute colours varied according to the contents of the containers.

1	Kaki	: Troupes	1	Khaki : Personnel
2	Bleu	: Rationnement	2	Blue : Food supplies
3	Jaune	: Matériel médical	3	Yellow : Medical supplies
4	Rouge	: Armes et munitions	4	Red : Weapons, Ammunition
5	Blanc	: Transmission, équipement personnel	5	White : Miscellaneous, equipment, personnel and civil

The parachute colours varied according to what they were meant for - khaki for personnel, blue for food supplies, yellow for medical supplies, red for weapons and ammunition, white for both equipment and personnel.

The original Bénouville Bridge, renamed Pegasus Bridge after the liberation, is on display in the park of the museum. Its capture by the glider-borne troops under Major John Howard was the first allied operation on D-Day, enabling the seaborne reinforcements to cross the Caen canal.

THE REENACTORS

Reenactors play a significant role during the annual D-Day celebrations. Their uniforms and equipment help bring the past back to life and preserve the memory of history-changing events. Even more importantly, they pay a tribute to those who lost their lives in the fight for liberty. The novel's chapters feature several pictures of the reenactments staged by the France 44 Association. Here are a few more and a photo of French civilian reenactors. The latter reminds us of the sufferings endured by the population during the Battle of Normandy and the contribution made by the French men and women who never stopped believing in freedom.

The France 44 reenactors' camp at the Merville Battery site.

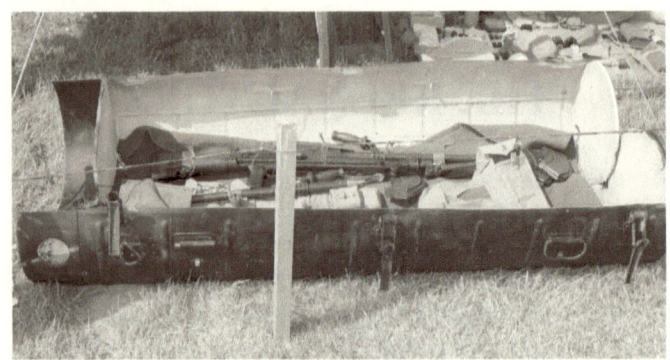

Weapons containers like this one were parachuted over Normandy along with the airborne troops.

Reenactors wearing replica blouses and trousers with the Airborne Forces insignia.

This is how a British officer's tent looked like in 1944.

Reenactors in civilian outfits - photo taken in Carentan.

THE SOURCES

The following is a list of the testimonies, books, websites and documentaries I found more useful as I sought to build a plausible historical background for the novel. In them the reader will find detailed information regarding events as they truly unfolded, and in particular the assault on Merville, the Normandy landings, the siege of Caen, the French Resistance, and on daily life and football in the United Kingdom during the war. Mentioning the authors is the least I can do by way of thanks.

EYE-WITNESS TESTIMONY

Di Cintio, Francesco, *interview with* **Gordon Newton** *and* **Geoffrey Pattinson**, *veterans of the Ninth Battalion*.

BOOKS

Ambrose, Stephen E., ***Pegasus Bridge - D-Day: The daring British airborne raid***, *Pocket Books (UK), 2003*.

Barber, Neil, ***The day the Devils dropped in - The 9th Parachute Battalion in Normandy***, *Pen & Sword Aviation (UK), 2002*.

Beevor, Antony, ***D-Day - The battle for Normandy***, *Penguin (UK), 2009*.

Bernages, Georges, ***La nuit des Paras***, *Hors série Historica, Heimdal (France), 2002*.

Bernages, Georges, ***Les Paras du Jour J***, *Hors série Historica, Heimdal (France), 2002*.

Bouchery, Jean and Charbonnier, Philippe, *D-Day Paratroopers - The British, the Canadians, the French*, Histoire & Collections (France), 2012.

Koenig, Thomas and van der Meijden, Adrian, *On his Majesty's service - Watch, Wrist, Waterproof*, Horological Journal (UK), August 2008.

Richard, Olivier, *Paras Britanniques - Les unités, l'équipement et les opérations des "Red Devils"*, E-T-A-I (France), 2010.

Rippon, Anton, *Gas masks and goal posts - Football in Britain during WW2*, Sutton Ltd. (UK), 2007.

Shilleto, Carl, *Merville Battery and the Dives bridges*, Pen & Sword Military (UK), 2011.

Strong, Michael, *Sid's war*, M. Strong (UK), 2012.

Tootal, Stuart, *The manner of men - 9 Para's heroic D-Day Mission*, John Murray (UK), 2013.

Waller, Maureen, *A family in wartime - How the Second World War shaped the lives of a generation*, IWM-Conway (UK), 2012.

Ziman, Herbert David, *Instructions for British servicemen in France 1944*, Bodleian Library, University of Oxford (UK), 1995.

WEBSITES

www.**6juin1944.com** (Normandy landings)

www.**abmc.gov/cemeteries/cemeteries** (American Battle Monuments Commission)

www.**batterie-merville.com** (Merville Battery Museum)

w w w . **b b c . c o . u k / w w - 2peopleswar** (BBC archive: eye-witness accounts)

www.**cwgc.org** (Commonwealth War Graves Commission)

www.**dday-overlord.com** (Landings and Battle of Normandy)

www.**education.gouv.fr** (French Education Ministry, French only)

www.**france.44.free.fr** (Historical reconstitution, French only)

www.**genuki.org.uk/big/paras** (British war cemeteries in France)

www.**ildday.it** (The first Italian Museum dedicated to D-Day, Italian only)

www.**iwm.org.uk** (Imperial War Museum website)

www.**mehstg.co.uk** (History of Tottenham Hotspur)

www.**memorial-caen.fr** (Caen Memorial website)

www.**memorial-pegasus. org** (British Airborne Museum in Normandy)

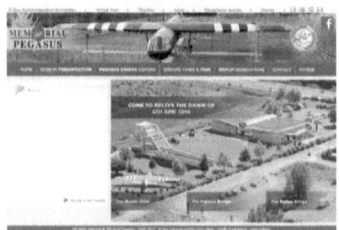

www.**paradata.org.uk** (British Airborne Museum)

www.**pegasusarchive.org** (Airborne 1940-1945)

www.**sgmcaen.free.fr** (Life in Caen during the Battle of Normandy, French only)

www.**soccer-history.co.uk** (History of football)

www.**tottenham-summer-hillroad.com** (History of the Tottenham area of London)

www.**ville-caen.fr** (Caen local government website, French only)

www.**wikipedia.org** (Online encyclopaedia)

DOCUMENTARIES

Bampfield, Andrew; Bour, Kim; Dale, Richard; Gordon, Pamela; Weale, Sally; *D-Day 6.6.1944*, BBC (UK), 2004.

Maire, Serge, *Il faut sauver le Dakota*, Galaxie Presse, France 3 Normandie, Planète (France), 2008.

Vecchiet, Jean-Michel, *Ils étaient les premiers*, Prismedia (France), 2013.

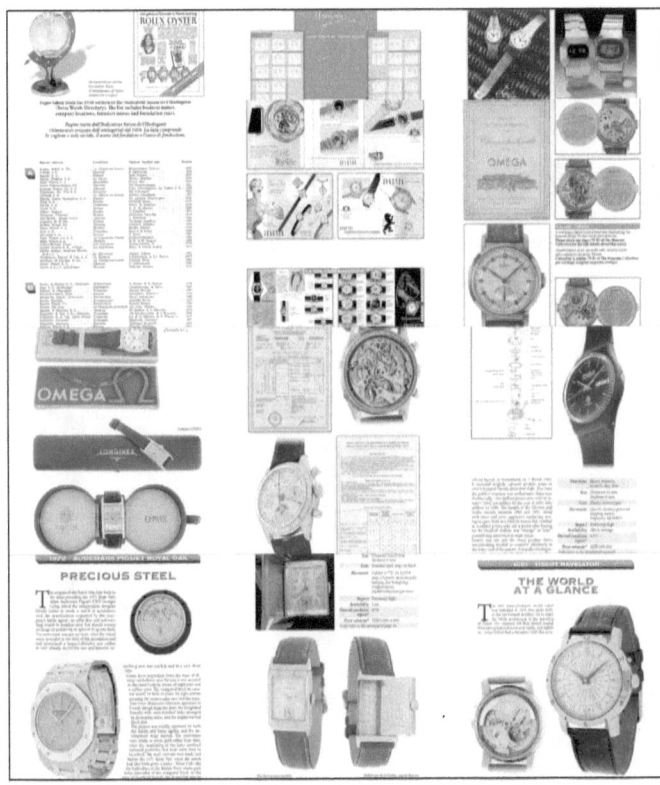

THE MUSEUM COLLECTION

100 milestones of 20th Century watchmaking

The Museum Collection is a voyage through time(keepers), an entrance ticket to an exhibition, a source of advice and inspiration for watch lovers seeking to build up the perfect collection. What is the "perfect" collection? According to this book's concept, it is the one featuring the most significant wristwatches of the 20th Century from a technical as well as style viewpoint.

Page count:
364, full color.
Binding Type:
US Trade Paper.
Trim Size: 8.5" x 11".
Languages:
English and Italian.
Price: $ 99.

This work takes into account a large number of timepieces by lesser-known manufacturers, along with the obvious "must haves". Several featured objects are within the reach of the average collector, who can buy Four-Star pieces - whose historical impact was very high, to put it as the book's descriptions do - for less than 1,000 Euros/Dollars.

The Museum Collection addresses itself to mature watch lovers who can appreciate the attractiveness of timepieces irrespective of trends, fashions and estimates, but not to them only. Its ambition is also to provide useful tips to those who approach the world of vintage watches for the first time, mostly after one or more experiences with modern products.

Welcome to a unique journey into watch collecting.

**A pictorial history of communication
and design in 20th Century watchmaking**

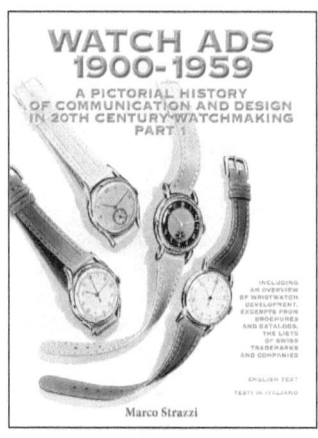

Part 1	Part 2
Page count: 360	**Page count**: 314
Binding type:	**Binding type**:
US Trade Paper	US Trade Paper
Trim Size: 8.5" x 11"	**Trim Size**: 8.5" x 11"
Languages:	**Languages**:
English and Italian	English and Italian
Color: Full color	**Color**: Full color
Price: $ 99	**Price**: $ 89

Watch Ads is a two-volume selection of images that take the reader throughout a century of communication relating to the watchmaking industry and provide an unusual look into the evolution of design, style and the public's tastes. Additional contents include pages taken from brochures and catalogs, certificates, user manuals, the complete list of trademarks and manufacturers as of 1958. The two books are sold separately

An extract from the foreword : "... Vintage ads convey something that no comment can express as effectively: the spirit of the time. The images, layout, wording and even font choice are a unique and unmistakable expression of how the manufacturer perceived its product, and of how he hoped the customers would perceive it, at the very time such product was available through retailers. They are living history. And not only that. The thousand or so selected images are also a faithful testimony of how design, style and the public's tastes evolved. The ambition of *Watch Ads* is therefore to turn into a tool allowing readers to figure out the approximate date of production of old watches …"

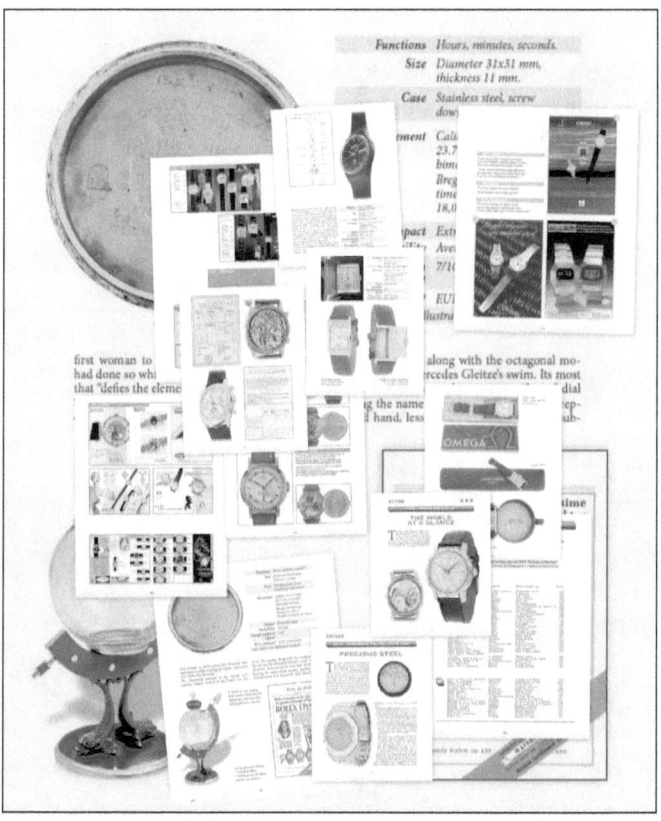

Marco Strazzi was born in Bologna (Italy) and currently lives in Lugano (Switzerland). After a twenty-year career as a sports writer, he became involved in communication related to the watchmaking industry. He is the author of five books on the history of timepieces, among which the three bilingual (English/Italian) volumes of the *Watch Books* collection - see pages 360-363.

Wingwatch marked his debut in the world of fiction. The novel is also available in French and Italian.

http://marcostrazzi.blogspot.ch